GREEN TEETH

I'm sure your own mother or grandmother told you about Jenny Greenteeths. We make a good story for a winter's night when the wind is howling down the chimney and the fire is casting long shadows on the wall. That's the best kind of night for stories. I bet you liked to curl up with a blanket and listen to tales about the bogeymen, the pixies, and the hobgoblins. Jennys belong in fairy stories, and like the other fae creatures, we're more real than your mothers would like to believe.

MOLLY O'NEILL

GREEN TEETH

orbit-books.co.uk

ORBIT

First published in Great Britain in 2025 by Orbit

1 3 5 7 9 10 8 6 4 2

A CIP catalogue record for this book is available from the British Library.

ISBN 978-0-356-52262-3

Typeset in Apollo by M Rules
Printed and bound in Great Britain by CPI Group (UK) Ltd, Croydon CR0 4YY

Papers used by Orbit are from well-managed forests
and other responsible sources.

MIX
Paper | Supporting
responsible forestry
FSC
www.fsc.org
FSC® C104740

Orbit
An imprint of
Little, Brown Book Group
Carmelite House
50 Victoria Embankment
London EC4Y 0DZ

An Hachette UK Company
www.hachette.co.uk

www.littlebrown.co.uk

For my parents

Chapter One

The witch looked surprised to see me, her eyes blinking furiously at me through murky waters. I don't know why she was so astonished. It was my lake she'd been thrown into; she should have expected I'd come and see if there was anyone worth eating.

It was an unseasonably hot day in early spring. The frogbit was just starting to regrow, bobbing up and down on the surface of the water, little green buds unfurling into the warm air. I was minding my own business like I always do, just doing a quick tidy up of loose roots at the base of the lake. The sunlight was glittering through the pond weed so I could see all the loose debris I hadn't spotted during the dark winter months. I chivvied away a school of scarlet-finned perch who were crowding around some sunken branches and began to drag them out of the mud.

I like to keep the lake looking neat and tidy. You wouldn't know it from the surface, but my lake is spotless, with excellent water circulation and the best crop of brown trout in western England. Even my frogs look smarter than those in inferior lakes, though they taste much the same. I may not be human but that doesn't mean I can let standards slip. Good lake maintenance is important for fish stocks and water quality, quite apart from the fact that I never could abide mess. A penchant for tidiness is not my most haggish feature to be sure, but then I'm not technically a hag. I've never been quite sure what it is that I am; apart from a Jenny, that is. Jenny Greenteeth, that's my name. And it's my mother's, and her mother's, all the way back upstream to the source of all the rivers and lakes in the country. It's my daughter's name too, though when she lived with me, I always called her Little Jenny and then she was Jenny in the Millpond by the Willow. I suppose my full name would be Jenny Greenteeth in the Lake at Chipping Appleby, but that's more of a mouthful than I like so I just go by Jenny. Jenny by name and Jenny by nature is what my mother said we are, silly old bat that she was. Not an actual bat though, I should make that clear. Nothing wrong with bats and they make a tasty snack of a summer evening, but I'd rather be a Jenny. Flying seems much riskier than swimming.

I'm sure your own mother or grandmother told you about Jenny Greenteeths. We make a good story for a winter's night when the wind is howling down the chimney and the fire is casting long shadows on the wall. That's the best kind of night for stories. I bet you liked to curl up with a blanket and listen to tales about the bogeymen, the pixies, and the hobgoblins. Jennys belong in fairy stories, and like the other fae creatures, we're more real than your mothers would like to believe.

If you thought those stories were old wives' tales, it might surprise you to know that most of what they told you is true. My teeth aren't green, that's probably the biggest falsehood, but they are long, and sharp enough to bite a fish in half. That's useful for a lake dweller. My skin is green, the same shade as the moss that furs the trees around the lake. My hair is green too, if I dry it out, but in the water it looks darker. I think I'm about the same height as a human, though it's difficult for me to tell. Usually when I see a human, they're either crawling away from me in horror or floating face-down in the lake. Not conducive to accurate height comparison.

Did your mother warn you to stay away from waters you couldn't see through? Did she tell you what might be lurking beneath a thick layer of lily pads, down in the silty waters of a lake or river, just waiting for a child to snatch up and drag down for her dinner?

It's good advice for a child living next to a lake with a Jenny in it, though it's been a while since I felt up to any of that rigamarole. There's a lot of eating to be got out of a child and most days I'm just not that hungry. I'd rather stick to fish or frogs or the occasional bag of kittens that some farmer throws in the lake. Right nice of them that is, I always thought, though it takes me ages to get the fur out of my teeth.

I usually get a few bags of kittens in the springtime – when all the animals are having their babies. So, when I heard the splash that day in spring that was what I thought – the first unwanted litter of the year had been delivered by an obliging young fieldhand.

I looked up from dislodging a rotten log and my immediate thought was that I'd have to track down a rabbit bone to use as a toothpick. I peered up through the water to see where the splash was coming from. I like to be quick about grabbing the bag, so the drowning isn't so slow. Panicked meat always tastes bad to me, and I may be a river monster but I do have principles. My mother used to call me soft for that. When I spotted the edge of the splash at the surface, I noticed the ripples were larger than I would have expected for a sack of kittens. My hearing isn't the best under water but now that I concentrated, I could hear some humans cheering. Or maybe humans laughing, or maybe even screaming. It's difficult to tell the difference, humans are always making a noise for some reason or another. Maybe they'd rolled a cart or something into the lake and were going to make a big fuss about hauling it out. That would be entertaining indeed. The villagers are wary of my lake and if I sneaked up and grabbed one of their ankles they'd be guaranteed to shriek loud enough to wake the dead. I chuckled at the thought.

Either way I wanted to investigate this disturbance, so I pushed off from the bottom and shot off through the water. I could feel my long hair streaming behind me as I swam, freshly combed out this morning, and I enjoyed the sense of the sunlight dappling on my skin. I opened my mouth to taste the lake water. There was something metallic that I could smell, possibly blood of some kind, but not much of it. The splash had come from the village side of the lake, and it took me a few minutes to swim over. I came up to just below the surface and peered through the frogbit.

A small crowd of humans was gathered on the shore, waving their little pink arms in the air. I didn't recognise any of their faces, but they all wore the dull linen clothes humans in the village had been wearing for hundreds of years, brown kirtles and britches and greying shirts. The people all looked much the same to my eyes, mostly too young for me to know any by name but too old to be playing childish games on my banks. One human, a male I thought, was standing facing away from me and shouting. He wore a big black hat and a dark overcoat of some kind, newer and less patched than the clothes of the others. He turned a bit so I could glimpse his face, small eyes and a pursed little mouth. His expression was twisted in anger, and he was pointing back at my lake. I thought he looked even sillier than the rest of them and sank back down from the surface.

Satisfied that the humans weren't going to come barging into the lake I looked around for whatever it was they had thrown in. There wasn't anything floating on the surface so the cause of the splash must have sunk to the floor. I floated about a yard below the surface and twisted around to see where it had fallen. There! Just below me I spotted a trace of tiny bubbles coming up through the weeds. I kicked my legs up and dived a little deeper, brushing the leaves aside with long fingers.

To my intense surprise a human was sitting on the bottom of the lake. A female human, I thought, with pale skin and big eyes. She was looking at me with an expression of shock and terror, as if I was a creature from her nightmares brought to life. I suppose that's exactly what I was. I could tell she was a witch because she was holding one hand up to her mouth and had conjured a small globule of air around her fist. She was trying to breathe from the glob, but she hadn't quite got the spell right and little bubbles of air kept creeping out of her nose and scurrying back to the surface. Every time she messed it up the main globule would shrink, and her fist would tighten a little, as if she was trying to hold the air there by sheer strength of grip.

I didn't think it was too clever of her to be sitting here trying to learn how to breathe underwater. Quite apart from the obvious hazard of river monsters, jumping into the literal deep end seemed an extreme way to practise, compared to, say, dunking your head in a bathtub. If this was a new trend among human witches then I didn't like it. I've already said that I like to keep a tidy lake and strange witches jumping in and causing a commotion would be extremely vexing.

I wasn't entirely sure what to make of her being here, but I did know that a Jenny always leads with her teeth. I opened my mouth wide and gave her my best smile. The witch's eyes bulged even wider and the glob of air at her fist exploded in a fizz of effervescence. I was sure that now her air was gone she'd be zipping off back to the surface and leaving me in peace. To my surprise the witch just sat there, opening and closing her hand again, trying to regain the spell.

I moved nearer, still smiling my toothiest grin. I have a lot of teeth, multiple rows on both top and bottom jaw, each needle-sharp and glittering. The effect is quite striking, so I'm told, and this has worked on every human I've ever met before, usually causing them to soil themselves and scream for their mothers. This witch stayed put. I reached out a hand towards her. She shrank back, but awkwardly, floundering around in the water like a landed carp. I inspected a little closer and realised why she was moving so clumsily. Her right hand and left foot had been shackled together. They were bound with some kind of metal manacles, newly forged and shining even in the dim light at the bottom of the lake. That explained the metallic taste on the waters I had noticed earlier. Why would a witch bind herself with iron and jump in a lake? It didn't make any sense to me, but witches are a strange breed, even for humans. Perhaps it was a kind of spell that she was trying to perform, which was why the humans on the banks were shouting and waiting for her. I still didn't think that was a good enough reason to be disturbing my lake.

I waited for the witch to free herself, but she kept thrashing around. I could tell she was getting weaker and weaker, her mouth bulging out with the last breath of air. She looked back at me, and I could see the fear in her eyes. Not fear of me, I thought, the fear of a dying animal caught in a trap.

Maybe, I thought, maybe she didn't jump in. Maybe those yelling creatures on the banks *threw* her in. Threw her like a bag of kittens. That seemed an extreme development and not a particularly welcome one. Witches being lobbed into the lake wasn't any better than witches diving in.

If she had been thrown in, then did that mean I should eat her? I frowned a little. I didn't relish that thought. I hadn't eaten a whole adult human in a very long time, and I'd never eaten a witch before. I wondered if they tasted different. It was probably bad luck to eat one. Adult humans were pretty gamey, not really to my taste at the best of times. While I was pondering this the witch gave a final wriggle and then a last bubble slipped between her lips, and she was still.

I sent a ripple of water towards her to check that she wasn't faking it. Nothing. Her body drifted in the water like a ragdoll.

Was she dead? It was hard to tell without having a closer look. Witches were famously tricky; I didn't want to go over and give her a prod in case she woke up again and cast a spell on me. I wasn't sure if I should leave her there or drag her up to the surface. If the humans on the shore had thrown her in, then they had probably meant for her to drown. Too bad for them if that was the case; I didn't want her to rot here and clog up the bottom of my lake. It would be very untidy. Should I eat her? I wasn't particularly hungry today, and if I ate now when she was fresh then I'd definitely get indigestion. That could put me off my game for days and I had a lot to do around the lake in spring.

The witch's black hair floated up around her like a dark cloud. It reminded me of Little Jenny's hair, way back when she still lived here in the lake with me. She'd had shorter hair then, only down to her shoulders. I didn't want to eat something that made me think of Little Jenny. That settled it then. I wasn't going to eat her, I wasn't going to let her rot here and I couldn't take her to the surface. I would have to take her somewhere else.

I grabbed the witch by her shoulder and pulled her over to me. She was thin underneath the billowing dress and I tucked her right underneath my arm. The manacles would have been heavy for her to lift, but Jennys are strong creatures, and the weight made no difference to me as I sped back through the water to my cave. One of the pike came over for a look as I swam but I shooed it away. It blinked mournfully at me and vanished back into the deep waters.

I don't like to brag but my cave is very cosy. You swim in through a submerged tunnel at the eastern end of the lake that leads into a small cavern full of trapped air. Once you climb out of the water there's enough space that you can walk ten paces to the back wall and ten paces from side to side. There's smaller tunnels that go back into the hillside but I've never explored them much. I keep my bedding section at the back of the cave and arrange my trinkets along the walls. You wouldn't believe the things people lose in a lake over a thousand years. There are stacks and stacks of old coins, stamped with the faces of a dozen different kings and lords. Glass bottles and earthenware cups; little statues and figurines carved from bone, antler and wood. I have an array of interesting skulls, one of each kind of creature that's fallen into the lake. My favourite piece is an old sword someone threw in the lake way back when I was just moving in. It is very fine and has some writing on the hilt though I can't read it.

I even have a will o' the wisp trapped in a glass bottle to give off light. I can see in the dark of course but I thought it would brighten the place up, so I bought it from the fairy tinker who does the rounds of all the magical folk in this part of the world. That was a mistake as now he's always dropping by and trying to sell me things and chatter to me. The wisplight is nice to have though, and I like the way it flickers.

When I clambered back through the tunnel I felt as happy as I always did when coming into my cave. There was plenty of space for the witch, but I wasn't sure where to put her down. I didn't want her to roll back into the water, but if I put her in my bed then she might mess up my nest. It sounds fussy but it takes a long time for me to organise rushes and reeds properly and I like to curl up small. Eventually I compromised by dropping her on the floor but sitting between her and the water. She landed awkwardly, face down, so I rolled her over. Her wrist and ankle were still shackled together. I lifted up the irons, wincing slightly as the metal touched my skin. Fairies don't like iron; it hurts us to touch it. Jennys are more resistant to it than the high fae, people are always dropping iron bits and pieces in our rivers and lakes, and I was better than most Jennys. I could touch it with only a stinging sensation, like holding a wasp. Once I had a good grasp on the shackles it was an easy thing to snap them apart. I unfolded her arm and laid her out in a more comfortable position.

I looked around the cave and picked up one of the neatly folded linen dresses the pedlar had sold me. I rarely bothered with them except when I did business with him but humans were fussy about clothes and I thought it would be less alarming to the witch if I was dressed. I slid into it, tugging the fabric down to my knees. Pleased with myself I looked at the witch's face. Her eyes were closed, and her chest didn't seem to be moving.

I thought about it some more. Humans are just like other land animals – they like to breathe air – but the witch couldn't breathe air with all the lake water still in her. I needed to get the water out. It was a new experience for me to think about how to stop a human from drowning. Maybe I could tip the water out.

I picked up her feet and lifted them into the air. The witch stayed motionless. I needed to be more aggressive. I lifted her off the ground, so she was dangling by her ankles and shook her up and down. She swung from my hands, hair trailing on the floor. I accidentally hit her head on the ground and hauled her up a little higher. I swung again. At first there was nothing but then I heard a great spluttering sound and brownish lake water started to spurt out of the witch's mouth. I kept on shaking her, until the floor was covered in watery bile and she'd stopped coughing any more up. Her eyes were still closed but her chest was definitely moving now. I was pretty sure that was a good sign.

I started to put her down again but realised I couldn't lay her in the regurgitated water. There wasn't really another good spot to drop her so I slung her over my shoulder and mopped up the mess before setting her back down. It was hard to tell in the wisplight, but I thought there might be some pinkish colour coming back into her face. I was pretty sure that was a good thing for a human.

Getting the witch breathing was a start, but now that I thought about it, my cave was probably too cold for a human. There are obvious difficulties with bringing firewood into an underwater cave, even if I were inclined to have a fire in my living quarters which I most assuredly am not. Jennys don't like fire, we're very much creatures of the water. Everything here is damp, which is just how I prefer it. I scooted a little closer to feel her forehead. She was warm to the touch, just starting to dry off from her dunking. Her clothes were still wet through and starting to chill. I decided to take off some of the layers humans like to wrap themselves in.

The boots were by far the trickiest part of this endeavour: hooks and laces and tiny knots. I tried very hard not to break any part of them but I did snap a few of the ties. I tipped them out over the tunnel entrance and then set them down on the floor. Next were a pair of knitted socks which I squeezed out and hung next to the wisplight. She was wearing some kind of thick kirtle, laced over a thinner linen smock. I could feel some interesting shapes in the pockets but resisted the urge to look. The laces on the kirtle were thicker than on the shoes and I managed to undo them without any breaks. Once I peeled her out of that I draped it over the sword, next to the socks. That left the smock, which I decided to leave on. It was light enough that it would probably dry off on its own now that the kirtle was off. After some reflection I decided to remove the human skull from my collection of bones and hide it behind my bedding nest. No need to alarm the witch when she finally woke up.

Now that she was breathing and out of her wet clothes, I thought about the other difficult parts of keeping a human alive.

She would probably be hungry when she came round. I could go and catch her some dinner, but I didn't want her to wake up and try and escape when I was gone. I'd brought a rabbit back here once, intending to keep it as a pet. It hadn't ended well. The stupid thing panicked and ran away and drowned in the tunnel. I hadn't even had the heart to eat it so I gave the corpse to one of the lake pike. Witches should have more sense than rabbits but they're still mortals and a half-dead witch who got herself thrown in a lake might have no sense at all. I gave up and sat down again, settling in to watch the witch breathe, her chest rising up and down.

She really did remind me of my daughter Little Jenny. She had the same small nose and big ears and the dark hair on her head was starting to curl the same way Little Jenny's had back when I first found her as a baby. That had been before I made her my daughter. The resemblance got me thinking about how to make a Jenny. Maybe I should make the witch a Jenny too.

Any Jenny can make another Jenny, but it doesn't happen very often. We don't give birth to our own babies. There aren't any male Jennys and frankly the idea of human reproduction makes me feel a bit sick. We make our children from the unwanted offspring of others.

In the time I've been living in the lake here at Chipping Appleby forty generations of humans have come and gone and I have only had the one daughter. She came to me maybe two hundred winters back. I remember it like it was yesterday. The lake had frozen over around the sides and the deer that live in the woods would edge along the ice to drink from the hole in the middle. I don't get out much in winter and it was even more unusual for me to be swimming at night, but the sky was clear and I wanted to watch the stars. I was floating on the surface near the middle of the lake when I heard a wail like a fox kit crying.

When I looked in the direction of the sound I saw a bundle of rags, dropped on the ice and a cloaked figure fleeing back to the shore. I hauled out onto the ice and tentatively scuttled over to grab the bundle.

Inside I saw there was a little baby human, abandoned naked and newborn. It looked up at me with big blue eyes and gave a little toothless grin. I could tell it was a baby girl and dangled a finger in her mouth to suckle on. She was still sticky with after-birth and blood so I took her into the water to clean her up. She shrieked a bit at the chill but baby humans like to swim and she bobbed around quite happily with me for a while but the lake was cold and I knew she wouldn't last long.

I remembered what my mother taught me about my own rebirth as a Jenny. I bit my own wrist open and put the wound to her mouth, dripping a little blood down her throat. When she swallowed it I brought her back under the surface and held her there until the water filled her lungs. The little body didn't last long before the final breaths of air left her but I cradled her in my arms until the change began. The curly dark hair straightened and pikelet-sharp teeth budded in her mouth like fresh grass. The baby blue eyes widened and grew darker, all the better to catch the light that filters into the lake. By the end of the night she was swimming freely, catching frogs on her own and I began to teach her the ways of a Jenny.

Seventeen years she lived with me until I found her a pond of her own to live in and very nice it was too, though she always was a messy child and I fear she doesn't keep it as tidy as I would like. It had been pleasant to have some company in the lake while she was growing up though. If I made this witch a Jenny then she probably wouldn't stay that long, being already a grown woman. She might not take to the change well. It was a bad idea, I thought, tucking my legs underneath me.

I watched the witch a long while. I could sense the day was ending; the sun would be dipping below the stand of apple trees at the western edge of my lake. The witch hadn't moved since I got her breathing, and I was starting to get bored. I decided to pick up one of the stacks of coins and amuse myself by sorting them according to which of the faces on them had the biggest nose. I leaned over her body to grab for the coins and that's when the witch started awake and opened her eyes.

Chapter Two

To give her credit, the witch only screamed for a minute or so. My face had been a few inches from her own when she'd opened her eyes and I'd been frowning in concentration as I reached for the pile of coins. The frown must have seemed like a terrible grimace. To make things worse I was so startled that I jumped, tripped over the witch's feet and yelped in surprise.

The witch scrambled backward, knocking over my neatly stacked coins and objects of interest. She looked around wildly, trying to find a way out through the back of the cave and made a run towards my bedroll. She slipped on the rushes and went down hard. By unhappy chance she landed right next to the old skull I'd thoughtfully hidden back there and screamed again.

I reached out an arm to reassure her and she shrank back against the wall. She reached for something in her pockets but realised that I'd removed her kirtle and she was just wearing the thin chemise.

I was trying to speak, but it must have been months since I'd formed words aloud in the air and my chest was full of water. I took a deep breath in and started to cough it up, bending over and retching it out over the tunnel opening. The witch looked at me strangely, bafflement starting to encroach onto her fear. I put out a hand again, raising one finger to indicate she should wait while I continued to clear my lungs. This was deeply embarrassing; I should have thought about surface speech before she woke up.

When I finally got enough air into my chest to speak I turned back to the witch. She had conjured a small fireball around her fist, not much larger than the bubble of air she had been trying to breathe from in the lake. She shook her fist at me, taking a tentative step forward.

'Get out of my way, hag,' she said. Her voice trembled as she spoke, echoing around the cave, but she stood firm.

I took another deep breath,

'C-c-c-c-aaaaa,' I started. Talking was always difficult after a few months of silence. I tried again.

'C-c-c-calm down, witch.' This time I managed the words and smiled, pleased with myself. The witch did not appreciate my smile and the fire at her hand dimmed a little.

'Let me out now,' she said, pushing her magic further to try and fan the flames.

'D-d-don't be silly,' I said, 'You're still half drowned. Put that nasty thing out and sit down before you faint.' I tried to be firm, conjuring up the strict voice I had used for Little Jenny.

'You can speak? Do you understand what I'm saying, hag? Get out of my way!' the witch said again, taking another step forward.

I eyed the fireball. I really don't like fire but here in my cave, at the heart of the lake, it wasn't enough to scare me.

'N-not a hag,' I said, dropping my hand and reaching back behind me.

'What did you say?' the witch asked, brightening her flame a little.

'I said, I am not a hag!' I called the lake to me, a whip of water extended from the entrance pool and lashed through the air. It wrapped around the witch's wrist, extinguishing her fireball. She gaped at it then looked back at me with a stunned expression. I released my hand and the water whip retracted back into the lake.

'My name is Jenny. Now sit down and stop messing about.'

This time my tone seemed to have an effect. The witch sat, squatting on the floor right where she had been standing. My bedding nest was a mess around her, rushes and reeds everywhere. I wanted to go and rearrange everything, but she was still very twitchy and I didn't want her to spook again.

I sat down myself so that I wasn't looming over her. I offered her a smile, but her eyes bulged again and I could hear the breath catch in her throat. It was very difficult not to scare humans, it seemed. I had assumed that witches at least were made of stronger stuff.

I wanted to be polite so I asked her if she would like a drink.

'I'm sorry, what did you say?' she asked.

'I said, can I get you a beverage? The lake water is too silty to drink down here but I keep a few bottles of small beer that I bought from the tinker.'

She continued to look stunned but nodded. I stood up again and very slowly moved over to where I stored my drinks. One of the benefits of the cave is that the drinks are always cool and refreshing so I took two small earthenware cups and poured us each a measure of beer. I made to hand the witch's cup to her but she recoiled immediately. I put it down on the ground in front of her and returned to my seat, holding my own cup and the bottle.

I could see her watching me out of the corner of her eye, so I took a sip of the beer. It was dark and hoppy, just the way I liked it. I smacked my lips, overexaggerating my enjoyment to encourage her. She picked up her own cup and took an experimental sip. Clearly it was to her taste because she drained the beaker and put it back down on the floor. I drank mine slowly, then leaned over to refill her cup, using movements that felt achingly sluggish.

She didn't flinch again, but I could sense the tension in her body the closer I came, and she noticeably relaxed when I withdrew.

We sat in silence for a while. I felt her eyes on me, focusing on my rows of teeth and long arms and legs. I wondered whether she would say anything again. Technically she was a guest in my home, so it was my responsibility to lead the conversation. What did humans like to talk about?

I coughed a little and she looked at me.

'Nice, um, weather we've been having lately,' I said. The witch didn't react so I pressed on.

'Very warm for March. Some years we're still getting snow but this year it hasn't even rained for a week.' Still no response from the witch. I thought that was a little rude. I was trying my hardest here.

'I, erm, I do enjoy a nice spring day, all the flowers blooming.' I gestured expansively with one hand. We both looked at where I'd waved: bare cave wall. I winced. I was very out of practice at this.

'I like spring,' said the witch in a small voice. She looked surprised at her words.

Encouraged, I nodded enthusiastically.

'Me too. Winter gets very dull down here, and I do like to see all the new life. Baby birds and lambs and tadpoles. Nice to see and nice to eat – ha-ha.' The witch nodded doubtfully. Inwardly I cursed. I shouldn't have brought up the topic of things I liked to eat. She had nodded though, and that was a good sign.

'Might I ask,' I started, 'what your name is?'

The witch looked up from swirling the dregs of beer in her cup.

'Temperance. Temperance Crump,' she said.

'Well, it is nice to make your acquaintance, Temperance,' I said. 'Like I mentioned before, my name is Jenny.'

'As in Jenny Greenteeth?' Temperance asked, cocking her head slightly.

'Indeed. I am a Jenny and I am called Jenny.' I tried to copy her head tilt. It must not have looked right because her expression became quite alarmed. I gave up and resumed a normal affectation.

'Have you lived long in the village, Temperance?' I asked, trying to keep the conversation flowing.

She nodded.

'All my life,' she said. To my horror I could see tears brimming in her eyes.

'I've lived there all my life,' she continued, 'and now I don't know what I'll do. All my neighbours – how could they do this to me? They grew up with me and suddenly they're all convinced that I'm evil. They tried to kill me.'

Temperance kept crying, great fat teardrops rolling down her cheeks and snot beginning to drizzle from her nose.

I was mortified. Crying humans were a new phenomenon. I wanted to pat her knee but I was pretty sure she wouldn't want me to touch her, so I just sort of mumbled wordlessly. I wanted her to stop so I handed her a scrap of cloth. She took the hint and mopped herself up.

'I'm sorry, Jenny. I'm not normally such a wet lettuce. It's just, my whole life has fallen apart in so little time. A few days ago I was living with my family, teaching my daughter how to sew. And now,' she paused to gulp, 'now it's all gone.'

'You have a daughter?' I asked, trying to distract her. She nodded enthusiastically.

'Ursula. She's just turned three. I have a son too, Josiah. Lord, my poor husband. He'll have to raise them himself now; they must all think I'm dead, drowned in the lake. Benedict will have to explain it to Ursula. My poor girl, she must be so afraid. Josiah's just a baby, he won't even remember me, but he'll grow up thinking I was evil. Oh God, how could I not have seen this coming?' She sniffled and dabbed at her nose again.

'Might I ask,' I began, trying to be tactful, 'what it was you were doing in the lake? A young witch like yourself, you should be popular with the village. Witches are right useful to keep around I should think.'

She frowned at me.

'How do you know I'm a witch?' she asked.

I couldn't help myself, I grinned at her.

'You did conjure a fireball and try to throw it at me,' I said, 'that gave me a fairly good inkling.'

'Oh, yes, well I'm sorry about that. You scared me when I

woke up. But you don't mind that I'm a witch? Most people think witches are evil.'

That made me laugh outright.

'God's bones, Temperance! Look at me! Do you think I'm in a position to be judging who's evil and who's not? Besides you're in my lake now, at the heart of my power. I'm not afraid of you here.'

She wrinkled her nose a little at that and then managed a watery smile. She had a very nice smile, I thought. Her teeth weren't sharp at all, but they were very neat and even. When she smiled little dents appeared in her cheeks, like a ripple passing through smooth water.

'I suppose that makes sense. It's nice to think there's at least one person in the world who doesn't think I'm evil.' She sniffled again. 'That's why they threw me in the lake. I was suspected of witchcraft and witches float in water, so they threw me in to see if I could float.'

I frowned. 'That doesn't make a lick of sense. Most humans will float for a bit, unless they panic and swallow a lot of water. And you sank anyway because they put those metal bonds on you. They must have known you would sink.'

She nodded. 'That's preachers for you. They care less about facts than about fear. That cursed parson probably didn't even think I was really a witch, just a woman who was cleverer than he thought she should be.'

'I don't understand,' I said. 'They threw you in for being a witch, even though they didn't think you were a witch but you actually are one?'

Temperance smiled again. I was pleased to have made her smile, even if I did think it was tinged with sadness.

'Maybe I had better start from the beginning.' She tipped her cup back and swallowed the last of it. I refilled both of our beakers again as she began to tell her story.

'I was born here in Chipping Appleby, almost thirty summers past. My father had a small farm, and he expected the whole family to work on it. He taught me how to till the land, shear a sheep and thresh the wheat in autumn. My mother taught me magic. She had learnt it herself at my grandmother's knee and taught it to me as soon as I was old enough to keep the secret. It isn't a flashy magic like in fairy stories. I don't know the spells a great wizard like Merlin or Ceridwen would use. What I learnt instead was practical magic. How to ease the birth of a calf or a child, how to pickle or salt food so it keeps long into the winter. She taught me the best spells to sing when I sowed barleycorn so the crop would grow fast and strong.

'I learnt to spark fire within my fingers to light damp wood and to conjure air to ease the breaths of a dying man. My mother told me never to call it magic, even among ourselves, but that was what it was.'

I settled back on my haunches as Temperance spoke. Her breathing had slowed to what I thought was a normal pace for a human and she smiled to herself as she spoke of her mother.

'Ma was what the village called a cunning woman. People came from all over to buy her medicines and ask for her help. She always gave it, charging those that could afford it and gifting those that couldn't. When she died, I knew it would be my turn to serve and to pass on the knowledge to my daughters.

'So that is what I did. When I was one and twenty I started stepping out with Benedict Crump. He was a few years older than me and had his own farm. Best of all he was sweet and kind and pleased to be courting a cunning woman and we wed the next spring. I waited five years for our first child to be born, using all the spells and prayers I knew and finally I had my Ursula. Two years later I had Josiah. I was happy with my family. There was always work to do, mouths to feed and grazes to heal, but I have ever liked to be busy.

'The trouble began this winter. We had a new parson move to the village. A widower named Asa Braddock. The whole village sat in St Swithin's Church the first Sunday to hear him preach. We had been six months since the old parson died and the village was keen for spiritual comfort. I had scrubbed my two babies clean for the occasion and pressed Benedict's good shirt. He had

given me a kiss in thanks and we walked off to the service hand
in hand. That was the last time I knew peace.'

Temperance paused to drink, her knuckles paling as she
gripped the cup. She set it down and squared her shoulders,
ready to begin again.

'Asa Braddock walked into the nave, his nose held high in the
air as if he was better than us. He wore new black robes, clean
and unpatched, and he twitched them around his feet so as not to
dirty them. When he looked out at the congregants, I felt every
villager squirm a little. Where we had previously sat proudly in
our Sunday best now we felt shabby, out of place and unworthy
to sit in church.

'Parson Braddock waited until everyone was off kilter and
then began. His sermon was vicious. He condemned us as having
sin in our hearts, embracing luxuries and the Devil and turning
away from the true faith. "Papist fripperies!" he thundered,
pointing a long bony finger at each villager where they sat. He
called for us to return to the church and practise good Protestant
values. The whole village was quaking in their boots. A baby
started to wail and its mother scurried to soothe it. Parson
Braddock looked out at us and accused us of worse and worse
things. Then he dropped his voice and hissed at us.

'"There are witches abroad!" he said.

'I knew right then that there would be trouble coming. We all
left that church chastised and quiet. That didn't last. Within the
week the village was buzzing with rumours. Parson Braddock
denounced witchcraft again the next week, and every week
after. Witches drank the blood of children, he said, they con-
sorted with the Devil and cursed good, pious folk. Soon people
were coming forward with stories of witchcraft: a sick child, a
failed crop. No names were mentioned but I could feel the village
starting to look at me. It was like they had been possessed. People
who had brought me their babies sick with colic or measles now
crossed the road to avoid me. Helping people had brought such
joy to my life, I felt the absence like a missing tooth. My kitchen
had been full of gossip and chatter, now it was empty. I put away

my herb collection and buried my spell book out in the woods. As I shovelled the earth onto the grimoire, neatly wrapped in a cowhide, it felt like I was digging my own grave. When I came home Benedict looked at the soil trapped under my fingernails and I saw my own fear reflected back at me in his eyes.

'Finally, the day before yesterday, it happened. Benedict had gone out to plough the northern fields. He'd left early and I was alone with the children. I was sweeping the front yard, trying to look meek and unassuming. Pastor Braddock came strolling down the path towards me, flanked by Hezekiah Bone. Hezekiah had never liked me, she'd wanted Benedict to court her instead, and she'd always been bitter that she'd ended up married to Oliver Bone. He was a decent man but he wasn't as handsome as Benedict and his fields were poorer and smaller.

'Hezekiah stood in my front yard and pointed at me. She smiled nastily.

'"Her," she said, speaking loudly and clearly, "Temperance Crump. She's a witch. She put a pox on my husband's crops. She caused our cow to drop a two-headed calf. She's made a deal with the Devil so as to enrich herself." She spat on the ground at my feet.

'Parson Braddock looked at me with his small pale eyes.

'"Temperance Crump," he said, "I am arresting you on the most serious and evil charges of witchcraft. You will be confined under the church and tried for your crimes."

'At first I thought it must be a bad dream, but then I heard the sound of my Ursula running out to greet the villagers. She clung to my skirts and Hezekiah stepped forward to wrench her away. I slapped at her hand and she leapt back, howling that I had slashed her with my devilish nails.

'Parson Braddock moved forward then and grabbed my arm. He was stronger than he looked and twisted it painfully behind my back. I cried out and Ursula started to sob. The pastor—'

Temperance choked. I moved forward instinctively but she waved a hand at me and I retreated. My presence would hardly be soothing to her.

'The pastor, he, he hit her. He backhanded her so hard that she flew across the grass and landed against the house with a crack. Hezekiah seized her and carried her back inside the house. Parson Braddock hauled me away as I screamed. I was too upset to try any spells, and I don't really know any defensive ones anyway. He dragged me to the church and threw me in one of the anchorite cells. He kept me locked in there all that day and the night with nothing to eat or drink. I was wild with worry about my children, about Benedict. The sound of Ursula hitting the wall of the house echoed inside my head till I screamed aloud to try to block it out. Once I started screaming I couldn't stop; I called for my husband, for my children, even for my mother, though she was ten years dead. It was the longest night of my life.

'The next morning two farm labourers hauled me out of my cell and into the town square. Benedict had been placed in the village stocks and he called out to me as I passed. I twisted to try to get to my husband and bit the hand of one of my captors, but he yelped and struck me across the face, hard enough to make me dizzy. I heard Benedict yelling at the man. The other labourer laughed at him.

'"You just mind your manners, Mr Crump. As soon as your slatternly witch of a wife is tried I'm sure you'll snap out of her spell and be out of those stocks before you know it."

'I almost started screaming again at that. If they weren't going to let Benedict vouch for me then surely Parson Braddock would win his case. I tried to order my thoughts, to think of an argument that would prove my innocence but my mind was too panicked.

'The two men dragged me in front of a small crowd of villagers. Parson Braddock was there, looking black and grim as a raven. He began to list my crimes, pointing out Hezekiah and citing her accusations as fact. When I tried to speak, he told the man who had hit me to cover my mouth to stop my "wicked spells".

'After that I don't remember much. Hezekiah was the only one to openly denounce me but no one spoke up for me or my family. I saw the faces of my oldest friends in the crowd. Some were tear-stained, others looked scared. I longed for them to meet my gaze, for any of them to offer silent comfort; their grim faces were more isolating than all Hezekiah's crowing. Parson Braddock expounded grandly on the nature of evil. He took full credit for having "sniffed out the witch". He did not call for a vote nor did he allow me to speak.

'Eventually he declared that I would be judged by God. He brought forth iron manacles and bound my right hand to my left foot. Then he led the crowd out to the lake, my two guards carrying me behind.

'He made a final prayer on the banks of the lake for God to judge my soul and smite down wickedness. I could hear Benedict still shouting in the village but then the Parson told the crowd of villagers to scream and shout, to pray for judgement. Soon all I could hear was their roaring. Then they threw me in.

'I'm a fair swimmer, I grew up in and out of the Caerlee river, upstream of where it flows into your lake. But when I was thrown in I forgot everything, I panicked and twisted in the water. The weight of the manacles and the awkward positioning of my limbs was preventing me from staying afloat and I was dragged down through the waters. I managed to get my left arm in front of my mouth and conjured up the air spell. I was breathing again but how long would that last? I didn't know a spell to break the handcuffs and the air would eventually run out.

'Then I saw you. I thought – forgive me, Jenny – but for a moment I thought that Pastor Braddock was right. I thought the Devil had come to drag me down to Hell, that I was evil after all. Then I lost the spell and blacked out. When I woke up I was here with you.'

Temperance was quiet for a while, sipping her beer and staring at the wall. I let her sit in silence for a bit. Then I tentatively spoke.

'How horrible that Pastor Braddock sounds. I wonder why he is so angry at witches?'

Temperance gave me a wobbly smile.

'I don't know, Jenny.'

'Well, he failed because you didn't drown — I rescued you, and I'm right glad I did. He seems very stupid. When you are feeling better I can take you up to the surface. If you go out the far side of the lake you can follow the Caerlee as it flows south and that will take you to the Oxford road. You can walk to Oxford and find a new farm to live on.'

I was pleased with the plan, and with my knowledge of the lands beyond Chipping Appleby. Most Jennys didn't know that. I was disappointed when Temperance didn't smile again.

'I can't leave my babies, leave Benedict. What would I do in Oxford? I've no money, no relations outside the village.'

'Oh, money's easy,' I said, pointing over at the pile of coins beside her. 'People are always throwing money in lakes. You can take as much as you like. Some of it is quite old but there's lots of different types. I traded just one for this wisplight here, and a waterproof bag to carry it in!'

Temperance's eyes widened as she took in the glowing bottle and then looked back down at the money.

'Jenny, these are gold coins! You've got hundreds of them.'

I grinned at her, forgetting myself, 'Yes, they're pretty, aren't they? I like the way they gleam in the light. I am sure you could buy another farm with them.'

'Jenny, this is a fortune, I could buy the whole village with this much coin.'

'Ah well, why don't you try that? They can't kick you out if you own the village.'

Temperance shook her head, 'I don't think it works quite like that, Jenny. With a few of these coins I could buy a new farm, though. I could send for Benedict and the children to come and—' She stopped short. 'I'm sorry Jenny, I couldn't accept your money, especially after you just saved my life. I'll come up with another way.' She looked sad.

I frowned at her.

'Please take the money if you need it. It's been sitting here with me for hundreds of years, I only spend it now and then when I want something I can't get here. I'd much rather some of it be put to use.'

'That would be a huge imposition,' Temperance started, then paused. 'Did you say hundreds of years? How old are you?'

That was a difficult question. I remembered at least a thousand winters but beyond that I'd rather lost count. I settled for saying simply that I was very old, older than the village church. That startled her.

'St Swithin's was built in 1218!' she said. I shrugged. I wasn't totally certain I knew what the year was now by the human counting.

'If you say so. It doesn't seem that long ago to me. So you can see I am perfectly happy here and you should take some of the coins.'

I could see Temperance wrestling with herself. Eventually she seemed to come to a decision.

'I will accept your offer and borrow five gold coins. Hopefully when I send for Benedict he can sell his farm and I can repay you.'

I was surprised. 'You would come back here to give the coins back?'

'Of course!'

I smiled widely. She flinched but only a little.

'It's a deal!'

Temperance slouched back, clearly tired from telling her story. My sense of the outside was telling me that it was late now, a few hours before midnight.

'I will go and fetch some dinner. You can eat and then go to sleep. Tomorrow night I will take you back to the surface with the coins.'

She smiled at me and I hugged that smile to myself as I slipped back down the tunnel. Since there would be two of us eating I decided to catch a fish for dinner. I came out into the lake and found the pike floating by the tunnel entrance. He was a wily one. I had been known to give him the other half of my catch so he followed me as I located a sleeping school of bream and snatched one. I waved my hand at him but he blinked big pikeish eyes at me and trailed me all the way back to the cave, even when I stopped to dig up some reed tubers.

Despite Temperance's smiles I had half expected her to make a break for it as soon as I left. To my surprise she was sitting where I had left her, knees tucked up under her chin and leaning on the wall. I clambered out and smacked the bream on the floor to kill it. I knew that humans were fussy eaters – always throwing fish innards back into the lake rather than eating them. I usually just golloped the fish down whole so it took me a while to locate a knife and gut the fish properly. I dropped the guts back into the lake and the pike snaffled them up and then swam back out. I presented the fish to Temperance along with half of the tubers.

She looked at it.

'Would you like me to cook it?' she said.

'As in, burn it?' I asked. She wrinkled her nose at me.

'No! I won't burn it. Let me show you.' She conjured a smaller ball of fire in her hand and began to pass it over the fillets. Then she stopped and put the fire out.

'I'm sorry, you don't like fire do you?' she said.

I shook my head but said, 'Go on, I want to see.'

Temperance lit the fire again and held her hand over the fish, muttering something under her breath. The fish meat changed, going from a waxy translucent pink to a flaky white. True to her word they didn't burn. She repeated the process for the tubers then served half of the food to me on an earthenware plate from my wall of trinkets. I gave the food a sniff. It smelt very strange. I took a small bite. It wasn't bad, just different.

I finished it off quickly, realising as I took the last tuber that humans didn't usually eat face first from the plate. I looked at Temperance and saw that she was eating with her hands, pointedly not looking at me. That meant she had looked at me and been embarrassed and was now looking away. Humans were very complicated.

When she finished eating Temperance washed the plate in the entrance pool and then dried it with a bit of her skirt. I consulted my bedding nest and fished out the least raggedy blanket. She took it from me a little tentatively but wrapped herself up in it willingly enough. Satisfied that my guest was as comfortable as possible I scuttled past her and began to tidy up my bedding. I put the skull back with the others and rearranged the reeds into the nest I liked. I folded myself up into it and said good night. Temperance said good night too, but I could tell she was still a little uneasy. I stayed as still as I could and breathed deeply but I don't think it fooled her. I fell asleep for real eventually, still listening to her shallow breathing and the faint lapping of the water at the cave entrance.

Chapter Three

I slept as deeply as a sunken log and when I woke up Temperance was still there, staring at the mossy wall of the cave in the flickering wisplight. I wasn't sure if she had slept at all. The purple spots many humans have under and around their eyes seemed larger and darker than before. I wondered if she continued to stay awake, would she turn purple all over or just continue to pale?

I was stiff from my sleep and wanted to get up. I coughed loudly and rustled the reeds and branches of my nest more than I usually do. I didn't want to startle her but Temperance stayed still, her chin resting on her knees. Her face was perfectly blank and pale, devoid of any expression, even when I scuttled past her to dangle my feet in the water. I looked back at her and tried to smile without showing any of my teeth. This was difficult to manage and a few of the first row popped out. I gave up and stopped smiling.

'Good morning, Temperance,' I said in greeting.

She looked over me and returned a weak smile.

'Good morning, Jenny.' Her voice was gravelly and dry and she resumed staring at the wall.

I stood awkwardly behind her. I didn't know whether to go about my morning routine as normal. I usually went for a quick swim and then tidied up the cave before heading out again to spend the day in the lake. It seemed that it would be impolite to leave my guest here alone and unentertained, but perhaps my presence was making her more uncomfortable. I decided to split the difference and jumped in the water to freshen up. Even though my cave is damp and dank I do sometimes feel dried out after a long sleep out of the water. Most Jennys sleep in their lakes but I have always liked having somewhere dry to keep my bits and pieces, and after a while I started sleeping there too. It is always pleasant, though, to dive back in and feel the cool lake revitalising me. The water was cold and crisp and I ducked underneath to brush out my hair.

Once I had soaked to my satisfaction I reluctantly hauled out into the cave again and began to straighten everything up. I redid my bedding nest and ran a rag over my stacks of trinkets and treasures. It doesn't get particularly dusty down here but it is important to keep everything clean and free from mould. Some of my older treasures rotted right away before I realised that I needed to clean them regularly.

Temperance had paused from her introspection and was watching me with an expression that seemed amused.

'I would not have expected such diligent housewifery from a lake dweller such as yourself,' she said. 'This place is spotless. You may come and help me clean the farmhouse any time you run out of work here.'

'You don't like to do it yourself?' I asked, picking up a small icon of a cloaked figure so I could wipe under the folds in the wood.

'Heavens no,' Temperance said, 'I've never cared for it much. Benedict likes things to be neat, and I do what I can to keep the place tidy, but with two children and a kitchen full of visitors all wanting their ailments tended to, it can get out of control fast.'

'Ah children, yes,' I said. 'When my daughter was young it was impossible to keep the cave orderly. I would send her out to play in the lake while I cleaned in here, then send her in here so I could tidy the lake.' I smiled at the thought of Little Jenny building towers and castles out of mud she had brought up from the lake floor. It had driven me mad at the time but I missed it now.

Temperance started at my words. 'You have a daughter?' she exclaimed, eyes widening. I nodded, still smiling, though I tried to cover my teeth again.

'Of course, Little Jenny. She lives in the millpond at Winchford. She must be nearly two hundred winters old now. I visit her there occasionally and sometimes she comes here.'

'Goodness,' said Temperance, 'what a thing to think about.' She paused for a while then said, 'Well in that case you must know what it is like to miss your children. I am missing my Ursula and Josiah very much this morning. I am worried especially about Ursula, she must be so frightened after seeing me dragged away. I have been praying that Benedict has been released and is caring for them.'

Her voice was so sad. I badly wanted to pat her shoulder but I was sure the touch of my long nails would panic her. I tried to cluck sympathetically but it came out as more of a gurgle. I think she took it as it was meant, though.

After a moment Temperance shrugged her shoulders and pasted on a smile.

'What time of day is it at the surface, Jenny?' she asked.

I thought about it.

'A few hours after dawn,' I said, 'before the time when the church bell rings for midday.'

She considered this. 'So around ten in the morning?'

I shrugged, copying her earlier movement. I didn't concern myself much with the human accounting of time. I knew the hours of church services that were announced by the sound of bell-ringing but even they seemed to change as the years went by.

'When will you take me to the surface?' she asked, starting to gnaw a little on her bottom lip.

'Whenever you like,' I said. 'There aren't any farmhouses near the south side of the lake but it might be better to go at night. Humans have very bad night-sight and no one will see you then.'

Temperance continued to chew her lip.

'The problem with that, Jenny, is that I also have very bad night-sight. I don't know if I can make it through the woods to the Oxford road after night falls.'

'Hmmmm.' She made a good point but going by daylight seemed dangerous too. I asked if she wasn't worried about running into the villagers if she left during the day.

'I think maybe if I left now then I could get a good day's walk in before having to stop overnight. It's a Sunday today so everyone will be at church until midday.' Temperance looked eager to go.

I didn't blame her for wanting to leave so soon. I loved my cave but it wasn't designed for human habitation and in her eyes I was probably still the nightmarish monster who had trapped her here. Her excuse wasn't even that flimsy. It did make sense for her to leave while the village was at church, and it would be another week before such an opportunity arose.

I nodded and reached behind me for the waterproof bag I had bought from the tinker with the wisplight.

'Here,' I said, handing it to her. 'Pack your clothes in this. You can get dressed on the banks and then you won't have to walk in wet clothes all day.'

She took the bag tentatively and picked up the socks and boots then hesitated. I realised I was standing in front of where I had hung her kirtle and she didn't want to come that close to me. I jumped back at once.

'I'll just go and check there's no one at the surface, shall I?' I said and slipped into the pool. The lake water still had the chill of winter to it despite the warm spring sunshine above. I kicked off from the bottom and swam a circuit of the lake, staying low enough from the surface to avoid being seen. The banks were deserted. Satisfied I wasn't about to be spotted I broke the surface and took a breath of the fresh morning air. It was unusual for me to do this but I wanted to be sure there was no one on the streets of the village or hanging around the houses that were nearest to the lake.

I couldn't see a single human, only an arrowhead of geese flying north through the cloudless sky. No movement on land, not even the rustle of a field mouse. I stayed there a little longer, just to be sure there was no one in sight. Finally, satisfied the village was all at church, I dipped back into the water and sank to the bottom.

When I returned to the cave Temperance had finished packing up her things and was trying to braid her hair into a neat plait. She wasn't having much success; the dark curls were knotted from her dunking in the lake and kept springing out at odd angles. Her brows were furrowed together in concentration.

When she saw me she dropped her hands and gave me a questioning look.

'No one on the banks,' I said. 'Are you ready to go? I'll have to carry you through the tunnel; you should conjure up another bubble of air to breathe from.'

She nodded but looked uncomfortable, twisting her hands. I was a little irritated by that. I knew she didn't want me to touch her but there really was no other way for me to get her out again.

'Um, Jenny,' Temperance started then stopped, looking even more awkward.

'What?' I asked, a bit grumpily I'll admit. She gulped but carried on.

'Last night, you said you might loan me some . . . I mean if you've changed your mind that is understandable, but I was wondering if you still . . .'

Realisation dawned on me. She was talking about the coins. I had assumed that was settled already.

'You mean you didn't pack them yet?' I asked, surprised. She shook her head vigorously.

'Oh. Well in that case . . .' I skirted around her and picked up a double handful of coins. 'Take what you need.'

Temperance considered the hoard I was holding out to her. She selected four large gold coins and a dozen of the smaller coppers. She looked up at me and smiled.

'I think the coppers should be much less than the fifth gold piece I asked for, but I'll need some small change for the road. I don't want to have to pay for lodging and a meal with a coin worth more than the inn.'

'You should take the fifth gold piece as well,' I said, 'You might need it when you are buying a new farm.'

She shook her head. 'Thank you, Jenny, but no. Your generosity is already too much.' She leaned down to tuck the coins somewhere in the bag. 'I swear on my power that I will return to repay this money.'

That was very pleasing. It would surely take her several years to organise a repayment but she would definitely be coming back to see me. Maybe she would even return several times to pay instalments a coin at a time. I was surprised at how happy it made me to think of future company. I had always thought I was content to live alone in the lake.

I nodded gravely and she straightened up, the coins safely stowed.

'Are you ready to go?' I asked. Temperance nodded, holding the bag close to her chest with both hands. I stepped back into the water and held out my hand to her. She took it tentatively and sat down on the edge of the cave, dangling her legs in the water. She let go of my grip and held her left hand to her mouth, whispering something into the curled fist. It was harder to see above water but I saw there was a shimmer in the air, like the sun heating a road in summer. She put her lips to the shimmer and took a deep breath. The shimmer fluttered but stayed in the air.

Satisfied that it was working she nodded at me again and slid into the water. Under the water the shimmer became a bubble, much larger and more stable than the one she had conjured the first time we had met. She took another breath from it, the bubble billowing in and out. I slipped an arm around her waist, pulling her towards me. We were about the same height but I was much thinner; my strength came from my nature rather than flesh and bone. I could feel the tension in her body as I held her by the waist but she didn't struggle in my grip. When I was

sure she wasn't going to pop the bubble of air, I sank us a little
further down and swam into the tunnel.

There was no light in the tunnel and I realised too late that
I should have mentioned to Temperance that she wouldn't be
able to see. She squirmed a little as the darkness consumed us.
I looked down at her. Her eyes were staring sightlessly and her
right hand clutched the bag of her clothing to her chest.

I decided to hurry and kicked off faster than I usually do. The
tunnel seemed longer than I remembered it but we were soon
bursting out into the main body of the lake. Temperance relaxed
a little as the light hit her and we swam through the pond weed
and gravel beds of the lake floor. Her head turned to watch as
we passed a school of minnows, their silver bodies glimmering
in the rays of sunlight. I hoped the pike wouldn't come out and
startle her.

We swam to the far east side of the lake. I surfaced just
above where the Caerlee flows out of my realm and turns to
the south. Temperance's bubble popped with a squeak as I
pulled her head above the water and she gasped for fresh air. I
let go of her waist and she trod water beside me, her chemise
ballooning out around her. I reached an arm out of the water
and pointed at the shore.

'Over there is the river. Come ashore there and start walking.
If you head due east from here then you'll hit the Oxford road
in about a mile.'

Temperance nodded and began to paddle to the banks. I
swam in beside her. She slipped as she dragged herself out of the
water into the reed beds that covered this part of the shore but
caught herself at the last instant. She hugged the bag of clothes
and money tight to her chest and stumbled forward, reaching
unobstructed dry land and heading towards the woods.

I stayed in the water, watching her walk away through the
trees. She turned back to pull on her boots and waved to me.

'Thank you, Jenny,' she called. 'I will never forget what you
have done for me.'

I felt a little heat fill my cheeks and sank back into the water to hide the colour. Temperance started walking again and soon vanished from view into the woods. I waited a while longer then kicked down and swam back to my cave.

The rest of the day was uneventful. I straightened up the cave, restacking and ordering the remaining coins from my hoard. When the cave was as tidy as I could make it I went back out to the lake and started taking a rough tally of the fish stocks. I had completed one before winter and it was a good habit to do them regularly. But I struggled to keep the numbers straight in my head and the fish were flightier than usual and I kept counting them twice. Eventually I gave up and floated freely in the water. The pike came up and nosed at my feet but I ignored it and eventually it swam away, looking elsewhere for food.

I was thinking about Temperance. She would have reached the road by now and was probably well on the way to Oxford. I wished I could know if she was doing well. It occurred to me that it could be many years before I found out if she had reached safety. I thought about how sad she had been this morning when she was missing her babies. Her husband and children must think she was dead. At least I had been able to send her off with the coins. Humans put such a store in coins that she was sure to be able to get by with what she had taken.

Hopefully Temperance would be able to send for her family once she was settled. They would probably be glad to leave Chipping Appleby now that Parson Braddock had come to take charge. I had not liked the sound of him at all. I thought that he was probably the man in black I had seen on the bank. I hoped he did not plan to make a habit of throwing people into my lake. Temperance had been relatively sensible for a human: probably as a result of her being a witch. If they threw in a regular human then it was entirely possible that they would be frightened to death before I could rescue them. Even if I was able to prevent their foolish hearts from stopping, could I trust a normal human to keep my secrets the way I had trusted Temperance? Having a Jenny in the lake was not something that humans wanted. I had kept a low profile for all these years and I did not want to have to leave Chipping Appleby.

I stayed in the lake, drifting just under the surface, my head tilted up to the air. Above me I watched the sun as it tracked across the sky and began to drop to the west. The sky faded from blue to pink to grey and the evening stars began to wink into existence. I thought about going back to the cave to sleep but it seemed to me that it would feel very empty. I remained floating until night had fallen and the waterbirds had all returned to their nests. Even the fish were sleeping.

Eventually I gave a deep sigh and slipped below the surface. I had been lying there so long that the frogbit was tangled in my hair and I paused to comb it out with my fingers before I went back into the tunnel. My hands were wound into my hair when I heard something. There was a strange sound coming from the eastern side of the lake. It sounded like something splashing almost methodically into the water: *splash, splash, splash*.

It was probably a deer that had fallen over whilst drinking and was struggling to get up in the mud. I kicked off towards it. I still wasn't feeling very hungry but maybe I could scare it into getting to its feet. At the back of my mind I also thought of Parson Braddock. Perhaps he had decided to see if he could find Temperance's body. I wouldn't mind dragging him down into the lake if he was sniffing around looking for trouble. I doubted he would taste good but the pike would probably enjoy sharing him with me.

I swam towards the noise then stopped sharp. Temperance was kneeling among the bulrushes at the edge of the lake, slapping both hands into the water. She looked tired and muddy, but her face was determined and as I watched she slapped her hands again.

'Jenny,' she called out, in a low whisper. 'Jenny, are you there?'

I broke the surface and looked towards her. She stopped smacking the water and waved at me.

'Temperance? What are you doing back here?' I called. She waved again, beckoning me over.

I swam over and pushed up off the muddy banks so that my torso was out of the water. I squinted at her.

'What is it, Temperance? Did something happen? Do you need to take some more money?' I couldn't think of another reason she would come back so soon.

'No, Jenny.' She sat down next to me in the mud. Our eyes were about level and she looked me straight in the face without flinching.

'I got to the road about midday and I was walking south-east. I was missing my family but I was hopeful. I was sure I could find a new patch of land to buy, and then I could send for my babies.

'But then I got to thinking — Benedict would never sell his farm. It's been in his family for generations, longer than anyone can remember. It would break his heart if he had to leave. And his brothers and sisters live in the village too, along with all their children. I couldn't ask him to leave all that behind, couldn't drag my children from their family.'

She paused, eyes flashing in the starlight.

'And I realised I didn't want to leave either. Chipping Appleby might be a tiny little village but it is my home. My mother was the cunning woman and her mother before her. I'm not going to let some out-of-town pastor keep me away from my home.'

I frowned, not quite understanding what she was going to do.

'But they all think you're a witch. And also dead. If you walk into the village they're going to run screaming that the witch has come back to life.'

She smiled at me.

'Exactly Jenny. They do think I'm a witch. I had forgotten that I was one. I was so upset by my arrest, by the village trying to drown me, that I was thinking like a farmer's wife and a mother, as if I had no defence other than my husband's word. But I am a witch! And I'm going to save myself.'

She picked up a package wrapped in muddy cowhide and brandished it at me.

'I looped back north and dug up my spell book. I have a plan, but I'm going to need some help, Jenny.'

'What are you going to do?' I asked. 'Curse Pastor Braddock?'

'No, not right away. I don't know any proper curses or attacking spells. What I do know is healing spells, and one of the spells in my book is for sicknesses of the mind. I can cast a spell that will make the whole village forget that I was ever accused of being a witch. They won't remember that I was drowned or arrested, I can just walk right back into my home and kiss my children like nothing ever happened.'

Temperance's face was fierce. 'And then I will find a way to drive Pastor Braddock out of town. I was naive and trusting but I'm wiser now. He'll find me harder to get rid of this time around.'

I considered her plan. It seemed a good one, but I still didn't see where I came in.

'What do you need from me?' I asked.

'If I am going to enchant the whole village I will need to make my spell very strong. I only have so much power, and for this kind of spell I need a few items to strengthen my magic. I was hoping you would help me find them, and that maybe I could stay with you while we prepare the spell.'

I tried not show my surprise that she wanted to come back to the cave. It wasn't like she had a lot of choices of where to go but I was still pleased.

'You are welcome to stay if you like, I would appreciate the company. As for the ingredients you mentioned, what exactly is it you require?'

Temperance smiled widely and reached for my hand. She squeezed it tight, ignoring the long, jagged nails

'Oh thank you, Jenny! I can't say how grateful I am for your help!' She patted my hand again. 'I was thinking about what I'll need as I was walking back here. Hopefully it won't be expensive, but it might be difficult to get.'

She put my hand down and started counting on her fingers.

'For a memory spell, I'll need pansies, crow feathers, anise leaves and a horseshoe. I should be able to collect some of those myself and I bought the anise from an apothecary three towns over.'

She paused and then continued:

'For the magnification part it might be a bit trickier. I need the fingerbones of a murderer, buried in unhallowed ground. I need a hair from the head of a kelpie. I need a candle with a wick of cotton from a bishop's cassock, and a drop of blood from a fairy, freely given.'

She finished and looked up at me. Her expression was hopeful. I considered the list.

'The last should be simple enough, I am technically a kind of fairy and it is no trouble to give you a drop of blood. The rest I am afraid I cannot produce myself.'

Temperance's face fell and I sighed deeply. I was going to have to do something I was sure to regret.

'I do, however, know someone who can help supply such items.'

'You do? Who is it?' she asked.

I grimaced. I really didn't want to say his name.

'Brackus Marsh,' I said, 'He is the one who sold me the wisplight, a pedlar of sorts. He's a scoundrel and a rogue, but he can source what you need.'

'Is he,' she hesitated, 'like you?'

I harumphed. She hadn't meant it as an insult but I didn't like to think of myself as similar to Brackus.

'I suppose,' I grumbled. 'We are both low fae. Brackus is a goblin; he buys up stock at the goblin markets and then journeys around selling things to Jennys, dwarfs and other types of solitary fae that do not like to travel themselves.'

'You don't like him?' she asked, noticing the edge to my voice. I shook my head.

'Not much. He's always hanging around and pestering me. He'll have what you need though – he has a huge pack full of every kind of magical ingredient or knick-knack.'

'How can we contact him?'

I pointed at the ash trees behind us and asked Temperance

to bring me a handful of leaves. She came back with an armful, the oval green leaves spring-fresh and bright. I folded each one into a little boat then lifted them to my mouth and whispered Brackus's name to each. I handed them to Temperance.

'Here, take these over to the Caerlee and set them off downstream. Brackus generally stays within the extent of the river. He'll get the message. If prior experience is anything to go by he'll be here within the day.'

Temperance gathered them in her arms and tripped off along the banks. I watched as she knelt by the river and sent off the leaves. I contemplated what I had gotten myself into. I did want to help Temperance but it was going to be a little strange having to share the cave on a more permanent basis.

Chapter Four

True to my prediction it took Brackus less than a day to receive our message and travel to my lake. I was sitting in the cave with Temperance, picking through a bag full of various bird feathers, when a bubbling sound came from the mouth of the tunnel. I looked over and saw the leaf boats I had sent downstream bobbing up and down in the water. They looked considerably battered from their trip and when I scooped them up they began to fall apart in my hand.

Temperance looked questioningly at me so I held the boats up for her to hear. Brackus had emptied out my message and spoken his own back to the leaves. I listened carefully as his voice echoed around the cave.

'My dear Jenny Greenteeth, I was surprised to receive your message and have made haste to visit you. I have pitched camp on the south shore and await you there at your leisure. Best, Brackus.'

His voice was the same as always, affectedly cultured as if he was addressing a fairy queen. It had amused me once, but now it rankled at me, like mockery. Temperance looked impressed.

'You were right, he was quick.' She began to slip her kirtle on, hands fussing at the stays. 'Can we go and see him now?'

I shook my head.

'Don't rush, Temperance. I don't want him to think we've just been sitting here and waiting for him or that we are overly keen to buy. Otherwise he will try to overcharge us.' I crushed the leaves in my hand and scattered the fragments over the water.

Temperance looked disappointed but resumed tying on her kirtle. She had found a length of twine somewhere in the pile of trinkets and was using it to keep her dark hair off her face. She adjusted it now, tucking a few stray curls behind her ears. I considered whether I should do the same – maybe it would make me look less alarming if I wasn't always peering out from behind a sheet of wet hair. Perhaps later; I had no intention of letting Brackus think I was changing my appearance for him.

Temperance continued to fidget for a while, counting her coins, smoothing down her dress and rearranging the crow feathers we had retrieved from the bag. Eventually I gave up.

'Come on then,' I hissed, my voice a little rougher than usual. 'Let's go and see the pedlar.'

Temperance jumped up and beamed at me. She placed the coins into her pocket and started towards where I was sitting at the edge of the water. I held up a hand.

'Now don't be too polite to Brackus. He's a very tricky type of creature – goblins are known to be deceptive and cunning. Let me do the talking.'

Temperance nodded at me, wide-eyed. I sighed and slid into the water. She jumped in beside me and conjured her breathing bubble. I took her hand and we swam out into the lake. This was our fourth trip through the tunnel, and the third that Temperance had been awake for. She was getting much better at it, the air blob was larger and more stable, and she didn't panic when the darkness closed in around us.

I could scent the woodsmoke coming from the south banks as soon as I emerged from the tunnel. Brackus always burned some strange kind of spice in his fires. It gave a bitter, acrid taste to the smoke, but it made the flames burn black, giving off no light. Useful for a goblin who spent much of his time trying to avoid being seen by curious human eyes.

Brackus knew me well enough not to stand too close to the

lake and had pitched his camp further away, several paces from the woods. I hauled out onto the banks, pulling Temperance to my feet beside me. She looked around blankly, not seeing the black flames until I pointed them out to her. Brackus's camp was a piddling small thing. He had hung a tarpaulin from four carved staffs, driven into the ground. Just in front of this cover was the dark fire, and sat behind it, on a three-legged milking stool, was Brackus Marsh.

Brackus looked much the same as always. He wore his hair short, the brown curls tickling over his pointed ears and out from underneath the red velvet cap he wore at a jaunty angle. A matching suit of burgundy velvet was adorned with an abundance of buttons, carved from ivory, bone, wood, jet. Gold braid was pinned haphazardly in the few gaps between the sea of buttons. His skin was a shining acorn brown, contrasting with his bright blue eyes and gleaming white teeth. He wore the same air of ineffable smugness that had irritated me from our first meeting.

I stomped over towards him, towing Temperance along behind me. Walking upright on land was difficult and I was out of practice. By the time I reached him I was out of breath and in a worse mood than ever. He looked up at me, grinning. He'd known exactly what he was doing when he picked this spot.

'Sweet maiden of the emerald lagoon,' Brackus said, jumping to his feet and grabbing my hand. He bent over it and kissed the air above my palm. 'It always brings me such pleasure when your sight befills my eyes.'

'"Befills" isn't a word, Marsh,' I said.

'Of course it is, verdant lady, though it hardly befits me to correct you.' I growled and snatched my hand away. Brackus smiled widely at me, then turned to look at Temperance.

'And who is this delightful young damsel you have brought to me, Jenny? Either my nose deceives me or there is something of a whiff of magic about her, the aroma of enchantment.' He reached for her hand and I smacked it away.

'Don't you talk to her, Marsh. Your business is with me.'

He pouted. 'May I not know the name of this illustrious

enchantress? It is so rare that I get to make the acquaintance of such an appealing young mademoiselle.' He bowed deeply, 'Brackus Marsh at your service, Miss . . .?'

'Temperance,' stuttered Temperance. She shot me a guilty look but pressed on: 'My name is Mistress Temperance Crump. It is a pleasure to meet you, Master Marsh.'

'Ahh, Temperance,' crooned Brackus. 'Such a sweet name for such a sweet lady. I am at your service, Mistress Crump, and you must of course address me as Brackus. All my worthy customers do.' He paused to eye the look on my face then amended, 'Most of them anyway.'

Brackus took Temperance's hand and guided her to his stool.

'Now, Mistress Crump, tell me what I may do for you.' Brackus adopted an expression of humble obedience, his large brown eyes almost brimming with helpfulness.

I slouched down on the floor between them, turning my face to Brackus. His expression didn't falter.

'I want to buy some supplies from you, Marsh. I have a list.'

'A list of supplies, Jenny! Goodness, and after all those times you told me you never wanted to buy so much as a button from me again!' He leaned past me to wink at Temperance. To my annoyance she giggled.

'What I want, Marsh, is three things. I want a murderer's finger, some kelpie hair and a bishop's cassock candle.' I counted them off on my fingers. Brackus adopted a countenance of pantomime surprise.

'Great heavens, Jenny, what would a simple river dweller like yourself want with those?' He nodded towards Temperance. 'Is Mistress Crump there truly a great witch?'

I resisted the urge to bite his face off.

'What my business is with these things is none of your concern. Can you provide them or not?' I snapped.

He rolled his eyes, 'Hold your horses, Jenny. Let me check my pack.' He dropped another wink at Temperance and bounced to his feet. He snapped his fingers and a large sack appeared at his feet.

'The first article you requested, my malachitinous delight, was the finger,' he paused, reaching into the bag, 'of a killer! The deadly digit of a death-dealing delinquent! Well, it just so happens that I have such a thing!' He withdrew a small leather pouch, displaying it to us. 'Behold! The fourth finger of Steven Cleghorne: the bloody blacksmith of Catford! His crimes are beyond imagination, he once—'

'Get on with it!' I interrupted. Brackus gave me a doleful look then placed the pouch at Temperance's feet.

'The secondary item, the hair from a kelpie's mane. Well, it just so happens that I was recently in the Highlands and picked myself a veritable skein of locks from those most foul-tempered mer-mares.' Brackus brandished a spindle, wound with multiple strands of what could conceivably be horsehair.

'Merely select the colour that is most pleasing to you, mi-ladies.' He bowed again and tossed the spindle to Temperance with a flourish.

'The final, and most unexpected artefact is truly a rarity. Many pedlars have never so much as seen this prodigious item, much less been able to source it. For whom, whom could sneak into a cathedral to steal a string from the very robe of a prince of the church? Whom would then have the wit, the wherewithal, and the wisdom to craft this precious fibre into a candle? Whom indeed . . .?'

Brackus paused for effect. I put my head in my hands. Temperance was wrapped up in his performance. He paused for a response but sensing that none would come, plunged onwards.

'Well, my dears, it just so happens, that I, Brackus Marsh, am whom!' He stuck his whole be-buttoned arm into the sack and brought forth a squat wax candle, grimy with ash and fluff. Brackus knelt before Temperance and offered it to her with all the pomp and circumstance of a knight pledging his sword. She took the candle with a look of astonishment, holding it as if it was a holy relic.

Brackus sprang back, holding his arms behind his back, looking like a cat that had caught a rabbit twice its size and had just dropped it on his owner's pillow. Temperance examined the three items carefully. I could see hope starting to bloom in her face. She looked back up at Brackus questioningly.

'Good sir, might I ask how much these items would cost?'

Brackus wrinkled his nose and hopped on one foot. He jammed his head to one side and appeared to consider the question very deeply.

'Dear lady, such items, the very cream of my collection. It would be a terrible loss to see them go, even if into such fair hands. For these divine articles, almost family heirlooms, I must ask—'

'How much?' I interrupted again. 'Spit it out, Marsh.'

'Seventeen gold pieces,' Brackus said promptly. 'As you are such a beloved and loyal customer, Jenny.'

'Highway robbery!' I exclaimed, 'These paltry things are worth no more than two gold pieces. I shall give you two and a half to show willing but not a penny more.' In truth I had no idea of their worth but it was always good practice to argue with Brackus.

Brackus acted as if he had been stabbed, reeling backwards and clutching at his buttons.

'Sweet Jenny, I could not allow these cherished belongings of mine to go for any less than fifteen gold pieces. They are almost irreplaceable, I should not even have shown them to you.'

'Three. And you may return to show me more items for sale in future; I will rescind your banishment from my lake.'

He smiled toothily, 'Such an offer is indeed priceless, but I still cannot allow these to go for less than ten gold pieces.'

'Jenny,' said Temperance, looking worried. I waved a hand to soothe her.

'Four. There – I have already doubled my initial offer, far more than you deserve.'

'Oh my sweet pea-green princess, would that I could accept but alas it would bankrupt me. Perhaps we shall not settle our differences today.' Brackus began to pack up, sorrowfully prying the items from Temperance's hands.

'Now listen here, Marsh,' I began, but was interrupted by a loud sob from Temperance.

She fell to the floor, tears streaming down her face.

'Oh, Jenny, Jenny, what are we to do? I only have two pieces of gold to barter with and if we cannot afford it than I will surely die.' I gaped at her sobs but she kept crying, mewling like a drowning kitten. Brackus looked uncomfortable and continued trying to inch the spindle of kelpie hair from her fingers.

'Dear Mistress Crump, I am sure it is not as bad as all that,' he said. Temperance's tears grew thicker and her sobs louder.

'Oh but it is, kind sir. I have been banished from my village by a wicked parson. Without this spell I will be separated from my beloved children for ever. A life without my babies is surely not worth living. I will cast myself into the lake to drown.'

'Please stop crying, my dear lady,' said Brackus as he stopped trying to confiscate the spindle. Temperance wailed and threw herself at him, clutching him to her chest.

'What shall become of my children, my sweet motherless babies? Oh, I am the unluckiest woman who ever lived.'

'Please, Mistress Crump – erm, Temperance – do stop your crying. I, ah, am sure we can come to some kind of arrangement. Was it two gold coins you said you had?'

Temperance sniffled. 'Yes, my whole worldly wealth. Scrimped and saved for over all the years of my life.' She grasped his shirt, wiping her eyes on the gold braid.

'Well, perhaps I was a little hasty in setting my prices, especially for such a good and worthy maiden such as yourself.' He patted her arm gently and tried to unwind her grip. 'Two gold coins it shall be!'

'Oh Brackus, you are such a sweet soul! Truly a gentleman in goblin form. I am so grateful for your kindness.' She smiled up at him, tears sparkling on her cheeks. 'Even with all our money gone I am sure my children and I will be happy to live in abject poverty, as long as we are reunited.'

'Poverty?' asked Brackus, nervously. Temperance nodded, flicking a tear away with an elegant finger.

'Of course, all our wealth will go this purchase; after this we shall be destitute. But you are so kind, Master Marsh, to let me spend it here. I shall think of you always when I am serving us gruel and tree-bark soup.'

'Ah, well.' Brackus hesitated. 'I am sure I cannot let you and your family be destitute. Perhaps we shall settle on one gold piece. That way you can save your family and not have to eat so much gruel.'

Temperance wailed again, 'You are too kind, Master Marsh!' She sobbed anew and insisted on kissing him wetly on both cheeks. He pried her hands off him as gently as possible.

'Of course, no need to thank me, Mistress Crump. If I may . . .'

Temperance retrieved a gold coin from her pocket and handed it to him. He bit it automatically, then nodded and bowed, stowing it away too fast to see and began to pack up his camp.

'Well, delightful as always, Jenny. I think I had better be off at once. I am due in South Wales tomorrow night and I must needs be on my way. Mistress Crump, I do wish you the best of luck with your endeavours.'

Temperance gave another sob and stepped forward to embrace him again. Brackus dodged it with another bow.

'As I said, a pleasure, and now I must be off!' He grabbed the cloak pegged over his stool and shoved it into his pack. Each of the poles that had been supporting it were snatched from the ground and collapsed like telescopes then tucked neatly at his belt. The dark flames were extinguished with a word. Brackus made a final bow, buttons glinting in the darkness, then snapped his fingers and vanished, leaving Temperance and I alone at the edge of the woods.

Temperance wiped her face and grinned at me.

'Mistress Crump!' I exclaimed. 'I offer my humblest apologies. I had thought you an innocent but you are clearly far trickier than I gave you credit for. How on earth did you know that would work?'

She laughed and tossed me the spindle. 'Brackus may be a goblin but he's not so different from mortal men. I've met many a human pedlar that could be his brother. All flash and fire when he controls the conversation but avoids real emotion like the plague. A man like that can't abide a woman's tears. I knew he'd do anything to make me stop. The final touch of poverty was a bit of a gamble but I sensed he had a soft heart underneath the bluster.'

She picked up the pouch of fingerbones and the candle and tucked them into her pockets.

'Now if I really want to impress you I'll sell them back to him at a profit.'

I spluttered, leaning over and coughing. I realised I was laughing at about the same time she did and we laughed together, the noise pealing through the midnight woods.

'Do you want to do the memory spell tonight?' I asked when I had caught my breath.

Temperance shook her head, her smile fading.

'I need some time to prepare, think of the best way to arrange the magnification. Can we do it tomorrow, after sundown?'

I nodded and started tramping back towards the water. Temperance caught me up and we stepped back into the lake together.

The next night was a new moon, the sky black and empty. Temperance and I swam up to the surface just after sunset. After much discussion we had decided to hold our ceremony on the eastern bank of the lake, closest to the village. That way Temperance's spell would have the least distance to cover, increasing its chance of success..

Since Temperance couldn't see well in the dark, I had to help her mark out the spell circle in the mud of the banks, carving it out with a stick of elm wood. When it was complete she stepped into the centre and began to scatter the pansies around her. The flowers fluttered to the ground, their petals wavering like moths in the evening breeze. Temperance was muttering something under her breath. Her voice was pitched too low for me to catch the specific words, but it sounded like an old language humans had spoken in the village many hundreds of years ago. I tried to pin it down to a time and decided I had not heard it spoken since the church had been built. Old English perhaps, or even Latin.

Once the flowers were arranged to her satisfaction, I passed Temperance the crow feathers and anise leaves. She placed a long black feather at each compass point then crushed the spice between her palms, rubbing it onto her forehead and wrists. The spicy-sweet scent of liquorice broke onto the air. Next was the horseshoe which she positioned at her feet, prongs facing towards the village.

When the basic ingredients were done I handed over the pouch of finger bones, which she tied to her belt, and a hair from the spindle which she wound around her wrist. The kelpie hair she had selected was grey and shiny with sea salt. I wondered if it had come from a sea loch. Finally I gave her the bishop's candle which she placed carefully on top of the horseshoe. She nodded at me and I inserted my left forefinger into my mouth. I pressed the fingertip hard down onto a tooth until I tasted cold blood. I knelt at the edge of the circle and dripped blood onto the candle: one, two, three drops.

Temperance smiled at me and gestured for me to step back, before holding out each hand at her waist. She closed her eyes and began to chant, speaking in the same dead language she had used before. I still couldn't get the individual words quite right but I thought I understood the meaning. It was something about sleep and dreams. The world around me seemed to blur, the water and the earth overlapping. It seemed nothing more than a vision, a daydream or a fantasy. I looked at Temperance's feet and saw the candle was now burning. The flame was white hot, the brightness scouring my eyes. I blinked hard and focused on Temperance, while stepping back into the lake. As I re-entered the water the power of the lake pushed the spell away from me and my mind sharpened once more. I could see the spell more clearly now, perceive where it blossomed in Temperance's hands. She brought them forward and I watched the magic billow up towards the village.

The charm was fuelled in part by my own blood so I could sense it travelling forward. The enchantment slid up the slope like rising floodwater, ensnaring scuttling mice, rabbits sleeping in their burrows. As it caught each mind it grew larger and stronger, the wave building as it washed over larger creatures; dogs, cats and pigs in the back yards of the nearest houses. When the magic reached the first cottage, I felt it trickle in through the gaps in the wooden shutters, into the sleeping minds of the couple that lived there along with their children. It was a gentle spell, a quiet magic. I could feel it touching those in its path like a mother's hand smoothing the forehead of a child woken from a nightmare.

'Be still,' the spell said, 'it was just a dream. I am here now, none of that was real.' The mother's voice was different as it echoed in each head, but in every mind the undertone was that of Temperance's voice. I could see her in their heads as she had been: a young woman hugging her baby and her little girl, laughing and kissing her husband or bandaging an injured arm for a neighbour. The magic dislodged something in their minds, washing away fear and hatred. I felt her frown at that, as she saw through the eyes of the people who had tried to drown her.

Temperance kept chanting. I felt the spell expand out of the first three houses and cross the street. It bloomed out again to include another half-dozen cottages. I heard Temperance catch her breath as the magic caressed the sleeping form of a man lying in a wide bed. He was holding two young children in his arms, soothing them even in sleep. Tears stained all three of their faces. Temperance almost lost the spell then, the candle flickered but she shook herself and pressed on.

The magic rolled over the empty church, skirting around the edge of the holy ground and lapped up to the parsonage next to it. I could sense Temperance's magic moving up to the walls and she took a breath, preparing to push into the enemy's lair.

The charm stuttered. There was something inside the stone walls reacting to the memory spell, a magic both brighter and darker than Temperance's. She pushed again, focusing all of her power on the walls of the parsonage, searching for an entrance. The candle at her feet flared up, its flame burning as fierce and white as a star.

The opposing magic didn't retreat. It oozed out of the house as tree sap, repelling Temperance's fluid magic like oil rolling over water. It dribbled forth, crossing the road and chasing out the memory spell. It built and built like a tide of mud, sloshing back through the houses and down the field towards where we stood at the lake's edge.

Temperance gasped, clutching the pouch with her left hand and holding up her right towards the wave. The candle was burning brighter and brighter so that it hurt me to look at it but the wave of magic didn't stop.

I realised that it was too strong for her, that she couldn't repel it. The ooze was going to envelop the both of us, doing who knows what damage to Temperance's human mind. I called to her to come back to the lake, to drop her spell and run but she didn't move. She was shouting the words of the spell, planting her feet in the ground and drawing all of her magic and all of her strength to fend off the ooze. The candle burned so bright that everything else was hidden; I could no longer see Temperance clearly, only the shape of her outlined by the blazing light. Then it went out.

Blackness rushed in, followed by the crashing wave of oozing magic. Blinded by that final flash I summoned the lake towards me and reached out with arms of water to grab Temperance by the waist and arms and pull her backwards. She landed in the lake with a splash and I drew up walls of water around the banks of the lake, infusing them with all the force and magic I had available to me.

The ooze welled up against the water walls, looking for a way in. It rose up, trying to overtop them, to reach around them. I pulled more water to me, enclosing the whole lake in a shining translucent dome of living water. The ooze kept probing. I stood firm. Here on my lake I could hold these walls for ever, I never doubted I was strong enough to keep it out.

Eventually the ooze subsided. It retreated back up towards the village, leaving a fine coat of magic everywhere it had touched. I could trace it as it went, sliding backwards towards the parsonage. When I was confident it wasn't going to return, I dropped the dome of water. It shattered into a million droplets that fell like rain around us. Temperance was sitting in the shallow water next to my feet. Her face was stricken and still. She had given everything to the spell and the strange magic had knocked her back seemingly without effort.

I crooked a finger and the remnants of the spell ingredients washed down the bank towards us. The petals and feathers were fragmented, the horseshoe blackened and slimy. I collected them in my hands then turned to look again at Temperance. She met my eyes and struggled to her feet.

'What was ...' she began, her voice harsh and cracking. I interrupted her.

'Not here,' I said, 'don't speak. Whatever it was is still there.' She closed her mouth and splashed towards me. I took her hand and we dived under the water, sinking down towards the tunnel. She didn't have the strength to conjure a bubble of air so I swam as fast as I could and pushed her up back into the safety of the cave.

Chapter Five

Once I had Temperance safely back in my cave I ducked back into the water and returned to the lake. Whatever foreign power had reversed our spell was still present in the village and I could not be sure it would not come down to the water to search out its challenger. If something emerged from the village, dripping that oily magic, I would meet it here at the water's edge. In my lake I was nigh untouchable; even the high fae would struggle to best me here. The strength of the Jenny is in the strength of her water and my lake is large and healthy.

The magic I had felt had been very strong, its power only matched at the very extent of my lake. I had not seen its like before, not in all my long years of existence. That worried me. What menace lurked inside that parsonage, poisoning the village and its inhabitants? Temperance's spell had been strong, she had been fighting for her homeland and had the borrowed power of Brackus's artefacts to feed the magic. The ooze had thrown her back as easily as a child crushing an ant. Was it another witch or wizard, a new Morgan or Nicnevin? I didn't see what they would want with a little place like Chipping Appleby. Were I a young sorceress, I would surely head to the great cities of London or York, not waste my time with country villages.

The night seemed dark indeed after the phosphorescence of Temperance's candle. I swam laps of the lake, gliding just below the surface of the water. Around me the inhabitants of the lake were uneasy. Fish scattered at my passing and the frogs, normally loudly calling for their mates, were silent. Even the sky was clear of bats or owls, a sheer blackness quilted with stars.

I paused after my fifth circuit, stopping just before the point where Temperance had cast her spell. The circle was broken, two slashes in the mud where I had dragged her backwards. Enough of it remained to look suspicious so I rolled a ripple forward to smooth away the markings. As the water trickled back to me I could perceive the contagion of the opposing spell, coating the water droplets like oil.

It tasted like wood, like fir trees and pine needles. It was almost sweet at first but the longer I held it on my tongue the more it congealed into something rotten. I saw a dark forest, so overgrown that light could not penetrate and the whole undergrowth was dead. No life moved, no wind stirred the fallen leaves. At the heart of the wood lay the body of a male deer, its great antlers twisted and caught in a tangle of creeping vines. The chest of the stag was torn open, the inside black and rotting.

I spat out the water. Something very severe was in that village; even the trace of its passing was pure malevolence. I gathered the contaminated water to me, reaching deep into the well of power at my core. I summoned the thought of tree roots curling in the earth, of limestone caves dripping with water. The poison was expelled and I breathed out again.

I spent the rest of the night in the lake, watching the village for movement. There was nothing, not even the barking of the dog or the soft *pfwhoop* of an owl snatching a dormouse. The effort of defending the lake and then purifying the water had tired me and I longed to return to my cave and sleep. Despite this, I stayed. The night seemed to drag on and by the time the eastern sky began to grey I was truly exhausted. Still I waited. Only when the sun had risen above the horizon, casting an incongruously pastel pink light over the village, did I sink back to the depths.

Temperance was still awake. I hauled out onto the cave floor beside her. She was trembling but for once I did not think I was the cause. She looked as tired as I felt; the purple spots beneath her eyes were now sunken and her skin was dull. Even her curls seemed flat and lifeless. The remaining items from the spell were where I had thrown them when I had brought Temperance back earlier. I picked them up and placed them neatly beside the rest of my collection. The bishop's candle had all burnt out, leaving only a ring of grimy wax. I put it with the rest anyway.

Temperance was still shaking as I knelt beside her. I took her hand and began to unwind the kelpie hair from around it. She had clenched her fists so tightly that the hair was stained with blood and stuck to her skin. The scent of flesh permeated my fatigue and I realised I was very hungry. Too tired now to go fishing, I would have to settle for bulrush roots. When I had disentangled the last of the hair I dipped her hand into the lake water to rinse off the blood. I ripped a strip from her linen shirt to bandage the cut.

'Thank you, Jenny,' Temperance said in a small voice.

I gave her one of my closed-mouth smiles and fetched a few roots from the pile near the entrance.

'Here,' I said, 'eat, you need to regain your strength.'

She looked at the tuber without much enthusiasm but the sense of my words got through and she raised it to her mouth to take a bite. I chomped on my own roots, trying not to think about the smell of blood.

When she had finished her bulrush Temperance looked at me.

'What was that out there? I have never felt anything like that before.'

I shrugged. 'I don't know. I've never felt it either. Whatever it is almost killed you and would definitely have knocked me out had I been on land. It's very strong and very bad.'

'Bad,' Temperance whispered. 'I almost didn't believe there was bad magic after meeting you. I thought the stories weren't true.'

I frowned. That certainly wasn't the lesson I wanted her to

learn from our collaboration. I might not have eaten her but I certainly wasn't good. I wasn't bad either, I simply was.

'There's bad magic and good magic just like there are bad humans and good humans,' I said, picking my words carefully. 'Most of us low fae aren't either one.' I took another bite of my tuber.

'But you said the force in the village was bad,' she pressed.

I nodded. 'I don't say that often. What's bad for prey might be good for the predator. My pike eat the frogs but they're not bad. Whatever is in that village is not just bad. It's wrong. It shouldn't be here. It shouldn't be.'

I paused, unsure whether to confess the next part. 'It scared me, Temperance.'

She looked at me, eyes wide and shocked. Then she said, 'It scared me too.'

I put down the last of the tubers. 'Get some sleep, Temperance, you must be exhausted. That force very nearly killed you. We'll be safe here in the daytime. Tonight I will go and look myself.'

'Isn't that dangerous for you?' Temperance's face wore an expression almost like concern. That was sweet of her.

'A little, but I am sure I can outrun whatever it is back to the lake. Besides, I am very good at sneaking around. It won't see me.'

I smiled a proper smile then, all my rows of teeth exposed and gleaming. Temperance shivered. I noticed as I prepared to sleep that she kept looking at me out of the corner of her eye. It wouldn't do her any harm to remember what I was. She had much worse things than me to face in that village.

After a tense day spent in the cave, I bade farewell to Temperance and headed to the surface. A pale sliver of moon hung low in the sky, casting the slightest wash of light over the village. I would have preferred to make this expedition in pure blackness where my night-sight would have given me the advantage. Alas, I was not prepared to wait another four weeks for the next new moon. I would have to count on my natural sneakiness and the coldness of the night to keep all the villagers indoors.

A northerly wind was blowing through the trees, catching at my hair. It seemed to whisper at my ears, urging me to go back to my lake. I was still stumbling a little as I strode forward, my legs not quite used to bearing my weight. Halfway between the water's edge and the first houses I gave up and dropped to my hands, scuttling forward on all fours. It was not the most elegant of gaits but I was much faster and more even. I chided myself for attempting the walk. All this time spent with Temperance had caused me to forget how un-human I was. That was a dangerous habit to get into.

I came up to the main street between two houses, sneaking around a metal and oakwood plough as I went. A hound of some kind stirred in the backyard of the left-hand house. It padded forward, sniffing at the air. A sheepdog, I could see it trying to sense my presence through the darkness. A dog was no threat to me but I did not want it to start barking. I drew in a deep breath and hissed through my teeth, as loud and threatening as I dared. The dog flinched as the noise hit its upturned ears and it stepped back nervously. I hissed again and the furred tail dropped. The dog backed into the house and whined.

I pressed on. The village was dark; there was no need for lanterns to light the streets in such a small community where no one went out after sunset. The main road was cobbled with flat blocks of limestone, smoothed over by the passage of many feet. I remembered the hullabaloo that had greeted the installation, many decades back. I put a tentative hand out onto the nearest cobble. There was no one in the street. I scuttled across the road and hid in a patch of long grass.

The parsonage was just past the village church. I headed towards it, going slowly and carefully. Despite the darkness I could tell the village had changed since the last time I had walked through it. The cottages, once wattle and daub and then wooden, had been upgraded again to stone. I traced a hand over the wall of one as I passed. Limestone again. I had not seen quarrying carts come past my lake; they must have come down the other road. Strange how much I had missed, living only a stone's throw from these people.

St Swithin's was as silent by night as it was noisy by day. I crossed right over the little graveyard, leaping over the dry-stone wall. The parsonage was in front of me now. It was the same type of small stone house as a dozen others I had already passed but it seemed to loom before me, dark and forbidding. I reminded myself that I was Jenny Greenteeth and this was my land, and pushed onwards.

I circled the parsonage, looking for a good spot to spy from. Like the other houses in the village the parsonage's windows were covered in neat wooden shutters, but it had one small glass window, set high up on the eastern side of the house to catch the morning sunlight. I checked around me a final time and then approached the wall. To my happy surprise the stone blocks that formed the exterior of the house were very easy to climb. I was able to worm my long fingers and toes into the gaps in the mortar, hauling myself up as easily as I had crawled from the lake. I pressed an ear to the wall and listened.

There was something there, two somethings at least. On the far side of the house was a normal heartbeat; dull, throbbing, human. Nothing strange about that. The other thing was strange indeed. I thought it was another heartbeat, but it was slow and uneven, as though the heart was struggling to pump blood. I could hear breathing, perilously close to the other side of the wall. Each breath was torturous, rattling. I pictured spittle flying from the unseen mouth.

I lifted my fingers from their position, leaning back on my toes, and reached up for a new handhold. My fingernails found a void, just underneath the glass window, and I dragged myself upwards as silently as I could manage. I hung there, hugging myself to the wall, waiting to hear if the one breathing would move. I didn't want to risk looking inside just yet.

My fingers started to go numb. The other human in the house had moved around. I could hear them coughing, chattering quietly and even sneezing once. I wondered how they could be so blind as to not sense the other presence in the room for what it was. Then again, Temperance had lived in the village for weeks and still presumed the parson was merely a man.

Something dripped onto my face and I flinched horribly and looked up. There was nothing above me. I began to think I had imagined it when another splash hit me just below the left eye. It was rain. I shuddered a little with relief and clutched the wall tighter. The rain fell around me, a light drizzle at first and then thickening to sheets of water. It was blowing in from the east now, pushing me against the house. A human might have fallen but I was a creature of water and the rain renewed my strength.

Eventually I heard the other human murmuring something about the rain and the heavy breather replied. Their voice was too low for me to catch but the floorboards creaked as they moved into the centre of the room. Perfect.

I tensed my fingers and pushed up. My eyes rose just over the edge of the windowsill and I saw into the room. The glass was smeared from the rain and my view was blurry. At the far side of the room was a woman. She was definitely human, with dark eyes and thin hair tucked under a starched bonnet. She was sitting on a stool next to the fire, stirring a cauldron. I couldn't smell much through the walls, but it looked like stew.

The other figure was the parson. He looked much the same as the only other time I'd seen him: pursed mouth, small eyes. He had removed his hat and was wearing long dark robes. Despite his best efforts they appeared more worn than when I had seen him at the lake, the hem was stained with mud and there were fraying threads at his left cuff. When I looked at him I didn't see anything strange, but my ears were still telling me that his heartbeat and breath were not human.

I dipped back down out of sight to think about the scene. The parson wasn't human, not a witch or wizard, but that wasn't enough. I needed to know more about what kind of creature it was. I rolled over the pieces of information I had. It was strong, it could appear human, it had a strange heartbeat and breathing pattern. The magic that had touched mine had tasted of forests, but not the ones I knew. It didn't seem English, or even Welsh or Scottish. Maybe a Norse huldra or even a spirit from Araby?

My thoughts were interrupted by sounds from the house. I looked back inside. The human woman was serving a bowl of the stew to the pastor. I watched as she handed him a spoon and poured a cup of dark red wine. He pointed to the fireplace and said something I couldn't make out. The woman went over and crouched down, poking at the fire with a spare log. The parson snapped at her, and she dropped the log. The woman reached into the fire with her bare hand, grabbing out hot embers which she placed in a copper warming pan. By the time she had filled it I could see her right hand was scarlet and swollen. The pastor nodded at her as she carried the pan into the next room, tears trickling down her face. She hurried back in and curtseyed. The pastor waved a hand at her and carried on eating.

She fetched her hat and cloak from a hook on the wall and then opened the front door. I froze. The woman turned left out of the front door and stepped onto the road. She would walk right past me as I clung to the wall. I dared not move for fear of attracting her attention. I stayed as still as a rock. The woman looked down at her hand. Even from where I perched, I could smell the cooked meat smell of her burnt flesh. I heard her stifle a sob. Still clutching her hand, she wrapped her cloak close around herself and hurried down the road. She did not so much as turn to look back.

Now that the parson was alone perhaps he would reveal himself. I looked back into the house. The parson sat at his small wooden table, neatly spooning chunks of stew into his mouth. A dribble of broth ran down his chin. He put down the spoon and I assumed he would reach for the napkin the woman had laid beside the bowl for him. Instead the pastor opened his mouth and a long dark tongue snaked out, lapping up the rogue droplets. It returned to his mouth as quickly as it had appeared and I blinked hard, doubting what I had seen. He picked up his spoon again and resumed eating. I focused on his mouth, squinting my eyes to try and glimpse the tongue.

I had no luck. The parson finished his meal and lifted the bowl up to his mouth to drain the last of the soup. He used the napkin to dab politely at his mouth then stood up, beginning to unbutton his jacket. The parson placed it neatly on the table, folding the arms out and back in on themselves. Next, he removed the white linen undershirt, pulling it over his head. He put it on top of the jacket and then stepped towards the fire. He stood there, wearing britches and boots, bare from the waist up.

The parson put his hands out towards the fire, squatting down on his calves to get closer to the heat. He smiled slightly, as if enjoying the warmth. He traced a finger through the ashes at the base of the flames.

Then he turned around and looked directly at me.

I went rigid, unable to move. The parson's face was still nominally human, the eyes, nose and mouth all the correct shape and size. Had I seen him from my lake I would not have noticed it, but as he looked at me now I felt the wrongness in him. His smile widened, revealing neat white human teeth, and he straightened, meeting my gaze as I peered down into the room.

There was nothing in that smile, it was as empty as a carved jack-o'lantern. His eyes were the same: dead, devoid of emotion, of fear, of pleasure. There was only a yawning hunger behind them. This was not a creature that would be satisfied with the flesh of humans. It could devour the very soul of the world and feel nothing but a desire for more. There was intelligence, yes, but focused on that single goal; filling that emptiness, that gaping void.

I knew what he was, but I didn't want to say the words. I didn't even want to think them, as if forming the shapes in my mind would somehow give him more power. A small part of my mind was thinking about Temperance, about how strong a witch she must be to have survived their encounter. I realised now that when I had fought off the ooze at the lake, it had barely been trying – that it could have crushed me if it had wanted to.

The parson took a step towards me, tucking his hands behind his back. I could smell that foul magic now, feel it sliding around me, sliding around my nostrils, my mouth, inside my ears. I saw the dead forest, the rotting carcass of the stag. It was beyond the natural circular death that comes to all mortal things. The parson's smile spoke of a putrefaction at the very heart of his being.

I couldn't move, couldn't breathe.

I took the only action available to me. I stopped holding on to the wall.

I had been clinging so tightly that the fall scraped my arms and legs against the stone and I landed hard on the grass. Freed from his gaze I took off at a run on my hands and feet, nails scratching at the cobblestones as I raced forward. I could feel the ooze snapping at my heels as I careened across the road and down the slope to the lake. I reached out, grasping the heart of the lake to me.

At twenty yards from the water's edge I leapt, swinging myself into the air and diving for the water. The lake leapt up to meet me and I swirled back into the depths. No time to waste here, I shot back up to the surface, ready to fight off the oozing magic. I could sense it still, lapping along the bank. I stretched my fingers out, preparing the water walls in my mind.

But the ooze fell back, slipping back up the hill and out of my perception. I knew somehow that it would not return tonight.

I was shaking, the water around me rippling from the movement. The parson's smile was stamped on my mind. Even now I saw his dark eyes before me. I wrestled with myself, trying to control the impulse to flee. It had been a very long time since I had known fear and I was out of practice at being courageous. I wanted to run, to swim out of my lake and head downstream, to put as much open water between myself and that creature.

Surely Temperance would eventually realise that I wasn't coming back and reach the same conclusion. Maybe I should duck back into the cave and we would run together. Whatever the thing inside the parson was planning – I still cringed at naming it – surely it would not reach past the extent of the river? I thought again of the depthless hunger. Would the river be far enough? Should I tell Temperance to run to France, or even further afield?

Something brushed my foot and I flinched, spinning in the water. The pike gave me a doleful look, then vanished back into the pondweed. I tried to calm myself, waving my hands back and forth through the silky lake water. Gradually, I felt my panic recede and anger took its place. A deep, reckless, selfish fury. This was my place. Mine. My lake, my fish, my pike. I was not going to be drummed out of my own home, not going to leave my lake and its inhabitants unprotected. There must be something I could do, perhaps with Temperance's assistance.

I ducked back below the water and headed for the cave. As I emerged from the tunnel Temperance looked up from where she was sitting and hurried over towards me.

'Thank heavens you're back, Jenny, I was starting to worry.' She took my hand to help me out of the water. 'Are you all right? You're trembling. Did you see the parson?' Her voice was tight with concern.

I waved her away and sat down heavily at the edge of the cave, leaning against the wall.

'Do you know what caused the opposing magic?' Temperance pressed.

I looked up at her, watching how her hands twisted in the front of her dress. I didn't want to tell her the bad news, knew that I had to.

'Yes, I saw him, Temperance. I know what he is.' I took a deep breath. 'Is there any more of that beer left?'

Temperance fetched a bottle and poured me a cupful. Serving one for herself she sat opposite me, cross-legged.

'Tell me, Jenny. I need to know what is in that parsonage,' she said, her voice firm.

I took a long draught then put the cup down on the floor.

'It's worse than I thought. The thing in the parson, it is the Erl King.' Even here in my home I shuddered to say his name.

Temperance didn't react and I realised she didn't understand.

'What is an Erl King?'

'*The* Erl King, Temperance, there is only one. I daresay one is more than enough for that world.' I reached for the bottle and topped up my beaker.

'You know how goblins and Greenteeths are the villains in your fairy stories? Well, the Erl King is the villain in ours. We don't know exactly where he came from, the tales don't say. The earliest stories came from the far east, from the Silk Road. For a while he was in Germania, in the Black Forest. That's when we first heard his name.'

'So he's a ... a spirit?' Temperance asked, raising her eyebrows in confusion. I shook my head.

'Not exactly. The way my mother described it, he's a hole, a rip in the fabric of the world. In the beginning they say that he was insentient, but enough mortal matter fell through the gap that he became aware. Now he roams the lands ever hungry, never satisfied.

'I do not know how he came to be here; there were no whispers from Brackus or my other fae contacts that the Erl King had come to Britain. I do not know why he is here, why of all places he has chosen Chipping Appleby to make his lair. Whatever foul purpose he has, I cannot fathom it.'

Temperance's face was pale.

'How do we stop it?' she asked. I shrugged.

'I do not know that either. Theoretically it must be possible, what is done can be undone. But that is higher knowledge, beyond my ken.'

Temperance was quiet for a while. I drained my cup and poured myself another.

'He saw me tonight – I could not prevent it. His magic chased me back to the lake. Temperance, I do not think I can protect you here. I think perhaps he intended for me to eat you when he threw you in the lake. Your spell last night will have disproved that notion. He knows you are here with me and is surely only biding his time before moving against the both of us. You should flee now and send for your husband and children if you can.'

'What do you mean "if I can"?' Temperance asked.

'They may have been too long under his influence. He may not let them go.' I said, wincing as I saw my words take effect. She paled and drew back.

'What will you do, Jenny?'

'I will stay here for now. This lake is my home and I will not abandon it. I will send word downstream to the other Jennys. The next time Brackus visits me I will tell him what I know and ask him to get the message out that this part of the world is not safe any more. Maybe then I will leave.'

Temperance was quiet for a long time. She sipped her own beer. After a while she spoke again.

'I can't leave. I tried once, I won't do it again. I will do whatever it takes to get my children out of that village. There must be a way. Perhaps I can meet my husband when he is out in the fields or sneak in after dark again. If I fail I will try again and again until the Erl King takes my last breath.'

I looked at this fragile human witch, emboldened by the strength of her words. If she was not done fighting then I wasn't either.

'I will help you, Temperance Crump, if you will let me.'

She smiled and took my hand, 'Gladly, Jenny Greenteeth. Gladly.'

Chapter Six

I managed to catch a little sleep that day, still tired from my expedition. When I woke, Temperance was already up. She was sitting at the edge of the cave, feet splashing in the cold water. Her right hand held a ball of conjured flame and she was summoning a gust of wind with her left. Periodically she would direct the wind through the blaze and bathe the far wall in a column of orange fire. The scorch marks on the wall indicated she had been doing this for some time.

I stretched and yawned loudly, crawling from my nest. Temperance threw me a quick nod and returned to scorching the offending wall. I watched for a while before interjecting.

'I am really not sure how effective fire will be against the Erl King. Most legends says that attacks only strengthen him,' I said, above the crackle of the flames.

'It's not for him,' panted Temperance as she threw another pillar of flame at my unfortunate cave, 'I just wanted to burn something.'

I considered this then began to tuck my bedding away so that a rogue spark wouldn't set the whole thing alight. I noticed a few empty beer bottles on the floor at Temperance's feet. She had made a good dent in my stash of drink. It would be difficult to get more once I had warned Brackus not come back again, I thought mournfully.

'Perhaps you could try again when you have sobered up a little? You are called Temperance after all, and it is usually considered a little unwise to be drinking so early in the day.' I nudged the last few bottles towards me with my foot and tucked them at the back of the cave behind my nest.

'It is not too early if I didn't go to sleep. It is merely a rather late evening,' slurred Temperance. She dropped her right hand, still burning, and reached for a bottle. On instinct I pulled the lake towards me and soaked her in a wave of water before she could burn the whole cave down.

She spluttered. The flame at her hand had sputtered and gone out. 'What was that for?'

'That,' I said, 'was to save us from the embarrassing fate of burning to death underwater. Don't you want to live long enough to die at the hands of the Erl King? You seemed quite keen on the idea last night.'

Temperance groaned. 'I did, I am. I was convinced and set on my path. That was before I started thinking about my husband and children trapped in the village with that thing. I started drinking to take my mind off it and just kept going. I think one of those bottles was stronger than the others; normally small beer doesn't have that effect on me.'

I inspected the empty flasks. She had indeed gone through a very old flagon of beer that had been sitting forgotten in the cave half as long as I had. The fumes alone were enough to make me feel a little dizzy; it was a miracle she was still standing upright, another that her breath hadn't caught fire.

'Nothing for it then,' I said, and pushed her backwards into the water. Temperance fell with a mighty splash. Resurfacing she shrieked like a banshee as she bobbed up and down in the icy lake.

'God's bones, Jenny, my blood will freeze in my veins. Get me out of here,' she yelled. I leaned over with a grin, not bothering to hide my teeth.

'Best thing to sober you up is a cold dip,' I said. 'It is why I never suffer a hangover. Straight into the water every morning – you'll never regret it.'

'Best thing for a river hag maybe,' Temperance groused, treading water, 'not a human.'

'It is good for everyone. And I am not a hag.' I watched her splash about, reaching for the edge of the cave. 'However, I will let that pass just this once as you are not in your right mind.'

'I'm sorry, Jenny, just get me out!'

I reached out an arm and pulled her out of the water by the collar. She looked like a drowned rat, black hair plastered to her scalp, but her eyes were clearer and she wasn't slurring her words quite as much.

'I will go and fetch us some breakfast,' I said, 'do not set anything on fire while I am gone.'

She glowered at me but nodded. I jumped into the water. The temperature was pleasantly cool and I smiled widely at her before sinking down and heading for the tunnel.

The lake felt incongruously peaceful after the events of the night before. It was another lovely spring day, the golden sunlight filtering through the water. Schools of fish grazed tranquilly as I swam by and frogs kicked back and forth on the surface. It was strange to think that just yards away in the village lurked a force that could threaten all of this.

I pushed the darkness from my mind and concentrated on the task at hand: breakfast. It felt like days since I had eaten properly and I was ravenous. I spied a shoal of chub near the western end of the lake. I floated over, moving silently through the water. Chub were a flighty fish who preferred the flowing waters of the rivers to still lakes and it was rare to see them in my lake for more than a few weeks a year. My mouth watered as I approached. A particularly tasty-looking specimen was lurking near the surface, underneath an overhanging tree branch. I could already taste the flesh, warm and succulent on my tongue.

I put on a burst of speed and streaked forward hands outstretched, only for the chub to scatter. Ripples criss-crossed the surface as they vanished into the depths. Someone had flung a handful of pebbles into the water, scaring them off. Fuming, I turned around to the bank. I was still loath to show myself to a human but perhaps I could cause some other mischief.

Brackus Marsh was standing at the edge of the lake, buttons and braid glittering in the sunlight, his leather boots shin-deep in the water. He tossed another handful of stones as I watched, whistling cheerfully. His pack lay safely back towards the trees.

I contemplated jumping out and giving him a well-deserved scare. Sadly I couldn't risk him running away in terror, since Temperance and I needed him to start spreading the word about the Erl King if we were going to stay here and fight rather than leave ourselves. There was also the unhappy risk of him not running away in terror which would make me look like a fool.

I settled for swimming right up to his boots and leering up at him. To my enormous satisfaction he yelped in shock when he saw me and staggered backwards. I rose out of the water, levering myself up so that I loomed over him impressively. I peered at him through mossy green hair.

'I am surprised to see you back so soon, Marsh. I would have thought you would be looking for easier pickings after your drubbing at our last encounter.'

He recovered his composure and bowed, still keeping a wary eye on me.

'Who could stay away from such a delightful presence as yourself, Jenny?' He cast a sideways look behind me at the lake. 'But I confess I was rather hoping to retrieve the spindle of kelpie hair I left here. It seems I accidentally gave you the entire thing rather than the single strand requested. A foolish oversight caused by, ah . . .'

'Caused by running away at top speed from a weeping woman?' I finished for him. Brackus nodded, a little nervously.

I considered telling him a deal was a deal but changed my mind. A little goodwill would be useful and what did we want with a whole skein of magical horsehair?

'Very well, Marsh. Give me a moment and I will retrieve your package. Perhaps I will see if Temperance wants to come up and say hello.'

Brackus hopped on one foot, the water splashing around him.
'She's not still, ah, upset is she?' he asked.

'Well, last I saw her she was throwing fireballs around my cave
so I'd say that more tears are not your most imminent concern.'

Brackus perked up at that.

'Oh excellent, excellent.'

I sighed and backflipped into the water. There went any
thought of catching fish this morning, I thought mournfully. I
would see if Brackus would cook us something after we returned
his spindle. When I bobbed back up in the entrance of the cave
Temperance glared at me, water still dripping from her face.

'Brackus is back,' I said cheerily. 'Fancy coming up to the
surface and tormenting him some more?'

She considered the matter, not looking thrilled at the prospect.

'He has probably got some food with him that isn't fish or
bulrush roots,' I said. Her stomach rumbled loudly.

'Fine,' she said, shrugging on her kirtle and starting to lace it
up, 'but what is he doing back here already?'

'He wanted to know if he could have the rest of the kelpie hair
back,' I replied, scratching my nose as I waited.

'Ha.' Temperance rooted around in the pile of ingredients left
over from the spell and retrieved the spindle. She threw it at me
and I kicked upwards and caught it one-handed.

'I'm only giving it to him in return for some breakfast,' she
said. 'No offence, Jenny, but my jaw needs a break from eating
bulrushes. No wonder your teeth are so sharp – it's not for eating
children, it's for chomping through inedible tubers.'

I cocked my head to the side. 'I resent that. I can also eat children. But I suppose they are multi-purpose teeth.'

Temperance stuck her tongue out at me and dipped a toe into
the water.

'Urgh, it's still cold. He'd better have bacon,' she said and
jumped in.

Brackus did indeed have bacon. He was so happy to get his
spindle back that we retreated into the woods and he cooked us
a mountain of food for breakfast. He served up fried eggs, fried

mushrooms and fried bacon along with porridge sweetened with honey and toasted sourdough bread liberally spread with butter and berry preserves. To drink, Brackus boiled us a pot of hot apple juice, spicing it with a stick of cinnamon that he carefully took out, dried and folded away.

Temperance fell on the food like a starving woman. I felt a little hurt at how quickly she wolfed down the meal but it was hard to deny how much better suited Brackus's food was for Temperance than my own lake-grown fare. Even I quite enjoyed it, rediscovering my appetite after a few days of trying to eat politely. Brackus ate as much as either of us, clearly relieved that we hadn't tried to haggle over the return of the kelpie hair.

When the last of the porridge had been scraped from our bowls Brackus sat back and retrieved a long wooden pipe. He added a pinch of strange leaves into the end and lit them with a snap of his fingers.

'So,' he said, drawing in a breath through the pipe and making the leaves glow, 'how did your spell casting go? You never did tell me what it was for.'

Temperance and I looked at each other gloomily.

'It was not,' I started, 'a total success.'

Brackus frowned, 'No problems with my products I hope? I do offer usage guarantees on all my items.'

Temperance shook her head, 'The spell worked fine, each item knitting into the magic like fine wool. I've never felt more powerful. Unfortunately it still wasn't strong enough.'

Brackus raised his eyebrows questioningly. Temperance looked over at me then put down her plate and began to tell him the whole story. She started from the beginning when Pastor Braddock came to the village. Brackus sat quietly, listening and blowing occasional sweet-smelling smoke rings into the air. Occasionally he would interrupt and ask a question. When Temperance reached the part when I saw the Erl King in his house he spluttered, inhaling far too much smoke. He stammered and tried to speak through fitful coughs. I gave him a slap on the back that might have been firmer than necessary.

When he stopped coughing he looked at me, wide-eyed with fear and surprise, not even grumpy about the slap.

'The Erl King. Jenny, are you sure? It wasn't an ogre, or a rogue sorcerer? I've never heard of the Erl King setting foot on our shores before,' he said, voice low and urgent.

I looked at my feet. 'I am sure. I am older than you, Brackus, and I have seen many things come past this lake. What is in that village is older than all of them, and worse too. I smelt the rot, tasted the decay in the water. It can only be the Erl King, come here from the continent for some dark purpose.'

Brackus sat back on his stool, raising his pipe to his mouth again.

'Well, if you are sure then I believe you. Blood of my ancestors, Jenny, the Erl King here in England. I never thought I would live to see the day. I wonder what he's doing here. I mean no offence but Chipping Appleby isn't exactly the centre of civilisation. What purpose could bring him to such a small village? I only come here because I enjoy winding you up so much.'

I hissed and he gave me a cheerful grin. Temperance laughed, breaking some of the tension that had descended at the name of the enemy.

'So what are you going to do?' Brackus asked, 'You're strong for a Jenny but the Erl King, he is in another class. I doubt any fae could go up against him, nor any common witch or wizard either.'

I shrugged. 'Temperance and I will do what we can. I can hold out for a little while if I use the strength of the lake. Perhaps I can draw him out down there whilst Temperance sneaks into the village and gets her children onto the road and away.'

Temperance gave me a shocked look. 'I didn't know you were thinking of doing that. It's a terrible plan, you wouldn't have a chance!'

'Can you think of a better one?' I snapped, rather grumpily. 'It won't be all sunshine and flowers for you either. If the whole village is under his spell then you'll probably have to kill your husband to wrest the children away.'

'All the more reason for not doing that then,' she said stubbornly. 'We should co-ordinate our attacks. You fight from the lake and I'll try and outflank him from the woods.'

'Oh, so we'll both die?' I retorted. 'That will be great for little Josiah and Ursula.'

Temperance puffed up and opened her mouth to respond but Brackus interrupted.

'Ladies, ladies,' he said, adopting a singsong tone in his voice. 'There's no need to fight about who is going to get to die heroically. Clearly both of your madcap strategies will result in the tragic deaths of the pair of you and probably everyone in the village.'

We scowled at him.

'Then what do you recommend, Brackus the goblin pedlar and famous tactical genius?' I snarled. 'If you have another notion I am sure that we would be happy to hear it.'

Brackus smirked and leaned forwards on his stool, tapping the pipe on his knee.

'I do have an idea, as it happens. Neither of you can defeat the Erl King separately. Even if you combined your strengths you know nothing of his weaknesses, nor how to destroy a force like that. I would warrant that neither of you two fine ladies have ever killed anything more hazardous than yourselves. You need to find someone who has. Someone with experience hunting down uniquely dangerous prey and mounting their heads on his walls.'

I groaned, realising where he was going with this. Brackus ignored me.

'You need, in short, to ask Gwyn ap Nudd for help.' He pursed his lips and puffed out a smoke ring to underline his point.

'I will not be going hat in hand to that knavish cockerel that thinks he's king of the fairies,' I said. 'It's beneath my dignity.'

'Well, I will,' interjected Temperance. 'I don't have any dignity; I'd ask the Devil himself for help. Who's Gwyn ap Nudd?

'He's a stuck-up arsehole with a crown,' I said before Brackus could reply. He winked and blew a smoke ring at me.

'Gwyn ap Nudd, my dear lady, is the Lord of the Fair Family, King of the Tylwyth Teg. He rules over the fae.'

'The hell he does,' I said, 'No one ever asked me my opinion on that and if they had I certainly would not have chosen Gwyn bloody Nudd for my king.'

'He rules over the *high* fae,' corrected Brackus, 'By name at least. Back in the old days Gwyn led the Wild Hunt; slaying dragons, rescuing maidens fair and generally doing a lot of fighting. If anyone knows how to defeat something like the Erl King it will be Gwyn.'

Temperance asked, 'Does he still hunt? How come I have never heard of him?'

Brackus sighed with the pleasure of one who rarely got to pontificate at length and settled into his story: 'He doesn't come down into these parts much. Even in their heyday the Wild Hunt stuck to the mountains and high places of the isles. Wales, Scotland, the moors of Cornwall, Devon and Yorkshire and the like. There is an old story about him getting kicked out of Glastonbury for wreaking havoc on the abbey there, so he might hold a grudge towards Wessex. That would account for there being little tell of him in this part of the world.'

'If he's such a great hunter,' asked Temperance, 'why don't we just ask him to hunt the Erl King himself? I would have thought he would relish the opportunity to hunt a prey that's so rare and dangerous.'

'Fat chance of a member of the high fae actually doing something useful, especially something that might mess up their pretty faces,' I said. 'I wouldn't trust any of those idiots to not make the situation worse.'

'Alas, Gwyn has not hunted big game for many years now. The Wild Hunt is transformed to a court, half faded from this mortal realm. I do not think we could entice him back to the field. However,' Brackus paused for dramatic effect, 'his knowledge has only grown with age and his mind is still as sharp as his long knives. Moreover he is the last of the great powers, the only one left from those days. Any others who could have matched him have long since passed over.'

'Do you think he would tell us what to do?' Temperance's expression was doubtful.

'Perhaps. The high fae are as changeable as the winds they ride,' said Brackus sombrely.

'That's not the only similarity they have to wind,' I muttered, 'garrulous old airbags the lot of them.'

'Surely we could persuade them,' said Temperance, ignoring my words. 'Even if they don't hunt any more this is still their land, they should care about the people on it.'

I opened my mouth to make another snide remark but she gave me a warning glare out of the corner of her eye. I contented myself with grumbling under my breath.

'The high fae are not like Jenny and I,' said Brackus. 'They don't have the same motivations as us. Time doesn't exist in the same way for them, nor space, nor life or death. They seek only amusement, distraction in any form from the ageless emptiness of their existence. For a while Gwyn led them in the hunt, now they sit and sing songs. They will feel no responsibility for you and yours.'

Temperance looked crestfallen. Brackus held up a hand.

'But' he said, 'if we can present the problem in a way Gwyn would find entertaining, that piques his interest, then maybe there is a chance he will help.'

'How can we do that?' Temperance asked.

'Flatter him,' I said, then returned her glowering look. 'Don't look at me like that, I'm right aren't I, Brackus? There's nothing the high fae love more than to hear about how special they are. We will bring you to the Court, put you in a pretty dress and you can bat your eyes at Gwyn. Spin him a tale about your poor lost village, leave out the part where you have a husband and two children, and cast him as the noble lord whose sacred knowledge can save you. He'll sing like a skylark if we catch him at the right moment.'

'That's certainly one option,' mused Brackus, looking over Temperance quizzically. 'The high lord has always had a weakness for fair maidens. Not much to my taste but I don't like to judge.' He frowned. 'She'd need a proper bath before we put her in front of him, and to change out of those rags, I don't think living with you is improving her looks much, Jenny.'

I hissed at him but didn't bother to argue. Brackus knew much more about those things than me.

'He's not going to expect . . .' Temperance paused, her cheeks and ears pinkening slightly, '*satisfaction* from me, is he?'

Brackus giggled. 'Oh I shouldn't think so. Chivalric courtship rarely gets down into the actual fun parts of romantic love. Besides, his wife will be standing right next to him when we appear to petition the Court. Lady Creiddylad was a famous beauty in her day, a standout even in an age known for them and the years have not dulled her loveliness. Gwyn fought a thousand battles for her hand, his devotion to her is famous and unchanging.' His voice softened a little at the mention of the queen; I detected a rare soft spot there. He caught me looking and cleared his throat. 'Gwyn will just be more likely to listen to a story from a pretty maid than a plain one.'

'Good,' said Temperance, 'so if I can get to the Court, find Lord Gwyn and tell him a good story he might tell me how we could defeat the Erl King?'

Brackus nodded. 'It's the best chance I can think of. If he doesn't know then you can always summon a demon and feed it your soul in return for some advice.'

'Let's ask Lord Gwyn first.' Temperance glanced at me. 'What do you think, Jenny?'

I wrinkled my nose. 'I don't love the idea of it. The high fae are unpredictable by nature. Cruelty comes easier to them than kindness and Gwyn ap Nudd didn't become their ruler by playing the harp; he bought that crown in blood and did not pause to count the cost. He is not as bad as the Erl King but only because he lacks the focus to be a true menace.'

I took in a breath and sighed deeply. 'For all that, I still agree with Brackus. This may be our only hope of learning how to defeat the Erl King. If anyone knows how to kill a thing like that it will be Gwyn, and if Brackus thinks you've got a fair chance of getting the information out of him then he might well be right. Whether that insight will be usable is another matter, but we can deal with that later.'

Temperance beamed at me. 'So you will come with me to try and find him?'

'Of course I will,' I said. 'I wish to protect my lake from the Erl King as much as you want to save the village.' She squeezed my hand, her face glowing with hope.

'What an interesting little quest,' said Brackus thoughtfully, 'it promises to be quite exciting. Perhaps I will join your company.'

I gaped at him, truly shocked by his words.

'Brackus Marsh, why on earth would you do a thing like that?' I gasped. 'There'll be no money in it.'

Brackus looked offended. My dear Jenny, money is not everything. Some things are more important.'

'When have you ever done something not for money?' I asked bluntly.

'Well . . . all right, not often. But this time is different, though there will, admittedly, be some benefit to me. I have a vested economic interest in the Erl King not consuming Chipping Appleby and moving on to places with more consistent customers of mine. Additionally, it has been a long time since I visited the faerie court and this promises to be an unusually entertaining trip. I suspect that young Mistress Crump was not entirely honest with me at our first meeting and it has been a while since I was played for a fool that easily. I will admit to being intrigued to see if she will repeat the performance for the high fae. If she can wring aid from the Lord of the Hunt as easily as she wrung profit from me then I will not feel nearly so foolish about the matter.'

Temperance and I looked at each other, unconvinced.

'It will be quite dangerous,' I said. 'I have heard the Court is a treacherous place even for one as politically adept as yourself. And if we succeed then there is still the matter of the Erl King to defeat.'

Brackus blew another smoke ring.

'Well, in truth – and if questioned I will deny ever having

said this — I am rather fond of you, Jenny. You are amusingly soft-hearted for a villainous swamp creature and I enjoy sparring with you at our meetings. I would be passing sorry to see you devoured body and soul by an ancient eldritch nightmare.'

I stared at him, too surprised even to object to the characterisation of my beautiful lake as a swamp. He flushed a little and coughed on his pipe. I could see Temperance smothering a smile out of the corner of my eye. I cleared my throat loudly.

'Right, well, very good. It is decided, the three of us will travel to the Court and seek out Gwyn ap Nudd to ask for his aid.'

Brackus grinned. 'A witch, a goblin and Jenny Greenteeth are off to seek the King of the Fairies,' he said. 'What a delicious disaster this could be.'

Chapter Seven

Having decided on our strategy, Brackus wanted to leave as soon as possible.

'If we set off now we can spend a whole day on the road before sunset,' he said whilst packing away his copper frying pan. 'That should be enough to get us to the Court tonight.'

'Is it truly that close to here?' asked Temperance in disbelief. I shared her surprise; surely I would have known if the heart of faerie was within a day's swim of my lake?

Brackus frowned a little.

'Not quite, it's hard to explain.' He rinsed out the cups we'd been drinking from and stacked them up. 'The Court is never in one place for more than a fortnight. The high fae get very restless.'

'But they'll be near us tonight? That's lucky.'

Brackus shook his head again. 'I don't actually know where they'll be tonight.'

'I'm not gaining much faith in this plan of yours, Marsh,' I said.

He shot me a long-suffering look. 'I don't need to know where it is. Gwyn's Court can only be reached by the Wild Roads. Anyone who steps onto one of the roads intending to find the Court will arrive there after a day of walking. It doesn't matter if he's in the Hebrides or the Scilly Isles; all we need to do is walk and we'll find it.'

Temperance's mouth fell open. 'That's amazing!'

I rolled my eyes behind her back but restrained myself from saying anything. Brackus flushed, the tips of his long ears reddening.

'Indeed it is, my dear enchantress, and so proves my point. I do not wish to linger here in the shadow of the Erl King and a wise witch would not spend a night out on the Wild Roads. The pathways of the fae are treacherous enough for those who tread them regularly, let alone a newcomer.'

Temperance looked at me for confirmation. I nodded. 'Brackus is correct – if this is the way to Gwyn ap Nudd we should try and get there tonight. The Erl King is not the only darkness in this world, and I will lose part of my power when we leave the lake and I am separated from its source.'

She nodded and we began to tramp back to the water's edge. Brackus watched as we stepped in, hand in hand.

'Don't be too long,' he called. I ignored him and pulled Temperance under. I swam us quickly back to the cave and packed up a few things: coins, a spare cloak and a chunk of amber that had washed into the lake three hundred years ago. I remembered my mother telling me the high fae liked amber. At the last moment I took the ancient sword, still holstered in a leather sheath that had defied the years underwater, and belted it over my dress.

Temperance was finished before me and we hurried back up to the surface. She took the waterproof bag from my shoulder and darted over to a stump to put on her stockings and boots.

I stood in the shallows of the lake. It seemed so alive to me: dragonflies hovering over the flat lily pads, frogs chirping on the bank. As I narrowed my eyes I could perceive fish swimming lazily beneath the surface. It had been years since I had last left the lake, and never at a time when I thought it might be at risk without me. For over a thousand winters I had lurked in its depths, and for a thousand springs I had rejoiced as the ice broke and new life returned. It was hard to turn away.

There was a splashing noise behind me and Temperance

waded over. Her dress was still wet from the swim and it trailed behind her.

'We'll be back soon, Jenny. I promise. I know it's hard to leave.' She put a hand on my arm.

I sniffed. 'It's just a lake, I'll be fine.'

She squeezed my arm and I turned around and squelched back to the shore.

Brackus was waiting for us in the trees. He had shouldered his pack and was whistling cheerfully.

'So how do we get to these roads?' Temperance asked. 'Are you going to snap your fingers again?'

'Ah, well, that is more of a goblin trick than an actual means of travel,' Brackus said shiftily. 'I mainly do it to impress my customers. No, we need an actual gateway to the Wild Roads. I believe there is one further into the woods.'

He spun on one foot and pointed uphill into the trees.

'That way to be exact, gentle ladies.'

I considered the direction. So far that morning I had been walking on two feet but I suspected that I would be too slow on a proper trek. Better to get it over with now.

I dropped down to my hands and feet. The others looked at me.

'Well, lead on then, Marsh,' I said grumpily, 'show us the way.'

We set off through the Appleby Woods. It was difficult for me to join in with Brackus and Temperance's conversation from my four-limbed crawl but I wasn't in much of a talking mood. I was already missing the lake. I hadn't seen the pike that morning. It was foolish to get sentimental over a fish, and beyond idiotic to be wondering if it was all right. It only followed me around because I fed it.

I pushed thoughts of its stupid fishy face out of my mind and concentrated on the woods around me. We had been climbing a small hill for a while, the forest thickening as we rose. Brackus seemed confident in his direction and I could hear him regaling Temperance with tall tales and flowery stories. It was deeply irritating but I was beginning to pant from the climb and didn't have the breath to contradict him.

The land flattened out after we crested a small outcrop of limestone, glinting golden in the yellowish light of the forest. Brackus paused to catch his breath and looked around.

'Over there.'

I turned to look where he was pointing. At first I saw only more trees, then my eyes caught on something. There was an arch of vines and broken branches, built beneath two tall apple trees. It didn't appear to lead to anywhere special but the more I watched the more I felt there was something odd about it.

As we approached I grew certain. We stopped in front of the arch and looked at each other.

Brackus smiled. 'There you go, I knew it was around here somewhere. Appleby Woods, bound to be an elf door with all these apple trees around.'

Temperance reached out a hand to trace the left-hand tree trunk. 'I never thought of it like that. Apple branches can make very powerful wands though, and the bark can be used for all kinds of ailments. I suppose it makes sense that it's important to fae too.'

'Very perceptive of you, Mistress Crump,' Brackus fawned. I snorted but he ignored me.

'How do we pass through onto the Roads?' Temperance asked, dropping her hand back and turning to us. 'Do we just walk through?'

'Not quite. Anyone can walk onto the Wild Roads; the fae are always happy to spirit away lost humans.' Brackus peered at the arch. 'So it became the custom for the local witch or wizard to put a lock on the door, meaning only those with the knowledge can pass through.'

'I've never heard that,' said Temperance. 'My mother was the local cunning woman before me and she would have told me.'

Brackus yawned. 'Well, it would have been before her time. Do you remember, Jenny? It would have been after the Normans came over and started writing stuff down. Kicked off a bit of a craze for ordering things.'

I cast my mind back. I did remember him telling me something about the elf doors, but I couldn't have said when. Brackus had always talked a lot, even as a young goblin. I settled for grunting in a vaguely confirmatory manner.

'How do we open the lock?' Temperance pressed.

'We don't have to.' Brackus smirked, 'Jenny and I aren't human, the lock isn't for us. Yon great-great-grandmother or whomever it was didn't concern herself with poor lower fae tripping onto the roads. We can walk through it whenever we like. You, on the other hand, are going to have a harder time of it.'

'Fine, how do I open the lock?'

'To tell you the truth, Temperance, I don't know. Never had to bring a human up here before.' Brackus squatted down and grinned up at her. 'Take a look and see if you can figure it out.'

Temperance sighed and stepped closer to the arch of vines and branches. I could see there were carvings in the wood and reached my hand out to trace them.

'Ouch!' I yelped, grabbing my hand back. The engraving had burnt my fingers as I had touched it. I glowered at the arch.

'Ah yes, you don't want to touch it, Jenny,' Brackus said cheerfully. 'It was designed so the likes of us couldn't mess with the spell.'

I hissed at him and slunk off to sit on the ground, sticking my fingers in my mouth to soothe them.

Temperance was still staring at the symbols carved into the branches. She was mouthing something, her fingers dancing just above the wood. The etching seemed to wrap around the whole arch and Temperance stepped between and around it as she followed its path.

After a few minutes she stopped and looked at us from the other side of the arch.

'All right, I think I understand what to do,' she said, 'I'll just come back to you and then we can step through togeth—'.

Temperance vanished. I leapt to my feet, hissing again. Then I whirled around to look at Brackus, who was urgently clambering to his feet.

'Quickly, quickly,' he called, 'You don't want to leave her on the other side alone.'

I took a deep breath and rushed through the arch. The world seemed to blur around me and Appleby Woods vanished. As I finished my step I felt my foot meet stone and I pushed forward. My sight cleared and I stood on a wide road, paved with great granite flagstones. A few steps away from me I saw Temperance, lying still and sprawled on the ground.

I hurried over.

'I'm not hurt,' she said, looking down. Her fingers suddenly clutched my arm, surprisingly strong and bony. 'Could you just—' she started and I ripped her whole arm off.

The thing that had been pretending to be Temperance howled at me. I wielded the arm as a club and smashed at it. It raised its face to me and I saw red eyes, no pupil, no whites. It growled at me and then made a break for it, hurrying back up the road.

I hurled the severed arm after it. Brackus appeared mid-air at just the wrong moment and got smacked in the face.

'Aarghh,' he said and sat down in shock on the flagstones. I looked around. A second Temperance was sitting at the side of the road. I was reasonably sure she hadn't been there before. I stomped over to her and wrenched her to her feet. She started to speak but I grabbed her face and tilted it so I could see her eyes. They were wide and dark brown.

I let her go.

'From now on we all stick together,' I growled. Temperance nodded. Brackus was still sitting in the road holding the offending limb. I went over and held out my hand. He shoved the wraith's hand into it and clambered to his knees.

'I know you won't believe me,' I said, 'but that was an accident.'

He grumbled and began to try and dab splatters of blood from his shirt.

'A happy, happy accident,' I continued. Temperance giggled but suppressed it when Brackus looked at her.

'I can't believe you just tore something's arm off,' she said. Her tone sounded almost admiring. I looked at her.

'You keep forgetting that I'm not human, Temperance,' I said heavily. 'There are scarier things than me out on these roads.'

'Exactly,' added Brackus, evidently giving up on rescuing his shirt, 'which is why we should be moving. It's still before midday, eight hours till sunset. We need to be walking all of that time to reach Gwyn.'

He walked past us and turned around. 'Come on then.'

'I thought you said it didn't matter which way we walked,' I said suspiciously. 'Why do you want to go that way?'

'Because, oh willowy hellcat,' Brackus said, 'that is the opposite direction to the way a shrieking wraith just ran, covered in blood and calling out for its mother. Every foul thing in these hills will be going after it. I think, therefore, we should head this way.'

That was a difficult argument to find fault with so Temperance and I followed him down the road.

The Wild Road wound between high moorland on either side, furred with purple heather and yellow gorse. The sky above us was bright blue, scratched with long lines of white cloud hurtling past in the wind.

It was so lovely I was tempted to stop and look around, to wander off the road and inspect the flowers, to roam over the craggy hills. I didn't. I kept my eyes fixed on the road in front of me, not stopping, not even turning. Brackus did the same. It took effort from both of us to keep Temperance on the road. She kept pausing to watch the clouds pass or bending to trace a crack in the pavestones. I stopped walking on all fours and tottered upright, gripping her arm both to keep myself stable and to prevent her from drifting off course.

Eventually, after Brackus stopped to snatch a quick drink from his flask, I saw her about to step off the road.

'What are you doing?' I hissed, grabbing her arm with more strength than I meant to. She tried to shake me off.

'I was just chasing that butterfly,' she said, her eyes cloudy. I shook her as I dragged her back to the centre of the road.

'There was no butterfly.' I pulled her face towards me. 'Listen

Temperance, there was no butterfly. There's no nature here, no birds, no insects, no creeping animals. Only fae. You need to focus on the road and keep walking. If you leave the road then you'll walk these hills for ever, until you become just like them. You won't have to worry about the Erl King then, you won't even remember why you came here.'

Her face was dreamy and I realised with a shock that she was thinking about it. Brackus came up beside us. His face was grim.

'We might have to carry her,' he said. 'If she steps off the road we'll never get her back.'

I looked at Temperance. Her eyes were already unfocused. I cursed myself for not preparing her better.

'I can carry her for a while,' I said, 'but don't you have anything in that pack of yours to prevent enchantment?'

He considered then shook his head. Something chimed in my mind.

'Here,' I said, thrusting Temperance at him, 'hold her a moment.'

She sagged in his arms, smiling up at him. I rummaged in my pack, then retrieved a neat parcel wrapped in leaves.

'Aha!' I said, brandishing it. Brackus wrinkled his nose.

'What is that awful smell?' he asked, trying to twitch away from it.

'Carp,' I grinned. 'I caught it last summer and was saving the other half for a treat. I brought it with me to cheer me up on the road.

'You can't think that she'll . . .' Brackus petered off.

'Oh yes I do think. Now open her mouth.' He grimaced and wedged Temperance's jaw open. I unwrapped the leaves. To my nose the carp was finely aged, the flavours developed perfectly. From the look of disgust on Brackus's face, he did not agree.

I broke off a handful of the fish and dropped it into Temperance's mouth. Brackus pushed it closed. At first there was no effect. Then her eyes bulged and she started to struggle. I reached out and pinched her nose, forcing her to chew the fish flesh. Her skin went bright red and she swallowed. Brackus let her go and she fell to the flagstones, retching mightily. As chunks of fish splattered the road Brackus turned green himself and backed off, clutching a handkerchief to his face.

After what seemed like an eternity of vomiting Temperance looked back up at me. Her face was still scarlet and drool was dangling from her lower lip but her eyes had cleared.

'What,' she said, 'on God's green earth was that apocalyptic horror you just fed me?'

'Rotten fish.' I displayed the rest of it to her. 'It's an old family recipe. Oh look, a little maggot.' I picked it out and tossed it in my mouth.

Brackus muttered something and Temperance gagged again.

'It worked though, didn't it?' I said, thinking that insufficient attention had been paid to the genius of my plan.

'Honestly I think I'd rather lose my mind next time, Jenny,' Temperance said, struggling to her feet. 'Just put that cursed thing away before I smell it again. Or better yet throw it on the ground and I'll burn it. If I'd known you had that with you we wouldn't even need to see Gwyn ap Nudd. Just one bite of that and the Erl King would probably surrender.'

I protested that I liked the taste just fine but both Brackus and Temperance refused to move on until I had folded up the fish again and stowed it at the bottom of my pack.

For all her complaining Temperance was a lot more focused on the road from then on. If I saw her eyes begin to lose focus I would catch her attention and pat my bag. She would generally straighten up after that.

We walked for hours and the landscape changed as we went. The moorland faded to sweet green hills, then to arable farms. No movement stirred in the picture-perfect farmhouses but there was something in the wheat fields. Brackus paused to stare at it but backed off, looking pale. We walked a little faster after that.

It was a relief when the farms gave way to foothills and then a high mountain pass. Rocky outcrops towered either side of us and the road was edged in thick snow. Snowflakes as large as thumbprints flurried down around us, each one melting before it hit the ground. It was hard going, and I felt the muscles in my calves burning. I was missing the lake and the strength it usually gave me. In a moment of thoughtlessness I opened my mouth to catch a snowflake on my tongue. Brackus reached out a hand and caught it just in time. I shook myself and nodded at him gratefully.

The sun was low in the sky by the time we reached the peak of the mountain. As we started down the other side we were suddenly walking along a coastal path. The paved road was gone, leaving only a goat track, dirt hammered hard as stone by the passage of many generations of livestock. To our left was the wide blue sea. Ahead of us Brackus stopped and looked around.

'We've left the Wild Roads,' he breathed, 'this is the mortal realm once more.'

I slumped forward, feeling the tension leave my body. Temperance sat down on a tuffet of grass and put her head in her hands. I put a hand on her shoulder.

'I know,' Brackus said, looking over at her. 'It's hard enough for Jenny and me to walk those roads. You did very well.'

Temperance's shoulders began to shake and I realised she was crying. I met Brackus's eyes and we sat down either side of her.

'I forgot who I was,' she sobbed. 'I forgot my children's names. If you hadn't stopped me I'd have run off.'

I rubbed her back. Brackus patted her knee.

'It's a necessary step,' he sighed. 'If you can walk the Wild Roads then you can face the Lord of the Hunt. They are one and the same in a way. He might have a pretty face but at his core that's what he is.'

I nodded. Temperance looked up at me, wiping teardrops from her cheeks.

'Thank you for walking them with me,' she sniffled, 'and for feeding me that terrible fish. Thank you too, Brackus.'

'Don't thank me for the fish,' Brackus said, 'I don't want my name associated with it.'

Temperance gave him a wobbly smile. She straightened and stood up again.

'Where now?' she asked, 'I presume that now we're off the roads the direction matters again?'

Brackus bounced to his feet. 'Very observant of you, my young mage. By my reckoning we are,' he spun around, 'about three miles north of Redruth.' He regarded our blank faces. 'In Cornwall,' he added.

'So we know where we are,' I said. 'Do we know where we're going?'

'Don't be so hasty. I do in fact know where we are going. This is Nancekuke Head, and inland from here, on that hill over there, is Nance Round, which is a very old hill fort. It's even older than you, Jenny, which is saying something.'

I growled at him, but my heart wasn't really in it. He smirked.

'Nance Round is one of the Hunt's favourite gathering places in Cornwall, right after Tintagel Castle. If the road led us here then that's where they'll be.'

I craned my neck to see where he was pointing.

'And what about that village in between here and there?' I asked.

Brackus looked again. 'Hmmnnn, I think it was just a few houses the last time I was in these parts. We'll have to go around it.' He slapped my back. 'All part of the fun of an adventure.'

I considered biting his hand off but I had already thrown an arm at him today. I let that one pass.

Climbing down the cliffs was less of a struggle than I expected. Brackus hopped from crag to crag with the agility of a mountain goat and Temperance tucked her skirt up and half scrambled half slid down. After the stress of walking all day I quite enjoyed the descent; the hard slatey rock of the cliffs provided lots of finger and toeholds and was rippled with veins of glassy quartz which gave it a pleasing look.

We reached the base with the last of the sunlight and turned south, skirting the edge of the little village and heading towards the woods. A narrow stream was running along the floor of the valley. I put my ear to the tumbling water but I didn't think there was anyone there. Temperance and Brackus stepped over the stream but I walked up until I found a pool wide enough to take a proper dip. The water tasted different from my lake, sweeter than the slightly acidic Caerlee. Too sweet for my palate, but it was pleasant to wash off the dust of the Wild Roads and I regained a little of my strength. I could see Temperance itching with impatience, so I hauled out and rejoined her and Brackus and we crossed the last of the valley floor. At the base of the hill was a stand of oak trees, welcoming us into the forest.

'Nance Wood,' said Brackus, pausing before the first oak tree. He looked back at us, 'From here on we'll be under the power of the Hunt.'

Temperance bit her lip. 'Do you have any advice? Should I avoid the food and drink?'

'No, it's not enchanted, but—' He slapped his forehead. 'We were going to dress you up for this!'

He chivvied her to a stray boulder. 'Tie your hair up,' he said, producing a long yellow ribbon from somewhere. She took it, beginning to braid it into her curls. Brackus took off his pack and stuck his whole head inside. Sounds of assessment filtered out of the bag. Temperance glanced over.

'Don't look at me,' I said. 'Appealing to men is really not my area of expertise. Eating them is more my thing.'

Brackus emerged, clutching a pile of yellow and white fabric. He shook it out triumphantly.

'Put this on,' he said, thrusting it at Temperance. She inspected it, holding it against her body.

'Where's the rest of it?' she asked, fingering the top. I couldn't really tell what she meant. It seemed like any other dress to me.

'Oh just try it on,' huffed Brackus. 'Trust that you're not my type. Here, Jenny and I will give you some privacy.' He turned around and stared into the woods. I moved over and stood next to him.

There was much scuffling and swearing behind us. I looked at Brackus but he was focusing his gaze on the oak trees.

'Never interrupt a lady when she's getting ready, Jenny,' he muttered, 'unless you've a hankering for a boxed ear.'

I didn't think Temperance would box my ear but I stayed turned away until she called out to us.

'Oh turn around,' she said grumpily. I peeked back. Temperance was wearing a long yellow gown, cut low over her shoulders and chest, with a high waistline that made her seem tall and elegant. Tufts of white fabric, some kind of thin filmy material, covered her arms. The effect was slightly ruined by the muddy boots peeking out from underneath the hem and the wild curls escaping from the ribbon Brackus had given her.

He looked her up and down. 'Almost right,' he said, 'may I adjust a little?'

Temperance sighed and held her arms out. Brackus sprang over and began tidying up her hair and tweaking the fit of the dress. I gave them both a wide berth, shooting what I hoped were sympathetic looks at Temperance from the sidelines. The goblin knelt before her, muttering a spell, and snapped his fingers. There was a shimmer in the air as a charm enveloped her boots, leaving them clean and polished.

Temperance picked her feet up, looking at them admiringly. 'Now that's a useful spell. You'll have to teach me that one.'

'I dress her in a gown fit for a goddess and she admires the boot cantrip,' Brackus grumbled. He stepped back. 'There you go, that'll have to do for now. What do you think, Jenny?'

I considered Temperance. She looked much the same as before. I concentrated harder. The dress did seem to fit her better, no longer stretching over her hips and crumpling under her arms. I didn't really think she looked much better than in her own clothes, though I supposed the yellow was nice. I liked yellow.

'I like yellow,' I said. Temperance's face fell and Brackus sighed. 'On you. I meant I like yellow on you,' I added. 'You look very, um, smart.'

Brackus smacked his face into his hand. Temperance smiled at me.

'Thank you, Jenny,' she said, then laid a hand on Brackus's shoulder, 'And thank you, Brackus. I would never have been able to pick out something so elegant.'

He pursed his lips. 'I could have done better with a few weeks' notice, but it'll do I suppose. You wear it very nicely, Mistress Crump.'

Temperance picked up her skirts and spun around. 'If everything goes the way I hope maybe I'll buy it off you to show my husband.'

I smiled to see her hopeful. The last rays of the evening sun played over the yellow silk, lighting it up as she spun. Then the sun dropped below the horizon.

'Come on,' I said, 'we'd better get going. Let's pray that Gwyn ap Nudd is in a helpful mood. Or at least that he doesn't kill us on sight.'

Chapter Eight

We heard the faerie court before we saw it. As we climbed the hill, Temperance was struggling with her dress and had bunched it up in both hands. She stopped walking as the first sounds filtered towards us and dropped the skirt. High laughter echoed through the oak trees, along with light music and assorted growling. It sounded like a troupe of bears were playing the harp. The Hunt was a wild place, so it wasn't outside the bounds of probability.

Brackus was ahead of Temperance and me, and he turned around to look at us, gesturing for us to catch him up. I helped Temperance up the last bit of the hill and gazed out at the open ground before us. Nance Round would not have looked like much by daylight. The few blocks of masonry that had persisted from its time as a fort were overgrown with moss and the bulk of the structure was a raised ring of earth, covered with long grass, daisies, and sunny yellow dandelions. Had Brackus not told us the spot was an ancient site I doubted that I would have noticed anything special about it.

The fairies' night-time additions, however, were spectacular. They had driven intricately carved wooden poles into the ground and hung bells and bright fabric streamers of every colour from the tops, turning the round into a huge tent. Balls of a soft white light hung in the air, casting a misty glow over the Court. Long trestle tables had been erected around the edge of the round, piled high with every kind of good food. Whole geese and swans were roasted and restuffed in their feathers, placed alongside heaped platters of honeyed parsnips and greens. Slices of fine white manchet bread were fanned out around silver dishes holding waxed cheeses. Strange fruits were scattered among the other plates, rare oranges and lemons and poppy-red pomegranates cut open to reveal the bloody seeds within. A suckling pig stared sightlessly out at the revels, a scarlet apple wedged in its mouth. Great copper and gold urns stood beside the food, awash with wines, blood-red and silvery golden, as well as spiced hippocras. As I watched I saw a faun wander over and dip an engraved wooden goblet into the red wine. The cup came up sloshing crimson liquid and the faun turned back to wassail the main company.

If the decorations and food were dramatic, the guests were something else. Every kind of fae seemed to have gathered together; tiny blue-skinned pixies hovered in the air, their glassy wings a blur of motion. Glaistigs, satyrs and centaurs with furred pelts of every hue lounged in a pile of rich velvet cushions, tossing glowing golden balls back and forth with each other and laughing. Skeletal fear-gortas lingered over the food, their wasted fingers dancing across plates of sweetmeats and honeyed fruit whilst brownies and redcaps hurried past underfoot. Many of my more distant cousins were there, other water spirits from other rivers. Pegs, Nellys, shellycoats and grindylows nodded towards me as I hesitated at the entrance to the court, my hand clutching the hilt of the sword for comfort.

Still scarcer creatures lurked around the edges of the gathering. The ground shook as a great monocular fachan, one of a Scottish breed of giants, thundered to the ground, using his single arm to ease his single leg to a sitting position. Most surprising of all was a gigantic cormorant that stood by the food tables, its mighty beak tearing at the skin of its roasted cousins.

And everywhere, there were the high fae.

They could only have passed for humans to the most casual

observer, though their forms were much the same. Each was tall
and slender, with long hair and colourful robes of painted linens
and pricelessly rare brocaded silk. Their skin and eyes were every
colour that could be imagined, often patterned after a favourite
animal or flower. Males and females alike wore glittering white
jewels; diamonds, pearls and opals, though I spied a few rings of
amber. They were almost all dancing, long skirts and tunics flying
out as they swirled, moving swiftly between each other.

Temperance stared at them, her eyed wide and admiring. Even
I, who rarely recognised traditional beauty, was taken by their
strange and graceful movements. Brackus nudged me.

'Look at the centaurs,' he whispered, 'the golden balls.'

I followed his gaze. What I had taken to be enchanted toys
were tiny glass globes, each containing a miniature fairy. As
I watched a piebald centaur toss one to a faun with chestnut
legs I could see the tiny creature bang against the glass, the
light flickering as its face twisted with anger and despair. I had
used wisplights my whole life, but this was something new and
horrifying.

Disgusted, I took a step towards them. Brackus caught my
arm, pulling me down so that I was forced to meet his eyes. I
scowled at him.

'That's the Jenny I know,' he said. 'You've never been one to
be taken in by pomp and circumstance. Take another look, and
try not to be dazzled.' I blinked hard, trying to shake away the
glamour, and turned. Where before I had only seen the cheek-
bones and delicate steps now I saw the cruelty. Where the high
fae joined hands as they danced I saw long, sharp nails cutting
into their partners' hands, drops of blood scattering when they
let go. None of the high fae deigned to check their path – if a
brownie was in their way they would trample over him, not
pausing even when he cried out. Shivering butterflies were
pinned in their hair, kept alive by the courtly magic. A cluster
of fae gathered around a beehive, conjuring blooms of illusory
flowers and laughing their bell-like laughs as the bees struggled
to collect the imaginary nectar.

I met Brackus's eyes and he nodded at me. I felt a shiver go down my spine and Temperance came up beside me and took my arm, holding on tight.

Together the three of us stepped into the Court. Brackus led us forward, circling the dancers as he led us towards the far side of the old fort, where the earth rose to form the back wall. The high fae did not pay us mind but the lower fairies looked at the three of us with curiosity. A few followed in our wake. I could hear them chattering about the human. Temperance's presence was a novelty, it seemed.

Brackus waited for a pair of dancers to move out of the way and then we beheld the thrones. Two great chairs were set on a high dais. A slim woman dressed in silver sat in the right-hand throne, but my eyes were drawn to the man on the left.

Gwyn ap Nudd sprawled in his seat, looking bored. He was intimidating even for a high fae. The icy green eyes of a wildcat blinked lazily out at the crowd, seeming brighter and keener for being set in the sun-browned skin of his face. A permanent scowl darkened his features, scratching deep lines into his brow. A thick fur cloak hung loosely from his shoulders over his bare chest, stitched from the pelts of wolf, fox, bear and otter. Most striking of all were the horns that branched from his temples, somewhere between the branching antlers of a stag and the curling horns of a ram.

Brackus halted before the dais and made a deep bow. Temperance curtseyed beside him. She glanced up at me from the corner of her eye. I knew I should bow but it rankled me to fawn at the feet of such a man. I compromised by nodding my head. Gwyn ignored me, focusing his cat's eyes on Temperance, her yellow dress lush and vibrant in the enchanted light.

'A witch,' he said, his voice as deep and low as thunder. 'It has been some time since your kind came to visit me. I had half thought magic had died out among mortal men. And you have arrived in the company of a hobgoblin and a river hag. Strange fellows indeed. Rise, mortal.'

Gwyn's voice carried, hushing the gathering behind us. I

could feel the eyes of the high fae scorching the back of my neck. Temperance stood up. I could see her trying not to fidget, holding her arms stiffly by her side.

'Do you know who I am, little witch?' Gwyn said, leaning forward in his chair. Somehow I doubted he was speaking English but the magic of the Court carried understanding to us.

'You are Gwyn ap Nudd, Lord of the Wild Hunt.' Her voice shook a little. I hoped I was the only one to notice.

'Yes,' rumbled Gwyn, 'It seems that you mortals have not completely forgotten me. What is your name, child?'

'Temperance, my lord, Temperance Crump. I am from Chipping Appleby, on the Caerlee river. This is Jenny Greenteeth and Brackus Marsh. They guided me here.'

'The land of the hollow hills,' Gwyn said, turning his head to inspect Brackus and me. 'I have not visited the valley of the Caerlee since the Old Times. Tell me, Temperance Crump, why have three such unlikely friends as yourselves come to visit my court?' He peered at her, fixing his considerable gaze on her face.

Temperance paused, struggling to speak.

'My lord ...' she stuttered, seeming frozen as a rabbit caught before a fox.

'My lord, we have come to ask for your aid,' interjected Brackus. The horned lord glanced at him without much interest.

'What help would one such as a hobgoblin demand from the Lord of the Wild Hunt?' The gathering fae snickered at his words.

'The Erl King has come to Britain,' I said, curling my hands into fists. Gwyn's attention snapped to me, quick as a striking hawk.

'The Erl King?' he said, looking as if he had only just registered my presence. 'The Erl King is a continental presence, reaping his victims from across the steppes and plains of the East. If he had turned westwards and followed the path of the setting sun to our island there would have been word. Such an event does not occur quietly. Since there have been no whispers it cannot have happened. You are mistaken, little water spirit.'

I gritted my teeth. 'I am not mistaken. I saw him, I felt his presence. I know the old ways and I know what he is. It is the Erl King, I am sure of it.'

A rustle went through the crowd as I contradicted Gwyn. He raised an eyebrow at me and peered with a little more interest.

'You speak very boldly in the presence of your king. Did you not learn respect as a hagseed?' spluttered an adjacent courtier, spitting the words through a mouth almost as cramped with teeth as my own.

'Peace,' Gwyn said, waving a finger indolently, 'let the creature say her part. It would be beneath my station to take offence from one of the low fae.' He beckoned me towards him with a twitch of his hand. 'If you are so sure of what you have seen then you will not mind sharing it with me?'

Confused, I stepped forward, nodding. His implacable eyes met mine and I gasped as his power gripped my mind. He was as strong as the Erl King had been but I was weaker away from my lake and he tore my thoughts apart between his hands as easily as a cat with a vole.

I fell to my knees, my eyes still caught in his gaze. Abandoning any pretence at resistance I opened the tattered barriers of my mind and showed him what I had seen in the parsonage. All at once I was back there, clinging to the wall, listening to the rattling breath, the sluggish heartbeat. The stench of decay filled my nostrils again and I saw the empty forest, the gleaming bone of the stag's open ribcage.

Then it was gone again and I was slumped on my hands and knees in the centre of the court.

'Hmm,' said Gwyn, twisting one of the silver rings on his left hand, 'curious indeed. The little maid speaks the truth. I would not have thought such a thing possible but there it is, all laid out in her mind.' He laughed, amused. 'After an age of existence it is good to know I can still be surprised.'

The Court laughed with him, the sound rippling outwards

from the throne. Temperance crept forward and helped me to my feet. Brackus draped my arm around his shoulder and I consented to lean on him.

'The Erl King has indeed come to Chipping Appleby it seems,' continued Gwyn, still ignoring me. 'What on earth can have possessed him to travel such a long distance and with such secrecy of movement? I had heard there were disturbances in Germania; the heydays of the Black Death are behind us now, but I cannot imagine that it is so bleak that he must flee to the banks of the Caerlee. I wonder if the old whispers about that valley ...' He drifted off, staring into the sky.

'My lord.' Temperance had stepped forward again. 'My lord, about the Erl King?'

Gwyn broke off gazing and looked back at her, his eyes refocusing as they settled on her face. He smiled, mouth curling upwards.

'What is it, sweet child?' he asked. 'Speak freely to your king.'

Temperance flushed but pressed on: 'My lord, there are many tales of you hunting the forces of darkness, defeating them all. Will you not seek out the Erl King and slay him too?'

'Why should I do that?' asked Gwyn with genuine surprise. 'He has not threatened me or mine. My court and my people are quite safe. You yourself are the first mortal to have visited the Wild Hunt for generations. The humans no longer show us the proper respect or make the old sacrifices and we have begun to splinter from their world. In another century we will be cleaved from this place entirely. It is no concern of mine what the Erl King does or does not do to this land since the Hunt will not be here to see it.'

Temperance's face fell. 'But you lead the Wild Hunt. Do you not wish to try your hand at besting such a foe?'

Gwyn snapped his fingers and a goblin in a page's smock appeared at his side bearing a double-handed cup wrought from antler and bone. Gwyn took the cup and raised it towards Temperance.

'This is the stirrup cup of the Wild Hunt. We drank from it every night for millennia, hunting down creatures that would make your Erl King turn tail and run. This court and I have slain countless beasts, mounting their heads on our spears and bringing their skins home to lay at the feet of our ladies.' He tilted the cup to his left to indicate the pale queen.

'I have nothing left to prove to my court, little mortal, nor to you.'

He tossed the cup back to his page and slumped back in his chair, dismissing us with a wave.

Brackus moved forward. 'My lord?'

'What now?' growled Gwyn. 'You try my patience with your incessant chattering.'

'My lord, if you do not care what befalls the Erl King then tell us how we may defeat him,' urged Brackus. 'A prince of the forest such as yourself knows more than any mortal or immortal yet living of hunting such strange creatures. If you would but share that knowledge then we could fight him ourselves, and not bother you further.'

'Gift you the knowledge of my years?' rumbled Gwyn, reaching for his wine goblet. 'Your demands grow each time you speak, goblin. What price do you offer for the thousand-thousand hunts I rode in, the fathoms of blood I spilt?'

'I have nothing of value to give you,' whispered Temperance. 'We have a little money, I can borrow more.'

Gwyn snorted. 'Coins for the hard-won secrets of the Hunt? Do not insult me, girl.'

Temperance looked over at me desperately. I could feel the chance slipping away from us. I retrieved the chunk of amber from my pocket, my hand brushing against the sword belt.

'I had heard the high fae liked amber,' I said, holding it out to him.

Gwyn glanced at it. 'Only that which has trapped creatures in it. Pure amber is mere tree sap and as creatures of the wild places we have that in abundance. You three are wasting my time. This audience is over, you may stay and enjoy the feast if you like.'

Twin guards stepped towards us, holding long spears tipped with sharply knapped flint.

'Please, my lord,' cried Temperance, falling to her knees. Brackus did the same. Swallowing my pride I joined them. What use was pride to me if the Erl King could not be defeated?

Gwyn ap Nudd barely looked at us, inspecting the contents of his goblet. The guards lowered their spears, preparing to shepherd us from the royal presence. I could see our last hope dying in the faded eyes of the Lord of the Hunt. Then something happened that I had not expected.

Gwyn's queen reached out and laid a delicate hand on his arm. He turned towards her, moving his right hand to cover hers. She whispered something to him, too quiet for me to hear. He opened his mouth but she kept talking, tilting her blonde head towards us.

'Halt,' Gwyn said, without moving his eyes from the queen's face. The guards stopped moving towards us but kept their spears pointed down. The queen finished speaking and smiled up at her husband. He raised the hand she had placed on his arm to his lips and kissed it tenderly. The queen blushed prettily and Gwyn motioned the guards back.

'Fortune smiles upon your strange trio,' he said, turning back towards us, 'or at least my lady does, and she is fairer and more constant than that fickle creature.' He cast a devoted glance at his wife.

'Lady Creiddylad has interceded for you and suggested a challenge. A chance for you to prove yourself worthy of my aid.'

I stood again, pulling Temperance and Brackus to their feet beside me. Gwyn smirked at us.

'There are two ways to vanquish a being such as the Erl King. One method is beyond low fae such as yourselves. The other way is what I propose for you. There are three tasks you must complete to open up this course. When you have finished all three then you will have demonstrated to me that you are capable enough to not disgrace my help. Return here and I shall tell you how to defeat the Erl King and you may then leave to pursue the final confrontation with my blessing and the blessing of the Wild Hunt.'

'Thank you, my lord,' said Temperance meaningfully, 'and Lady Creiddylad, my deepest gratitude for your kindness and compassion.'

The queen inclined her head gracefully but did not say anything. Gwyn continued as if Temperance had not spoken.

'Have you heard of the Twrch Trwyth?' he asked. Temperance looked blank. Brackus shook his head.

'The Twrch Trwyth is a great wild boar, the King of all Swine so they used to say. I hunted him myself many centuries ago but released him after capture rather than slay such an exceptional beast. He wanders across the isles of Britain and Ireland, using both Wild and mortal roads. The key to banishing the Erl King is found with this boar.'

Gwyn paused to take a swig of wine. Smacking his lips he returned his attention to us.

'Hunt down the Twrch Trwyth but do not kill him. Instead you must trap him and hold him fast. When you have caught him take out a comb of silver and brush the bristles that grow from his back. As you do this you will comb out the poison that infuses the bristles and it will go into the silver. Bring this comb back to me and I shall give you the second task.'

He sat back, clearly pleased with himself and took another drink. His page ran forward to refill his cup.

'Where might we find this boar, my lord?' I asked.

Gwyn guffawed loudly, slapping the arms of his throne. 'Even if I knew that I would not tell you! Only the finest trackers can seek him out; he cannot be found by spell or spoor. That is why this is a challenge. If you cannot meet the Twrch Trwyth and best him then you would die before you even approach the Erl King and I will have been proven wise to keep my counsel. I would advise that you hurry. The Erl King will be weakest in the long days of midsummer. Your best chance will be to complete your three tasks at the summer solstice. When the nights begin to grow again, so will his power.

'The last thing I shall say to you is to beware the beast's cunning. He was a man once, cursed long ago to dwell in the form of an animal and has lost none of that intelligence, even as his mind fell into pain and hatred.'

Gwyn laughed and waved a lazy hand at us. We were clearly dismissed for good this time. Temperance and Brackus bowed and we backed away into the crowd.

Brackus shepherded us behind one of the long trestle tables and brought us all cups of small beer and a platter of fruit. I snapped off pieces of the sugar confection closest to us, spun into the shape of a water dragon.

'What do you think?' whispered Temperance, in between bites of an apple.

'Better than nothing,' Brackus answered, 'and not as good as I had wished for. I had hoped that we would have some more solid advice on what to do next. I've no idea how to find this boar Gwyn is on about.'

'You haven't heard of it?' Temperance asked. Brackus shook his head.

'I think I might have,' I said, trying to reach for the memory. They looked at me. 'I think my mother mentioned it to me once. All I remember is that it likes woodland. Old woodland. Cannock Chase, Sherwood, the Forest of Dean. Places like that.'

'Well thank you for that, Jenny,' said Brackus. 'Boars like forests. I was about to suggest we set off for Salisbury Cathedral but with that pearl of wisdom I think we're on the right track.'

'Don't snark at me, Marsh,' I hissed at him, 'coming here was your idea and you've never even heard of the damned creature.'

He swelled up like a bullfrog, but Temperance interrupted him before he could respond.

'Don't bicker, you two are worse than my three-year-old.' She sighed. 'It might be a little obvious but at least it's a start. If the boar likes ancient forests then maybe we should pick one and wait for it to turn up.'

We all gloomily contemplated the thought of sitting in a forest waiting for a magical boar to come and attack us.

'I suppose it's better than going back home to be eaten,' I reflected.

'Not much better,' said Brackus.

'Do you have another plan?' Temperance asked. Brackus sipped his beer and yawned but did not reply.

'Maybe we should sleep on it and rethink in the morning,' I suggested.

'Is it safe to sleep here?' Temperance asked, eying the swirling fae suspiciously. 'I don't wish to insult either of you but I do not think I would feel at ease among these fairies.'

'Probably not right here,' Brackus said. 'Let's go back down into the valley. This lot should be having too much fun to bother us, especially if we stay out of the forest.'

We slunk away from the party, dodging gibbering phantoms and selkies as we went.

The woods were dark and I had to guide the other two through the trees. Eventually we came out into the meadow at the edge of the village.

Temperance plopped down on the ground. 'I'm too tired to go any further. Let's just rest here for now.' Neither of us had much strength to argue with her and sank to the ground as well.

'What about the comb that Gwyn said we will need?' Temperance said, shuffling backwards to lean against one of the oak trees. 'Do you have one, Brackus?'

'I'd have to check my pack, but I don't think so. It's not the sort of thing I would usually carry around; most of my fairy customers wouldn't want such a luxurious item and the few witches I visit wouldn't use it in a spell.'

'Surely you know where we could get one?' I asked, curling up between the tree roots.

'Not in this part of the world. We'd have to go to a large town, one wealthy enough to keep a silversmith in business. Though I suppose we'll be travelling anyway to try and find this Twrch Trwyth creature. Like you said though, Jenny, we'll worry about it tomorrow.'

Temperance stretched out on my left, with Brackus leaning against the oak on her other side. He muttered something and sparks flew from his fingers, dancing into the air.

'That should give us some warning in case anything gets bored of the feast fare and decides to come down the hill in the middle of the night for a snack,' he said, swaddling himself in his cloak. 'If something does, I recommend you hit it first and ask questions later.'

I huddled up to the nearby roots. Closing my eyes I reached for sleep, trying not to think about my lake. As I drifted off the last thing I heard was Brackus beginning to snore.

Chapter Nine

I awoke to the smell of fresh flowers. A sweet aroma of roses and geraniums, floating on the morning breeze. I smiled, eyes still closed, and stretched out a hand to my side. My fingers grazed soft silk, probably Temperance's yellow dress. Then she murmured in her sleep, the noise coming from the opposite side of me.

I jerked my eyes open. Lady Creiddylad was kneeling over me, her hand hovering just above my shoulder. I hissed and scuttled backwards, my spine pressing against the tree.

'Don't be afraid, Jenny,' she said soothingly, 'I only meant to wake you up. It's morning.' Her face was calm and her voice melodic, like the sound of a wooden flute. I reached over and nudged Temperance awake.

'What are you doing here?' I asked, as Temperance blinked the sleep dust from her eyes then gaped at the queen.

Creiddylad smiled at me. The effect was startling; the warmth of her expression lit up her face, like a sunset painting the clouds in pink rays.

'I thought I would come and break my fast with you before you set off on your quest. I brought food.' She gestured behind her at a wicker hamper. I cast it a suspicious look. That had definitely not been there a moment ago.

'Breakfast,' questioned Temperance, still looking half asleep. 'You want to eat breakfast with us?'

Creiddylad tossed her something gold and gleaming. She caught it in both hands then held it up to the light: a tiny glass jar of honey.

'Come and eat,' the queen said. She stood up and walked over to the hamper. She picked up a blanket of olive-green velvet and shook it out, spreading it out over the grass. Temperance followed her over while I shook Brackus awake. He woke muttering and confused.

'Brilliant protective spell, Marsh,' I said while he was getting his bearings. 'Gwyn's wife managed to walk right past it.'

'Who?' he slurred. I pointed at where Creiddylad was unpacking fine pottery plates and goblets from her basket. 'Mercy me!' Brackus leapt to his feet and hurried over, brushing his hands over the buttons on his shirt and adjusting the gold braid.

'My lady,' he said, bowing deeply, 'what an unexpected honour. Had we known you would grace us with your presence we would have been waiting, would have prepared something for you!'

'Nonsense, Master Marsh, you are a guest at my court. It is for me to entertain you, is it not? That is the ancient law of hospitality.' Creiddylad extended a hand towards where Temperance was sitting. 'Please join us. Jenny, come and sit by me.'

Brackus plopped down on the blanket. I scrutinised the fairy queen but try as I might I could not detect any hint of danger in her face. I lowered myself to the ground in the spot she had indicated. The velvet blanket was achingly soft under my hands, the plates dazzlingly painted in blue and white.

'Thank you, Jenny. May I serve you a cup of something? We have small beer, apple juice, spring water?' She indicated a row of coloured glass bottles that were nestled in the wicker basket, each sealed with golden wax.

'Water will be fine, thank you.'

Creiddylad selected one. She cracked open the stopper and poured out a cup. Turning back to the hamper she took out pastries and fruit, platters of grilled mushrooms and fried eggs. Butter was served in a pat stamped with a swirling pattern of interlocking Gs and Cs, ready to be slathered onto glossy, freshly baked rolls. With a smile Creiddylad retrieved a jar awash with a dark liquid, cracking open the lid as she handed it to me.

'Pickled herring,' she said. 'Try it. I hear it is a delicacy among river spirits of the east coast.'

I reached inside with a bone-handled knife, spearing a chunk of fish and bit into it. The half-sweet half-sharp flavour filled my mouth and the flesh was succulent and tender.

'Delicious,' I mumbled, looking at the queen, 'my thanks for thinking of it.'

She beamed at me. 'You must take the whole jar of course. It is an underappreciated taste among my court.'

'My lady, might I ask—' I began, but she held up a hand gently, cutting me off.

'Eat first, Jenny,' she said, 'we will talk afterwards. You have a long road ahead and will need your strength.'

I met Temperance's eyes and she shrugged slightly and reached for a roll. I helped myself to the food, heaping a plate high with some of everything. It was all delicious, impossibly fresh and with that round, filling sense food has in times of plenty.

Temperance and Brackus feasted alongside me, drizzling honey over hotcakes and pinching flakes of sea salt to top yellow-hearted eggs.

Creiddylad made her own plate, slicing rolls in half to fill with eggs and rashers of bacon. She nibbled at the creation so delicately that a less suspicious eye than my own would not have noticed that she put away three such sandwiches. She caught me watching and winked.

'I send out a maidservant at first light to fetch eggs and milk from a local farm wherever we go. One of my indulgences.'

'A human servant?' Temperance asked. 'A changeling?'

'Oh, just one of the nixies,' Creiddylad said. 'She leaves gold and blesses the hens with good laying before she goes.'

I could tell Temperance wanted to say something to that but she stayed quiet, chewing thoughtfully on a mouthful of mushrooms.

Brackus kept trying to engage the queen in conversation, offering compliments and courtly ripostes. She simply nodded politely in between bites, and he eventually resorted to simply gazing at her.

Even to my normally uninterested eyes, Creiddylad was profoundly beautiful. Her white-gold hair was caught up in a net, pinned in place by a halo of pearls. A crescent moon was painted on the cream-coloured skin between her dark eyebrows, the curve echoing the perfect circle of her face. The only imperfection was the queen's uneven eyes, one violet, one green.

She was as fresh and lovely as a bank of spring flowers gilded by a late frost. It was difficult for me to remember her sitting alongside Gwyn, who was all chaos, thunder and glowering darkness. I had rarely seen two less matched people. Perhaps that contradiction was what had bound them together for all this time.

I reached for a final piece of bread to mop up the last splashes of egg yolk and refilled the queen's cup. She drank and then began tidying the spread away. She poured water into a silver bowl for us to wash, laying out a towel beside to dry our hands. I sat back and fought the urge to pick at my teeth.

When everything was stowed away Creiddylad folded her hands neatly in her lap and smiled at us.

'Now that we have eaten,' she said, 'let us move on to business. You may be wondering what I am doing here. I did not have a chance to speak with you directly at the Court last night and I wanted another opportunity to meet you before you leave on your quest.'

'Thank you, my lady,' burbled Brackus, 'it is truly an honour to break bread with you.'

I thought that perhaps the only honest compliment he had ever made. Creiddylad patted his hand gently, causing Brackus to flush scarlet.

'You are sweet to say so, Master Marsh, but it is not honour that I come to offer you. Though the Twrch Trwyth pales in comparison to the Erl King, it is still a most dangerous adversary, one that has inspired legends for many years. I fear that none of you have much experience in hunting even mortal boars. Would I be correct in that assumption?'

I nodded. 'I have seen them occasionally drink from my lake, though not since the village grew more populous. Even in the old days I never preyed on them.'

'I thought so.' The queen paused. 'I would very much like to see you succeed in this endeavour. I have thought about what help I can offer you. I am tied to the court, by bonds of both love and duty. Even if I were free to accompany you, I cannot imagine that I would be of much assistance. But there are other things that I can contribute. Three things will I gift you, for three is the most magical of numbers.'

'Lady Creiddylad, we would never presume—' started Brackus.

'Please, Master Marsh, I want to help.'

Brackus settled down, and Creiddylad began again.

'The first gift I can offer you is knowledge. The Twrch Trwyth is unpredictable in many ways, but consistent in a few. He returns to the same places each year for the solstices and the changing of the seasons. The spring equinox is in ten days. The boar feels the shift from darkness to light. He will go to Glastonbury, travelling through the Mendip Hills. If you want to catch him soon then your best opportunity will be to waylay him as he passes through the gorge at Cheddar.'

Brackus withdrew a scrap of parchment and began scrawling notes with a stick of charcoal. Creiddylad continued:

'The second gift is this.' She reached to her head, removing a shining comb from where it was tucked into her hair.

'Use this comb to brush out the poison on the boar's bristles,' Creiddylad said. 'It was wrought by dwarfs using their own magic and will contain the venom better than one made by mortal smiths.'

She handed it to Temperance who turned it over in her hands. I could see that it was silver, smooth and beautifully made.

'Finally, I offer one of my most prized possessions,' sighed the queen, 'as much as such a thing can be possessed.' She raised her fingers to her mouth and whistled like a field hand.

At first I saw nothing and heard only the echoes of Creiddylad's whistle. Then something rustled in the woods behind us. I twisted to look, just in time to see a great hound burst out from among the oak trees. It lolloped over to where the queen sat and barked at her playfully. Creiddylad laughed and reached out a hand. The dog approached, bending its head down to be patted and shaking its tail.

'This is Cavall,' she said, scratching behind its ears. 'The greatest hound who has ever lived. Such a fine hunting dog was he that my husband adopted him as his own, extending his life while he runs with the court. The last and only time the Twrch Trwyth was caught, Cavall was the one who brought him down. Take him with you and he will be happy to chase the boar again.'

I looked at the dog. It was tall, leaning down to lick Creiddylad's ears as she sat on the ground and laughed up at him. I hadn't much experience with dogs other than the black-and-white sheepdogs the village farmers kept. This was a different kind of creature entirely. Its body was slim and rangy, with long legs and a long nose. Its coat was a brindled brown, with a splash of white at his neck and tail. It looked over at us with doggish interest before padding over to Temperance and putting its head in her lap and yawning.

She laughed and began to stroke its head. Creiddylad smiled again.

'I am pleased he has taken to you so quickly!' She leaned over to stroke the dog's hindquarters. Cavall rolled over so she could scratch his stomach more easily, wagging his tail again.

I wasn't sure what to make of the dog. Creiddylad and Temperance were reacting to it as if it were a toddling child, but it didn't seem much more interesting than a sheep or a deer or any other four-legged land creature. It probably tasted similar too. I decided not to mention that to the queen.

I realised they were both looking at me, having asked a question I hadn't heard. I gambled with a nod. Temperance looked pleased and shifted over to make space. Clearly I had assented to touching the beast.

I crawled over, reaching out a long finger to prod the dog's back. It felt lean and bony. I didn't really feel the attraction but I smiled at Temperance and the queen anyway. The creature did have nice fur, long and silky. I thought it would make a lovely coat, or perhaps a rug. I decided to keep that thought to myself as well.

Cavall twisted his head around, peering down his snout to regard me with beady black eyes. Temperance patted its neck and he opened his mouth, panting contentedly.

'It is a wrench to let him go,' said the queen, 'but I fear he is getting restless now that Gwyn no longer hunts. He deserves to stretch his legs and run, not stay here as a lapdog.' She stroked his ears tenderly.

I didn't think that the dog looked distressed at being petted and cosseted but the queen seemed certain. In any case the beast was sure to be useful as we hunted down the great boar and I did not want to contradict her.

Brackus coughed politely, moving closer to the queen.

'Lady Creiddylad,' he began. 'You have shown us unrivalled kindness and generosity. I am sure all three of your gifts will be invaluable as we continue on this quest. However, I must ask –' he paused awkwardly '– why have you decided to grant us this most substantial aid? I have visited the Court before and never have I seen you intercede the way you did last night, nor have I heard it related by others.'

Temperance waggled her eyebrows at him, as if to tell him to stop talking before Creiddylad took offence.

The queen nodded. 'Quite a reasonable question, Master Marsh. It is indeed a rare thing for me to interfere with my husband's rulings. Perhaps the reason for that scarcity is that it is rare for someone to come to the Court asking for help in such an endeavour. Our petitioners request money, favours, magic. The three of you ask for help in a quest.

'Ah my children, I know you that are old compared to a mortal like Temperance here, but to me all three of you seem alike in your youth. For ten thousand years I have walked this earth, treading on roads both mortal and fairy. I wed Gwyn when we were both younger than you are now, and our love was a shining thing, bringing light and happiness to us both. It was a time of epic quests, a time where it was common to slay a dragon and rescue a damsel, to risk life and limb for honour and glory. The world was larger then, or so it seemed it was to me.

'When the Romans came from over the southern seas, we retreated to our mountain fastnesses and waited them out, still hoping for one final blaze of splendour. Our hopes came true when they left and Arthur came to power. He brought back the old ways and invited all to come to his court at Camelot. You cannot know how sweet that time was for Gwyn and me; we found we were young again, our love was remade. Those years of chivalry and adventure were the happiest of my life.'

Creiddylad stopped speaking. Her face was shining but I thought there were tears in her eyes.

'Mayhap we should have left then. Arthur died on Mordred's sword and the world fell apart without him. The kingdom he had built shattered and Gwyn and I returned to the Hunt; sadder, wiser and older. Since then the Hunt has faded from a great force to the shadow court you saw last night. We are fading still. That is not a wholly bad thing. I am ready to leave this mortal earth of mankind. But I still think of those glorious years with bitter fondness.

'Then last night you came to my court, craving assistance to slay a monster and save your village. I remembered the old days. I saw the shadows of Arthur's knights in your faces. There is no Merlin left to guide you on your path so I resolved to do what I could to take that place.'

Creiddylad wiped away the tears that had dripped down her cheeks. I watched her face. It was still beautiful, but as she had spoken I had seen some of the numberless days start to carve their passage on her face. Lines had formed, then deepened around her mouth and eyes, scars of a thousand laughs, a thousand tears. Her hair glinted silver and the hand she held up to brush back a strand was mottled and papery. I glanced at Brackus, but he still stared at her in total adoration.

'Fifty years ago I think Gwyn would have helped you himself, but he is too far gone now. You will have to do this alone. Complete the three tasks and I will guarantee that Gwyn will tell you the rest of the way to defeat the Erl King.'

We were quiet when the queen finished speaking. Temperance leaned over to stroke her hand and Cavall whined. Creiddylad smiled and the years fell away from her again, her face luminous.

'I entreat you not to waste your pity on me. I have lived a long and eventful life, blessed with love and adventure. I am happy that you have come here and are allowing me to help you. It may be the last good thing I do in this world.'

'Thank you for telling us that, my lady. We are honoured to hear it,' said Temperance. I nodded, realising to my surprise that I truly agreed. Behind me I heard Brackus sniffle.

Creiddylad shook her head and rose to her feet.

'Now, I must not keep you any longer,' she said, 'Take the dog, the comb and the advice and be on your way. Eight days of walking should bring you to Cheddar Gorge, which will give you one day to prepare.'

We scrambled up and the queen kissed each of us on the cheek, not flinching at my damp green skin. It was as strange an experience as I had ever had, but not altogether unpleasant. Brackus bent over her hand in his most exotic bow and she laughed aloud. He looked as pleased as if she had given him a bar of gold and practically skipped back to my side.

'Jenny, Brackus, Temperance', said Creiddylad. 'Fair weather and good fortune keep you safe until we meet again.' She seemed to glow from within, moving eastwards so that the rising sun was at her back. I blinked and then she was gone, leaving only the faintest smell of lilies on the wind. The basket and blankets were gone too; in their place sat leather satchels. I bent to inspect the closest one. It was stuffed with neatly packed food, a cloak and a small pouch of bronze coins.

Cavall whined again then jumped up. He barked twice then tossed his head to the north.

'Well,' I said, picking up one of the satchels. 'We have a week of walking ahead of us. Let's move out.'

Chapter Ten

The journey from Cornwall to Cheddar Gorge was uneventful, marked only by a change in the weather. The golden days of early spring yielded to sheeting rain carried on westerly winds that soaked through our cloaks and harried our steps. I discovered quickly that a lifetime spent underwater had not prepared me for the misery of being dripping wet on land, scrambling with bare hands and feet through muddy roads. Temperance became silent and sullen as the rainy days wore on and even Cavall's boundless energy seemed to ebb once the rain had scattered all potential chasing targets.

Brackus alone seemed unaffected by the weather. The tarpaulin that he usually erected over our campsites was able to be buttoned into an overcoat that kept him warm and dry and his boots were sturdy and waterproof. The raindrops only touched his face. If his expression ever faltered then a quick glance at me seemed to perk him up again. For a while I thought that it was the sight of my struggles that was cheering him so but the effect was much the same during the rare dry intervals.

I grew to suspect that his constant smirking was the result of the glamour he had agreed to cast on me so that we might travel human roads without alarm. He had claimed to be altering my appearance to that of a wizened grandmother but I doubted that would make him giggle into his collar ten times a day.

As it happened I did not think the glamour was of much use anyway. We rarely saw another traveller on those long muddy roads through Cornwall. I glimpsed occasional cottages clinging to the hillsides as we walked but the road north passed mostly over moors and heaths, where the earth was too thin to support farming. Black-faced sheep peeked out at us from the shadows of high granite tors, chewing thoughtlessly as we passed before them.

I left the rations Creiddylad had given us to Brackus and Temperance and caught my own food from the handful of streams we crossed. I stuck my head in each, looking to see if anyone was at home and enjoying the chance to bathe and recoup a little of my strength. The water was rarely inhabited by anything more than frogs and fish but as we passed into Devon I did meet another Jenny in a tributary of the Torridge river. She refused to come out to meet my companions but generously shared a large trout with me and gave me another to take on my way. When I emerged from the stream, dripping and cheerful from the rare interaction with my own kind I found Brackus and Temperance huddled under a spreading oak tree. As I scuttled towards them I felt a wave of hot dry air flow towards me.

'Marsh, is it you doing that?' I shouted, retreating before I dried out too much.

The heat vanished and the misting rain immediately fell to fill the air.

'Sorry, Jenny,' Temperance called. I hurried over to join them. The witch looked refreshed, her clothes had dried out and the curls that had been plastered to her face were now springing in their usual dark halo. I glowered at Brackus.

'Did you have to push the spell out so far?' I asked. 'What if someone had come past and noticed it?'

Brackus shook his head, grinning. 'Not me, Jenny. Temperance asked me if I knew any spells for heat. I taught her the cantrip and she cast it better than I ever have! We've a powerful witch among us, Jenny.'

I looked over at Temperance who was smiling widely and I battened down my bad mood.

'Well done,' I said, genuinely pleased that she would be able to dry out properly from now on. Temperance went pink with pleasure.

'Well, Brackus is a good teacher. The credit should really go to him.'

Brackus smirked at me and I snorted.

'I always knew you had a gift for producing hot air, Marsh. Come, let's get going again.'

The roads became busier as we headed through Devon and into Somerset, filling up with shepherds driving stocks to market and merchants leading donkeys loaded down with packs. The rain eased and we began to see the lands we were walking through. The high moors ceded to low farmland, sheep gave way to fields budding with new growth. I was steadier on my feet now, able to walk upright for hours at a time without leaning on Temperance, though as each day wound to a close I would revert to all fours for the final few miles.

We turned westwards and began to head towards the rising form of the Mendips. At the end of the seventh day we made camp at Brent Knoll, in the shadow of the lonely hill. Brackus lit his dark fire and he and Temperance bunched together around it. I still disliked the flames but joined them to share their conversation. Cavall flopped down on top of my feet and yawned. I slid my feet out from under him and he looked up at me as if I had slapped him.

'Cursed beast,' I muttered. He whined at me. I gave him a tentative prod with my toe and he rolled over. Temperance reached over to scratch his stomach and he wagged his tail.

'We should reach the entrance to the gorge tomorrow,' said Brackus, reaching for a stick and beginning to sketch out a map in the ashes. 'This,' he said, marking out a long wavering line that made a sharp angle back on itself, 'is the path of the gorge. We will need to make our move before the boar reaches this point where it widens out.' He scored a mark across the line of the valley and drew a north arrow beside it.

'All right,' Temperance said, furrowing her forehead. 'And how exactly do we make our move?'

Brackus dropped the stick. 'I am not completely sure, my dear. Hunting is not exactly a pastime I have indulged in, except where necessary to keep hunger at bay. I was hoping that Jenny here, as our resident ambush predator, would have some ideas.' They both turned to look at me. Even Cavall tilted his head my way.

I was a little thrown by this. There was quite a large difference between hunting fish or snatching an unwary faun from the edge of my lake and bearding a wild boar in the open. I stroked my chin to play for time.

'Can you tell me a little more about the gorge?' I asked. 'Are there any lakes or streams nearby?'

'Not in the main corridor.' Brackus pointed his stick at the eastern entrance of the valley, 'There are some small streams here. The gorge rises to over a hundred feet on either side but it's too steep to climb, it's just sheer rock face. There are no good spots to hide on the valley floor, and it's fairly narrow. I expect that is why Lady Creiddylad suggested the gorge would be a good place to strike.'

I inspected the drawing, leaning over with a finger to trace the strokes in the mud.

'Do you have anything in that pack of yours that might be of use, Brackus?'

The goblin shrugged. 'Some ropes. Not enough to weave a net from. I imagine even a mortal boar could break through them easily enough.'

I turned to Temperance. 'What about you? Any hunting or restraint spells?'

She thought about it. 'I could probably make a lure that would at least draw the boar over to have a look. It wouldn't be strong enough to hold him for long, especially when we try to comb him. And we have Cavall of course.' She patted the dog.

I turned it over in my mind. Temperance's lure, Brackus's rope, Cavall and me. Surely I could make something out of that. Something flickered; the bones of a plan took shape, blurry but definitely there.

'I might have something,' I said slowly, 'but we're all going to have to work very closely together. And it could be very dangerous.'

Brackus gulped. 'Dangerous for all of us?'

I shook my head. 'Mainly dangerous for me.'

Brackus relaxed. 'Well, that's all right then,' he said and grinned at me.

The entrance to Cheddar Gorge rose up before us. Brackus had been accurate when he described the cliffs as sheer. Greying limestone crags jutted out over scree slopes, with only a handful of trees to seek shelter behind. We walked through the valley, the three miles taking us over an hour to cover. At the north end I clambered up one of the sides with Temperance and we looked down into the ravine. Brackus was waiting at the bottom and Cavall was nowhere to be seen, presumably racing around with excitement at the various smells and shapes of the canyon. I tilted my head back to watch a hawk hovering in the late afternoon sky.

Suddenly Temperance turned to me. 'Are you sure about this plan, Jenny? It seems very treacherous for you. It is not too late to change your mind. I'm sure we can come up with something else.'

I shook my head. 'We are out of time. The boar will arrive tomorrow and if we miss this opportunity then it could be years before we find him again. Even with Creiddylad's intercedence we don't even know if Gwyn will remember the next task by then. I think Brackus may have been overstating it when he said the Lord of the Hunt's wits had not faded. We need to do this now.'

She sighed, looking out at the wooded slopes behind the cliff edges.

'I know that makes sense but I don't want you to get hurt. Brackus and I will be out of danger, you will be the only one at risk. It doesn't seem fair.'

'Well I am the strongest of us, I doubt either of you two could go up against the Twrch Trwyth. Besides, a part of me is almost excited at the thought. After a thousand years in my lake my life could use a little danger to keep it fresh.'

Temperance patted my shoulder. 'Thank you, Jenny. I know that you've done so much for us already. I wish I didn't need to keep asking for your help. I feel I'm a bad friend to ask you to put yourself in danger, but I'd be a bad mother if I didn't try to give this plan the best chance of success.'

I smiled at her. 'You're a good mother. And though I am not particularly experienced in the matter I would say that you are a good friend too. Come now, let us walk back and find the best spot to lay this trap.'

The day before the spring equinox dawned bright and clear. We did not know what time the boar would pass through the gorge so we arose with the sun and scattered to our positions with only the briefest confirmation of our tasks. Brackus hurried off to the northern entrance, trailed by a bounding Cavall. Temperance and I walked down into the valley together. The floor was still draped in shadow, the sun too low to permeate over the eastern cliffs. We reached the point of our divergence, a crooked whitebeam tree.

I nodded to Temperance and to my surprise she threw her arms around me in a hug. Stunned, I tapped her back awkwardly.

'Good luck, Jenny,' she said, releasing me. 'I know you can do this.'

She turned away and slipped behind the tree. I stood there gawking for a moment then shook myself. The eastern cliffs were especially steep in this section, rising almost vertically from the road. I flexed my fingers and toes and began to climb. It was easier than scaling the wall of the parsonage; I did not have to worry about being quiet and could leap from ledge to ledge with abandon. I was enjoying myself by then and grew careless. A rock slipped out from my feet and only a tuft of grass saved me from an ignominious fall. I resolved to concentrate more.

I found a good spot, tucked beneath a protuberant rock bed that would keep me shielded from sunlight even at midday.

I turned around so that I was looking down at the floor of the gorge, crouching down on my ankles. I could not see Temperance, though I knew she was still behind the whitebeam tree. I hoped she had been able to climb it and was even now casting her spell from the safety of its branches.

I patted the coil of rope at my waist, then realised with a jolt of surprise that I was still carrying the sword. I had almost forgotten I had it with me, had not unsheathed it once since leaving the cave. I had nowhere to leave it now, I would just have to keep wearing it.

The morning passed into afternoon. Long hours of squatting on a tiny ledge of rock were beginning to cramp my legs. I tried to flex my muscles, to keep them from falling asleep. The sun had passed overhead, lighting up the valley and was now beginning to travel westwards, the rays flashing in my eyes.

I realised I had not seen another traveller all day, despite meeting a handful passing through the gorge yesterday. Was there a local tradition that kept the canyon empty on the day before the equinox? It would at least make it easier for us to complete our tasks if we weren't worrying about prying mortal eyes.

Another hour passed. I estimated it was mid-afternoon. We had thought the boar would have come by now. I began to worry that I had missed it, dozed off without noticing and awoken too late. Surely Temperance would have come and got me if that was the case? Unless she had fallen asleep as well. I wrestled with myself. It was a stupid notion, but now I had thought of it I wanted to go and check with her. It would only take a moment for me to ask, I could be back in position in no time.

I decided it was worth it and began to warm up my legs to begin the climb down when a horn sounded from the north. Brackus's signal. I whipped around. The horn rang out again and on the wind I could detect the faint baying of a hound.

No time now to mess around by talking to Temperance. I would just have to trust that she was ready. I leaned out as far as I dared, peering down the road to the north. Nothing yet. I unwound the rope from my waist, looping the ends around my hands. I patted the silver comb, hanging by a leather thong around my neck. Everything seemed to be in place.

More barking came from the north. It sounded like Cavall but the tone was deeper than normal, baying out joyfully. I could hear faint squealing as well, similar to the village pigs. I hoped that was the boar and that the first part of the plan was in place.

Thundering hoofbeats echoed through the cliffs, growing in tempo and volume with each passing minute. Cavall would be chasing the boar down the valley now, skirting close enough to nip at its ankles. I trusted the silly creature had the wit not to get gored. Creiddylad's generosity might crack if we got her favourite pet killed.

The hoofbeats got louder and as I stared out I saw a dark shape come into view. It was a large blur, a deep muddy-brown, that sharpened into the shape of a huge boar. I thought it was easily five feet tall, judging by the size of the boulders it was rushing by. Long stained tusks curled out from its mouth, dripping saliva as it galloped. Hooves the size of dinner plates clattered on the stones of the road, aiming occasional kicks at the hound snapping at them. Cavall was right on his heels, dodging back and forth to drive the creature onwards. The boar was furious, almost reaching him with each kick, but kept running.

They were still a few hundred yards away, but the distance was closing fast. I thought the boar's patience was wearing thin and any moment now he would stop and make a stand. I was hoping that would happen close enough to Temperance's tree.

Cavall reached out to bite the boar's left hind leg, drawing blood which spattered onto the grass. The great beast ground to a halt, turned around and bellowed at the hound. Cavall skipped backwards, his black eyes not moving from the hog. The boar rushed at him, lowering its tusks in an attempt to impale the dog. Cavall jumped to the side at the last minute and risked a chomp of the boar's ear. It roared at him and tried to turn around. Cavall held his ground, ears pricked and tail held confidently high.

I whistled and Cavall glanced up. He darted to avoid another strike from the boar. I whistled again and Cavall ran forward, leaping into the air. He sailed over the rump of the beast and landed neatly on the other side. With a final bark of farewell he bolted back the way he had come, hopefully looking to return to wherever Brackus had set him.

The boar bellowed after him but didn't chase. It snuffled around in the grass, shaking out the leg Cavall had bitten. It didn't seem inclined to rush on with its journey. That was good. We wanted it shaken from the interaction but calm enough to accept the lure Temperance was about to send out.

The giant pig trotted forward, testing its injured leg. It hopped a little, grunting as it shifted its weight around. It walked forward again, stopping right in front of the whitebeam tree. It was still sniffling along the ground, tearing up chunks of grass to munch on. Suddenly I smelt the faint aroma of liquorice on the air again. Temperance was casting her spell.

At the foot of the tree little white shapes were beginning to bubble up through the earth. The boar sniffed, lowering its nose to the ground. A cornucopia of fungi was growing up alongside the roots. Beefsteak, dryad's saddle and hedgehog mushrooms blossomed from the side of the tree, opening umbrellas out up to the sun. The boar regarded them thoughtfully then began to munch, the sounds of mastication floating up through the canyon.

The scent of liquorice strengthened and flowery scarlet elfcups and rose-coloured wood ears popped up, their bright colours intended to catch the boar's eyes. Still more broke through the grass, bulbous white puffballs and lacy cauliflower fungus. Temperance was laying a path of mushrooms from the tree to the foot of the eastern cliffs. The boar followed the trail, snuffling noisily at the treats. It paused right beneath me to graze on a particularly flavoursome crop.

I tensed my legs, trying to judge when to spring. Temperance had promised me that the enchanted mushrooms would calm the boar enough that it wouldn't immediately kill me, but the effect would only last so long. I needed to go precisely when the boar had eaten enough for the soothing spell to take hold but before it had eaten its fill and decided to move on.

Minutes flashed past. When was the right moment? Brackus and Temperance had completed their parts perfectly, I could not risk messing up mine. Below me the boar paused, turning its head to the south, a ribbon of fungus draping from its mouth. I froze – had I waited too long?

The boar snorted, then lowered its head to continue eating. I decided I had to go now. I shoved all my courage into my shaking legs and jumped.

I landed catlike on the boar's back, looping the twist of rope around its head. The boar shrieked and bucked wildly, kicking out with both back legs and twisting its torso to try and shake me off. I clung to the rope with one hand and wound the other into the bristles, trying to stay balanced.

The hog screamed with rage, and began to leap four-footed into the air, curving its whole body as it bawled. My grip slid and I almost fell. The stony floor rocketed towards me, and I dug in with my feet, pulling myself up moments before my face smashed into the ground. I slammed into the boar's side, coarse, spiky bristles scratching at my skin.

The boar bucked and the force of its movement threw me upwards. I rode the wave of momentum and scrabbled to wind my fingers into the rope. A fresh series of bucks and twists almost threw me again, each landing knocking the breath out of me. I tightened my nails on the rope, digging it into the boar's flesh and it screeched again, bucking like an unbroken horse.

I needed to let go of the bristles with my right hand so that I could reach for the silver comb that was swinging at my neck. The thought seemed almost suicidal. I instructed my fingers to unclench but they wouldn't. The boar slammed its side against the rocks of the cliffs. I ducked just in time to prevent my brains from being smashed out by a rocky overhang.

I had managed to loosen a few fingers and was preparing to make a grab from the comb when the boar unexpectedly stopped twisting. I paused. Had Temperance's calming magic finally taken effect? I snatched the comb from my neck, snapping the leather cord, but before I could begin to coax it through the bristles the boar snorted and began to run.

It raced back to the centre of the valley and sprinted southwards, with me still clinging to its back. I squeezed my thighs, trying to slow the beast but it howled with fresh fury and sped up. The gait of the pig was incredibly bumpy, flinging me back and forth as it galloped on. I was still holding on to the rope with my left hand, now the only thing keeping me mounted.

The silver comb flashed in my hand as we passed through a patch of sunlight. Somehow I had to try and brush this thing. I brought my hand up to the back of the boar, where a raised spine of bristles jutted out. A tiny part of my brain was wondering if touching the poison would affect me. The rest of my brain was incoherent panic. I wanted to scream but I could barely suck in enough air to keep breathing. I jabbed the comb into the hair, scraping it through the bristles rather than brushing.

The boar's wrath reached a new level of ferocity at this indignity, and it put on a burst of speed. We were nearing the southern end of the gorge. I didn't know whether I had captured enough poison so I kept combing the bristles as fast as I could and clung on.

Without so much as a yelp the boar skidded to a stop. I lost my grip and shot into the air, tumbling over its head and rolling forward through the stony grass. I smacked my head against something hard and dropped the comb. I heard a savage growl and looked up. The boar was a few feet away, its tiny eyes brimming with outraged frenzy. Its tusks looked terribly sharp from this angle. I tried to lever myself up but the blow to my head was making me dizzy and I scrabbled on the grass.

The boar raised its haunches and charged. I lifted my arms and braced for the impact, closing my eyes in anticipation. It never landed. I opened an eye to see Cavall had leapt in front of me and was snarling at the boar. His hackles were up and his lips drawn back to reveal teeth. There was no trace of the affectionate lapdog that had tried to lick Creiddylad's ears or even the barking hound that I had seen from the cliffs. This was a creature of the hunt. A distant part of my mind was finally understanding the appeal of dogs, vowing never to eat a drowned puppy again.

The boar feinted left and right, trying to reach me. Cavall met every move, drool beginning to drip from his slavering jaws. The boar roared at him, blasting hot mushroom-scented air. The dog didn't flinch, maintaining that low threatening growl. For a moment I thought the boar would attack anyway, having been driven to the point where its reason had fled. My hand felt the hilt of my sword and tightened around it. Perhaps I could scare it off with that.

Before I could draw the blade, the boar stopped roaring. It backed off, never taking its eyes off us. Cavall let it go, standing over me like a warning; he had ceased growling but his mouth was still twisted into a snarl. The boar's hind feet clattered onto the road. It rumbled once more at us then took off south, disappearing into the flat plains of the Somerset Levels.

I sighed and collapsed into the grass. My head was aching but the dizziness was starting to fade. I felt something fall onto my chest and peered up to see Cavall, nosing at the silver comb he had just dropped. He was looking deeply pleased with himself. I raised a tentative hand and patted his head the way I had seen the others do.

'Good, ah, good boy, Cavall.' He barked happily and began to lick my face. It was truly disgusting but I allowed it. I thought the dog had earned the right.

I lay there in the grass for a while, catching my breath and holding the comb to my chest. Slowly I felt my mouth curve in a wide grin.

'We did it, Cavall. We completed the first task. I can't believe it actually worked.' I felt days of pressure sliding off my shoulders and laughed up at Cavall as he barked.

I heard someone calling my name and sat up to see Temperance running down the gorge, Brackus a few steps behind her.

'Jenny,' she yelled, looking around wildly.

'Over here,' I waved at her. She hurried over, bunching up her skirts to allow her to run faster. She sat down next to me, raising a hand to the rapidly growing bump on my forehead.

'My word, Jenny, are you hurt? I was putting everything I had into those mushrooms but it wasn't as effective as I had hoped. When I saw that thing take off with you on its back I thought for sure you'd be killed. I was trying to run after you but you vanished around the corner before I could even get out of the tree, and then Cavall came baying past, with Brackus behind him.'

She paused for breath.

'I'm not injured,' I said, 'I actually feel fine.'

'You hit your head, Jenny. I can see a lump the size of an egg forming on your brow. Sit still and I'll rustle up something for the pain. Do you have any broken bones? Any cracked ribs? No, don't shake your head at me, you haven't even stood up yet.'

Brackus staggered over, panting, and fell to the ground.

'Stop fussing over her, Temperance,' he gasped, 'Greenteeth are hardy creatures. She'll tell you if she needs help.'

Temperance ignored him. 'Such a pity about the comb but it couldn't be helped. We will have to try again. Maybe the boar will come back this way after the equinox? If we have a little more time then we could buy enough rope to weave a proper net.'

I looked at her, confused. 'What about the comb?'

Her face fell. 'Well, Jenny, we don't blame you. We couldn't have predicted the boar would take off like that. It might have been too much to ask of you even if it had stayed by the mushrooms – what with the way it was bucking. There's always a second chance for . . .'

Temperance's voice petered out as I waved the comb at her. Brackus chuckled.

'You always were a tricky one, Jenny, I'll give you that,' he hooted. Temperance's mouth fell open.

'You didn't,' she said. I grinned at her and tossed her the comb. She caught it then looked up at me astonished. 'You're telling me that not only did you successfully ride the Twrch

Trwyth for a mile through the gorge without falling off, but you also combed his hair at the same time?'

'It was not so very difficult,' I deadpanned.

'Jenny Greenteeth, you are a marvel. Come here.' She wrapped her arms about me. Brackus joined in and the three of us shared a glorious embrace. Cavall pranced around us barking enthusiastically.

When we broke apart Temperance looked down at the comb.

'The first step to defeating the Erl King,' she whispered. Brackus reached out and she handed it to him. He lifted it up to the light and whistled.

'Is it wrong to admit that I didn't think you could do it?' He winked at me. 'I won't be underestimating you again, Jenny.'

He tucked it away in a buttoned pocket. 'One task done, two more to go. We'd better look for another entrance to the Wild Roads before that boar comes back to finish us off.'

Chapter Eleven

We camped up on the eastern escarpment. The sun was getting low by the time Brackus located what he thought was a door to the Wild Roads and none of us wanted to travel there by night. Brackus pitched his tarpaulin over his telescopic staffs and we lay down, still giddy with our success.

'I wonder what the next task will be,' Temperance pondered aloud, as she fended off Cavall's attempts to steal her dinner. 'Another animal to hunt? A puzzle to solve?'

'I think it will be killing something this time.' I reached for my jar of pickled herring, popping the lid with a twist. 'Something really terrifying. A giant or a dragon.'

'How would that help us defeat the Erl King?'

I shrugged and speared a chunk of fish with a fingernail. 'It's a traditional quest isn't it? Maybe Gwyn just wants us to overcome obstacles rather than actually collecting tools. I doubt we're going to comb the Erl King to death.'

'Creiddylad said the poison was in the comb now,' Temperance said, giving up and halving her sausage with Cavall.

'I still don't see how a comb is going to help, even if it is poisonous. I'm thinking dragons.' I bared my teeth and growled dramatically, flapping my arms in the air. Temperance laughed.

'There are no dragons left,' said Brackus from his stool by the fire.

'Not in the lowlands maybe, but there must be lots in Snowdonia, or in Scotland.'

Brackus shook his head, 'Not a single one.' He kicked a stray branch back into the cooking fire. 'They all died out after the Normans invaded. Precious few giants left these days either.'

I frowned. It had been long years since I'd seen a dragon fly overhead but I had presumed they had merely taken different paths.

'Are you sure, Brackus? What happened to them?'

He kicked the branch again. 'No one knows. They were always popular targets for knights but before the Norman conquest they could still maintain their population. Then they just stopped breeding. The ancient ones died of old age with none to take their place.' He sniffed. 'Terrible pity I always thought, though I expect the mortal farmers didn't mind the change.'

'Did you ever see one?' Temperance asked, fascinated.

'Not up close,' I admitted, 'though they used to fly over the lake once or twice a year. I don't remember when I stopped noticing them. How about you, Brackus?'

'Once,' Brackus said, his voice dreamy. 'When I was young. This would have been oh, eight hundred years ago? Back when this would all have been called Wessex. One of those Aeth-kings was on the throne. Aethelbald, Aethelbert, Aethelred? The famous one.'

'Aelfred.' I said. Brackus nodded.

'Sounds about right. I was up near Chester, trying to sell something to one of the hedge wizards I knew. I was walking back along the old Roman road when I saw it. A great scarlet lizard with wings wide enough to blot out the sun. It wheeled overhead, looking for a place to land.'

Brackus grinned at us. 'I almost passed away on the spot. I recovered just enough to dive off the road into a ditch. Ruined almost all of my goods. The dragon came down not a hundred feet away, to drink from a lake. You can't imagine the smell, acrid and sulphurous, like the very fires of hell. And the heat

Jenny, you would have hated it. Even at that distance it was as hot as a smithy in June.'

'Did it see you?' gasped Temperance.

'If it had I wouldn't be around to tell the tale,' winked Brackus. 'When it had drank its fill it took off again, wings beating the air so as I thought a storm had come through. I pulled myself out of the ditch and began to traipse back to Chester. Everyone I passed wanted to know if I had seen the dragon overhead. I drank out on that story for years.' His face fell a little. 'Of course that was when mortals still spoke with us and believed in dragons.'

We sat in silence for a little while, then he sighed again.

'So I doubt we'll be looking for a dragon, Jenny. I'm inclined to agree with Temperance. I think we're still searching for some kind of weapon. Or the parts of a spell. Either way we'll find out tomorrow night.'

I stared into the fire. Temperance shuffled a little closer to me.

'Whatever it is, I'm starting to believe that we can face it,' she said. 'That we can find a way to win.'

I glared at her, in mock outrage. 'Now! You said earlier that you had total confidence in me.'

'Well, you were about to go and wrestle a wild boar,' she grinned at me. 'I didn't want to show any doubt.'

'Have a little more faith in me,' I huffed, 'I haven't let you down yet.'

'Nor will you. We're on a quest and a knight doesn't disappoint their maiden fair.'

I smiled at her imagery. 'Ha! Some story this would be. I don't think I'm particularly well suited to the role of knight.'

'Then I'll be the knight and you can be the maiden,' Temperance said. 'I'll end up rescuing you.'

I looked over at where Brackus was trying to defend his own dinner from the hound. 'What about those two?'

Temperance pursed her lips, considering. 'Cavall can be the noble steed. Brackus can be the treasure; with all those buttons and braid he shines like a pile of gold already.'

I pealed with laughter as Brackus lost the battle with Cavall and looked over at us.

'I can hear you, you know,' he said grumpily, spurring Temperance and me into further giggles. 'And this outfit is extremely fashionable.'

This did nothing to diminish our laughter and he stomped off, Cavall bounding along at his heels. Temperance's smile faded.

'What?' I asked. 'He'll be back soon.'

'Not him,' she said, 'I was thinking about knights and maidens. And Creiddylad and Gwyn. I was also missing Benedict. I haven't spent so long apart from him since we wed.'

'Tell me about him,' I said, curious to know what sort of a man had such an effect on my friend.

Temperance smiled; her face warm with the memory.

'He looks like a farmer. Like the land itself. His hair is the blond of ripe corn, his eyes the blue of a summer sky. When I sprained by ankle in the fields his arms were strong enough to carry me home, his hands gentle enough to bind it up again.

'Every day he comes home with a wildflower or a snail shell or a handful of berries. He goes down on one knee and presents them to me and I pay him with kisses. When Ursula was born, he carried her around the village, boasting that she would be as clever as her mother and he carved her an applewood crib with dancing bears around the rim.

'He keeps the children from getting under my feet when I'm working and gets up in the night when they cry.'

She paused, hooking a lock of hair behind her ears, and met my eyes.

'Oh, we fight like anyone. He's no more perfect than I am. But never for a moment have I stopped loving him. When I saw Gwyn and Creiddylad, that's what it felt like. Silly I know, to compare myself to one of the great mythical romances.'

'You're risking your life for him, and for your children,' I said, 'facing legendary foes and travelling the length of the kingdom. That sounds like a classic love story to me.'

Temperance smiled at me. 'It would be an epic romance or

an ordinary act of motherhood. I suspect you know something about that.'

I thought of Little Jenny and nodded. We sat together in silence, waiting for Brackus to come back.

The second doorway to the Wild Roads was different from the first. Instead of an arch of trees Brackus had found a plain wooden gate standing in the middle of a field. It looked well maintained; the latch didn't squeak as Temperance opened it. I would not have glanced at it twice had it not been unconnected to any fence, standing alone and vaguely ominous.

Temperance walked through the gate to no effect before we could stop her, then came back round the side.

'Shall I try the spell I used on the last one?' she asked, reaching for the latch again.

'Wait a moment,' I grabbed her wrist. 'I don't want to rip any arms off today. We'll all go through together. Brackus can lead the way. We should have done that the first time. You can go next with your spell and I'll bring up the rear.'

'What about Cavall?' We looked down to where the dog was sitting at my feet, wagging his tail.

'We could call him after us?' I suggested. 'He's part of the Court after all, he should be able to come through.'

'I don't want him to get lost.' Temperance knelt down to smooth a hand over his head. 'Especially after he saved you from the boar.'

'Well what do you suggest? I'm not carrying him through the gate.'

I ended up carrying Cavall through the gate. Brackus and Temperance went through before me, arm in arm. I scooped up the dog. He was surprisingly bony and wriggled around as I held him, managing to thoroughly lick both of my ears whilst barking happily.

We stepped through into freezing mist. I peered around, looking for my companions. A shape veered out of the fog to my left and I almost dropped Cavall. Brackus waved at me, Temperance still holding onto his elbow.

'Is that you, Jenny?' he said, voice echoing strangely in the grey-green miasma. I clutched the dog.

'Prove yourself,' I snarled.

He sighed deeply. 'Still reluctant to trust me, oh apple-eyed demoness?'

I put down Cavall. He ran over and jumped up at Brackus. A few buttons pinged loose as his claws scrabbled at the velvet shirt. That made me feel a little better; the dog was really growing on me.

'This place is even worse than I remembered it,' said Temperance, releasing Brackus's elbow. She wafted a hand through the haze leaving swirling shapes in the water vapour. 'I can barely see the road. Do you still have that rope with you, Jenny? We should tie ourselves together so we don't get lost.'

I fumbled in my pack and produced the rope. There wasn't really enough to knot us individually so we settled for gripping it in our hands and walking in a line. Temperance fussed over Cavall and wanted to fashion him a collar but he vanished into the clouds before she could grab him.

We heard him barking and yelping as he romped through the gloom around us.

'Leave him be,' Brackus said before Temperance could panic. 'He'll be just fine on his own and catch us up when he gets bored or hungry.'

We started walking. It was somehow both better and worse than the last time we had been on the Wild Roads. Better because there was nothing to tempt us off the road and we had Cavall's exploits to blame any unexpected rustling noises on. Worse because within a few minutes the reeking fog had permeated our cloaks and drenched us with sticky, grimy water. Brackus was leading the way but the haze was so thick he had to keep stopping to check we weren't wandering from the road.

'You would think,' I griped, after walking into Temperance's back for the tenth time in as many minutes, 'that we wouldn't have to spend so much time worrying about getting lost. Seeing as how there isn't a specific direction we're going in.'

'Hazard of the road, I'm afraid.' Brackus tapped out in front of him with his heel. 'It didn't trap us last time with all the pretty sights. Now it's trying a different trick.'

Something cold touched my hand. I yelped and spun. Cavall gazed up at me through the gloom, snuffling around the flap of my satchel. I took back my earlier softening towards the beast.

'Bloody dog,' I grumbled, 'away with you. Go on. Skedaddle. Just because I've decided not to eat you doesn't mean you can creep up on me.'

I could hear Temperance snickering ahead of me. We traipsed on. The fog persisted as we marched along the road. I thought we had been walking for hours, perhaps days, but that was wishful thinking. Temperance made occasional attempts at conversation but it was strangely difficult to hear the words through the blanket of mist without shouting, and somehow we all felt that wasn't a wise idea.

My feet were aching and blistered by the time I sensed the mist was changing. It seemed to be getting lighter ahead of us. I looked behind me. Yes, we were definitely walking towards some sort of light. My spirits lifted as the fog started to thin out, the air warming. Brackus stopped less often and Cavall reappeared and began trotting alongside us.

The air cleared and suddenly we were walking uphill, through a green forest, punctured by craggy outcrops of weathered limestone.

'Are we —' Temperance hesitated '— out?'

I sniffed the air. It smelt clean, the corruption of the wild fog nowhere to be found.

'I think so. Brackus, do you know where we are?'

The goblin looked around, tilting his head back up to see where the path went.

'I believe,' he said, 'that we're in the Pennine Hills.'

Temperance and I offered him identically blank expressions.

'Bumpkins,' he muttered. 'Centre of the country. Near Nottingham.' I nodded then bugged my eyes questioningly at

Temperance when he turned back around. She shook her head, equally lost.

'Which way do you think we should go?' Brackus asked, looking back at us.

'You don't know?' I frowned. He shrugged.

'I haven't been to every spot the Court frequents, my lakelette.'

I hissed at him but my heart wasn't really in it.

'I think we should go uphill,' offered Temperance. I looked at her with surprise.

'Why do you say that?'

'Well, for a start, the Wild Roads left us walking in that direction. It makes sense to keep going that way. For another,' she pointed up the slope, 'that's the direction Cavall just ran off in. He probably knows the way home.'

'Very prescient of you,' murmured Brackus. Barking filtered down from up the hill so we set off after the noise.

The road soon degraded into a rocky path, strewn with small boulders. I guessed that it turned into a channel when it rained; potholes were filled with soft sand that squished between my toes when I stepped in them. We climbed up and up, the forest looming in on either side. Eventually, when I thought I could not go on, the road flattened out. It wound onwards, finishing at the face of a huge smooth cliff. At the base of the rock was a small gap, barely big enough for a man to squeeze through.

We paused outside.

'A cave?' I asked. Brackus winced.

'Ugh. I hate caves. So damp and dark and full of horrible crawling things.' He flexed his hands and shuddered.

I opened my mouth to reply but stopped. From deep inside the cave I heard the sound of a dog barking. The noise reverberated up. Brackus wrinkled his nose.

'Go on then. But you should go first, Jenny, you're better at this sort of thing than me.'

I rolled my eyes and ducked underneath the slab. I scrambled down a rocky slope to what looked like a carved pathway. As

I looked around I could see I was standing at the end of a long cavern, stretching out before me and disappearing around a corner. Cavall's barking was echoing from the far end of the cavern, along with faint music.

Temperance slid down alongside me. She conjured a ball of fire to light the blackness, jumping when she saw me beside her. In the yellow glow of her flames I could make out lines of glittering stalactites hanging from the ceiling like icicles edging a cottage roof.

'This place is huge,' breathed Temperance, raising her hand. 'You should move here, upgrade from the lake.'

I smiled at her then checked behind me. Brackus was kneeling at the entrance slab, sticking his head into the cavern.

'Get on with it, Marsh,' I called, 'there's nothing to be afraid of. Don't you want to see your lovely queen again? Temperance has even lit a candle for you to keep the darkness away.'

His reply was lost as he stepped forward onto a patch of slippery calcite crystals and tumbled down the slope. He rolled to a halt at our feet, jumping up and dusting himself down. I noticed that he'd lost a few more buttons, leaving only fraying threads on his velvet jacket. Temperance reached out and rearranged the gold braid to hide the worst of it.

'Come on then,' she said, stepping back and turning towards the sound of the music. I followed after her, Brackus hurrying behind.

As we walked on, the stalactites around us became thicker and longer, until the whole ceiling was a mass of sparkling white spires, cascading down the walls like a frozen waterfall. When we turned a final corner the Court was laid out before us.

It was much the same as it had been at Nance Round: heaving tables of food, a miscellany of low fae zipping to and fro. The high fae danced in the centre of the cave, their faces totally focused on the steps. Instead of coloured streamers, glowing lights had been conjured and placed inside the druzy, crystalline geodes that grew from the walls. Flashes of purple and yellow lit up the court as they celebrated another night of feasting.

Gwyn and Creiddylad were seated on thrones at the far wall of the cave, Cavall stretched contentedly at their feet. As we stepped towards them the dancing fae stopped, moving aside to clear a path for us. It fell eerily quiet as we walked between them; their strange eyes seemed to will us to trip. I wondered if one of us fell, would the fae resume dancing, stamping over us before we could rise?

We stopped in front of the Lord of the Hunt and his lady, and bowed.

'Stand up.' Gwyn's face was cast into shadow and I could read neither anger nor joy in his features. I glanced at the queen who gave me a dazzling smile.

'You are strangely swift to return to my court, little voyagers,' Gwyn said. 'I trust you have not disappointed me?'

Brackus passed the comb to Temperance who stepped forward, offering it to the lord with a curtsy. He raised it to his lips, running the edge against his tongue. He frowned then spat to the side.

'It seems I have underestimated you three. Or perhaps my soft-hearted wife has a hand in this early success?' He glanced at Creiddylad, scowl softening into something like tenderness. 'I cannot fault you in this, nor in anything, my love, but I would ask you to let them complete the next task alone.'

Creiddylad met her husband's gaze innocently enough but there was mischief dancing in her mismatched eyes.

Gwyn returned his attention to us.

'Very well. Now that you have completed this task I will reveal the next. The second thing you will require to defeat the Erl King is an ingot of pure iron.'

'Iron?' I asked, puzzled. Gwyn nodded.

'Iron. About five pounds' worth should do it, I would say.' He laughed at our expressions. 'Don't look so surprised. Not everything is mystical and convoluted. Sometimes what you need is something simple and strong, and what could be simpler and stronger than iron?'

'My lord,' started Brackus, 'it does seem simple, but I imagine there is a catch?'

'Would it be a quest if there was not a catch?' Gwyn laughed again, the sound booming around the cave like a roll of thunder. 'It is true you must fetch iron but it cannot be any common iron. Six days west of here is the Penrhyn Ddu, the Black Peninsula. The first Britons mined for iron there, the Romans too in their time. There is an old legend that a star fell to earth there, forming the ore deposits. Star iron is what we need. Travel to the Black Peninsula and bring back the raw metal. My smiths will smelt it into an ingot for you while you complete your third task.'

'It still seems quite simple, my lord,' offered Temperance.

'Truly child, that is all you must do.' Gwyn leaned back in his chair. 'A warning though. The Black Peninsula is a treacherous place, even for such folk as your companions. The veil between the mortal world and the Wild Roads has worn very thin. It is a test of your mettle. Fitting, no?'

He turned to smile at his wife, already losing interest in us. Creiddylad touched his cheek.

'Husband,' she said, her voice sweet.

'Very well,' Gwyn groused. 'Refill their supplies. No more magical help.' She beamed at him.

Cavall jumped up as we turned to go, barking at his master.

'You too, hmm?' Gwyn slapped the dog's side. 'Go on then, boy. I doubt he'll be of much use but he seems to have taken a liking to you. And it keeps him out from under our feet.'

Cavall barked again then bolted down the steps towards us. Temperance patted his head. We backed away, bowing again. Cavall led us over to the nearest table of food and yapped at us until I tore a leg off a roast duck and gave it to him. The dog satisfied, the rest of us began to eat.

'Iron ore,' Brackus muttered, 'seems straightforward enough. Whatever this Penrhyn Ddu place is like it surely can't be much worse than the Wild Roads were today. I'm sure we can figure it out. This is looking up.'

'How much iron ore will we need to make five pounds of iron?' Temperance asked, slicing herself some cheese.

'About double I think.' Brackus was fidgeting with his buttons. 'Can we get out of this cave now?' he blurted.

'Oh come on, you're not still bothered are you?' I waved an arm at the cavern. 'It's been standing for years, it's not going to collapse in on us now.'

'I. Just. Don't. Like. It.'

'Fine.' I checked my satchel. It was newly refilled and bursting with food. 'Temperance, are you ready to go?'

We ended up having to bribe Cavall out from under the table with another duck leg. He ran alongside us happily as we left, holding both joints in his mouth. Getting out of the cave was more of an ordeal than getting in had been: neither Temperance nor Brackus were able to get up the slippery rise alone. I ended up having to hook my toes underneath the roof slab and lean back to haul them up one by one.

'Should we stay near here in case Lady Creiddylad wants to visit us again?' Temperance said, looking around for a likely camping spot.

To my surprise Brackus shook his head. 'She's already replenished our supplies and promised Gwyn that she wouldn't interfere. Let's just make a start.'

We walked all the way down the hill and pitched camp by starlight in a little valley at the base. Brackus cast his protective spell again and we passed an undisturbed night.

The following morning dawned blue and clear. After a breakfast courtesy of Creiddylad's fresh supplies we set off down across the fields, heading west. It was a lovely day, almost comically picturesque with larks and blackcaps warbling in the trees as we passed underneath. Brackus began to whistle and Temperance threw sticks for Cavall to fetch. By midday we had reached a muddy track that seemed to lead roughly in the right direction and picked up some speed. Almost all thought of the Erl King had fallen away from me and I was about to join in Brackus's whistling when we turned a corner and ran straight into a party of three travellers coming the other way. Soldiers, I thought, with swords swinging at their hips and boiled leather armour.

Brackus lifted his cap and the three men did the same. They eyed Temperance appreciatively and bade her a good day. Then the first man looked at me. Disgust and fear flooded into his face. Temperance followed his gaze and froze in shock.

'Jenny,' she whispered, 'the charm.'

The other men reached for their weapons, gloved hands tightening around sword hilts. I looked down at myself, confused. In a moment of shocking horror I realised that Brackus had forgotten to glamour me this morning.

Chapter Twelve

I looked up to see the lead soldier raising his sword in the air, about to strike. He brought it down in a slashing motion. The blow would have split my face apart had I not leapt backwards. I lost my footing and fell down, landing heavily on my rump. The soldier struck again, the sword hissing through the air. I rolled over so that the blade hit the muddy ground where I had been moments before.

The soldier's face was twisted in disgust as he yanked the sword back and stepped towards me. There was fear in his eyes, and he held the sword out in front of him as if fending off a wild animal.

Behind him I heard Temperance call out to me. The other soldiers had pushed her behind them and unsheathed their own swords. They ran forward to stand on either side of the first man, Temperance hard on their heels. She was pulling on the arm of the left-hand soldier, trying to get him to drop his weapon.

'Stay back there, miss,' he snarled, turning his sword to where I crouched on the road. 'If it gets past us you'd better already be running.' He ripped his arm free of her and she tripped and went down in the road, clutching her ankle.

'What kind of cursed creature do you think it is, Sergeant?' the right-hand man asked.

The leader shook his head, 'A demon of some kind. I don't know. Watch out, though, it's fast as a viper when it moves.'

I bared my teeth and hissed at them. The sergeant stood his ground but the other two paled. I could see sweat beading on the forehead of one; the other's sword quivered almost imperceptibly.

'Steady, lads,' called the sergeant, raising one hand. 'It won't get past all of us. On my mark jump forward and circle it. Aim for the back of the knees, stop it leaping at us. I'll go for the head.'

Temperance was struggling to get up. Brackus was next to her, rummaging for something in his pack. I had managed to get to my hands and knees; I was slower, weaker than I was used to, and the refreshing strength of my lake felt very far away. I felt the unfamiliar tang of fear in my chest and tried to push it down. Three armed soldiers were fiercer opponents than I had faced in many years but I imagined men still bled the way they had when I was young.

The sergeant brought his hand down and all three men ran forward. I launched myself at the sweating man, grabbing his sword arm and twisting. It snapped like a pane of lake ice. He screamed horribly and dropped his sword. Still holding onto his broken arm, I brought up a foot and kicked him hard under the chin. He fell backwards and I landed on top of him. He was out cold before we hit the ground.

The second man yelled and broke towards me. I caught the blade of his sword as it swung, the cold iron biting at the skin of my hands. I growled and thrust it back at him. He staggered and slipped but caught himself and came up again, still holding onto his sword. The sergeant barked at him to get back in line.

My hands were bruised but miraculously not cut by the blade. I snarled at the two men again but they had the measure of me now.

'Both at once,' said the sergeant. 'It can't keep us both off. One, two . . .'

A blast of wind smacked into them, throwing them backwards. I whipped my head around.

Temperance was standing in the road, one arm around

Brackus's shoulders. Her other hand was outstretched, air shimmering above her open palm. She said something I couldn't hear
and the blast hit them again, building strength as it battered
them back.

'She's a witch,' called out the sergeant, raising a hand to his
face to peer back at her. 'Put an end to her, I'll deal with this.'

The second soldier began staggering up the road towards
Temperance. I could tell each step was a struggle as he fought
to place his feet steadily. Temperance focused her gale against
him, but he kept coming, the sword in his hands dragging along
the ground.

I tried to go after him but the sergeant blocked my path. He
was older than the other two, solidly built, and the sword in his
hands was steady.

'Oh no you don't, you fiend,' he said, stepping sideways, eyes
never leaving my face. 'She'll get what's coming to a witch, and
you'll get what's coming to you.'

He struck again. The sword whipped past my face, missing
by half an inch. He growled and moved forward. The sword
missed again. Behind him I could see the other soldier trudg-
ing forward, almost within reach of Temperance. Brackus was
nowhere to be seen.

The sergeant took advantage of my distraction and brought his
own blade down. I ducked under it, moving forward, then leapt
for his throat. He screamed as my teeth sank into the meat of
his neck, biting down through flesh and grazing against bones.
I shook my head, tearing loose a chunk and spitting it out before
clamping my teeth down again. He dropped the sword, collaps-
ing forward against me.

I shoved him off, just in time to see the last soldier raising his
blade to Temperance. I screamed at her as he prepared to strike.
Brackus winked into existence behind him and smashed the
copper cooking pan against his head. The soldier crumpled onto
the road and was still.

'Jenny,' Temperance called, limping towards me, wincing
every time she put her left foot down. 'Are you all right? You

caught that sword with your bare hands, they must be cut to ribbons.'

She reached me and picked up both of my hands.

'It's not my blood,' I said, trying to soothe her. 'They're sore but not cut.'

Frowning she turned them over, raising my palms to her face. 'Not a scratch. You must have the Devil's own luck.'

'What about you?' I tilted her face back up. 'Your ankle, is it broken?'

'I think it's just a sprain. Could have been a lot worse if Brackus hadn't knocked out the soldier.' She favoured the goblin with a smile. He returned it with a wink then looked over at me sombrely.

'I'm sorry about that, Jenny. I should have glamoured you this morning. I just forgot about it after all the stress of being in the cave.' His face was drawn and pale. I waved a hand.

'Mistakes happen. I forgot too.'

I turned back to where the sergeant was lying. The blood pouring from his neck had slowed to a bubbling trickle and he was jerking horribly. His sword lay just outside his grasp and his fingers were twitching as he tried to touch the hilt.

'I'll finish them off and dump the bodies in the field,' I said, crouching down beside him. 'You two go on ahead, I'll catch up.' I bent down to his neck, opening my mouth. The sergeant's eyes flickered, and his panting quickened.

'What?' Temperance fell to her knees beside me. 'You can't kill them now. They're no threat any more.'

I goggled at her. 'They attacked me. Unprovoked. I was just walking down the road.'

'Yes, but they were frightened of you. They don't deserve to die like this.' She reached out a hand to place on the sergeant's throat. Her fingernails touched the edge of the wound. I snorted.

'Don't be soft-hearted, Temperance. They tried to kill you too, remember?'

'Only after I cast the wind at them.'

'Yes, to save me. Because, as I mentioned, they were trying to kill me. Three armed men against one defenceless creature.'

'You're carrying a sword, and you've ably demonstrated that you're hardly defenceless,' Temperance pointed out. My hand went to the hilt. I had strangely forgotten all about the sword.

'I didn't draw it. And they tried to kill me for what I am.'

'But they didn't realise you weren't a threat and can you blame them? They pushed Brackus and me behind them. They were trying to protect us.'

I looked at Brackus in disbelief. 'Are you hearing this? Would you care to join in?'

He shrugged. 'I don't much care either way. You may as well end them quickly.'

'I can heal them,' Temperance insisted. 'It won't take too long.'

'And when they wake up again and come after us?'

'I'll do the memory charm. They won't remember anything, not even meeting us.'

'Because that worked so well the last time you tried it,' I scoffed.

Temperance flinched. 'Don't throw that in my face. It was working fine until the Erl King interfered.'

'But is it really worth the risk? What if we wake up tomorrow morning with pitchforks at our throats and not enough magic left to defend ourselves? Didn't you learn anything from being thrown in my lake?'

'That was the Erl King.'

'You didn't think so at first. There's a reason for that. Most of the time when this happens it's not the Erl King or witchcraft or the high fae,' I yelled. 'It's just humans being human.'

'I'm human too!' Temperance shouted back at me.

'You're a witch, it's different.'

'I'm just as human as these men,' Temperance said, gesturing at the other two, still lying motionless in the road.

'Well, I'm not human. Which is exactly why these three attacked me. Without even a second thought.'

'So you want to prove them right by slaughtering them when they're helpless?' Temperance laughed humourlessly.

'Maybe they were right. Maybe you are the one who has forgotten what I am,' I spat at Temperance, baring my teeth. She blinked but didn't shrink backwards.

'I haven't forgotten. You rescued me from drowning. That's who you are. This . . .' She pointed at the wound on the sergeant's neck. 'This isn't.'

'Yes it is.' I stood up. 'I'm done arguing. Heal him. Heal them all if you want. If they come after us again then I'll put them in the earth.'

I stalked off up the road. When I turned back Temperance had placed both hands on the sergeant's neck and was whispering something. I looked away. I didn't care to see her waste her power on such malicious creatures.

'Brackus, would you come up here and glamour me?' I snapped. He walked up to where I was standing, his face troubled.

'Don't sigh at me like that,' I muttered. He reached out and prodded me on the forehead. I felt the cantrip slither over me.

Brackus gave me a doleful look.

'Not you too.' I was seething still.

'Don't explode at me, Jenny.' He paused. 'I know you're angry but don't take it out on Temperance. It was me who forgot to glamour you. Those soldiers were just reacting.'

'You forgot, well so what? I forgot too. I had forgotten . . .' I broke off, looking back down the road. Temperance had moved over to the man whose arm I had snapped.

'You forgot what? Forgot that this world belongs to the mortals now, that we can no longer roam un-glamoured?'

I glared at him. 'Jennys never roamed freely anyway. I had forgotten that . . . Oh, it doesn't matter. Leave me alone, Marsh.'

He sighed heavily and went back to Temperance. I could hear him persuading her to spend a little power to heal her own ankle. I stood looking west and fumed. I wasn't even sure if I was angry at Temperance or at myself. I suddenly felt a desperate yearning to be back in my lake, away from the judging eyes of humans.

I didn't want to watch Temperance's fury turn to fear, the same fear I had seen in the soldiers' eyes.

Eventually Temperance finished up and she came up to me.

'They'll wake in about an hour with no memory of seeing us,' Temperance said. I cleared my throat and stared above her head.

'You're still angry with me?' she said incredulously.

'I'm not angry. I just want to keep walking. We've wasted too much time already.' I looked around.

'Fine,' she responded. 'Let's walk.'

We didn't speak again that day, or the next. By the end of the third day of silence between us we had settled into a miserable stalemate. In the mornings Brackus would come over and glamour me while we ate a breakfast of Creiddylad's supplies. Then we would start walking westwards. Temperance and I didn't speak. Brackus tried to make conversation with one or both of us but usually gave up by mid-morning. Even Cavall seemed downcast, trailing after Temperance or me, tail between his legs. We avoided most towns, skirting around Chester and following the old Roman road into North Wales.

As we left England the villages grew smaller and the land rose up around us in jagged mountains and hills. Tumbling streams rushed down from the heights and raced under old stone bridges towards long flat lakes. It was the start of lambing season, so the hillsides were empty of sheep, though the villages were loud with the baaing of the ewes.

There was fresh meat aplenty for purchase, and Cavall dined well on stillborn lambs. Brackus could make himself understood in Welsh and with some practice I remembered some of my old fluency. There were conversations that went easier between women, so I spoke more to the Welsh villagers than I had to any mortal but Temperance in long years.

I felt Temperance's eyes on me whenever I spoke to a human. Her face was pointedly blank, but she never looked away until I had finished. I began to suspect she thought that I could not be trusted around them. The notion stoked my anger and I hugged it to my chest, letting it warm me. I had rescued her from drowning and bargained with the high fae and risked my life with the Twrch Trwyth but it seemed none of that meant anything as soon as another human appeared. The fragile trust that I had worked so hard to build between us had been swept away so easily that I doubted it had ever been real. In her eyes, I was probably only a little better than the Erl King, a lesser evil to be endured for the greater good. I did not know why the idea of this cut me so deep, but it carved a moat between us, one that I did not know how to cross over.

We never stopped overnight in the towns, preferring to camp out in the open. I was wary of more trouble, spending the first few days after the attack looking over my shoulder, but the roads were clear of anyone but farmers or merchants. Eventually I began to focus on the path ahead. Brackus wanted to talk about the Penrhyn Ddu, about what we could expect there. He asked questions of everyone we passed on the road.

Most of them had no answers to give, not having travelled there. A few knew it but were not aware of any mining industry. Brackus was frustrated. He went over everything the travellers told him as we sat together in the evenings. Occasionally he would ask our opinion. If directly queried I would reply but as soon as Brackus tried to draw Temperance into the conversation I clammed up. Temperance did the same. A part of me was impressed at her level of pettiness. It equalled my own, which I had honed through years of living alone in the lake. It made it easier to hold on to my resentment.

Occasionally Brackus would explode and harangue the pair of us. He would shout and threaten to leave the quest. We sat and listened, wearing identical sullen expressions. I began to wonder if the whole journey had been a mistake. Should I leave and go back home? I missed the lake every day, not only in my heart but with my body, which weakened with every moment it was away from my home waters.

I decided to stay. This was still my best shot at defeating the Erl King and I didn't want to abandon it. If Temperance had similar thoughts of desertion she didn't share them. When Brackus went off in a huff one evening, she set her mouth into a thin, hard line and reached out to throw another log on the fire. Our friendship might have guttered out but she wasn't going to quit now. I stroked Cavall's ears as he lay with his head in my lap and stared into the fire until Brackus came back.

We took the direct route through Snowdonia, walking down the Pen-y-Pass between Snowdon and Glyder Fawr. The road had narrowed to a sheep track and we had not passed another traveller since dawn. The light was fading as we chased the setting sun west. Brackus paused on a rocky bluff, the dusk painting the mountain behind him a bloody red.

'We should reach Llanberis by nightfall, and make camp on the outside of the village,' he said, pointing down the valley to where small slate-roofed buildings clustered at the midpoint between two lakes.

He turned back to me and smiled. 'Maybe you could catch us some fish in the lake, Jenny. The carp here is supposed to be delicious.'

Temperance sniffed. I shot her a look and stuck my nose in the air.

'I wouldn't want to offend anyone by catching innocent creatures,' I said. 'I know how sensitive some people can be.'

Brackus groaned but Temperance didn't so much as blink. I stomped past Brackus and back onto the footpath. They let me gain a head start before following me. I suspected Brackus was trying to talk Temperance around. I doubted he would have any more success with her than with me. I was glad of the break; I'd spent all day going over the last few barbs Temperance and I had exchanged, and all that thought had stewed into a splitting headache. I longed for the cool waters of my lake, soothing away my troubles.

I peered down into the valley, at the long glacial lake below. I'd have a long swim there this evening and try and regroup a little. To my right a thin white waterfall was clattering off the slaty rocks and falling into an overflowing pool that spilled across the path. I splashed into the puddle, then paused in the middle and looked around for Cavall. Temperance and Brackus were still making their way down the path behind me but I couldn't see the hound anywhere. I whistled for him and the sound startled a pair of crows, who rose cawing into the sky. The closest one wheeled towards me and I ducked, late enough that I felt the whoosh of her wings as she skimmed my face. I stepped back cursing and lost my footing. I slipped to the ground, falling at a bad angle and tumbled off the edge of the path and down the slope. I didn't fall so far, maybe only a couple of yards before colliding, feet first into a boulder.

The agony was immediate, hitting my senses even before I heard the crack of bone splitting. I lay stunned, in the wet grass, trying to process what had happened. It took me a moment even to understand that the sensation was pain. I had felt discomfort before, irritation and fatigue but never pain like this. Safe in the arms of my lake I had never so much as sprained my ankle. The feeling was shocking, incapacitating. I didn't know what to do with it. I felt like a landed pike, unable to do anything but snap at the fisherman who had reeled me in.

Above me the crows were circling. I heard Cavall bounding towards me and managed to pull myself up just as he stuck his nose in my face. I pushed him away and looked down at my legs.

My left ankle was definitely broken. It looked like a messy break, too, with a chunk of bone almost piercing through the green skin of my leg. I prodded it, hoping vainly that it would simply go back in. The result was a wash of pain so blinding I thought it had snapped again. I glanced back up the hill where Brackus and Temperance were hurrying down to me. Temperance would probably be able to fix this if I asked her, I realised. The idea was enough to make me lie back down in the grass.

'Jenny, Jenny,' called Brackus, reaching me and putting his hand on my forehead. 'Are you all right? Are you hurt? We saw you slip but we were too far away to do anything.'

'I'm fine,' I grumbled, batting his hand away, 'it barely hurts.'

Temperance knelt down beside my leg and laid a hand on my ankle. I hissed in pain.

'It's a nasty break,' she said, reaching into her pack and pulling out a waterskin to hand to me. 'You should rest for a moment before I try to heal it. Lucky this happened before nightfall really, we may as well camp here.'

I batted the water away, frustration and embarrassment bubbling up inside me.

'If you two hadn't been so slow then maybe I wouldn't have been standing around waiting for you,' I snapped. 'Am I supposed to be grateful that you're deigning to heal me with your precious magic?'

Temperance dropped her hand as if my leg had burnt her. I instantly regretted my words, but it was too late. She glared at me.

'If you hadn't stormed off for no reason then you wouldn't have slipped. And now I have to waste power that I should be saving for the quest, or for my family, on your stupid leg.'

'No one asked you to do anything,' I snarled, doubling down on my anger and baring my teeth a little to try and make her recoil. Irritatingly she didn't so much as flinch. 'I don't need your help and we're not camping here.'

'Jenny,' Brackus said, 'be reasonable, you're not going anywhere with that. Calm down and let Temperance patch you up and we can start again tomorrow.'

I clenched my teeth and hauled myself up, leaning on the boulder and trying not to put weight on the injured ankle.

'You can stay here if you want. I'm going to go and camp at Llanberis.'

Brackus gaped at Temperance who merely rolled her eyes and stood up.

'Fine,' she said, 'lead on then. Since you're so clearly independent and incapable of accepting help.'

I took a tentative step forward, resting a tiny bit of my weight on my left foot. Red-hot agony stabbed at my leg and I immediately leaned back onto my right leg. I tried to hop, grazed my left leg against the hillside then fell again. Brackus caught me under the arm and lowered me to the ground.

'You've made your point,' he said. 'Temperance, come and heal her before she gets up again.'

Temperance shrugged. 'She said she doesn't want my help. If she's changed her mind she can ask nicely and admit I was in the right.'

A grim sense of satisfaction went through me. It was so much easier to be unreasonable in a pair, to have a proper feud. Brackus clutched at his buttons.

'Blood of my ancestors, what did I ever do to deserve this? To not only meet the two stubbornest women in the world but end up trapped with them on the side of a Welsh mountain.'

'I'm not trapped,' I said, 'I can move quite well on all fours if it doesn't affect the delicate sensibilities of those present.'

'Not at all,' Temperance scoffed.

I pulled myself up onto my hands and knees and began to crawl. My left ankle dragged behind me, occasionally catching on rocks and branches and sending spasms of pain through me. Temperance walked behind me; her arms folded. Cavall capered alongside, occasionally letting me lean against him when I needed a quick rest.

It took me until the moon was high in the night sky to reach the edge of the first lake. I crawled right into the shallows and let the icy meltwater cool the burning pain of my ankle. I couldn't heal myself here, this was not my lake, but I was still a water creature and the water helped.

'Too late to buy any supplies in the village,' Brackus observed morosely. 'And I can't tell where's a good spot to camp.' He looked down the valley. The village was completely dark; not even a candle glimmered from between the shutters.

'There,' he said, 'the castle. Jenny, can you swim over and meet us there? It was abandoned the last time I passed through this way. We should be able to camp undisturbed in the ruins.'

I looked to where he was pointing. A small circular keep rose on the western shore of the lake, dark against the darker sky. It looked like a sensible spot to camp, and I would certainly be able to swim easier than crawl. I nodded and slipped into the water, kicking off with my right foot before. To my surprise the lake was empty of anything but fish. An ancient body of water like this would have been a prime spot for a Jenny or one of their Welsh equivalents. I breathed in the water, enjoying the chilled freshness after a week in the dry air. I passed a shoal of sleeping carp. They did look fine, and I was tempted to snatch one for myself. I resisted. I couldn't have carp on my own and I wasn't going to get carp for Brackus or Temperance. Therefore no one would have carp and we would all be miserable together.

This was cold comfort as I surfaced in the shadow of the stone tower and began crawling up to it. I arrived before Temperance and Brackus, who had offered to carry my pack, so there was nothing to do but curl up against the old stone walls and try to sleep.

Chapter Thirteen

The dawn light filtered through gaps in the stone wall of the keep, prying its way under my eyelids. I blinked awake. It was cold enough that my breath billowed out in front of me in clouds. I waved a hand to disperse them and looked around. Temperance and Brackus were huddled on the other side of the tower, sleeping back-to-back. The embers of a cooking fire gleamed beside them.

I pulled myself up and gasped as the bone shards in my ankle stabbed at me again. I slumped back and tentatively felt around the area. It looked swollen; the green skin had darkened to a blue-ish black as blood had pooled in the area. The fragment that had threatened to break the skin was now held in place by the inflammation. Even brushing my fingers across the area was torture.

I considered my options. The sensible thing to do, the only reasonable thing to do, was to get Temperance to heal me. I would probably still need a day of rest before we set off again, but we would only lose that one day.

If I had read Temperance correctly then I wouldn't even need to ask her, let alone apologise. All I would have to do was wait for Brackus to ask her and then accept the help. I could let the mood of the last few days wash away. But I didn't want to – I was in the right! She had shared her power with men who had tried to kill us both.

A small voice in my mind told me that I was being unreasonable. The voice sounded irritatingly like Brackus. I smothered it.

A breeze whispered through the fallen walls, carrying with it
the smell of the lake. I remembered the relief of the cold mountain waters and began to shuffle out of the tower. The castle was
far enough away from the village that there were no humans in
sight. I tensed my body as I levered myself down the hillock to
the water's edge. I went straight into the lake, enjoying the cold
sting against my ankle. I floated in the shallows, listening to the
sounds of the valley.

Snowdon rose up behind me, snow-capped and gleaming in
the morning light. The grassy slopes glittered with frost and
dew and the wind whistled between the mountains to ripple
the glassy waters of the lake. I could sense the fish swimming
beneath me and remembered how hungry I was. I had almost
decided to get out and go and retrieve my pack when there was
movement outside the castle.

Temperance and Brackus were making their way down to
the lake. Both wore their packs and Brackus was carrying mine.
Cavall skipped at their heels, clearly keen to get moving. I swam a
little closer to the shore, beaching myself on the smooth pebbles.

'How is the leg this morning, Jenny?' Brackus asked, whip-
ping out his stool and sitting down. 'You looked fast asleep when
we came in last night so we decided not to disturb you.'

'Still broken,' I said, deliberately not making an effort to
enunciate my speech. 'The water helps, though. I should be ready
to leave soon.'

'Now, Jenny,' Brackus said, 'be a good sort and let Temperance
patch you up. You know how slow you were yesterday, and you
can't crawl all the way to the coast dragging a broken ankle
behind you.'

I said nothing, and merely kept floating and glaring at him.
Brackus pulled his hat off and fanned himself.

'The thing is, Jenny, we really can't afford to keep losing time
on this. The longer we take to complete these tasks the longer
the Erl King has to establish himself in Chipping Appleby. If

you won't ask Temperance for help, then perhaps it's better that you stay here.'

I froze. Brackus continued, looking unhappy,

'You've got the lake here and you'll heal much faster in the water than if you keep agitating the injury on the road. Stay here, Temperance and I will carry on to Penrhyn Ddu and when we have the iron we'll come back and collect you. It'll probably be a couple of weeks but you'll have the whole lake to swim around in.'

My jaw fell and I goggled at Brackus.

'You're leaving me?' I stuttered.

'Well, if you won't let Temperance heal you then I don't see we have much of a choice. I'm really sorry, Jenny, and I'd say the same thing to Temperance if she was in your position. I think you're both being ridiculous but unfortunately ...' He let the words fall away.

I looked from him to Temperance. She had her arms folded in front of her, her face deliberately blank. Her mouth twitched. I realised that they both thought I would give in. In that moment I knew I would do anything rather than admit defeat.

'Fine,' I said, shrugging my shoulders. 'I'll see you back here in a few weeks. Take the dog with you, I don't want to have to look after him.'

I sank back into the water and dipped below the surface. The water was clear enough that I could see Temperance and Brackus standing on the bank. They looked like they were arguing. Brackus dropped his head in his hands then nodded. They made their way back up the hill and away from the lake. Temperance looked back and for a moment I thought she was going to call for me. Then she whistled for Cavall, who was sniffing around in the hedges, and disappeared from sight.

Wonderful, I thought. Well, I didn't need them anyway. I had been doing fine on my own for a thousand years, I would do fine again. Maybe I would be gone by the time they came back for me; if they came back at all. People rarely did in my experience – they left and didn't return. I sank to the bottom of the lake and proceeded to wallow in self-pity.

A week after they'd left, I was beginning to regret my decision. My ankle was still painful but I could feel the bones starting to knit themselves back together. Another fortnight and I would probably be able to walk again. I spent most of my time swimming in the lake, feeding on the carp and doing some basic maintenance. If this lake had ever been inhabited, then the owner must have left a long time ago. Sheep bones and fishing rods littered the lake floor and the weeds were a tangled mess.

The water was much colder than I was used to; the dozens of mountain streams flowing down from Snowdon and Glyder Fawr ran with water from the melting snow. If I came to the surface and the sky was clear then I could see the peaks on either side of the valley. At the western end of the lake a small channel led into a larger lake, which in turn flowed into a small river. When I swam to the edge of the second lake I could taste the trace of salt on the air, and estimated I was about ten miles from the coast. I remembered Brackus had said that once we reached the coast we would turn south again, heading to Penrhyn Ddu. He and Temperance would be there already.

I thought about them almost constantly, probing my grievances the way I had prodded my broken ankle. If I thought of other things then my anger would cool and I needed to be angry, needed to keep the wound fresh.

I floated near the surface of the second lake as a rainstorm swept through the valley, and watched the drops patter on the water as if through glass. I wondered about the villagers, if they had all their ewes and newborn lambs under cover and out of the rain. I was just deciding to swim back to the first lake when something grabbed me around the waist.

I was shaken back and forth in the water, limbs flailing around. I managed to put an arm to my waist and found a giant hand, fingers clenched tight. I yelled out, using all my strength to try and pry the enormous digits loose.

'Let go,' I yelped, trying to remember the little Welsh I knew. *'Aros, aros!'*

The hand stopped waving me around and a dim shape appeared out of the depths of the water. It was huge, as tall as the castle tower, all scales and fur. Golden eyes glinted from a reptilian face set with long tusks, and a long tail snapped back and forth along the lake floor, stirring the sediment. An Afanc. I had heard of these creatures before, ancient, rare and dangerous.

You are not human, a voice echoed in my head in slow, careful English. *What are you?*

My name is Jenny Greenteeth, I thought, still trying to loosen his grip on my stomach, *I'm just travelling through, I didn't think anyone lived here.*

Green Teeth, the Afanc repeated. Something flared in his face, and he dropped me. *A Gwyrdd Gen,* he said. *I have not seen your kind in long years.* He flicked himself up so that his face, almost the size of my whole torso, was in front of mine. *I had forgotten you were so small.*

I floated in the water, trying to resist the urge to flee. *Is this your lake?* I asked.

One of them. He pushed back suddenly and circled me. Despite his size the Afanc was incredibly nimble in the water, propelling himself with four long arms that ended in bone-white claws. He flipped up and eyed me from the surface.

You are travelling through, hmmmm? Travelling from where to where? His English was improving as we spoke, the words in my head becoming clearer.

Well . . . I hesitated. *To Penrhyn Ddu. But I injured my ankle so my companions went on without me. They'll meet me here on the way back.* I eyed the Afanc warily. *I didn't realise the lake was occupied, I can haul out and wait in the castle.*

There is plenty of space here, the Afanc snorted. *I won't mind the company.* He looked around. *Come, I've got half a sheep stashed under a rock somewhere.*

He ducked back into the water and headed for the northern bank. I followed, keeping a wary distance. As the Afanc swam he seemed to diminish in size, shrinking almost imperceptibly until by the time he trotted out of the water he was only a little taller than I.

He paced over to a slab of slate and flicked it aside as if it weighed nothing. Clearly the strength did not lessen with the body size. Beneath the slab was the promised half-sheep, neatly skinned and chilled by the cold air. The Afanc extended a claw and sliced off a leg which he then tore in two. He tossed the smaller half to me as I waited in the shallows.

'Come out and eat in the air,' he called in a deep, rasping voice, 'projecting thoughts in English gives me a headache.'

I looked down at the meat and splashed up onto the banks. The Afanc stretched out on the pebbles and began to eat. His great jaws ripped chunks of mutton straight from the bone, which he threw back and swallowed whole. I sat next to him and took a tentative bite. The meat was fresh and bloody and delicious. I fell on it with enthusiasm.

As I ate, I noticed how comfortable I felt, sitting next to the Afanc, the both of us gnawing meat off the bone. I didn't have to cut clumsily with a knife or take small bites. If anything I probably had the better table manners of the two of us.

'Good meat, no? The sheep of this valley have a special flavour to them. I only wish I had more to share. Come back in autumn and you could feast on berries,' the Afanc said, waving at the thorn bushes that edged the lake. 'Alas, I don't keep them through winter and I get precious few offerings from any of the villagers any more.'

'Neither do I,' I said morosely. 'The mortals have forgotten the old ways. It's the same everywhere.'

The Afanc nodded.

'I just travelled down to the coast and across to Man to go and visit the Glashtyn, an old friend I had not seen in years. Can you believe that I found no trace of him? He had simply vanished from the world. A creature who had stalked the island waters for centuries gone with the falling tides.'

I looked across at the Afanc and saw grief written in the

creature's scaled face. I reached out a hand and rested it on his arm.

'The world is changing. I too have lost friends to the slow decay of time.'

Faces flashed before my eyes, before I could blank them out, push them back into the furthest recesses of my mind.

The Afanc placed a clawed hand over mine.

'We must make new friends while we may then, Gwyrdd Gen. I am pleased to have met you. Now tell me, what brought you to these waters?'

By the time I had finished telling my story we had finished off the rest of the sheep. The Afanc extended one long claw and began picking fragments of mutton from between his teeth and flicking them into the water. Minnows snatched them up and swam away.

'The Erl King, hmmmm, that's a very bad business,' he said after a while. 'I hadn't sensed anything amiss. You said you were from the Caerlee? That's Thames waters, and I rarely travel east of the Severn these days. Still, something like that is dangerous for all of us, especially with our numbers fading each year.'

I nodded, turning over the clean mutton bone in my hand.

'What I do not understand,' the Afanc continued, 'is what you are doing here. The mortal witch offered to mend your ankle, but you chose to remain in Llanberis? That seems like an uncommonly foolish act.'

I bristled. 'She shouldn't have left with Brackus, I was in the right.'

'I understand there is a time component to this quest of yours, hmmmm? How long should they have waited for you to drown your pride?'

'She wasted her magic on people who tried to kill me! She doesn't even seem to understand why that would upset me.'

The Afanc's reptilian face was difficult to read but he managed to project an air of scepticism.

'It's more than that.' I floundered for the words that would explain the twisting fear inside of me. 'It was so easy to forget these past weeks. To pretend we were just three travellers, three equals . . .' I paused. 'Three friends. The soldiers saw a monster and the thing is, they were right. That's who I am, that's why I have the strength to go on this quest, to help Temperance and yet she spends her power healing those who would kill me, after everything I've done for her.'

'They tried to attack her too, no? Shouldn't she be allowed to choose to forgive and heal for her own sake?' rumbled the Afanc.

'It's different. They tried to kill me for what I am.'

'Her village tried to kill her. Don't you think that she understands what it is like to be feared? It sounds to me like she is trying to be more than what they think of her. Are you angry because she expects you to try too?'

I grimaced. It didn't sound very logical when he put it like that.

'You just don't understand,' I said, turning my face away to look up at the crags of Snowdon.

A scaled hand gripped my neck and hauled me around. The Afanc had me by the shoulders, my feet dangling above the lake waters. He shook me like a cat with a mouse.

'Do you know how long it has been since I spoke to another fae?' he asked. 'Seventy-five winters. Twice that since I saw another of my own kind. Do you think I care for respect, for gratitude?'

'Let me go!' I screeched, twisting to claw at him. He shook me again.

'Do you think you will care about those things when the Erl King sucks the life from your lake?'

'So I should just roll over and apologise? Apologise for saving her life? Say I was wrong to try and end a threat to the both of us?'

'Yes!' bellowed the Afanc, loud enough that a cloud of starlings burst from the thorn bushes and streaked across the lake.

I hung in the air considering my options. The Afanc regarded me with golden eyes.

'Well, maybe,' I said grudgingly, 'but they've gone now. They'll probably be at the mine already. And my ankle is still mending, I can't catch them up.'

The Afanc swung me back and deposited me on the beach.

'I can fix that if you ask me nicely,' he said. 'It will be good practice for you.'

I glowered at him. The words seemed like lead in my mouth; it was impossible to push them out into the air.

'Would you,' I began, 'kindly help me with my foot.'

The Afanc waited, tilting his head to the side. I ground my jaw as I realised what he was waiting for.

'Please.'

He grinned, revealing long rows of yellowing teeth.

'Since you ask so politely,' he rumbled. He dropped his tail into the lake and flicked it at me. A silvery thread of water extended out of the lake, twisting fluidly in the air, and wrapped itself around my ankle. It dipped up and about, until the whole of my left leg was covered in a web of water. I couldn't feel anything strange, only the chill of the lake.

'Now what?' I asked the Afanc, still a little grumpily. He winked at me, and the loose coils of water snapped taut. I howled in agony and clutched at my leg. It was exactly as painful as the break had been.

The loops of water fell to the ground in a splash and began to trickle back to the lake. I rubbed my ankle. The bones had snapped back into place and the bruising had vanished. I looked up at the Afanc who was definitely smirking.

'You could have warned me,' I grumbled. He shrugged.

'If you wanted it done kindly you should have asked your witch friend. I don't do nice. Besides, your pain is the price for my power. There has to be a balance.'

I shut my mouth and continued probing at my ankle. I clambered up and tentatively put some weight on it. It bore me with only a little aching. I glanced at the Afanc, belatedly remembering my manners.

'Thank you.'

'You are quite welcome,' he said. 'This is the most interesting thing that's happened to me in years.'

I looked down at the lake, to where the river leaked out of the western shores. The Afanc sighed.

'You'll be off now, I expect. Swim down to the coast then haul out onto the land and follow the shoreline south. When you pass two small islands then you'll have reached the right place. Be careful. A star is dangerous, even one fallen and guttered out.'

'I could stay a little while,' I said, haltingly. He shook his head.

'You have work to do. I wish you the best of fortune with it. Perhaps if you succeed and feel the inclination to travel again you will come and visit me. I am sure we both have stories to tell.'

'I would like that,' I said, and managed a smile for him. He nodded at me, and I slipped back into the water and kicked off, heading west.

Chapter Fourteen

The beach was long and flat, the sand a dull beige under the grey sky. The sand was empty, but I could see fresh pawprints looping back and forth. I thought they could be Cavall's. I traipsed along the edge of the dunes, between the clumps of salt grass.

I paused in front of a mound near the far end of the beach. It was about ten yards tall, covered in the same long grass as the dunes but there was an opening cut into the side, tall enough for a human to crawl through. The earth was a reddish ochre, the colour of rust, veined with a metallic grey rock. I thought that was probably a good sign.

I peered inside. 'Hello? Brackus, Temperance, can you hear me?' No response. I straightened and looked around. Pursing my lips, I gave a long, low whistle. For a moment there was nothing but the wind rustling through the trees, and then there was movement in the distance. I saw a dark shape bounding through the grass.

Cavall raced towards me, not bothering to come to a full stop and instead bowling straight into my legs. I grunted but forbore to shout at him. He snuffled around my skirts, looking for a treat.

'Where are the others, boy?' I asked, tilting his chin up towards me. He cocked his head and led me off to the side, where the leather packs Creiddylad had given us were covered in leaves. He barked once then pointed his nose back towards the mound.

I walked back around and ran a hand over the earth covering the mound. It was packed in hard, bound together by the grass roots. I wondered how long Brackus and Temperance had been inside. I looked at the sky – it was just past dawn. They wouldn't have gone in just before nightfall so they must have been at least a day in there. A voice whispered that I had come too late, that even now they were lying dead inside the mound. I squashed it.

I looked back at Cavall.

'If I'm not out soon you go back to the Court,' I said to him. He yawned and began to scratch behind his ear. I was reasonably sure that even if he understood what I had said he had no intention of obeying. I sighed and crouched down at the entrance. The smell was foul, like stagnant milk and rotten eggs.

I grimaced and wormed my way inside. The tunnel was so narrow that I had to kick myself forward inch by inch with my toes, my stomach flat on the ground and my arms extended out in front of me. Each kick knocked me against some new rock protruding from the floor or banged my head against the ceiling. The weight of the earth overhead seemed to press down, crushing the air from my chest. I couldn't seem to catch my breath, my lungs constricted by the closeness of the tunnel.

I told myself I was no larger than Temperance, that if she had passed through then so could I. I tried to picture my lake in my head, imagining swimming through the water, kicking forward so easily. I kept going, pretending that the dirt around me was nothing more than lake water.

After a few minutes more I stopped and called out. My voice was croaky from the dust but echoed loudly through the tunnel. I looked up at the sides. It was all rock now, a glittering grey stone, but I couldn't sense even a vein of iron ore.

I slithered on, my arms and legs against the rock. Something poked me in the side and I panicked. I investigated and my hand closed around the hilt of my sword. Why on earth hadn't I taken it off? I considered unbuckling it but was distracted by a noise further down the tunnel.

'Brackus?' I yelled. When the echoes died down I heard the noise again. I scrabbled forward, reaching out and pulling myself along with both hands, when the ground fell out from beneath me and I was falling.

I woke in sunlight, at the lake. I was floating on the surface, breathing in the sweet lily-scented air. The water was coated with pink apple blossoms and curling green leaves. Below me I could feel the movements of the fish as they swam. I glanced over at the village. It wasn't there. A grey-robed druid, her long hair twisted up on her head, ambled along the edge of the lake gathering reeds. After a moment I shook my head. What was I looking for? Everything was the same as it had always been.

I yawned and stretched myself back out in the warm water. Dragonflies hovered over my head and swifts darted in and out of the water, snatching up mayflies. Fluffy white clouds hung in the sky, bright against the clear blue.

Something stirred in the lake beneath me, disturbing the fish. I frowned and looked around. Little Jenny burst into the air just in front of me.

'Made you jump!' she called, in the old greenspeech I had taught her. I affected horrified surprise as she splashed me.

'Made you jump, made you stare, made you lose your underwear!' She howled with laughter and launched herself at me. I grabbed her in my arms and ducked underneath the surface then kicked back up and flung her into the air. She screeched in delight, bombing back into the water.

'Again, again,' she called. I threw her further so that she splashed down closer to the centre of the pool. Every time she would try to sneak up on me underwater and every time I caught her and hurled her away again.

'Mama, do the whirlpool,' she grinned, her sharp white teeth glittering in the sunlight. I called to the lake and twisted it in my fingers. The currents obeyed my command and swirled into a vortex. Little Jenny giggled and climbed onto my shoulders to jump in, spinning around and around in the maelstrom. I followed her and we spun together, holding hands. I snapped my fingers and collapsed the whirlpool, propelling us up into the air so that we landed with another great splash.

We surfaced, still laughing so hard I could barely breathe. Little Jenny looped her arms around me in a hug and I squeezed her tight, looking down into her eyes.

They were the same mossy green as my own.

I dropped her and swam back.

'You're not her,' I said. 'She's gone.'

The sun blazed overhead and the scene vanished into white light.

I blinked hard and I was back in the mound. The tunnel had opened slightly and there was a junction in front of me. I shook my head, trying to get the hallucination out. I scraped my skull against the roof and growled. Whatever was in this mine was trying to test me. I didn't think much of that. I knew my own mettle already. It might explain where Temperance and Brackus had wandered off to, though.

Something gleamed in the left-hand tunnel and I smelt the fresh-blood scent of iron. I bit my lip then shuffled forwards.

This time when I opened my eyes I was back at Gwyn's Court. He and Creiddylad were dancing alone under a canopy of stars. The queen spun so fast that her skirts were a blur, her white-gold hair spilling long and loose down her back. However quickly she spun Gwyn was always there to catch her. He lowered her into a dip then lifted her up, hands around her waist.

She smiled her heart-breaking smile and spun away from him again. I sat watching as they repeated the dance, their bare feet crossing the soft grass of the clearing. There was no music, and even their footfall was muted but they seemed to keep their own time.

Finally they swirled to a finish, eyes lost in each other's faces.

They broke apart and stepped towards me. Gwyn made me a deep bow, Creiddylad an elegant curtsy. Confused, I glanced down and realised I was sitting on the carved throne. Clapping came from in front of me and when I looked back up the Court was full of high fae. Gwyn led them in a toast, raising his stirrup cup towards me.

'To Jenny Greenteeth,' he boomed.

'Jenny Greenteeth,' echoed the Court. I heard a familiar voice at my side. Temperance was seated on the other throne, wearing Brackus's yellow dress. She lowered her cup and drank, red wine staining her lips.

'This isn't what I want. This isn't real.'

Gwyn leered at me and the Court was gone.

It was easier to break free of the phantom Court than to let go of my daughter but it still left a bitter taste on my tongue. I wanted desperately to have a drink of water and wash the taste of the dusty tunnel from my mouth. The walls were wider still here, and I was able to crawl on hands and knees rather than wriggling. I saw the glittering of metal on the wall and raised a finger to trace the looping veins of iron that rippled through the rock. I reached for a knife before realising that I'd never be able to pry it out of the fresh basalt. The capillaries of the ore seemed to thicken as the tunnel led on. I readied myself for another vision and set off.

I sprawled on the muddy road near Nottingham. The soldiers loomed over me. Temperance and Brackus were nowhere to be seen.

'Some kind of hag,' said the soldier on the left, 'better kill it before it gets too close to a village.'

'Horrible thing,' the sergeant grimaced. 'I heard tell they were humans once. What kind of a life is that? It's a kindness to put an end to it.'

He lunged forward with his sword. I grabbed at it but it sliced through my hands, plunging into my chest. The iron burned me even as it carved. I felt the sword piercing my ribcage, into the chest cavity. I grinned at him, blood frothing at my mouth.

'Fool. Monsters don't have hearts,' I hissed, springing for his throat.

I stood inside a castle, warmth blazing from a fireplace. A tall man sat at a round table, a golden circlet on his tawny head. His face was merry as he watched the other men around him laughing and drinking. A red-haired woman sat beside him, a dutiful smile on her lips. I looked around, taking in the rich wool hangings, tapestries depicting battles and meetings.

An older man dozed in a chair by the fireplace, long white beard wafting slightly in the draught from the chimney. I looked back to the table. The tall man was giving a speech, pointing at various young knights. The company cheered each one, slapping them on the back and making jokes. One of the men smiled bashfully over his drink. His blue eyes kept darting to the woman's face.

I stepped forward, noticing the sword at the tall man's hip. Someone grabbed my arm. Turning I saw the old man, his furry white eyebrows drawn in confusion. He looked familiar, as if I had met him before.

'You're not supposed to be here,' he said, and pushed me away from him.

I was sitting by the edge of my lake in the rain. Brackus was standing in front of me, his cap in his hands. The normally neat brown curls were plastered to his scalp, raindrops dripped down his nose.

'I'm so sorry, Jenny,' he said, face sorrowful. 'I've got bad news.'

'No!' I yelled.

A knight threw a gleaming white sword into the air. A pike flashed in the murky water of the lake. The Twrch Trwyth lowered its horns and charged. My baby daughter looked up at me, dark eyes trusting as I dipped her below the water. A white dragon roared, flame gushing from its mouth to coat the flank of an even larger red dragon. Temperance flinched as I smiled at her. The blue-eyed man kissed the red-haired woman, his hand lifting up her face. Gwyn ap Nudd laughed at me, his heavy antlers shaking.

The Erl King stared at me as I clung to the wall of the parsonage. I gagged at the rotten smell of the dead forest, the rib-bones of the stag glinting in his eyes. In the corner a woman crouched, clutching her burned hand. Behind her were more figures, both men and women, young and old. An eyeless child crept forward to cling to the skirts of his headless mother. Beyond them was the dark emptiness of the yawning void.

The face of the parson twisted as the Erl King smiled at me.

'Jenny,' he whispered. 'Are you coming for me, Jenny?'

I opened my mouth and screamed. Temperance sputtered into existence to my left, Brackus appearing on the right. Their shrieks intercut with mine, as the Erl King laughed.

He walked forward and took Temperance's hand, crushing it between his own as he looked at me. She screamed as his nails cut her skin. He raised her palm to his lips in a mockery of a lover's kiss. He laughed again and looked over at me.

I grabbed for Brackus and threw myself backwards.

I woke falling. The tunnel floor had vanished. I fell for a heart-stopping second before landing on hard rock. I looked around, rubbing the elbow that had taken the brunt of the impact. I was in a wide cavern, a dome almost. Botryoidal iron coated every surface, like giant metallic bubbles. I winced as I registered the iron biting at the exposed skin of my arms and legs. Two figures slumped in the centre of the cavern. I picked myself up and hurried over.

Brackus and Temperance lay in peaceful sleep, cool, but not ice-cold. I shook them both but was not particularly surprised when neither were roused. I dug a finger under Temperance's chin and felt the slow thudding of her pulse. Alive, then. Brackus too had a heartbeat but his cheek was starting to blister where it lay against the iron floor. I took his hat off and wedged it under his head. I slid off Temperance's boots and borrowed her socks, giving a little sigh of relief as I put a barrier between the floor and my feet.

I squatted back on my heels and considered. This felt more real than the other visions but I still wasn't completely sure I was awake. The dome had no entrance or exit that I could see – not even one to explain how I'd fallen in here – and I got the sense that wherever I was, it was not wholly in the mortal realm.

I patted my sword, drawing a little comfort that it at least had made the trip with me. As I moved my hand away I felt something in my pocket.

It was the chunk of amber I had grabbed as I left the lake, meaning to offer it to Gwyn. He had scorned it as mere tree sap. I turned it over in my hand, finding ease in the smooth warmth of it. It seemed to glow as I stared at it and I noticed for the first time that Gwyn had been wrong. Though there was no insect or bird trapped inside there was something. A single apple pip, just a mote in the golden eye of the amber.

I pocketed it and began to look around the cave, investigating every crack and crevice. A faint humming seemed to be sounding as I approached the walls. I placed my ear to one of the bubbles of iron. A low thudding was permeating through the rock. I pulled away, startled. It seemed familiar. I put my head back and realised where I'd heard it. It was a heartbeat, drumming to the exact rhythm that Temperance and Brackus's had. I had thought there was something strange about how slow their hearts were. They had somehow attuned or been attuned to the rhythm of the cave.

I stepped back, moving slowly into the centre. This cave was alive. I thought back to what Gwyn had said about this place, the falling star. I had assumed he had been speaking metaphorically but it seemed it was true. I was in the heart of the living star, trapped and sunken into the rock.

I sat down on the floor, careful to keep my dress smoothed

beneath me. Now that I was listening to it, I could feel the thrum of the star, resonating within my own chest. I still didn't understand what to do. My friends were unconscious, we were all entombed underground, and the vision of the Erl King was gnawing at me still. It had seemed realer than the previous ones.

I rested my head on the warm metal floor, ignoring the sting of the iron. I listened to the thump of the star's heart. I wondered how long it had been here; if anyone else had been trapped here before us.

Trapped.

I scrambled up. The star was trapped. Endless lonely eons since it had crashed to earth. I remembered the freedom of swimming in my lake, twirling in the clear waters. The star must have felt like that as it raced through the night sky, all the wonders of the universe before it. No wonder it was keeping us here, snaring us the way it was snared.

I had to free it, release it back into the world, but how? I dropped a hand to my sword but dismissed the thought. I wasn't going to be able to carve my way free and, somehow, I felt that was the wrong kind of answer.

The amber. I picked it out of my pocket and I felt the heartbeat quicken around me. This was the solution somehow, I just had to figure it out. I touched it to the wall, placed it in the centre of the floor, held it aloft. Nothing.

Tree sap, Gwyn had said, only valuable if it captured life. I thought about that. Sap was the blood of the tree. The apple pip was the heart of a tree that was yet to grow. It was life, life frozen in time, just like the star. Could I harness it, bring it back?

I held it tightly in my fist. Blood of the tree, seed of the tree. And nothing was stronger than tree roots. They curled down deep and slow, splitting rock and stone in their quest for water and food. The star was buried in this half-world, too weak to break free. If I could help it escape maybe it would let us go too.

I sat down again and began scrabbling at the floor. The iron burned the palms of my hands and when I tried to dig my fingers in I did nothing more than break two of my talons for my troubles. I left the amber and went back to my friends. They had both left their packs at the entrance to the cave but I found a small rock hammer clutched in Temperance's hand.

I returned to the centre of the cave and began digging. It was filthy work, the clanging sound of the hammer on the rock echoed in the cave and every blow sent a jolt through my body. Metal dust began to puff up from the hole I was creating and as I breathed it in I felt it scorching the insides of my throat. The heartbeat of the star was quickening, drumming in my ears and I began to worry that the cave would collapse on me before I had a chance to finish.

'Please,' I whispered to the star, 'I can help you, but you have to let go, you have to meet me halfway. Release the pain and let me in.'

I started digging with renewed purpose until I had a hole about a handspan deep. I picked up the amber and smashed it open with the hammer. It splintered into glittering shards and I picked through them until I found the apple pip. I swept the rest into the hole so it formed a base then placed the pip on top. Then I replaced the material I had excavated, smoothing the surface over like any mortal gardener.

Nothing happened for a long moment. I bent over and breathed on it, trying to impart a little moisture but my mouth was so dry.

It needed water. I scanned the room desperately. There was nothing but bare rock and the gently breathing bodies of my friends. I held out an arm, looking at the dark veins that webbed below my skin, but I knew blood wouldn't do.

I looked over at where Temperance lay. I thought about how I had screamed at her, pushed her away from me and let her walk into this darkness alone. I thought about Brackus, my oldest friend, who I had cut off for daring to try to care for me. I remembered Gwyn and Creiddylad's hands intertwined, the wet-dog smell of Cavall, and the empty blackness at the heart of the Erl King. I thought of Little Jenny and the last time I had seen her.

I gasped and a single tear rolled down my cheek. I leaned forward and let it drop onto the ground.

For a heartbeat there was nothing. Then there was a great rumble and the ground seemed to shake. A golden sapling burst through the floor, thickening and reaching out as it grew upwards. Golden tendrils spiralled through the cave, roots swelling and flowing away from where I sat, covering the entire ground in a network of living wood. They spread up the walls, at first fine as dandelion seeds but thickening into great rivers of golden sap.

The heartbeat was quickening and I rushed to where my friends lay, clutching their hands to me. There was a great creaking sound as the rock bent and snapped, folding and fracturing into new patterns. The tree spread its branches wide, pale yellow blossoms blooming then budding into honey-coloured apples that thudded to the ground. New trees burst from each fruit, until the cave was an orchard that strained and pushed at the walls and broke through.

I looked up just as the first tree reached the apex of the metal dome. The yellow-orange branches spiralled like a whorl on the trunk of a tree and there was a final gasping boom as the roof cracked and sunlight filtered in and all was white light.

Chapter Fifteen

Something wet was touching my face. I groaned and opened my eyes. Cavall was leaning over me, his silky ears brushing the tip of my nose. He was whining and licking my cheek. I mumbled incoherently and tried to sit up. Every joint in my body felt like it had been stretched, every muscle and tendon felt crushed. A thumping ache pounded at my temples. I wavered, clutching onto Cavall to haul myself up. He stood patiently.

The sun was just rising in the east. I squinted at it. I had a feeling that was wrong, that when I had last been awake it hadn't been evening yet. Had I somehow slept through the whole night? My hands twinged and I looked down to see they were scratched from the tunnel.

My memories slotted into place. I spun around, trying to work out where I was. Was this still some kind of illusion? I was standing among tall salt grass, behind the beach. The others were nowhere to be seen. About fifty yards away was the mound we had crawled into. I started stumbling towards it, Cavall staying close to my legs.

I paused at the edge of the mound. Where before the hill had been covered in grass, now an enormous, gnarled apple tree had burst from the centre, sending roots rippling out to break open the sides as they searched for water. Fat golden apples dripped from boughs garlanded in fragrant white blossoms. Sunlight glittered through the leaves, sparkling like stars.

The entrance I had used yesterday was gone. I circled the mound twice, looking for a way in. I found the satchels we had left, covered in a thin layer of sand. That really made me worry. How long had we been underground? How had I got out? The last thing I remembered was the cave roof cracking.

I crouched down in front of Cavall.

'Where are the others, boy?' I asked. 'Can you find them?'

He wagged his tail and took off towards the beach. I rushed after him, losing sight as he crested over one of the grass-covered dunes. When I caught up I found him sitting next to Brackus, who was lying perfectly still on the sand. Heart in my mouth I knelt beside him and tentatively shook his shoulders. He murmured under his breath and yawned. Not dead then, that was a start.

I scooped him up in my arms and carried him back to the mound. He was surprisingly light underneath all the velvet and buttons; I wondered if that was a goblin trait. Cavall nipped impatiently at my ankles as I paused to slide a satchel under Brackus's head.

'I'm coming, I'm coming,' I said, standing back up. This time he led me further inland to where a holly tree grew, gnarled against the wind. Beneath the green and gold leaves sprawled Temperance, her eyes closed, loose tendrils of hair blowing in the sea breeze. I squatted down and grabbed her feet, pulling her out into the open.

'I've got you, Temperance, you're safe now.' I tilted her face up towards me. Her eyelids fluttered and she whispered something I couldn't hear.

I picked her up and hurried back, carrying her in my arms. Brackus was coming around by the time I laid Temperance beside him.

'Bloody hell, Jenny,' he croaked. 'What on earth happened down there? I lost track of Temperance. I had the strangest

hallucinations, there must be some strange vapours underground. Did you pull me out? Wait, what are you doing here?'

I shook my head. 'I saw things too. I woke up over that way.
Cavall led me to you.' I reached out a hand to pull him up.
'Gwyn did warn us it was a strange place.'

Brackus winced, rubbing his cheek where the iron had left
a mark like a bad sunburn. 'True enough. Mayhaps Cavall
pulled you out.'

I sat beside him, 'The entrance is gone. Either we crawled
out some other way or fell into some scion of the Wild Roads
and it dropped us out.'

Brackus frowned, 'The entrance is gone? Did we get the ore?
There must have been some down there, I still feel the sickness
of it in me.'

'I didn't see any by you or Temperance.'

'Damn.' Brackus smacked the red earth beside him. 'All that
for nothing but nightmares? We'll have to find another way in.'

I nodded gloomily. Temperance twitched and we turned to
look at her. Cavall lay down by her head and barked. Her eyes
shot open.

'Ursula!' she cried, looking around wildly.

'It was a dream, Temperance, you're safe. This is real,'
Brackus soothed, reaching over to pat her hand.

She blinked at him. 'Real?'

I crawled over to her side, 'I promise this is real. We're out
in the open again.'

Some of the tension faded from her face and she gave a
huge sigh.

'You would not believe,' she said, 'the things I saw.' I
smiled at her.

'Oh I'd believe you. Dragons and magic and −' I paused '−
well, let's leave it at that.'

'Let's. I don't want to think about it ever again. It was truly
horrible, I thought I would never get out.' She paused, chewing her lip.

'It was the star,' I said, pleased with myself for having

figured it out. 'It was trapping us inside, until it could free itself. I don't think it meant to hurt us; once I could untangle it, it let us go.'

'I don't mean from the cave,' Temperance said. 'From the dream. I was standing in front of the Erl King and you grabbed Brackus and left. You left me.'

'I remember that too,' Brackus added, 'I thought it was part of the dream.'

Temperance shook her head vehemently, 'It felt real. Realer than the rest. You left me with him.'

I flushed. 'I couldn't reach you. It was just a dream, Temperance. I got you out of the cave.'

She looked at the hand the Erl King had grabbed. The sun-tanned skin was unblemished, the scratches that he had inflicted had washed away with the rest of the dream. She shivered and dropped her right hand, wrapping it in her skirt.

This wasn't going the way I had planned. I coughed and Temperance looked up at me. The relief of being released from the cave was beginning to fade from her face and the suspicion that had grown between us was resurfacing.

'I, uh, well I'll explain on the road, but I had rather a change of heart,' I said, trying to force myself to meet her eyes. 'I acted like a child. I'm sorry. I'm truly sorry.'

She paused, nodding to herself, then she reached out for my hand. I gave it to her and she didn't flinch at the touch of my skin. She held my hand between hers and looked me straight in the eye.

'Thank you, Jenny. That means a great deal to me. Here, let us both forget the past and try do better in the future.'

I smiled at her, feeling some of the load that had weighed me down lift a little

'Finally,' Brackus wheezed, leaning away to cough vigorously. 'Have we got any water in the satchels?' he huffed.

I grabbed the nearest one, scowling at its weight, and opened it. Inside the satchel was filled with pebbles of glittering iron ore, neatly packed with linen.

'Look,' I gasped, 'the iron we needed. It's all here.'

Temperance scrambled over and peered over my shoulder. Her mouth fell open.

'Is it real?' she asked. I poked one of the nuggets. The familiar bite of iron burned the skin of my fingertip.

'It's real,' I grinned. Temperance sighed and fell back into the grass.

'Thank goodness for that. I really did not want to go back down that mine.'

Brackus was still coughing, 'Can you check the other bags for water?' he rattled. I checked the remaining satchels. They were as we had left them, half full of Creiddylad's supplies. I threw him a waterskin.

'Do you know what this means?' Temperance said, abruptly sitting up. 'It means we've completed two of Gwyn's tasks.' She bounded to her feet. 'We're more than halfway done!

'One more task! If we've managed these two then we can manage one more. We could actually do this.'

She beamed down at Brackus.

'Come on, let's go. We need to find a door and get back on the Wild Roads.' Cavall yapped enthusiastically at her words and she bent down to ruffle his fur.

'Very well, very well,' Brackus said, climbing a little unsteadily to his feet. 'Jenny, come here so I can glamour you. I think we passed a door before the village. And, Temperance, you'll have to carry the iron, I'm still feeling a little unsteady.'

Brackus's unerring instinct for finding doors to the Wild Roads was proven accurate again. The door was located about two miles east of Abersoch. It was different again from the ash arch or the wooden gate, consisting of a single jutting rock at the edge of a forest.

'We just walk at the rock?' Temperance asked doubtfully.

'Even easier,' Brackus grinned. 'You just walk around it. You won't notice the difference but eventually you'll turn the corner and find yourself on the roads.'

'That seems strange,' I said. 'What if I just fancied stretching my legs?'

'Then this would be a foolish place to do it,' Brackus answered. 'Shall we?'

I ended up carrying Cavall again as Temperance worried that he'd get dizzy and she was laden down with the iron. We stepped forward and began to walk around the stone, Temperance muttering the witch passwords under her breath. It didn't feel any different from walking along the lane we'd taken to reach the door. The rock was taller than me and wider than my outstretched arms. I kept expecting to see the Wild Roads unfold before me but every time I stepped around the stone I saw the same green fields. Cavall started wriggling, anxious to be put down.

Finally on our fifth lap the light changed and I was walking forward onto the Wild Roads. I dropped Cavall and looked around. We were standing on the top of a mountain, the summit dusted with a fine layer of snow. I traced a finger over the nearest surface, revealing grey rock beneath.

'Which way?' voice sounded from behind me. I shrugged.

'It doesn't matter, at least both are downhill. See which way Cavall wants to go.'

We looked at the dog. He sniffed around then bounded down the slope to our left. Brackus peered down the track and followed after him.

It took us all day to climb down the mountain. The path was incredibly steep and narrow. Temperance in particular struggled not to accidentally step off, weighed down as she was with the satchel of iron. Brackus was a little better but kept stepping on loose rocks and sliding forward. Eventually we decided I should walk in front, the better to catch my companions if they fell. Cavall raced up and down the slope barking merrily at our struggles.

Just as I thought we were nearing the bottom of the mountain the light changed again and we were walking down a long flat road.

'Are we back?' panted Temperance, leaning over, her hands on her knees.

'Aye,' said Brackus, twisting around. 'Well, almost. We're in Scotland.'

'Where in Scotland?'

'No idea, I've only visited a few times.'

'How can you tell, then?' I asked. Something buzzed near my ear and I slapped at it.

Brackus winked at me. 'You don't get midges like that south of the border. Besides . . .' He pointed up to the moors that towered either side of the road. 'Heather, thistles, rain clouds. This is Scotland.'

Cavall whined and bumped into my shins. I looked down and he tilted his head towards the east.

'All right,' I said, 'Scotland or not, let's go.'

We followed Cavall as he trotted down the road. He splashed through a stream that ran alongside the path then bounded up the slope on the other side. We sighed collectively, looking up at the steep moor, then grudgingly began climbing after him.

Dusk had fallen by the time we reached the hilltop. It was crowned with a circle of menhirs, jagged and raw against the darkening sky. Cavall trotted in between two of the standing stones and vanished from view. When we hurried after him we stepped into the Court.

This time the dancing stopped as soon as we appeared. The high fae nearest to us inclined their heads and stepped aside, clearing a way through the gathering. We walked over to the back where Gwyn and Creiddylad had placed their thrones.

'Another success?' Gwyn said, when Temperance placed the bag of iron ore at his feet. I noticed he drew his boots back slightly, as though affected by the mere presence of the metal. 'I must admit I am impressed by your diligence. Only two months have passed since I saw you last. I had thought you would be gone longer.'

Two months, I thought, confused. Temperance looked similarly baffled.

'My lord, it has only been three weeks,' she said.

The Lord of the Hunt grinned nastily. 'Time under the hill does not match up with the mortal world. Be grateful it was not two years.'

Temperance opened her mouth to argue but Gwyn waved his hand. I looked at Creiddylad for support. Her eyes were sympathetic but she said nothing. Temperance stepped back, letting his words sink in. I saw her clenching her right fist in the folds of her skirt.

'Now, the final task.' Gwyn beckoned to a servant who removed Temperance's satchel. 'The third item you must procure, and the rarest. Bring me the horn of a unicorn.'

Brackus gasped. 'My lord, surely there are no unicorns left on this island?'

Gwyn sat back and smiled, 'They are rare now, it is true. Perhaps half a dozen still live, all on the Isle of Skye. Find one and slay it. Cut off the horn and return here with it. Then I will show you how to create a weapon to defeat the Erl King.'

Creiddylad laid a hand on her husband's sleeve.

'My love,' she whispered, 'is there no other way? I am passing fond of those beasts.'

Gwyn shook his head. 'Silver infused with rare poison. Iron from the heart of a falling star. The horn of a unicorn. That is the only way.'

'Didn't you say there was some other method of killing the Erl King?' the queen pressed.

'None that now remains to us,' Gwyn sighed. 'Sigmund could have slain him with his sword Gramr, or Roland with Durendal. Even Arthur with Excalibur could have ended his days. Alas those days have passed and all knowledge of how to forge such weapons has gone with them. The blade I will show you how to make will not kill the Erl King, but it will destroy the mortal form he has taken and banish him from these lands.'

Creiddylad looked down at her hands. Gwyn reached out to touch one.

'My love, if you would rescind your support of these

petitioners merely say the word. The unicorns will continue unmolested.'

The queen paused. I held my breath, feeling the tension crackling across the Court.

'No, beloved. Let these three continue. All things must come to an end,' said Creiddylad. She turned her pale head to look down at us. 'I trust you to hunt with the swiftness and accuracy prized by this Court.'

I nodded and Brackus bowed. 'Your will be done, my lady.'

'Indeed,' rumbled Gwyn. 'Go now, and do not linger here. You have a long journey to Skye, and a hard task before you.'

We bowed again and left. Cavall followed at our heels. I looked back to see Gwyn kissing his wife's hand.

As soon as we left the circle of menhirs Temperance whirled to face me. Her voice was strained and I could tell she was close to panic.

'Two months! We were under there for two months! Jenny, did you know?'

I shook my head.

'Only a week passed before I came after you; I must have been there almost the whole time.'

Temperance trembled and raised a hand to her head. Brackus caught her other arm and steadied her.

'It's not so bad,' he said soothingly. 'It is mid-May still. We have six weeks before midsummer. We may have lost some of our time but we need not give up hope.'

'It's not that,' Temperance said, her voice shaky. 'Two months under the hill. A month before then in Cornwall and Wales.' She broke into sobs.

Brackus extracted his stool from his pack and I helped guide Temperance to it. She was breathing too fast and I could tell the air wasn't going into her lungs.

Brackus and I exchanged looks and crouched down on the ground beside her, taking a hand each. He began whispering some sort of cantrip and I just held her hand, stroking it the way I had stroked my daughter's when she had had a nightmare. It took several minutes but eventually Temperance got hold of her breathing and stopped gripping our hands.

'Sorry,' she whispered. 'Josiah was twelve months old when I last saw him. He's already a quarter as old again. They change so fast, I've probably missed his first steps, his first words. He might not even remember me. Ursula will, she'll be so worried. I almost wish that she would forget me, and the wishing breaks my heart all over again.'

I bit my lip. There was nothing to say that could make this better. Even if we succeeded there was no buying back that time. Temperance sniffled and wiped her eyes.

'Shall we rest here for tonight?' Brackus asked, looking around at the hillside.

'It's early evening still, we could walk another few miles tonight,' I said. We both looked at Temperance. She grimaced and stood up.

'Let's go.'

It took us a full month of travelling to reach Skye. The Scottish roads were narrower and more winding than those south of the border and we were lucky to make ten miles a day. The slow pace was frustrating, but it was difficult to stay angry when I looked out at the beautiful country we were walking through. Rugged mountains, purplish red moors and glassy lochs were everywhere. As we walked northwards the villages got smaller and farther between. This presented a challenge as Lady Creiddylad's supplies had only lasted a week. Brackus and Temperance bought more food whenever we passed through a town, but there was rarely enough for sale to sustain them for more than a day. Cavall roamed far and wide. Often we did not see him from day to day. He would emerge from behind a tangled bush or down a slope, often with half a rabbit hanging out of his mouth.

I fished for my own food in the lochs, feasting on fresh salmon and trout and delighting in the sweet, if only temporary, relief of the waters. Occasionally I would see the flash of a horse in the cold waters but the kelpies stayed at a distance, not bothering me. I wasn't so confident that they would ignore my companions so encouraged them to make camp further away from the water's edge than they would have preferred.

Kelpies were not the only fae we saw. Wisps were common, especially as we crossed over the high moors, casting their pale flickering light through the thick fog. Dwarfs passed us on the roads, lifting their glamour to greet Brackus and barter for something from his bottomless pack. At night, when the three of us would huddle for warmth against a boulder or tree, we could sometimes hear the wail of a local banshee.

Temperance particularly disliked this, and rarely slept well on those nights. She grew paler and more tired as the days went on. We were back on speaking terms but there was still an awkwardness between us. We both leaned on Brackus to keep our spirits up. He was the most used to frequent travel and enjoyed the challenge of finding food and shelter. His chattering, which remained constant even through sleeting rain and midge bites, was a great aid. I did not, of course, tell him as much.

The day before we reached the coast Brackus decided to pitch camp early, under the sprawling branches of an ancient oak nestled at the foot of a hill.

'We all need a proper rest,' he said, driving his telescopic poles into the ground and flinging his tarpaulin over the top. 'A good fire, the rest of that rabbit and my last bottle of small beer should lift our spirits.'

Neither Temperance nor I had the strength to argue so we built the fire and clustered around it, pouring out small cups of beer. Brackus was in a talkative mood and regaled us with a few of his favourite tales of adventure. Temperance sat and listened quietly, but I made the effort to grumble and poke holes in the narrative, just to show willing. When the fire had burned down to embers we retired for the night.

I dozed fitfully, waking what felt like every other minute to Brackus's snores. Temperance was lying in between us, which was the only thing preventing me from poking him. When I awoke for the fifth time I sat up, fully intending to thump him awake. Starlight shone down on the empty bedroll next to me. Temperance was gone.

I scrambled up and looked around. Cavall had snuggled up to Brackus and was making little yipping noises in his sleep. I paused. If anything had snatched Temperance, Cavall would have alerted us. Still a little concerned I padded around the tree. Out of the lee of the trunk the wind caught at me, and I shivered. I ducked my head down and saw indentations in the grass, about the size of Temperance's boots. They led away from the tree and up the hill. I decided to follow them.

At the top of the hill sat Temperance, her cloak wrapped around her, and her face tilted up at the stars. She was rubbing her right hand with her left, pulling at the skin absentmindedly. She turned as I approached and gave me a wan smile.

'Couldn't sleep either?'

I shook my head. 'That goblin snores like a dragon and the dog is worse. Do you want company? I only came up here to check you were all right.'

'Company would be welcome,' Temperance said, 'come and sit with me.' I sat down in the grass. Temperance offered me her cloak but I shook my head, enjoying the cool stillness of the night.

'I was just thinking about my children,' she said. 'I haven't told you much about them, have I? Josiah is a sweetheart, the easiest baby I've ever known. Ursula was such a handful from the time she could crawl, but so smart. She already knows her numbers and can mark out her name in the dirt with a stick.'

Temperance gulped and drew in a steadying breath.

'I know Benedict will be taking good care of them; they won't be hungry or dirty and he knows the lullabies that sends them to sleep. But what if they pick up a cold that takes a turn, or cut themselves and the wound gets infected? I never worried about all the thousand common things that could hurt a child because I knew I could protect them. What if that happens and I'm not there to save them?'

'Interesting,' I said thoughtfully. 'I thought you would be

worrying about the Erl King. He seems like a much more serious threat to your children.'

Temperance twisted to look at me. For a moment her face was completely blank. Then she cracked up laughing. I stared at her, nonplussed by this reaction. I waited for her to stop but she just got louder and louder, falling backwards and lying on the ground, convulsing with giggles.

'Oh my word, Jenny,' she gasped, struggling for breath, 'that is truly the most incredibly tactless thing I've ever heard anyone say.'

This confused me even more. My words had, on reflection, not been particularly comforting, but I didn't see why that would cause Temperance to laugh so hard that tears were bubbling down her cheeks.

'I didn't mean—' I started, but Temperance cut me off, waving her hand in the air.

Something snapped in the grass behind us, and Temperance dropped her hand. I whipped my head around to look. Cavall bounded up the hill towards us and threw himself on me.

'Get off me, you ridiculous dog,' I complained, trying to stop him from licking my face.

'Come on,' Temperance said, 'let's head back, we really do need some rest. I'll cast a spell of silence over Brackus.'

I wrestled the dog off me and followed her down the hill, Cavall trailing behind. By the time I reached the bottom she had cast the cantrip and tucked herself in for the night. I paused for a moment looking down at her face, youthful in sleep. Then I rolled myself back up in my cloak and let my tiredness carry me away.

Chapter Sixteen

We arrived in Kyle of Lochalsh late in the next afternoon. Brackus vanished off towards the foreshore to find someone willing to ferry us over to Skye. The day had cleared up from the looming grey of the morning and the horizon shone bright and blue. Cavall appeared at my feet, and I grabbed him by the scruff of his neck and looped a makeshift rope collar around him. He looked up at me with hurt eyes.

'Don't moon,' I said, 'we can't have you running off again before we catch the boat. You've caused enough trouble as it is.'

He sat down and sprawled theatrically against Temperance's legs, deliberately not looking at me. She smiled.

'He looks mortally offended,' she said, and reached down to scratch behind his ears. 'Do you think he'll recover in time to help us track down a unicorn?'

'I don't know,' I said. 'I don't even know if we can make him understand that's what we're after without a scent trail or something.'

'Maybe Brackus has something in his bag.'

'He'd have mentioned it by now. Can you do some kind of finding spell?'

Temperance frowned. 'I could try I suppose. It would help if I knew what unicorns really looked like. I've never even seen a drawing. Are they truly just horses with a horn?'

'I've never seen one either. Brackus will know, though.' I knelt to rumple Cavall's fur. He whined and twisted away from me.

'Don't be so dramatic, Cavall,' I teased. I rummaged in my pack, finding the last leaf-wrapped portion of rotten carp. 'Here, have some of this.'

Temperance retched as Cavall leapt to his feet and fell on the fish. Brackus reappeared, hurrying up from the shoreline.

'Come on,' he called, 'I've found someone who'll row us over, but we have to go now.'

I grabbed Cavall's leash and the three of us rushed down to the edge of the water. I could taste the salt on the air, but the sea was so sheltered that there were almost no waves. A tall figure in a long dress stood by a battered rowboat. As we got closer her features sharpened into view. Curly ginger hair tucked up beneath a headscarf and bright blue eyes, the colour of the sky. The woman squinted at us suspiciously, then said something to Brackus in heavily accented English. He looked over at us.

'She wants extra for the dog,' he said, looking down at Cavall.

'Why?' asked Temperance. Brackus shrugged and began packing our satchels into the boat.

'More weight,' said the woman. Her accent was just about comprehensible, the r's rolling like mist over a loch. I looked over at Temperance who sighed and dug her hand into her pocket. She withdrew one of the gold coins from my hoard.

'I don't have anything smaller,' she said, reluctantly handing it to the woman. The woman frowned and, lifting the coin to her mouth, bit it. Her eyes widened as she inspected the dent.

'Tis too much,' she said, handing it back. Temperance shook her head.

'It's all we have.'

The woman considered, then pulled up her dress to reveal a small hatchet strapped to her leg. She grabbed it. All of us took a step backwards but the woman placed the coin on one of the seats of the boat and chopped at it with the axe. Something pinged and the woman straightened.

'Here,' she said, holding out half of the coin. Temperance took it tentatively and put it back in her pocket.

The woman grinned at us and gestured to the boat. We piled in and she pushed it out onto the water, wading through to climb over the side. She rowed with practised ease, slicing the oars through the water and rarely looking behind her to check the direction. The three of us passengers sat in front of her while Cavall climbed up on the edge, his ears flapping in the breeze.

Skye billowed on the horizon, a great green jewel rising up from the sea. To the south a large rectangular castle looked out over the straits.

'Caisteal Maol,' said the woman, seeing us looking at it. ''Twas the old seat of the local thane. Tis empty now.'

I wondered how far we would have to go. Gwyn had not specified exactly where the unicorns dwelt, and Skye was a large island.

The sound of gravel crunching along the keel of the boat broke my reverie. I jumped out to help the woman pull us ashore. Cavall leapt out and splashed along beside me, paddling in the cold seawater.

When we reached the beach the woman helped Temperance and Brackus out onto the sand. I unleashed Cavall and he scampered off to the north. Temperance shook her head and turned to thank the woman.

'Why are ye here?' she asked. 'Tis a lang way fra' home for the likes o' ye.'

Temperance hesitated and glanced over at me.

'We're looking for something,' she said eventually. 'Something strange.' The woman nodded.

'Aye, well this is a strange place. Hope you ken what you're doing.'

'Do you know where we might find –' Temperance paused '– what we're looking for?'

The woman gave her an appraising glance. 'Go to Kilbride, where the red hills meet the black peaks. If there's something strange on this island that's where it will be. Mind how ye go.'

Temperance nodded and shook the woman's hand.

'If ye have any trouble with the locals give them my name, Flora MacDonald. Tell them I rowed you out here. I've family on the island and they'll mind the name.' Flora gave us a last look then pushed her boat back out to sea.

We stood on the beach and watched as her boat vanished towards the mainland.

'Should we set off now?' I asked Brackus. 'How far is it to Kilbride?'

He rubbed his nose. 'Let's camp here tonight. Tomorrow we can find a local and ask for directions.'

'Fine, but you don't want to camp this close to the water. We should go up into the woods.'

He groaned at me but picked up his satchel. 'You are too paranoid about kelpies, Jenny; they're not going to bother you.'

'I'm not worried about me.' I shouldered my pack. 'I've never swum in these seas before; if something drags you in I might not be able to get you out.'

Brackus rolled his eyes and started up the hill. We pitched camp next to a stand of elms. Cavall sneaked up when we were cooking supper and begged until Temperance threw him a strip of dried meat. We sat quietly after eating and stared into the dark flames of Brackus's fire.

'We should probably talk about it,' muttered Brackus eventually, lighting up his pipe.

'About what?' I said, poking a stick into the fire.

'About this unicorn we're supposed to be hunting. We need to come up with a plan.'

I sighed. 'Can't we do that later? I don't want to think about it now.'

'We've been not thinking about it for a month,' insisted Brackus. 'We've finally reached the island and we need to start talking about it. It's really no different than hunting a deer or fishing for salmon. We already tracked down one magical creature.'

'I know. It feels different though. Unicorns are . . .' I trailed off.

'Special.' Brackus finished for me. 'I've never even seen one but it does feel wrong to be hunting them. I suppose that's a good sign though. If we weren't so nervous about killing one then we wouldn't be good people.'

'Or does it say that we're bad people for knowing it's wrong and doing it anyway?' I added.

Brackus gave a half smile. 'A thorny philosophical dilemma, Jenny.'

Temperance rubbed the back of her hand. 'To be honest with you I don't really care if it is wrong or right. It's the only way to defeat the Erl King and save my children. I would do just about anything to achieve that.'

'Even kill something as pure and rare as a unicorn?' Brackus probed, leaning forward. 'Kill it yourself, not me or Jenny. Hold the knife in your hand and bring it down on an innocent creature?'

'Yes,' said Temperance simply. 'I would.'

Brackus leaned back, blowing a smoke ring into the air. 'Very well then. Just so long as we're all clear. So how should we do it?'

'Can we bait it with magic?' I inquired. 'That worked with the boar.'

'The Twrch Trwyth was a man cursed into the form of a boar, not an inherently magical being. Unicorns are more powerful, they're one of the oldest kind of fae.'

'What about that old story about virgins attracting them?' Temperance asked. I noticed her glancing at me out of the corner of her eye. Brackus shook his head.

'Well, why don't you tell us about them and we'll come up with a plan?' I snapped, growing impatient.

Brackus blew another smoke ring and settled down to speak.

'Unicorns came into being with the first of the high fae. Legend tells us that they were born from the waves crashing on the beaches of Britain and cantered forward, fully formed. They are similar to horses but smaller, maybe a little taller than Cavall here, and with cloven hooves. Their coat is said to be as bright and shining as the moon, and they prefer to come out only on moonlit nights.

'They are famously shy, rarely appearing before humans or fae and swift to flee if confronted. Their horn, which is what we seek, grows up to a foot in length. Some sources say it is made of bone or enamel or even diamond. All agree, however, that it cannot be removed whilst the beast lives.'

'Are they dangerous?' I asked.

'I have never heard of anyone being killed by one, but I have never heard of anyone catching one either.' Brackus sent another smoke ring towards the fire.

'Oh good. So we don't know if one can even be caught.'

'Surely you must know something else, Brackus?' Temperance asked. 'Something useful.' The goblin grinned and tapped the edge of his pipe on his knee.

'I do. Unicorns were born of the sea. They dwell in the mountains and hills but return to drink the salt water at night. Our best chance therefore is to wait along the seashore for one to come down to the water and then block off their retreat. Since the boatwoman suggested Kilbride was a likely spot I propose we start there.'

'And when we have trapped one,' I said, 'what then?'

'Then you can grapple it and Brackus or I can cut its throat,' Temperance said.

Brackus winced. 'I'll leave the throat slitting to you, Temperance, it's not really my speciality.'

I raised a hand. 'Isn't there something we're missing here? It's summer in the far north. It hasn't been properly dark all week. How can we trap them at night-time if it never gets dark?'

'Ah,' Brackus said. He looked a little taken aback. 'I hadn't considered that. Well it does get darker; the sun drops below the horizon and the moon comes out. We will just have to hope that they will be forced to come out in the twilight.' He rapped his pipe on his knee again, warming to his theme. 'You know this is probably a better opportunity for us as we will all be able to see, rather than just Jenny.'

I didn't think this was a particularly good plan but it was getting late.

'Fine,' I admitted, 'but I'm not going into the sea after it. Jennys are freshwater creatures only.'

Thus agreed we settled in for the night. I struggled to stay awake for a long time, to see if Temperance would wander off again but she showed every sign of being in a deep slumber and eventually I lost my battle and slept.

The next day dawned bright and sunny. We left the woods and headed west, following a rough cart track along the coast. A thin ribbon of land was farmed, mostly sheep grazing around stocky granite cottages. Behind the fields the moors rose up around us, caked in peat and purple heather. At midday we passed a cheerful pair of farmers, driving a small herd of rugged red cattle. Brackus dodged through the impressive horns to ask the men for directions. It turned out that they spoke no English at all but after some enthusiastic sign language, and a sly cantrip of understanding, they told us to turn left at the edge of the moor before the forest.

Temperance was very taken by the furry cows and wanted to stay and ask more questions. She and the farmers tried to make themselves understood by shouting loudly and cheerily in their own languages whilst Brackus and I attempted to drag her away.

'Bloody countryfolk,' complained Brackus. 'We're on a famous quest and she wants to ask questions about livestock. Come on, Temperance, we've only a week till midsummer.'

We managed to pry Temperance away and set off again. We missed the turn-off to the south-west, so small was the path, and had to walk back to find it. I was not looking forward to clambering over more mountains but to my relief the path ran through a low green valley. To the north towered an enormous hill. Its lower slopes were grassy but the top half gleamed red in the sunlight. We skirted around the foot of the hill and the valley led us out to the sea again.

Across the sea loch I saw dark mountains on the horizon, jagged and sharp as they rolled towards the sea. I thought of the boatwoman's words: red hills and black peaks. This must be the place.

Temperance stopped and took a deep breath of the salt air. She looked back at us.

'Where should we camp?'

'Further along the coast,' Brackus said, pointing. 'There should be a stream between the black hills and the red. We'll camp there.'

It took another hour to walk over and find a good spot. The ground was marshy and soft and so open that there was nowhere to lay an ambush. Eventually we decided to split up. Brackus would walk over to the black hills' side of the stream, Temperance would stay on the slopes of the red hills, and I would sit in the stream. If any unicorns came down the valley we would wait until they passed and then try and stop them on their way back.

'What about Cavall?' Temperance said, stroking the dog's muzzle.

'Cavall can stay with one of you. I don't want him running around scaring off the unicorns. Let him go when you approach and he can help us close in on them.' I eyed Cavall who was wagging his tail hopefully. 'Stay.' He flopped down and yawned at me. I glowered at him then turned to Brackus.

'Will we wait all night?'

He shrugged. 'Unless you have somewhere better to be.'

I gave him a half-hearted hiss and then slipped into the water of the stream. It was still fresh despite the proximity to the sea loch and I could taste the heather and peat on the snow melt. I couldn't sense anyone at home. Even the fish were small: little minnows dancing on the currents. It was strange to be in such a shallow stream, too turbulent for plants to grow in. I felt uncomfortably conspicuous as I lay on the stream bed. I reassured myself that the light bouncing off the surface would be sufficient to hide me.

The pale-yellow sun continued to sink behind the spiked black mountains to the west. I lay alert, waiting for something to happen, for the unicorns to come down the mountain and drink from the sea. I wondered what the term was for a group of unicorns. Was it still a herd? It seemed very mundane for ancient fae. I tried out words in my head: a drove, a flock, a swarm. I didn't have the right vocabulary to describe them. Brackus would probably know and be pleased to tell me. I would see if I could bear to ask him.

A bird spun over the river, a gull of some kind. Hoofbeats rang out to the north of where I squatted. I was sure it was cloven hooves and swirled in the current, trying for a better view. A magnificent red stag paused on the edge of the stream. He scanned the horizon then lowered his antlered head to drink. I paddled a little closer, trying to count the points of his antlers. Sixteen velvet spikes crowned the great russet head. He drank slowly, as if confident nothing on the island could threaten him, and I thought he was probably right. Wolves were near as rare as unicorns these days and it had been long years since a bear had wandered past my lake.

The stag finished drinking and left. I waited to see if anything else would come. I was disappointed. A fox, a handful of rabbits and a few river voles were all the evening visitors I had. When the sun broke over the eastern horizon I climbed out of the stream and headed to where Temperance had been waiting. I found her cooking a breakfast of rabbit stew, Cavall unhelpfully underfoot.

'I thought we should eat before we go to sleep.' Her face was cheerful but her voice wobbled a little.

I sat down beside her and sniffed the cooking pot. I thought I would rather have gone fishing but I smiled appreciatively anyway.

'It's only been one night,' I said as Brackus straggled over to join us. 'It would have been wildly lucky to have seen a unicorn on our first real night of looking.'

Temperance nodded and bent over the pot, stirring vigorously. Brackus shot me a worried glance and took a seat beside me without comment.

A second night passed. Temperance was getting nervier by the hour. Creiddylad had said that the best chance of defeating the

Erl King was to fight him during midsummer, the days between the twenty-first and twenty-fourth of June. It was now less than a week till the summer solstice. I could see her mouthing numbers when she thought we weren't looking. A day to travel to the court, time to forge the weapon. How long would it take to travel back to Chipping Appleby? If the court met somewhere remote then we would never make it back in time. I wanted to reassure her but the same thoughts were troubling my own mind.

On the third night at Kilbride we settled into our now familiar positions. As I waded into the stream I saw a flash to the west as Brackus signalled he was in position. I sank below the water to wait. Above me the gibbous moon was dull as it hung in the sky, washed out by the rays of the sun still filtering from the west. As I looked at it doubt crept into my heart. Surely the unicorns would not bother emerging for such a pitiful sight. I floated in the water, trying not to panic. I closed my eyes and focused on the soothing feeling of the stream washing over and around me.

Something splashed along the edge of the stream. I opened my eyes. Hoofbeats, too small for a deer, too delicate for a sheep. I stayed very still. The splashing continued. The hoofbeats were heading downstream, towards the beach. When they passed I rose up slightly and risked a look.

Four horses were cantering down the stream. Each was small, less than ten hands high, and delicate. The cloven hooves flashed a silvery grey and the coat and manes were a pure chalk white. I straightened a little more and saw the spiralling horn that grew from each equine forehead. They were undeniably strange and rare and lovely and my heart ached to have to hunt them. But I squared my shoulders and pushed off the riverbed to swim downstream.

I caught them up when they reached the edge of the sea loch. The unicorns slowed to a trot as they plunged into the water, going in up to their knees and sloshing around with evident pleasure. I thought three of them were females, with a stallion a little taller than the mares. One of the mares had a younger look; she kicked up the surf beneath her hooves and whinnied.

I watched carefully as she walked back and forth along the gravelly beach. I planted my feet on the base of the stream, ready to spring.

A flash came from the west and I leapt forward. I yelled and ran towards the unicorns. Their heads whipped up and saw me. Two dodged left, two right. I stayed on the left, following the younger mare and the stallion. Brackus had jumped out and was closing in on them; hopefully we would drive them towards Temperance.

A baying sound came from the north and Cavall emerged just in front of me. He snapped at the unicorns' hooves, blocking their escape across the moor. I was close enough to spring and jumped for the younger mare. My hands scrabbled for purchase and I wound them into her long flowing mane. I threw myself backwards, using my weight to bring her down. Cavall lunged towards us and took a bite out of one of the flailing legs. Brackus hurried over and pinned down the front legs. It took his full weight to do this; the unicorn was small but unnaturally strong.

'Temperance, get over here,' he yelled. The witch arose from behind a clump of heather, her face uncertain.

'Quickly,' I called. 'She's struggling and we can't hold her for ever.'

Temperance stepped towards us, her hand going to the knife at her belt. Suddenly the stallion was in front of her, horn held down as if to impale her. Temperance darted out of the way but the unicorn stepped backwards blocking the way to us.

'I can't get past,' Temperance shouted, ducking from another blow.

'Throw a fireball at it,' I hollered, wrestling with the back end of the younger mare. Temperance brandished her fist at the advancing unicorn and mumbled something. Her hand exploded into flames. Out of the corner of my eye I could see the beast flinch but try for another strike.

Cavall growled and hurtled off behind me. I twisted to see the other two unicorns galloping directly at us. Their horns were lowered, looking frighteningly sharp. I looked at Brackus.

'Can you hold her alone?' he asked. I nodded doubtfully and he took off after Cavall, his hands twisting something in the air.

It took all of my strength to keep the unicorn pinned down. I had neither the magical power of my lake nor the advantage of being in water. I lost track of the fights around me, focusing only on keeping the mare down. I tried to evade the hooves but took a solid kick to the chest that knocked all the breath from my body. I ignored it and carried on. Even a stab from the horn would not be too worrying, provided Temperance survived long enough to heal me. The important thing, the only thing that mattered, was holding onto the unicorn.

Suddenly the stallion screamed and fell back. Temperance had cast a wind at it and ran past as it pushed against the wall of air. She crouched beside me. Behind us Brackus and Cavall were fending off the other two mares. I could hear one of them snorting and squealing.

'Quickly,' I gasped, 'Temperance. The knife.'

Temperance had it clutched in both hands, left over right. Trembling, she raised it to the unicorn's white neck. I found a last reserve of strength and held down its head with my foot, still holding onto the chest with the rest of me. I could see its eyes rolling, dark brown and terrified. Temperance set her face and brought the knife down.

Without thinking I kicked the blade out of the way. It tumbled on the ground next to us. I rolled clear of the unicorn and it staggered to its feet and took off across the beach. The other three caught up with it and they vanished towards the mountains.

I glanced up at Temperance. The look of shock and betrayal on her face cut at my heart.

'What in God's name, Jenny?' she whispered, still crouched on the gravel.

'I'm sorry,' I said, 'I just couldn't.'

'You just couldn't?' She was yelling now, her voice echoing out across the sea loch. 'My children could die. My whole village could die and you just couldn't? I thought you were with me on

this, I thought we were allies, I thought we trusted each other.'
She paused for breath. 'My baby has probably already forgotten
me. My daughter, my husband, every day they live in fear, in
danger. Why, Jenny, just tell me why?'

I sat back, wrapping my arms around me. 'I'm so sorry,
Temperance,' I said again.

Brackus arrived beside me, panting hard. Cavall ran at his
heels, a dark streak of blood down his side.

'What happened, did it get loose? Sorry, Jenny, I shouldn't
have left you.' He bent over, hands on his knees and wheezed.
'We should probably find a different spot for tomorrow night.'

'It didn't get loose,' Temperance said, her voice cutting
like a whip. 'Jenny let it go. She kicked the knife right out of
my hands.'

Brackus's mouth fell open. 'But, why?' he asked.

'Its eyes,' I stuttered, 'I couldn't – its eyes.'

'What about its bloody eyes,' screamed Temperance, 'meant
that you had to damn my children? You had no problem killing
those soldiers on the road! I had to plead with you for their
lives. But when it comes to a dumb animal suddenly you're all
soft-hearted.'

She was literally fluorescing with fury, sparks flying from her
fingers. As she clenched them into fists I saw flames bursting into
life along her knuckles.

I did nothing, only sat there and let her rage and pain break
over me like a tidal wave. My ears were roaring, blood rushing
to my head. Brackus straightened up and moved in front of me.
I could hear him trying to reason with Temperance. The fire at
her fists dimmed a little. He turned back to me.

'Jenny,' he said, stooping down in front of me. I didn't meet
his eyes. 'Jenny, you have to tell us why.'

I felt the resolve with in me snap and the tears began to flow.

'It had – it had—' I stammered, struggling to get the words
out. 'It had Jenny's eyes.'

'Your eyes are green,' Temperance snapped. Brackus raised
up a hand.

'Not our Jenny's eyes,' he said, and his voice was painfully sad, a tone I had only heard from him once before. 'Little Jenny. Her daughter.'

'Her daughter back down south?' Temperance sounded more confused than angry.

I sobbed harder, unable to force out the words.

'She's dead.' Brackus said, in the same sorrowful voice. 'She died about fifty years ago. She had brown eyes like the unicorn, I suppose.'

'I'm so sorry, Temperance,' I gasped, 'I put her away, didn't think about her. All these years it was easier to pretend she was alive, that we were estranged. I wanted so much for it to be true that I had half convinced myself.'

The flames at Temperance's fists went out. She sighed and sank to the ground.

'And the little unicorn, it reminded you of her?'

I gulped, snot dripping horribly from my nose. 'Not just the unicorn. You. You remind me of her. She was bold and brave like you; you even look like her a little. I felt that by helping you, in a way I was helping her, that she wasn't truly gone. I saw her again when we were under the hill, and it all came back to me again, everything I had buried inside myself. The unicorn was just the final straw.'

Temperance crawled over and put her arms around me, hugging me close. I sniffled and tried to wipe my face.

'What happened to her?'

'She passed,' I whispered. 'Fae aren't living so long any more. The magic is going out of the world. There was nothing to be done, she just passed.'

Temperance shivered. 'I can't imagine,' she said, 'what it must be like. To lose a child.'

I turned to look at her. 'Yes you can. You've been imagining it since March, since we found out about the Erl King. You've faced losing your children every day and I just wrecked your best chance to stop it.'

Temperance's face was wet with her own tears.

'I'm glad you stopped me,' she said. 'I'm glad I didn't do it. And I hate that I am. You might have saved my soul but damned my family. I'm so tired, Jenny, I don't know what the right thing is any more.'

Cavall snuffled at our feet. I smiled wetly and reached out to stroke his soft fur. Brackus moved closer to us and put his arm around my other shoulder.

'You two will set me off,' he murmured, pretending to dab at his eyes. 'Shall we get some sleep and re-evaluate what to do in the morning?'

I nodded and we clambered to our feet. Brackus patted me on the back and turned towards the east. Cavall barked. I looked down at him. He was facing behind us, his ears cocked forward, tail high. I spun around.

The four unicorns were walking towards us down the path of the stream. Their heads tossed in the cool night air, their horns glossy. The stallion was in the lead, the younger mare beside him. They halted ten yards away. The stallion gave us a penetrating look then stepped aside. A fifth unicorn stood behind, an older mare. It was frailer, weaker than the others, the mane and tail thinned with age.

She slowly clip-clopped forward, every step painfully slow. She stopped directly in front of me. Temperance pulled at my sleeve but I was not afraid. I reached out, stroking her long nose with my hand. The coat was silky to the touch. The old mare snorted and began to lower herself to the ground. I knelt next to her and she laid her head in my lap.

Temperance looked at me and I could tell she was thinking about the knife in her belt. Her right hand twitched. Then she knelt beside me and reached out to stroke the mare's neck. Brackus stood beside us, Cavall whining quietly at his feet.

The other unicorns lowered their horns to the ground. The old mare in my lap began to tremble, her breathing coming unevenly now. The stallion came forward, dipping his head over my shoulder to nuzzle at her ears. I stroked her once again and she whinnied gently. The tired eyes closed and the unicorn disappeared beneath my hand. The long spiralling horn fell into my lap, the last remnant of her existence.

The stallion drew back. I held out the horn to him but he nickered and returned to the other mares. I looked down at it, tracing the whorls of pearlescent white bone.

'Thank you,' Temperance whispered. The unicorns gave us a final look then turned and raced back towards the dark mountains.

Chapter Seventeen

I woke the next morning still clutching the unicorn's horn in my hand. Brackus was already poking at the fire, coaxing a pot of porridge oats into edibility. Temperance lay beside me, staring up at the sky. Cavall wandered over and licked my face. He still had a thin raised scar on his side from the night's attack. I traced it with a finger. Temperance had done a decent job of knitting together the wound and he didn't flinch at my touch. That was a good sign.

I turned my attention back to the tapered horn in my hand. It felt as smooth as polished wood but cold, as if it was drawing in heat from my touch. Despite the chill it didn't feel malevolent. I thought of a cool cloth being placed on the fevered head of a child. Perhaps it would break through the Erl King's blight in the same fashion.

Brackus began to dole out porridge. He passed me a small wooden bowl and I started methodically spooning it into my mouth. Temperance grimaced and blew on hers. I watched her a little awkwardly. We hadn't spoken since my outburst last night and the return of the unicorns.

'May I see it?' Temperance asked, putting down her bowl. I didn't need to ask what she was referring to, handing over the horn without comment.

She turned it over in her hands, eyes widening.

'It's heavier than I thought,' she commented, weighing it with her hand experimentally. 'I imagined it would be light as a twig.'

'I suppose it's pretty sturdy,' I said. Brackus nodded, leaning over Temperance's shoulder.

'I was rather worried when those two mares pointed them at us and started charging. Could have run us straight through.' He chewed a spoonful of porridge. 'That must be why we can use them in weapons; wouldn't be much use if they were weak enough to snap.'

Temperance placed a hand on either end, as if to apply pressure.

'No,' I yelped, making a grab for it. She gave me a sardonic look.

'I wasn't going to break it, I just wanted to see if it had any resistance.'

'Let's save the experimentation for Gwyn's smiths, shall we?' Brackus lifted the spiralling horn from her hands and wrapped it in a piece of fine green silk. Tucking it inside his pack he sat back down and resumed his breakfast.

Temperance regarded her own bowl with distaste and turned back to me.

'Do you want to talk?' she asked. 'About your daughter, I mean?'

I heaved a sigh and put down my porridge.

'There's not that much more to say. I found Jenny about two hundred years ago. I raised her in the lake and found her a nice mill pond when she was old enough. You know that already.'

I prodded the crust forming on top of the oats.

'She was one of the last young Jennys that I had heard of. We were getting rarer and rarer even then. It took a while for us to notice the rivers were emptying. We've always been solitary folk. Even once we did notice we didn't realise it was part of a pattern. I certainly didn't feel any different. Brackus still came by once or twice a year to pass on the gossip and to try and sell me something. What else would matter to me?'

I paused, staring out at the shining grey sea loch.

'When Brackus arrived out of the blue one day it didn't occur to me for a moment that something bad could have happened to Little Jenny. Even when I saw his face all sad and crumpled. You had to tell me twice, Brackus, do you remember?'

The goblin nodded at me. 'You didn't understand the concept at first. Then you thought I was joking. Then . . .' He stopped.

'Then I screamed at you and told you never to come near me again?' I finished.

'Among other things.' Brackus nodded again. 'You were quite frightening.'

'You did come back though,' I remembered, 'twice a year, same as always. I was as rude as I knew how to be, and you still came back.'

Brackus smiled at me, but there was sadness in his eyes. 'I had fewer and fewer friends as the years passed. I wasn't about to lose one of my oldest and dearest sparring partners.'

'Thank you,' I said, looking at him directly. 'Thank you for coming back, even after I screamed at you.'

The tips of his ears pinkened and he waved a hand at me. Temperance patted my hand.

'Do you think,' she said, furrowing her brow, 'that once we defeat the Erl King the magic could come back?'

I considered the question. It was a pleasant thought, but I doubted it was realistic.

'I don't think so, Temperance,' Brackus said gently. 'The fae were diminishing before the Erl King came to Britain. It may even be why he came. Don't worry too much about it. All things must come to an end.'

We were silent then. I finished off my cooling bowl of porridge and began to pack up my things.

'Come on,' I said. 'One more day on the Wild Roads and then the Court, and then home.'

'Home, where we will attempt to fight an all-powerful demonic nightmare?' asked Brackus.

I grinned at him. 'Exactly.'

He grumbled but got to his feet. Temperance offered Cavall

the remains of her porridge but he turned his nose up and began sniffing around the edge of the camp.

'Did you see any doors as we walked over from the beach?' Temperance asked, rolling up her cloak.

'No, the last one I noticed was about three days south of the crossing.'

'We have to walk all the way back?' I groaned.

'Not necessarily. I can cut a new opening to the roads.' Brackus cracked his fingers.

I scowled at him. 'Then why did we spend all that time looking for the others?'

'Because, my dainty emeraldine doll, it takes a lot of effort. It's much easier to simply use a door that exists than to make your own.' He straightened up. 'But in this case it's worth it.'

'So should we cut one here?' Temperance indicated the hillside.

'Best not. I'm not going to build a permanent door, merely cut a hole and shut it after us. It can have, ahem, adverse effects on the mortal landscape.'

I narrowed my eyes. 'What kind of adverse effects?'

Brackus avoided my gaze. 'Let's just say I'd rather not destabilise any mountainsides. We can go down to the shore and do it there.'

This answer did nothing to allay my concerns. A quick glance at Temperance suggested she had similar worries. Neither of us had any better suggestions so we tramped down to the beach, Cavall trotting at my heels.

Brackus stepped out onto the sand. Looking around for a suitable spot he began to mark out a pattern with the thin end of one of his telescoping staffs. It started simple enough, two long lines running parallel to the sea, but as he went on adding extra lines, I began to see what it was he was drawing. It was a bridge, as if flattened and viewed from above. Cavall padded out next to him, messing up one of the lines. Brackus swore and banished him, sulking, back to us.

'Jenny,' said Temperance, bending down to grab Cavall by the scruff of the neck. 'We've been at odds for a while now.'

I looked down at her as she hugged the dog, choosing her words carefully.

'I'm tired of it, tired of not trusting you. When we fought on the road to Wales . . . I think we were both at fault. You took the first step after the mine, but I couldn't let it go yet. I'm sorry for that, I should have – I don't know. I still think I was in the right but I can see your point of view. I don't know if I'll ever fully understand you but I do want to try. More than that, I think I realise now that I don't always have to agree with you to see you as a friend and an equal.'

She scratched at the back of her hand as she continued.

'I wanted to say that I trust you will try to do the right thing, just as I hope you trust me, even if we have different ideas about what that right thing is. So can we be friends again?'

I held out my hand for her to shake and she took it and pulled me into an embrace. Surprised, I managed to return it, though I was out of practice. Temperance smiled at me and I grinned back at her, relieved.

Brackus hollered over at us from where he had finished repairing Cavall's damage.

'Keep your hand on that dog!' he called. Temperance winked at me then began walking over to him. I grabbed Cavall and scooped him up into my arms, following behind.

Brackus met us at the western end of the sand bridge. He pointed eastwards, between the two main lines.

'Right, all you have to do is walk between the lines. Don't smudge or step on them, just keep walking and keep your eyes on the horizon. I'll be right behind you.'

'Will you close it after us?' Temperance asked. Brackus beamed.

'That's the beauty of the beach, it'll wash away in a few minutes when the tide comes in. Hurry now, I don't want it to wash away until we're on the other side. That would not be good.'

Temperance and I exchanged looks and hurried forward, Cavall writhing in my grip. I felt the change more clearly this time. Where before I had barely noticed the transition, this felt like walking down a slope and missing your footing. We both tripped forward. Temperance caught herself but I had a faceful of dog and went down hard. Cavall yelped and tried to disentangle himself. I scrabbled around, hearing Brackus sniggering behind us.

'Now I see why you prefer existing doors,' Temperance said, trying not to laugh.

'My apologies, Jenny.' Brackus stepped over me and offered a hand. 'An accident, I assure you. A happy, happy accident.'

I growled at him but accepted the hand. He pulled me up and I looked around. Today the Wild Roads had deposited us in a cave. I peered around, spotting an entrance in the distance, another behind us. Not a cave but a tunnel. I wondered if the idiosyncrasies of the caster affected the form the roads showed to them. Brackus's laughter had died out, and he was looking around nervously.

I forbore to tease him and instead slapped him on the shoulder.

'Come on, we'll be out in a few minutes.'

He gave me a weak smile as we set off. It soon became clear, however, that it would take longer than a few minutes. No matter how far we walked the entrance never seemed to get any closer. The ground was flat and smooth, and I took to counting steps with my eyes closed. After five hundred paces I would open my eyes and check again. The circle of white light was the same size. I turned to look behind me, wondering if we should have gone the other way.

Brackus caught my arm.

'Don't look back,' he muttered. I smirked at his worried expression and made to keep turning. 'I'm serious,' he said, 'it's bad luck to look back underground.'

'Come on, Brackus,' I said, 'it's the Wild Roads not the depths of Hell. There's nothing behind us.'

'Please, Jenny,' he said, 'just don't.'

I rolled my eyes but nodded and we started off again. I still thought Brackus was being ridiculous but the further I walked the more I could sense something behind us. It wasn't a sound, or a shape, but something scratched at my mind, urging me to turn around. I ignored and kept walking. Cavall remained unaffected, racing up and down the tunnel, barking at the shadows and barking at the echoed replies of his voice.

I lost track of time. How long had we been walking in the tunnel? There was no way to tell; even the daylight at the end didn't seem to be changing. I began counting steps again. Surely after ten thousand we would reach the end.

Twenty thousand three hundred and fifty-nine steps later we staggered out into the soft evening sun. I collapsed onto long grass, rolling over to bask in the sunlight. Cavall stepped on my chest and snuffled at my face.

'Are we out?' Temperance asked.

'Yes,' Brackus confirmed, sinking down next to me and stretching out.

'Thank goodness,' I sighed, opening my eyes. The tunnel mouth had vanished. 'That was the worst one. I think I'm catching your fear of caves, Brackus. Not ideal for someone who lives in one.'

Neither of them replied. Cavall stepped forward, tangling my hair under his paws.

'Get off me, you stupid dog,' I grumbled, pushing him off. I sat up and looked out. We were sitting on top of a high flat hill. To the west unfolded a heavily wooded valley, the green trees washed in the gold of the late sunshine.

'This looks familiar,' I said uncertainly. Brackus sat up.

'I don't wonder that it does,' he laughed. 'This is Cleeve Hill, Jenny. Your lake is not fifteen miles east of here.' Temperance's eyes flew open and she sprang to her feet.

'We're home,' she whispered. A grin lit up her face. 'We're home!' she yelled out to the valley below.

'Not quite,' put in Brackus. 'We still need to call upon Gwyn.'

'Yes, but to be so close, and with all three tasks completed.' Temperance's face was flushed. 'And with three full days till the summer solstice.'

She threw herself down beside me and leaned over, her hair gleaming darkly in the sunlight.

'We're home, Jenny!' she whispered. I blinked a little and smiled at her. She bent down and kissed me loudly on the cheek. I flushed scarlet and she grinned at me.

'Let's go, I want to find the Court!'

'We've been walking all day,' moaned Brackus, pulling his cap down over his eyes. 'Can't we have a little rest first?'

'We can rest after,' wheedled Temperance, plopping down next to him and whisking the cap away.

'Fine.' Brackus began to clamber upright. He spun around; hand raised up to shade his eyes from the setting sun. 'That way,' he pointed.

We sloped off in the direction he had indicated. The sun had dipped below the horizon and the sky was a lavender-grey. In front of us I could see the soft glow of the hovering lights. A huge pavilion was erected on the crest of the hill. Laughter and music filtered out of the tent flaps. A huge giant sat outside, craggy faced and ancient. He nodded at us and pulled the hangings aside.

Inside the court was dancing. This time there were no guests but the high fae. They danced back and forth in perfect synchronicity. I spotted Gwyn and Creiddylad and we skirted the couples and headed towards them.

'You have returned to my court for the third time,' rumbled the Lord of the Hunt. 'Have you succeeded in your final commission?'

Brackus knelt and placed the green silk at his feet. He unwrapped it carefully, revealing the unicorn horn.

Creiddylad gasped and the Court fell silent. Gwyn said nothing, merely glowered at us.

'Master Marsh,' Creiddylad said, 'may I?'

Brackus offered her the horn. She reached out with delicate fingers and plucked it from his hands. She raised it high, as if flourishing a wand. It seemed to shine in her hands, reflecting silvery light onto her beautiful face. Then she lowered it and fine lines fractured through the fine skin of her face.

'This was not taken but freely given,' she said, turning to

her husband. 'And the more powerful for it. I would not have believed such a thing possible.'

He reached out. I thought he would take the horn but instead he took her hand.

'Strange times indeed, my love.' Gwyn looked back at us and snapped his fingers. The page appeared at his side. 'Bring the comb and the iron.'

The servant disappeared behind the throne, returning with a neatly wrapped bundle atop which lay the silver comb. Gwyn took them and settled them in his lap.

'Now,' he said. 'I made a bargain with you. Pay attention, I shall not repeat myself.'

Brackus delved in his pack and withdrew his charcoal stick and scrap of parchment. Gwyn raised an eyebrow then continued.

'Three tasks have you completed and three trophies have you won. The silver, impregnated with the poison of the Twrch Trwyth, represents England, the realm of earth. The iron, smelted from the heart of a falling star, is Welsh fire. The alicorn, or horn, taken from a creature born of the Scottish sea, is water. By combining these ingredients I can forge a weapon that will banish the Erl King from these shores.

'I shall take the comb and the iron and forge a blade around the alicorn, leaving a handspan free for a hilt. Strike the Erl King with it and he will lose his mortal form.'

'How do we get close enough to stab him?' Temperance asked.

Gwyn shrugged lazily. 'However you like. I know not the details of your village; make a plan and waylay him.'

Creiddylad coughed softly. Her husband glanced at her and then turned back to us.

'If I were you I would try and catch him unawares. He will not sleep but the human he has occupied must. It may take a while for him to awaken the host body and direct his power through it at you. Now,' he clapped his hands, 'let us proceed with this blade of yours.'

The servant reappeared, bearing the stirrup cup Gwyn had

brandished at us the first time we came to the Court. He knelt
before his lord, holding the cup aloft. Creiddylad took the bundle
from her husband's lap and withdrew the silver comb. She whispered something to it before placing it into the chalice.

Next she unwrapped the bundle to reveal a dull grey ingot of
metal. It seemed to resist the glittering light of the candles, sucking in rather than reflecting the fairy illuminations. Creiddylad
held it carefully, keeping the cloth between the skin of her fingers and the bite of the iron. She dropped it into the cup quickly
and I saw her wince with relief. Creiddylad returned to her
throne, twisting one hand into the folds of her dress.

Gwyn rose. Behind us the dancers swirled to a standstill.

'I made a vow to these travellers. Now I shall keep it. I
summon my court to bear witness.' His voice was suddenly
incredibly loud, echoing across the pavilion like thunder.

The fae drifted towards us, forming a neat arc around the
thrones. As they drew closer I felt cold pinpricks run up my arms
and down the path of my spine. Most kept their eyes on their
monarchs but a handful looked inquisitively at us, the sharp,
inhuman symmetry of their faces making me shiver. Temperance
shuffled closer to me and took my hand. I squeezed it tightly.

Gwyn said something in a language I did not understand and
the servant holding the cup let it go. I jerked forward instinctively to catch it but it hovered in the air, as steady as if it rested
on an invisible pillar.

Gwyn spoke again and though I still could not parse the
words, the meaning became clear to me. The very sound of his
words seemed to scorch the air, the white-hot heat of the midsummer sun rolled over me and the smell of cracked dry earth
filled my lungs. The cup did not move but began to glow from
within; the silver of the comb already beginning to melt.

I felt the warmth rolling off the goblet pushing down my
throat with each breath, probing at the corners of my eyes and
up my nose.

Sweat beaded on my forehead and trickled down my back
before evaporating off in the next instant. My skin dried and

began to crack. Gwyn stayed statue-still, his image blurring in my eyes through the haze of heat. I stole a look at Brackus. He was crouched over, hands covering his face as protection from the temperature.

Gwyn spoke again and the temperature rocketed. I could tell that I was only experiencing a fraction of the heat burning in the stirrup cup. The iron was starting to glow red and yellow, the sharp edges of the ingot beginning to blur. My throat was bone dry now, every inhalation sent fire into my chest. I held my breath, to try and prevent myself from cooking from the inside out.

Gwyn held out the alicorn, angling it above the chalice so that the spiralled end pointed down. It seemed impossibly fragile in his hand and I suddenly worried that it would shatter in the heat. I took a step towards the Lord of the Hunt. The earth beneath me was dead and burning hot to my bare feet. I felt my soles blister and pop. I moved forward, wincing each time I brought my feet down. The heat was all around me, catching at my clothes, at my eyelashes.

Before I could reach him Gwyn brought the horn down, plunging it into the stirrup cup. Not a drop of metal spilled onto his hand but I could tell the effort to keep holding the alicorn was immense. A trail of sweat dribbled down his left temple, and he gritted his teeth. Creiddylad moved to his side, reaching up to place a hand on his shoulder. He stiffened with new resolve and I saw his knuckles tighten around the alicorn.

Finally, when I thought my throat would catch fire from the heat, Gwyn groaned and withdrew the alicorn. It glowed in his hand, the metal too bright to look at directly. Creiddylad whispered a word of banishment and the heat fled in a whooshing wave.

The servant appeared again, dragging a tall wooden barrel that sloshed with water. The part of my mind that hadn't burnt out in the heat wondered how he had kept it cool. Gwyn stepped forward and dipped the alicorn into the bath. He moved back as steam erupted in clouds, flowing over the edge of the tub.

There was silence for a moment as the court collectively caught its breath. Gwyn picked up the stirrup cup from the air and handed it back to the servant. Creiddylad whispered something in his ear and he smiled down at her.

'Well,' he said, turning back to us. 'It should be cool enough to retrieve.'

I eyed the steaming barrel doubtfully. Temperance and Brackus seemed similarly disinclined to stick their hands in it.

'Go on,' said Creiddylad, 'I promise it'll be quite cool.'

The three of us exchanged looks and then Temperance moved hesitantly towards the barrel. It came up to her chest and for a moment her head and shoulders vanished behind the billowing steam. She leaned over the edge, submerging her arm up to her shoulder in the bubbling water. An unnameable expression fluttered over her face and she leaned in, the unicorn horn clutched in her hand.

It was thicker than before; the metal had moulded to every curve and swell of the spiral. The dull grey of the iron had changed, infused with the glimmer of the elf silver, so that the whole length shimmered like a dark pearl. Temperance tilted it at an angle and I saw that the whorls of the spiral had sharpened into razor edges, twisting down into a needle-fine point.

My eyes flickered from the newly forged dagger to Temperance's face. She was still looking at the blade, mouth slightly open in wonder. Brackus moved closer to me. I wondered if he too could feel the force of the weapon Temperance was holding. It wasn't malevolent as such, but the strength of it was palpable. For a moment longer we hesitated, then Temperance lowered the dagger and stepped towards us.

'Here, Jenny, hold it,' she said, offering me the hilt end. 'You won't believe how strong it makes you feel.'

I touched the edge of the alicorn. The iron sparked at my fingers and I drew my hand back.

'I think you'd better keep hold of that,' said Brackus to Temperance. I nodded.

'It is not a weapon for fae hands,' Gwyn rumbled when

Temperance looked as if she might protest. 'Keep that safe, little witch. Should you succeed in banishing the Erl King it would be wise not to leave it lying about.'

Temperance nodded slowly. 'Should I bring it back to you?'

Gwyn laughed delightedly, 'Why no! All your efforts deserve some reward and who knows if the Erl King will be the last dark force you or your descendants must face. They say Sir Bedivere threw Arthur's sword into a lake when the king died. Maybe your friend Jenny can keep it for you in her pond.'

I wrinkled my nose at his description of my beautiful lake as a pond, but a warning look from Brackus convinced me to let it slide. Gwyn sat back on his carved chair and accepted a cup of wine from his servant.

Creiddylad stepped forward with the cloth she had taken the iron from. She began to wind it around the length of the alicorn, covering the dagger completely, fastening it with a ribbon from her wrist. She turned back to Temperance.

'You have everything you need. We will wish you speed on your journey.'

Creiddylad snapped her fingers and I felt the satchel at my side fill up with supplies.

She turned to Brackus.

'Master Marsh, it has been a pleasure.'

Brackus made a deep bow. Creiddylad smiled at him and raised him up, kissing him on both cheeks.

'I do not think we will meet again. Be well, Master Marsh.'

Brackus smiled at her but there were tears in his eyes.

'My world will be a darker place without you in it, my lady,' he said. She laid a hand on his cheek.

'You must find a new light then. It would sadden me greatly to think of you in the darkness.' He nodded before stepping back

Creiddylad looked at me. I met her gaze straight on and held out my hand. She took it and shook it warmly.

'Jenny Greenteeth. I have known many of your kind, and you remind me of the best of them.' She gripped my hand. 'Yet in other ways you are unique. There is something about you, Jenny . . .' She trailed off. 'Regardless, I am glad to have met you. I hope you find your peace.'

'Lady Creiddylad,' I said, rising to stop her from leaving.

'What is it, Jenny?'

'Do you really think we have a chance? Against the Erl King?'

The queen looked up to where Gwyn sat, twisting a ring on his left hand.

'Truthfully I do not know. He is an ancient and wicked foe,' Gwyn said. 'That dagger can cast him out. But that does not mean it is a certainty that you will have that opportunity. He may destroy you before you get close enough.'

Creiddylad smiled. 'You three are formidable too, though. You have met every challenge and conquered it. There is something about you; the witch, the hag and the goblin. By rights you should have killed each other after a day on the road but you joined together as one. You made it to our court by the Wild Roads and then returned three times. You caught the Twrch Trwyth and bound him to your will. You travelled under the hill and surfaced blessed with star iron. You found the last unicorns and they offered you a horn.'

'There is some hope then?' I asked.

'You remember what I said the first time we met, Jenny? There is always hope.'

Chapter Eighteen

We camped half a mile back from the crest of the hill. The waxing moon hung yellow in the sky above us, a rising reminder that the full moon of midsummer was only days away.

Temperance fell asleep still holding the alicorn dagger, wrapped in the fabric of the high fae. Brackus lit his customary dark fire and sat down beside it. He retrieved some of the bread from Creiddylad's fresh supplies and began to toast slices on the flames. I moved next to him, accepting alternate bits of toast and fending off Cavall who had an incredible sense of entitlement to other people's food.

Brackus snickered as I lost my second slice to the sneaking dog.

'You'll have to be faster than that when we set off tomorrow,' he said as he dodged Cavall. 'The Erl King might be even more of a challenge than a hungry dog.'

'It's all good training,' I grumbled, aiming a fake kick at Cavall. 'Besides, I don't think we can distract the Erl King with toast.'

Cavall retreated, his tail wagging, his prize clamped in his jaws. Brackus's smile faded.

'Do you think we're ready?'

'Can you be ready for something like this? If we all make it to Chipping Appleby without chickening out then I'll consider that a win. Frankly, Brackus, I didn't think you would make it this far. I wasn't sure I would, for that matter.'

'Well, there's not much for me to lose these days,' Brackus said, shuffling his feet closer to the fire. 'I'll admit though, when we were under the hill in Wales and saw that vision of the Erl King, that was almost enough to make me want to give up.'

I shuddered. 'I remember. It felt just like seeing him in the parsonage. I wonder if he could tell where we were.'

'Do you think he knows we're coming back for him?'

'Yes.' I looked over at where Temperance was sleeping. 'I think he knows. I think he knew the moment I saw him in the parsonage all those months ago. That's why he let me go so easily. I think he's toying with us, letting us entertain him.'

'He doesn't think he can be beaten?' Brackus asked.

I frowned considering. 'It's hard to tell. I've never heard of him being defeated before. He's certainly not afraid of us, though he took the trouble to try and eliminate Temperance before she discovered what he was.'

'Even if he doesn't think we can win, Gwyn and Lady Creiddylad do,' said Brackus.

'You know how I hate to put my faith in the high fae.' I said, sticking my nose in the air. He grinned at me.

'Sadly, Jenny, on this occasion I don't think you have much choice.'

We were quiet for a while before I spoke again.

'Brackus?'

'Hmm?'

'I've been thinking ...'

'You want to be careful overheating your brain after today,' he said, grinning.

'I'm serious. I want to talk about Temperance.'

'Go ahead.'

'I know she wants to be the one to cut down the Erl King. I think that's a good plan. But we need to make sure she gets that far.'

Brackus gave me a hard look. 'What are you asking me, Jenny?'

'I'm saying that even if we bring him down, odds are that we won't all be walking away. Temperance is young, she has a family. If it comes to it, I'll put her life before my own.'

'Are you asking me to do the same?'

I swallowed and met his gaze. 'No, I'm asking you to protect her first, to choose her before me if it comes down to it.'

He looked over at where the witch was sleeping. Temperance was curled up around Cavall, the pair of them snoring gently.

'You value your life so little?' he asked.

I smiled at him. 'I value my life a great deal. These last months, travelling with you both, I feel young again. I want to live, want to go back to my lake and tend to it. I want to see more of this country while I still can. I want to buy trinkets from you and argue over the cost. I want to sit and talk to you about Little Jenny and remember the good times I had with her. I want to meet Temperance's children and tell them the old stories the humans have forgotten.

'I know now, the person I am, and the person I want to be. Part of that is fulfilling this quest, whatever it takes, whatever the cost.'

Brackus rubbed his forehead, 'You want to slay a dragon and save a damsel?'

'I do. Promise me, Brackus.'

He sighed deeply. 'I promise, Jenny. But you must promise me to fight, not to throw your life away either. You're one of the few friends I have left, not to mention a loyal customer.'

I reached out a hand to him. 'It's a deal.'

We shook and I grinned at his glum face. 'Cheer up,' I said. 'Most likely we'll all die, then you won't have to worry about business any more.'

'There's the bright side I've been missing, Jenny,' Brackus muttered.

I sighed and lay down on the ground, drawing my cloak tightly around me. My mind wandered to the lake, less than a day's walk from where I lay. I longed to be back in the water, to twist through the shoaling fish and ride along the currents. I drifted off to thoughts of green water.

We decided to camp on Cleeve Hill for another night and spent the day going over strategy. Temperance had never wielded a knife in anger before and Brackus drilled her in a few basic manoeuvres. We agreed to go in just after sunrise on the solstice, early enough that the Erl King's human body would be sleeping.

'I'm not sure if he will truly be weaker during the day than at night,' Brackus panted, as he dodged a wild blow from Temperance, 'but since it doesn't matter to us we may as well take the chance.'

'Very well,' I said, moving out of the way of Temperance's flailing arm. 'So let's review the plan in total.'

'Again?' groaned Temperance.

'Yes, it's important,' I snapped. I settled back into my seat and began again.

'We leave here tomorrow night, taking the road north to Winchcombe, which we should reach about midnight. From there we turn east, aiming to walk into Chipping Appleby at dawn. No one should be out on the streets, but Brackus will glamour you and me, Temperance, so that no one can recognise us.'

'Or the pitchfork gang will be after us,' said Brackus under his breath. I ignored him.

'We will proceed directly to the parsonage, which is the first house past the church. It's a two-room cottage and the parson will be sleeping in the second room. We will creep in, as quietly as possible. Then you, Temperance, will stab him in the heart.'

Temperance nodded and wiped the sweat from her eyelashes.

'I'll give him this,' she stabbed the air, 'and that!'

'Very good,' said Brackus. 'It is a little harder to stab someone corporeal but you get the idea.'

'I'm sure it's much more satisfying too.' Temperance wheeled and thrust her eating knife dramatically into the air.

'That's one way of looking at it.' Brackus turned back to me. 'What about after we've defeated the Erl King?'

'Wine, revelry and song,' I said. 'What else?'

'I mean,' he added, 'what are you going to do when you've just stabbed the parson to death and the village still thinks Temperance is a witch?'

I paused to consider this. 'Maybe the influence of the Erl King will go away when we banish him. If not we can do the memory spell again.'

'And the dead parson?'

'Maybe he won't die?' said Temperance hopefully. 'Maybe once we burn the Erl King out he'll be human again.'

'Isn't that wishful thinking? You'll still have stabbed him in the chest,' I asked.

'Yes, but I still don't want to kill anyone I don't have to. Maybe I can try to heal him once the Erl King goes.' Temperance made another darting stab with her dagger. 'If not we can bury him in the woods.'

'Very well,' I said, glancing at Brackus who shrugged.

None of us slept well that night. I spent most of the few hours of darkness staring up at the stars. I had spent thousands of summer evenings like this looking up at the same sky. Some with Little Jenny, some with my own mother, now both long dead. Mostly I had spent them alone with only the inhabitants of my lake for company. I thought about those numberless nights and was glad to have Temperance and Brackus with me for what might be the last one.

The morning dawned hot and humid. The long sunlight hours dragged endlessly and we eventually set off a few hours before dusk. The road to Winchcombe wound through the edges of the Cotswold hills. The moon, almost full, rose to cast a silvery light as we walked. Cavall bounded up and down the slopes chasing rabbits and foxes. Bats swooped overhead hunting the flying insects that filled the air. Occasionally I would hear the soft thrum of wings as an owl swooped down on a mouse

The light of the moon was strong enough that even Temperance could see her way without tripping. We walked together in silence, each of us lost in our own thoughts.

I anticipated using only my nails and teeth on the Erl King if it came to a fight. Perhaps the sword would be useful too. I glanced at the others as we reached the outskirts of Winchcombe. The silver dagger was tucked neatly into Temperance's satchel. I had no idea what Brackus planned on using as a weapon. I had never even heard of goblins fighting. I hoped for my friend's sake that he had some experience.

Cavall came back to our heels as soon as we turned east towards Chipping Appleby. I patted the back of his head and he whined softly

Half a mile out from Chipping Appleby fine threads of light began to filter through the trees in the east. The coming of the dawn soothed my fractious mind. Around me I could sense the familiar signs of home. To the north of the road the Caerlee was bubbling happily away as it tumbled towards my lake. The song thrushes and blackbirds began to sing as the daylight reached their roosting places, joined soon after by nightingales and robins. The smells of the forest filled my chest as I breathed in the cool morning air, sweet and fresh. I could hear the scurrying of voles and other small creatures in the undergrowth, and in the distance the bark of a fox. A fine veil of dew coated the leaves of the trees and sparkled on the delicate spiders' webs strung between them.

I was still glamoured as a human but we didn't pass anyone on the road. That was strange. Even at this hour I would have expected to see someone: a farmer walking out to his fields, a messenger or merchant heading towards Tewkesbury. I wondered if it was a coincidence or a bad omen.

At the western edge of the village the road crossed the Caerlee. The river passed under an ancient stone bridge that had been old even when I had been new to the lake. It was built from large square blocks of rough-hewn limestone, glinting golden in the morning sunlight. Three arches supported the roadway above the glassy waters of the river. This was usually where I left the river if I was travelling north-west, up to where my daughter had lived.

We paused at the edge of the bridge.

'All right,' Brackus said, turning to Temperance and me. 'Is everyone ready? Temperance, you should take out your dagger now and I can glamour it to look like a trowel.'

He put his pack down and dug around inside it. He withdrew two long knives, each single-edged and wickedly sharp. He muttered something over them and a shimmer ran up and down each one as the glamour took hold. Temperance handed over her dagger and the goblin repeated the charm.

Temperance took the dagger back and held it in her left hand, feeling the weight of it. She passed it to her right and gripped it tight.

Brackus glanced at me. 'Are you ready, Jenny?'

I nodded, patting Cavall at my side.

Brackus straightened and brushed down his jacket, his hands adjusting the buttons and braid. Temperance unwound a ribbon from her wrist and tied her hair back.

'Whatever happens,' she said, looking at Brackus, 'please know that I am forever grateful for your help. It is an honour to have been on this quest with you.'

Brackus swept into a bow. 'Likewise, Mistress Crump.'

Temperance turned to me. 'Jenny . . .' She faltered and I saw tears gleaming in her eyes. 'You saved my life the first time we met. Since then, you have been the truest friend I have ever known. I . . .' She broke off and threw her arms around me.

I felt my eyesight blurring and nodded dumbly, patting her on the back. Her dark hair tickled my nose but I managed not to sneeze.

Temperance let go and smiled at me.

'Let's go show this pastor whose village he has been messing with,' she grinned. Brackus and I laughed.

'Lead on then, Captain!' I said.

Temperance squared her shoulders and stepped onto the

bridge. Brackus and I followed close behind her. As I drew closer
to the lake I could feel its strength flooding back to me. I realised
how weak I had been since I had left, that I had been tired and
thirsty for months. I longed to step off the bridge and jump into
the cool waters, to feel the sweet touch of the currents dancing
over my arms and legs, combing through my hair.

I focused my eyes to the front, following Temperance as she
crossed the bridge and walked towards the edge of the village.
I pulled strength from the lake, walking upright and proud. On
my left, Brackus was nervous, casting twitchy glances into the
fields and gardens on either side.

The first few houses were on the left of the road. Each of
them was closed up, the shutters still drawn down for the night;
the only sign of life a handful of scraggly chickens picking in
the dirt. Temperance paused to peer at the second house but
hurried on.

We passed through the edge of the village into the centre.
There were cottages on both sides now, cutting off a lateral
retreat. The cobbled streets were empty, the only sound that of
our own footsteps echoing back at us. It seemed too quiet to my
ears, but I had never been in Chipping Appleby at this time of
day. I glanced at Temperance, but she seemed unfazed, her eyes
looking straight ahead, her left hand wrapped in the fold of her
dress where she had hidden the alicorn dagger.

The church appeared on the left, the limestone walls gleaming
golden in the early morning light. The graveyard surrounding it
looked more unkempt than I remembered. The grass had grown
long around the mossy headstones, and the stony path that
wound to the church door was thorny with weeds.

I thought it was strange that the parson the Erl King was pretending to be had let that slide but I had no time to pursue that
thought because we were outside the parsonage.

Temperance paused long enough to check that we were still
at her side. Satisfied, she approached the door. It was broad and
sturdy, built from oak timbers and fastened by a heavy iron
latch. She muttered something under her breath and ran a hand

over the door then snatched it away as if removing a charm. She nodded at us and then lifted the latch and opened the door.

It swung open on silent hinges, revealing a dark room within. I put a hand on Temperance's shoulder and stepped past her, my bare feet quiet on the stone floor of the cottage. My eyes saw through the darkness of the interior. The room was much the same as I had seen it last. The ashes of a fire lay cold in the grate. An abandoned meal sat on the wooden table, leather boots kicked off and left untidily at the foot of a chair. I closed my eyes and listened.

The uneven rattling breath was coming from the next room. I could hear the sluggish heartbeat pumping blood. It sounded like the parson's body was asleep. No other signs of life were present in the cottage, not even the minute thrum of a mouse's heart.

I beckoned to the others and they stepped cautiously into the house. Brackus had drawn his long knives and held them out in front of him. Temperance was clutching the alicorn dagger, her knuckles white around the pearlescent hilt. They moved carefully towards me and I pointed at the bedroom.

It was even darker in the next room, and I could tell Temperance and Brackus were struggling to see. I wished for my wisplight lantern and walked into the room so my body wouldn't block the thin bands of light peeking through the window shutters.

The Erl King lay on a four-poster bed in the middle of the room. Linen drapes cast black shadows across his face, but I could tell it was the same man I had seen months ago, first at the edge of the lake, then in this very house. He seemed smaller now, wearing a faded nightshirt. Dark hair, longer since the last time I had seen him, was spread out across the pillow, and his thin mouth was relaxed in sleep.

The old rot filled my lungs, the oozy, bitter blackness rose up around me once again. I fought the urge to scream and run; the creeping wrongness of the sensation was nauseating. I froze, wrestling for control of myself. For a moment I wasn't sure if I could manage it, but I held my breath, trying to fill my head with cleaner thoughts. I set my shoulders and planted my feet firmly on the ground.

Brackus followed me, raising his knives defensively. I turned and beckoned to Temperance.

She stepped forward, placing each footfall carefully so as not to trip over anything in the darkness. I met her eyes and nodded. Temperance circled the bed, hand still clenched around the dagger. Outside the shuttered window I could hear the wind start to pick up, whistling through the gaps in the rafters.

Temperance stopped, leaning over the sleeping body of the Erl King. She held up the dagger. I could see every edge, every curve of the alicorn. She angled the blade so that it hovered directly over his chest, her arms steady and true.

I felt the wrongness again, but it was different this time. It wasn't just the innate horror of the Erl King, it was something else. It felt almost . . . familiar. I remembered back to the night I had first seen the parson for what he was. I concentrated hard, shutting my eyes and bringing back the sensation of the rain, the cold wind blowing me against the stony wall of the cottage.

I had been looking at the parson, sure that he did not know I was there. I had felt safe, secure in my power and my abilities. I had been wrong then.

I opened my mouth to protest just as Temperance brought the dagger down. She was fast, moving so quickly that the knife was a grey blur. She struck down towards the heart of the Erl King then gasped.

Her hand hovered above his chest, unmoving in the still air. She tried again, but now her hand wouldn't even rise again to strike.

'What is it?' I whispered, confused. She shook her head, baffled and scared.

'My hand is frozen,' she muttered.

'Something's wrong,' I said, rushing forward to help her retrieve the alicorn. 'I don't know what, but something is wrong here.'

Temperance looked at me, eyes wide and scared.

'Jenny,' she said, 'what . . .'

Her hand suddenly opened and the dagger fell. Another hand rose to snatch it from the air. The Erl King smiled up at us.

'Thank you, Temperance, I was looking for that.'

A rumble like a stamping giant blasted through the room. The posts of the bed shook and the floor quaked beneath my feet. I scrambled forward to pull Temperance out of the way as one of the rafters dislodged from the ceiling. The heavy pine beam fell to the floor right where she had been standing. Brackus skittered backwards as the whole room shivered and broke apart.

My vision blurred and fractured, all the heat vanishing from the room. I fought to stay upright, one arm holding Temperance so she wouldn't fall. I could no longer see Brackus or the Erl King.

Laughter shook the walls around us, low and harsh. I lashed out with the arm that wasn't holding onto Temperance, swinging wildly at nothingness.

'Well, aren't we bold,' said the laughing voice.

I spun to see where it was coming from but it seemed to echo from all around us. Something ran into my side and I almost struck it before registering the buttons and braid.

'Brackus,' I snapped, yanking him towards us.

'Jenny, Temperance,' he said, his voice high with fright. 'Can you see anything?'

I was about to answer when the low voice laughed again, and I heard the sound of hands clapping.

My eyesight stabilised. The bedroom and the cottage were gone, the illusion wiped clean from my mind. The three of us were standing in a wide empty barn. Filthy straw clogged the ground and grey sky leaked through holes in the roof.

A figure shimmered into view directly in front of us. The Erl King smiled, stretching the parson's face into a rictus grin.

Temperance recoiled so fast that her foot twisted in the straw and she sprawled to the ground. She stared at her right hand. Long black scratches were blooming on the skin, smelling of rotten flesh. I watched the Erl King's glamour peel away from her like a snakeskin and knew I must be similarly revealed.

The Erl King laughed again and sent a wave of putrefaction washing over us. I gagged, bending over at the waist from the smell.

'Give up, Mistress Crump, Master Marsh, Jenny Greenteeth. Yes, I know your names. I knew you were coming even before I saw you under the hill. Thank you for waiting there for me. It took a while to find my way through the star's labyrinth of dreams. If you had left any sooner I wouldn't have been able to mark you.'

He gestured at the scratches on Temperance's hand. 'The mind of this parson is full of all sorts of useful notions. What is that his Bible says? "Do not let your left hand know what your right hand is doing." Charming thought. It is only seemly that I should help you back to the path of the righteous.'

The Erl King snapped his fingers and a pair of human men appeared at the doorway.

'It seems that the old witch we thought we had drowned has returned. Escort her back to her old cell, would you?'

His voice was measured and polite but the whiplike air of authority cut behind every word. The men rushed to obey his orders.

Brackus ran to Temperance's side, brandishing his long knives. I stepped between Temperance and the humans, keeping my eyes on the Erl King. I stole a look at the two human men and snarled, rippling my lips back from rows of scythe-sharp teeth.

'Get back,' I hissed, infusing each syllable with all the malevolence I had buried for months.

They hesitated but kept moving. The urge to obey was clearly stronger than the threat of my fangs. I squared up, ready to take them on. Behind me Brackus had helped Temperance up and they came up to cover my flanks. Temperance was shaking but had conjured a pillar of fire in her left hand, while Brackus still held his knives, Cavall snarling at his side.

I pushed down the nausea and took a step forward. I dodged around the humans and scrambled forward on my hands and feet. I got within a few yards of the Erl King when all the strength sapped from my body. I fell to the ground, unable to move. It felt like death, like all the life in me had faded, been snatched away. The only senses left to me were sight and sound.

Footsteps came up behind me and a boot in my side rolled me over. Temperance and Brackus lay on the ground, equally pale and motionless. The Erl King smiled mirthlessly down at me.

'None of that, Jenny,' he said. 'Now I know we're going to be friends. You can expect a visit from me later—'

His voice cut off. Cavall had launched himself across the barn, burying his teeth in the parson's throat. He shook his head to and fro, trying to tear out chunks of flesh. The Erl King screeched and grabbed the hound by the scruff. He ripped Cavall away from his throat, lumps of bloody gore going with him.

He screamed, the sound warped through the tattered fragments of his neck, as the dog snapped at him. As I watched the flesh of his throat was already knitting itself back together. He grabbed at the alicorn dagger. 'Wretched hound!' the Erl King roared, spearing Cavall through the chest.

As the blade pierced him, Cavall went limp. I heard Temperance screaming as I watched in shock. The Erl King withdrew the dagger, wiping it on his side as the dog fell to the ground. I tried to reach out, to stroke the soft fur, but my limbs still refused to obey me. Cavall looked at me, pain in his eyes, and whined. I heard a distant hunting bugle, calling low and sweet and insistent. Cavall raised his head and then he was gone, leaving only the crackle of magic and the faint echo of the fae horns that had called him home.

The Erl King snapped his fingers again and someone grabbed at my feet, dragging me out of the barn. The weakness in my body persisted as I was heaved through the village. My escort paused outside another cottage, fumbling with the entrance to a cellar. He opened the doors and kicked me in. I fell awkwardly, registering the impact but feeling no pain. The cellar doors slammed above me and I was left alone in the dark.

Chapter Nineteen

I came to when the fine rays of light filtering through the planks of the cellar turned from yellow to red. The strength in my legs was coming back and I managed to pull myself upright. I peered through one of the gaps. The village was bathed in the rich orange light of a sunset. A handful of human villagers wandered along the streets: an elderly woman carrying a bucket from the well, a pair of children running past her and giggling. It all looked surprisingly normal: no broken-down buildings or kitchen gardens left fallow.

I inched a little closer to the planks, pressing my face against the spyhole. I couldn't see any trace of where Temperance or Brackus might have been taken. I watched the old woman vanish around the back of one of the cottages, thinking hard. Should I make a run for it? Head for the lake and swim downstream, putting Chipping Appleby behind me? No. I had come too far for that now. Then what to do? The alicorn knife was now in the hands of the Erl King, along with the last of our hopes. Months of preparation, of hoping against hope. Blood, sweat and tears and all of it for nothing. He had overpowered the three of us without seeming to try.

I thought of the Erl King kissing Temperance's hand in the dream that had not been a dream, the deep scratches that had vanished when we woke up. She had told me afterwards it had felt real. I should have listened to her, pushed past my own shame at having taken Brackus and left. Even now the Erl King's poison was coiling in her hand.

The red sun was sinking further to the west, shooting out its dying scarlet beams of light to silhouette the houses and trees. Last-chance territory, I thought, we're in the end of days. Can't go back, can only go forward.

I'd start by trying to find the others, scope out the lie of the land. The Erl King hadn't killed me yet. He must have some purpose, some need for a creature like myself. Maybe that need, whatever it was, could be turned against him. I was down but I wasn't out of the fight just yet.

I stepped away and began by checking over myself. No cuts or bruises anywhere on my arms or legs. I ran a hand over my head, probing for a lump where I had hit the floor. Nothing. Now that I had been standing up for a while, I realised how strong I felt; the old power of the lake was seeping back into my muscles, into the marrow of my bones. My eyesight was sharper, even my sense of smell seemed more acute. I noticed all of this and put it away in my head to think about. My renewed proximity to my lake hadn't saved me from the Erl King's illusions, and I wasn't going to trust my eyes until I'd put him in the ground.

I headed to the door and paused, my hand hovering just above the wood. I was neither glamoured nor cloaked. Then I pushed the heavy timbers, snapping the rusty deadbolt, and stepped out into the last light of the evening. I wasn't going to hide who I was any more.

The grass was warm and dry under my feet as I padded forward. The barn from last night was the closest building so I slipped in through a side door. I looked around for my pack, for anything dropped by my friends, but the barn was empty. In the centre where Cavall had fallen, there was only bloodstained straw. I crouched down and touched the ground. I remembered Creiddylad telling me his life was bound to the Wild Hunt. He'd been recalled to the Court and I knew there would be no more help coming from the high fae. We were truly alone.

I would miss him though; I'd miss him pushing his nose into whatever I was eating and sneaking up on me and making me jump. I'd never had much time for dogs before, but he'd been a good one and there was a gap in my chest that he'd wriggled his way into that felt empty now. He was safe and far away from here and that would have to do.

Pushing the thoughts of Cavall away, I left the barn. I headed south, towards the centre of the village. I walked straight-backed and proud down the middle of the road. I took a sharp left almost without noticing and found myself walking on grass again, heading down towards the shores of my lake.

Only the very embers of the daylight remained, edging the reeds in gold. The water was smooth and still and so very beautiful I caught my breath. I hurried forward, almost tripping in my haste and ran in up to my shins. The lake was cool and refreshing. I bent down to trail my fingers through the lily pads and frogbit. For a moment I forgot everything else but joy at the familiar sensation.

Someone coughed behind me. I stopped, every muscle tensing.

'I am pleased to see you, Jenny. You must have missed your lake.' The Erl King's voice was silky as the evening breeze which carried it over to me. I straightened up, still looking out over the still waters.

'A great deal,' I said, turning to face my enemy. The Erl King still wore the body of the parson, a small and neat man. He was a few inches shorter than me but from where he stood on the bank our eyes were the same level.

'I hope you are satisfied that I have kept it well for you.' He inclined the parson's face slightly towards the lake. 'I hear that you have always been particular in that regard.'

'It looks well from what I see.' My gaze flitted to the parson's hands. 'But I no longer entirely trust what my eyes tell me.'

The Erl King smiled at me. His parson's face seemed unused to the expression.

'You're a quick learner, Jenny.' He reached out a hand and beckoned me closer to him. I moved forward before my head registered the gesture. I wrested back control just as my fingers were hovering above his.

'Go on, Jenny,' he said, and I found myself resting my hand in his palm. He gripped it tight and I turned back to look at the lake.

It really did look the same; I could sense the fish swimming below the surface, the water circulating from the west to the east. I let out a long slow breath. The Erl King's hand tightened on mine and he pulled me back to face him. The placid expression of the parson was gone, replaced by dark burning eyes and a twisted smile. Teeth glinted white as bone and the sense of putrefaction was all around me. I cringed backwards but the Erl King held me fast.

'Eyes open, Jenny,' he hissed, his voice a death rattle. 'This time you will not run.'

I forced my breathing to slow, to quieten the thumping of my rabbit heart. I opened my eyes and met his gaze, as steadily as I could. He grinned horribly at me.

'Such courage from a little naiad, Jenny. I confess I had not expected it. The Rhinemaidens fled from my path when I crossed over their river and even the old fathers of the Tigris could not stand against me in the old days of their majesty. Yet you, a low sprite from the merest drizzling creek in some backwoods island.' He tightened his grip, nails digging into my skin. 'Where did you find that spirit, Jenny?'

I hated hearing my name in his mouth, my mother's name, my daughter's name, but I tried not to flinch.

'This is my place,' I said, trying to keep my voice steady. 'You came to my place and started threatening my people.'

'Your people, Jenny? From what I hear you've been terrorising this village longer than me.'

'Hear from who?' I shot back.

'Your tinker friend and I have been having a most productive conversation.' The Erl King smiled again. 'The witch hasn't been quite so chatty but perhaps you can bring her around.'

There was something wrong around his eyes; the skin was

slipping a little, revealing the scarlet flesh beneath. I blinked hard and clenched my spare fist to keep it by my side.

'Have you hurt them?' I hissed.

'Now why should I do that, Jenny?' he tutted. 'The pursuit of pain has never been a vice of mine. The inevitable end result of pain, perhaps, but the process ... It has always seemed unnecessarily messy to me.'

'You swear they have not been harmed?' I pressed, taking a step forward despite myself.

'Well, not at my request. They may have incurred a few minor injuries. There was, I believe, a scuffle.'

He pronounced 'scuffle' with amusement, wrinkling his nose to spit out the word and smirked at me. I felt my nails begin to dig into my palm and forced myself to loosen my fist.

'I need to see them.'

'Don't believe me? I never lie, Jenny. Isn't that part of my legend? Lying is a mortal defect, for humans and low fae such as yourself.' The Erl King raised a finger and prodded at the loose skin under his eyes. 'You may see them later if you like. Once we have finished this conversation you may go where you will.'

I snorted. 'You'd let me go free?'

'You are no threat to me, Jenny. I have no wish to confine you.' He let go of my hand and waved behind me towards the lake. 'When first we sparred, right here at the water's edge, you could match my strength, but I was weak then. Now I could knock you aside without a pause. I already have.'

He smiled in a way that he clearly thought benevolent and flourished his left hand. The alicorn knife appeared in his grip. I lunged for it, intent on stabbing it into his smug face but he only laughed and skipped back.

'Steady, Jenny! And we were having such a nice chat.' The Erl King pointed the dagger at me and I felt my legs go weak again, the strength draining from me.

'It's a powerful little trinket, this knife,' he said, tilting it slightly. 'You could do some damage with this. Maybe not kill me entirely but certainly cast me out of this mortal form and knock me out of the game for a few generations.'

'What game?' I snarled, teetering a little on feet that were going numb.

'The Game, Jenny. Dark versus light. Life, growth, sunshine and flowers on one side, and on the other?' He grinned horribly, the parson's face almost totally lost now. 'Me. And you for that matter. All the dark things that crawl and kill and rot. That's why you're here having this conversation with me, because you and I, we are alike.'

I recoiled so violently that I tripped over and splashed down in the shallow waters of the lake.

'I'm nothing like you. I'm here to fight you,' I said, filling my tone with as much vehemence as I could summon.

The Erl King squatted down before me.

'Killing comes naturally to you, doesn't it? Even now you're thinking about how to kill me. Is that a naturally "good" aspect of your personality, do you think? Come now, there is no one else here to deceive. Perhaps you thought you could play at being good for a while, perhaps you even convinced your friends. But we both know that they'll never fully trust you.' I flinched at that and he winked at me. 'And they'd be fools to. You are what you are, what you were made to be.'

'I know who I am,' I shot back, scrambling for a response. 'I might not be perfect but I'm nothing like you. I'm not good but I'm not all the way bad.'

The Erl King laughed again and stood up.

'Who told you that? A half-rotten apple is a rotten apple. Things are either one thing or another. Don't be so picky, Jenny. We all must be as we are made. Come, walk with me.' He turned and began to head up the slope. I scrambled to my feet and followed, warily keeping myself between him and my lake. It was darker now, the sun having slipped beyond the western woods. But my eyes could still see the path of the Erl King as he walked around the lake, heading towards the eastern banks.

'When we first met, Jenny, I'll own that I was not at my best.

Your witch friend's survival and subsequent memory spell came as rather a shock to me. I was vaguely aware that there was something in the lake, but I had assumed that it was merely a nixie. The idea that something like yourself was living there had not occurred to me. Still more of a surprise was that you had not eaten the witch.'

He paused to allow me to catch up, 'She wasn't to your taste, eh?' He grinned, starlight glinting on bone-white teeth, then carried on.

'When I found myself fending off an unexpectedly powerful bit of magic with the same flavour as the hedge witch, I was rather confused. I threw my own strength at it, would have extinguished her power totally, had you not covered her with your water magic. Then the pair of you vanished.

'I knew you were up to something when I sensed you under the hill. I knew you would return, having cooked up some scheme.'

He bent to pick up a pebble and skimmed it across the lake. 'I was pleased to see you again.'

'Why? Why would you want me to come back?' I asked, watching the ripples die away. 'To bring back Temperance?'

'The hedge witch?' The Erl King scoffed. 'I hardly think so; that one knows nothing of her heritage. The humans here have lost all connection to the land. No, I need someone who has been here longer than anyone. Someone who knows the secrets this village holds.'

I frowned at him. 'Chipping Appleby? It's a bend in the road. It's never been important to anyone who doesn't live here.'

'Don't play dumb, Jenny,' he snapped. 'If it is so insignificant then why would I be here? Why would you be here? One of the last Jenny Greenteeths in the country. Do you think you survived this long by chance? Your hedge witch friend, do you think they all have that kind of raw power? Even your little goblin assistant, do you think he returned here so often out of friendship?'

I shrank back and he laughed at me.

'Your Chipping Appleby is a seat of power. One that has been carefully removed from the histories and myths to keep its secrets safe. And you, Jenny Greenteeth, you are going to help me take that power.'

'Why would I do that?' I asked. 'Even if what you're saying is true, you've invaded my home, tried to kill my friends. Why would I ever do anything but spit in your face?'

'Because I can offer you something that they can't.' The Erl King leaned in and grinned at me again, 'Peace, prosperity and another daughter. One that won't needlessly die young.'

My retort died in my throat. His word caught at my mind like a thorn.

'What do you mean "needlessly"?' I whispered.

'Well, with all the power of this place there's no reason why you should keep all the benefits for yourself. I can show you how to divide it, to give both you and your new daughter all the power and long life you need; and when the time comes I can create another lake upstream for her.'

'I only have what the river brings me. It may never bring me another child,' I said, my voice rasping.

'Don't humans breed like rabbits? I can bring you a dozen and you can take your pick.' He chuckled, 'Why limit yourself to one? You can have all the daughters you want, a regular little family of Jennys, freed from want and age and death.'

I saw my daughter's face in my head. I saw her duplicated, triplicated. A laughing family of happy, green-skinned girls smiling at me with their needle-sharp teeth. The image bit like a knife sliding between my ribs, straight to my heart.

'So, Jenny.' The Erl King had stopped and was standing, hands in his pockets. 'What do you think? Will you stay here and help me with a few little things and buy the future you've always dreamed of? Or will you jump in the water and swim away?' He gestured to the end of the lake, where the Caerlee flowed east towards Oxford.

I took a step towards the water, eying him as I did so. He didn't move.

'Go on, Jenny, it's your choice. Family or lonely freedom.'

I took another step, dipping my toe into the edge of the lake. The Erl King stayed where he was. He was really willing to let me go.

I thought about the darkness in his eyes, the image of the rotting forest. I tried hard to picture Temperance and Brackus but their faces kept slipping away from me, replaced by my daughter's, by the dream I had seen under the hill in Wales.

I turned back to the Erl King.

'What would I have to do?' I asked.

A human woman slid a pair of rough earthenware goblets onto the table and scuttled back, keeping a wary eye on me. From across the table the Erl King smirked and reached for one of the cups.

'Thank you, mistress,' he said to the woman who was now pressing herself to the wall as far as she could get from me.

'Yes, thank you,' I said, tilting my own cup in her direction before sipping. The wine was strong and well spiced. I ran the unusual flavours around my mouth before swallowing. The Erl King had brought me to a large house in the centre of the village. I had caught a glimpse of scared-looking children in the loft as I had been shown to my seat by the mistress of the house. A sturdy looking man I vaguely recognised had brought in an armful of neatly chopped wood and built up a fire before shepherding his children back out into the night. I wondered where they would stay now that their house was occupied.

'Do you like the wine, Jenny?' The Erl King's voice scratched at my thoughts. I took another sip and nodded.

'Paltry stuff, but the mortals value it, and it is useful to demand that which they treasure.' He drained his cup and snapped his fingers. The woman detached herself from the wall and hurried to refill it. He caught her arm as she tried to step away.

'Bring us another bottle.'

She trembled as he looked at her.

'Sir, there's no more left. You've cleaned out the village.'

The Erl King tightened his grip and she winced in pain.

'I – I think there's some communion wine somewhere,' she said, clearly trying not to stutter.

'There's a good girl,' he said, releasing her arm. The woman fled the cottage.

'Well then,' he said, once the woman had gone. 'I expect you must be longing to understand exactly what it is I am trying to accomplish here. I'm afraid that you must be patient with me; a life as long as mine must take a while to tell.

'I came into being many thousands of years ago, when a group of nomads broke off from their tribe and called a new god into being. For a long time I stayed there, fighting with the other spirits, accepting mortal sacrifices. The humans moved often and I moved with them, snapping at their heels with sickness and death to keep the offerings flowing. I had children, nine strong sons and nine dark daughters, creatures you would call high fae.

'As the nomads grew in number and strength they spread out, moving across the great eastern continent, through deserts, plains and ice forests. As they went I found myself splintering, losing aspects of myself with each group. Each fracture left me weaker than before and my children left one by one to follow their own peoples.

'Finally, I took my last daughter and headed towards the setting sun. We settled in a dark forest at the western end of the steppes and established ourselves in the minds of the people living there. For hundreds of years we strengthened our hold over the tribes, feeding on the sacrifices they gave to the woods, as well as the bloodshed from the constant fighting. My daughter grew strong in her own right and moved south, to establish her own place. Occasionally I would even reunite with my other children as they followed an invading horde west, but they would always return eventually, leaving the western forests bloodied and quiet.'

The Erl King paused and took another long draught of the wine. He regarded me over the brim of the cup.

'If everything was so wonderful in the forests, what are you doing here?' I asked.

'The magic began to die from the forests. I imagine you have seen it here, the fading of the mythic beasts, the ending of the old ways. It began in the heart of civilisation, in the cities of Samarkand and Baghdad, then spread out like lye in the rivers. When the dark forests grew silent, I knew it was time to leave.

'So I journeyed west, following the setting sun to the edge of civilisation. I had heard of your little tribal island, always war-torn and full of strange creatures. I knew that I could establish myself here, at the heart of the British magic. And here I am.'

'In Chipping Appleby?' I queried, surprised.

The Erl King grinned at me again. 'You really don't remember, do you? Chipping Appleby, such a sweet little name for a sweet little village. Chipping means market, did you know that? The market in the apple trees.'

I shrugged, nonplussed. The woods around the village were full of apple trees, though none of the mortals tended them any more. I even vaguely remembered hearing the old residents of the village using the word 'chipping'.

'I suppose that makes sense,' I said, not sure where this was leading.

'The best place to hide something is in plain sight,' said the Erl King. 'What better place to hide a place of great importance than a place of no importance. Can you think of nowhere that might be hidden?'

I frowned, still not understanding. Why was the Erl King so fixated on Chipping Appleby? The heart of British magic would be Avalon, but that had been lost for centuries.

My jaw dropped. Avalon. I remembered my old language now. Avalon, Abbalon. The isle of apple trees. . A place hidden in plain sight.

'Avalon,' I whispered. The Erl King nodded gravely.

'Avalon is here, and therefore so am I.' He finished his goblet and put it down on the table, leaning towards me. 'I am going to harness the power of Avalon. That is how I will establish my hold on this island and build my final kingdom. That is how I can grant you your heart's desire.'

'What do you mean, establish your hold?' I asked, still reeling from his revelation.

'I mean, bring back the wild places, the low and high fae. Grasp the Wild Roads and tie them more closely to this realm. Rule as the new lord of the forests.' He looked at me. 'Nothing that would upset a Jenny.'

'What about the mortals?'

'There will always be mortals. I shall bring them back to the old ways; blood sacrifices, castles and chieftains. This island at the edge of the world, how easily it can slip back into darkness. In a few dozen years no one on the continent will even remember it. Your witch will have to go, but others like her will spring up. Perhaps life will even be better for them.

'All I need from you is the centre of Avalon. At the crux point, the source of Britain, there is a well. It has been lost to time ever since Arthur found his rest there. He lies dreaming, surrounded by his knights. There I will make my sacrifice and draw night back across this land. So tell me, Jenny, do you know where it is? Will you show me?'

I swallowed hard, trying to think. That left the second question.

This whole fight had been doomed from the beginning, bringing nothing but blood and pain. We had been fools to think that we could defeat the Erl King by force of arms. I had been playing at being human, drifting away from who and what I really was. I wasn't the hero of any story, certainly not this one.

I stared at the floor, thinking of Temperance and Brackus. There was nothing I could do for them now. I had to be sensible, to make the least bad choice, I just didn't know what that was.

I thought of the journey across Britain, Gwyn's fading court, the last Afanc, the dying unicorn. I remembered my daughter's face.

In my mind I saw the future the Erl King had promised, tinged green and gold.

'Yes,' I said.

Chapter Twenty

I spent the night curled up in a corner of the room, a worn rag rug wrapped around my shoulders. I had known without asking that I would not be allowed back to the lake. For all the Erl King's talk of a choice it was clear that he would not be letting me leave before I showed him the well. He remained in the chair, occasionally refilling his wine glass.

I lay on the floor, staring across the room into the hearth fire as it fell into dying embers. Memories of the old world were coming back to me. Much of what he had said to me was familiar, as if hearing the words had undone some mental lock, revealing hidden knowledge I had shuttered away.

I had come to Chipping Appleby a few years before the death of Arthur, when it had still been known as Avalon. I remembered the fight, the last battle of the civil war that had ended with his passing.

The exact details were still vague and shimmering in my mind but I remembered Merlin, that greatest of wizards. He had cast a spell that had removed all memory of Avalon's previous incarnation, turning it into the small village it had been ever since. The knowledge of the heart of the kingdom had been washed from the fabric of the world, leaving even the high fae ignorant as to its whereabouts.

Now with the Erl King's words it had returned. I probed back through my memories, like a tongue worrying at a loose tooth. I remembered standing at the well, remembered speaking with Merlin. Try as I might though, I could not think how to reach the place. Merlin's words were achingly close, I could hear the rumbling voice, see the candlelight playing over his face.

I watched the last of the logs glow, and breathed in the bitter smell of woodsmoke while turning the uncovered memories over in my head. When I was not remembering the past I was worrying for the future. The Erl King was a being of true evil, but I sensed that he had been honest with me, to an extent. I tormented myself with doubts for hours but when the dawn light filtered through the shutters I could see no other path.

The new day was announced with a knock on the door from the burly man who had brought the logs yesterday. He came in, bearing a tray of scones. The Erl King dismissed him with a snap of his long fingers and began pushing the food into his mouth. As I stood up and wandered over he pointedly did not offer me one.

'So, Jenny,' he said, through a mouthful of pastry. 'Any luck processing those memories of yours?'

'I almost have it,' I said, watching stray flakes flutter from his lips. 'I remember knowing where it is. I think if I just walk around the village I might be able to find it.'

He shrugged and brushed away crumbs. 'As you like. You may wander freely on open land but stay out of the water and the woods. My magic will restrict you if you try to leave without permission.'

I nodded. 'What about my friends? I must have your word that they will be unharmed.'

The Erl King put down his plate. 'The goblin will stay confined in the anchorage cells until you have completed your tasks. The witch, well . . .' He leaned back and looked at me. 'The witch is another matter.'

A cold weight settled around my throat. 'What do you mean?' I snapped at him.

He smiled at me, 'Well, I am a parson after all. I shall not suffer a witch to live. My village congregation would accept no less.'

'Don't be ridiculous,' I said, my heart beginning to pound. 'You were the one who whipped them into that frenzy to begin with. You charmed them.'

'Only a little,' said the Erl King. 'They were surprisingly easy to convince, even for humans. And that is beside the point. A witch born at Avalon is a threat that cannot be tolerated. She could disrupt my spell.'

'So keep her locked up! She couldn't escape last time, she would have drowned if I hadn't rescued her.'

'Which is exactly why we are having this conversation, Jenny. You caused this mess, you will clean it up.'

I gaped at him. 'What do you mean?'

'I mean that you are going to take your witch friend and throw her in the lake.' He held up a finger. 'But this time there will be no rescue – you're going to slit her pretty neck first. You're going to do the job properly.'

'Absolutely not!' I hissed. 'Temperance is my friend. I'm not going to kill her.'

'Either you can do it or I can do it myself; and I warn you, Jenny, if I have to do it then it won't just be the witch going in the water. It'll be her husband and children too.'

I froze, yearning to snarl back at him, to close my sharp teeth around his throat. I could almost taste the blood on my tongue, hot and savoury. My mouth watered and I nearly sprang. The Erl King watched me, the slightest twitch of amusement in his expression, as if waiting to see if I would lose my composure.

'Did you think you'd all live happily together, Jenny? Mortals and fae will never mix. You'll have your new daughters, her family will be fine, and your beloved pike will have a good meal.'

I looked at the Erl King. He was no longer even attempting to hide his smile. I realised that as much as he wanted me to obey him, another part of him wanted me to fight, wanted me to have to stand in the stocks whilst he murdered Temperance and her family and threw them in the lake. I floundered for a solution, a way out, but I was too panicked to think of any. I thought of Ursula and Josiah and I knew what Temperance would want, even if I couldn't ask her. I buried my feelings and made my face a stone.

'As you want,' I said, fighting to keep my tone calm. 'Today?'

He wrinkled his nose as if disappointed. 'Let's not linger over it, shall we? Get it over with this morning and then I shall let you go looking for the well.' He snapped his fingers again and the burly man reappeared at the door. 'Cecil here will escort you to the cells. Don't glower at me like that, Jenny, this is all for the best. And don't go thinking you can trick me, I have dozens of eyes in this village and all of them will be watching you. Waiting for blood.'

I dropped my gaze and fled the house.

Cecil seemed afraid to meet my eyes and hurriedly led me through the village. I already knew where the anchorage cells were located, tucked in at the south end of the church, but I let him walk ahead. There was something in his face that said the Erl King could see through his eyes, like a worm coiled in his brain. I didn't want to make anything worse for him.

The village was as silent as it had been the night before, the only movement an early morning breeze rustling through the wildflowers that clumped on the side of the road. We skirted the edge of the church, reaching the small anchorage cells. I placed a hand on the cool golden limestone.

'These were built as a place of faith,' muttered Cecil. 'Not of captivity.'

I looked at him again, surprised by this outburst.

'All things change,' I rasped at him. He fumbled with a set of keys and unlocked the left cell.

Temperance lay slumped at the foot of the far wall. Her hair was tangled and dirty. Tears stained her face. Her wrists and ankles were bound with clumsy iron weights. Beneath the manacles I could see her skin had been rubbed red and raw. Her right hand was blackened, something dark twisted beneath the skin: the Erl King's mark.

'Temperance,' I whispered, staggered by how she looked. I had expected cuts and bruises but the dead stare in her eyes scared me more than the Erl King in his fury.

She looked up at me. 'Jenny, you're here.' She struggled to
her feet and shuffled towards me. I stepped forward and caught
her before she fell. As I held her up I could smell blood from her
wrists, feel the shaking in her bones. She squeezed my hand, and
I felt the strength that I had come to depend on these last months.

'Thank heavens you're alive. Are you hurt? What's happened?
The last thing I remember is you being dragged out of the
barn.' Temperance pulled back to look me in the face. 'Where
is Brackus?'

Behind me I could feel the gaze of the Erl King burning out
through Cecil's eyes. My fingers tightened around her arms.

'I'm so sorry,' I said, staring intently into her face. 'This is the
only way to save them.' Her brown eyes widened and I willed
her to understand, to absolve me of what I had to do. She met my
gaze, a wrinkle of confusion appearing between her eyebrows.
Her eyes flitted over my shoulder to where Cecil stood, fidgeting
nervously with his keys.

'Jenny?' Temperance said, her gaze darting back to meet
mine. I watched as the realisation bled into her face, that this
time I had not come here to rescue her. She shook her head and
tried to back away but I held my grip, holding her fast.

'No, Jenny, please,' she whispered. I closed my eyes so I
wouldn't have to see her face.

'Jenny, Jenny Greenteeth.' Temperance was still talking.
'Please, it's me, it's me. Look at me, whatever he said I know who
you are! It'll be all right. Look at me!'

I opened my eyes; I owed her that much. Then I growled
at her, letting my lips ripple back, revealing row upon row of
pointed teeth. Temperance gasped and began to shriek.

'What have you done? You've betrayed us! How could you, I
knew I never should have trusted you.' Temperance reached up
to claw my face, hissing and spitting. I grabbed the back of her
head, winding my fingers through her hair to grip the collar of
her coat. Then I turned and began to drag her out of the cell.

From the second cell I could hear Brackus yelling. His screams
interwove with Temperance's, boring into my head so that I

wanted to sit down with my hands over my ears and sob. I kept going.

I was as gentle as I could be but Temperance fought like a wildcat. She dug her heels in, kicking and screaming at me. It was only a short way to the edge of the lake but with all the fight Temperance was giving it felt like miles. I glimpsed humans peeking out of houses as I passed but none interfered. I wondered where Temperance's family were; if they even knew she had come back to them. I hoped they were out of earshot.

I hauled Temperance from the road into the long grass that surrounded the lake. She stumbled and swore loudly, cursing my mother for a fool who should have drowned me rather than let me live.

As we neared the water, she let loose an unearthly howl, throwing herself at me. I staggered, trying to fend her off without hurting her. I saw Cecil running after us, slipping a long knife from its sheath.

I had to be quick to grab Temperance's arms and hurry her down to lake before the Erl King could decide to take over. I splashed forward, going in up to my shins. The water curdled around us, sediment swirling up around my feet.

Cecil lingered on the shore, clearly unwilling to get his boots wet. Temperance continued to shriek and thrash cursing me in truly acrobatic foul language.

I stole a look back at where Cecil was waiting, searching for an easier way, any other way. He smiled back at me, and I knew I had the Erl King's attention. I had to do this.

Gripping Temperance's shoulder, I took a deep breath and stepped behind her. 'I'm sorry,' I whispered and drew my sword. The hilt felt hot in my grip as I raised it to her throat. She grabbed at her neck, the iron handcuffs jingling.

For a moment I almost lost my nerve, wavering as to whether I could do this. As if she felt my hesitation Temperance renewed her struggle, opening her mouth for a final scream. I slashed the blade in a single fluid motion. Blood spurted forward, a bright scarlet arterial spray that spattered on the lake water.

Her scream cut off and she fell limply against me. I threw her forward, so that she fell face first into the lake. Her body arced perfectly downwards, landing with a splash. She lay motionless in the water, her long dark hair fanning out around her. I pressed a foot into the small of her back, driving her deeper as the water turned red with her blood. Then I pushed her body away with my foot, shifting the currents so that she was dragged down, into the centre of the lake, sinking out of view. I could sense the shape of her as she descended through the water, unmoving but for the blood that continued to flow.

I replaced the sword in its scabbard then turned and waded back to shore, trembling and nauseous. I tripped and fell forward, landing on my hands and knees in the mud. Tears splashed into the mire, as I howled in grief. When there was no more breath left in me I looked up, my bloodstained hands still shaking. The Erl King flashed a twisted grin at me through Cecil's face and then his presence vanished, leaving the poor man staggering and weak. I lurched to my feet and looked back out at the lake, now calm and smooth again. I dunked my hands in the water and let the blood swirl away from me. The sword in its scabbard dragged in the water. I sneaked a quick look at Cecil, still doubled over and wheezing, then ripped the sword belt off and flung it into the water. Cecil glanced up at the sound of the splash but I glared at him and strode past, heading up the bank and back to the village.

 Chapter Twenty-One

I wandered the village, lost inside my head, trying to black out the thoughts of Temperance. Each turn seemed to bring back old memories, blurred faces brought back into focus. I remembered the first time I had come to Avalon, leaving the lake I had grown up in with my mother. I had arrived at night, swimming upstream like a salmon until I had reached where the Caerlee widened into a lake. The river had surrounded Avalon on three sides back then, making it appear an island to those who approached. I had been heading further to the north, to where a sprite had told my mother that there was a village that had dug a new millpond. I had intended only to pause for the night at Avalon, but by the time morning came I knew that I had found my home.

For those first few years I had stayed undisturbed in the lake. I had seen humans coming back and forth along the banks, though they had never disturbed me. I brought up the memory of Merlin's face, trying to remember the night we had met. He had appeared one evening, standing at the southern edge of the lake. I remembered the smell of blood that had clung to him, the grime that had covered his face. The memory was fragmented but I could see him standing on the shores and then somewhere else, a cave lit only by a glowing sphere of magic. He had said something to me then but I could not regain the words. It must have been a memory spell, maybe one of the last enchantments he had ever done. The echoes of it held me firm even now.

I lifted a hand to stroke the trunk of a wizened apple tree. Though it seemed ancient, these trees were the grandchildren of the grandchildren of the ones that I had walked under in my youth. Behind me Cecil coughed. I ignored the sound. He'd been following me all morning, traipsing a few steps behind as I wandered through my memories. I still couldn't frame the image of the well at the centre of Avalon. I could almost picture it, but as I tried to focus it slipped away.

I frowned and reached up to pluck an apple from the laden branches overhead. It smelt a little ripe for my taste so I threw it to Cecil. He caught it gracefully and inspected it suspiciously before biting. I picked a greener apple and sat down at the base of the tree. I considered whether to risk talking to Cecil. The ease with which he had caught the apple suggested that the Erl King wasn't piggybacking inside his head. I decided against it and chomped into my apple. The hard fruit gave way to something soft.

I examined the fruit. It was riddled with small maggoty grubs. I began to pick them out, tossing each into my mouth. Their flesh was sweet from consuming the apple. I pulled out a longer worm and slurped down the moist flesh with gusto. A gasp of horror came from my left and I looked up to catch Cecil staring at me in horror, his own half-eaten apple forgotten in one hand.

I smirked at the expression on his face. It was pleasant to be unabashedly inhuman for a change. Temperance had . . . I threw up a wall around that thought. I dropped the apple, the maggots spilling out on the ground.

I scrambled up and began to run, scuttling through the village on all fours. I could hear Cecil lumbering along behind me as I dodged back onto the main street. I vaulted the wall into the graveyard, landing in the soft green grass. The church loomed ahead of me and something else clicked into place. I could feel the power of the ground swelling underneath my feet. I remembered Temperance's spell, circling around the churchyard boundaries.

I had assumed that was the holy ground. I had been right, but the source of that blessing had been far older than the church. A perfect hiding place.

Cecil staggered into the graveyard as I made for the church doors.

'Wait!' he shouted, red-faced and panting. He blocked my path. 'You can't go in there.'

I tried to slip past him, but he stepped to meet me.

'This is the place,' I hissed at him, irritated. He met my eyes, clearly determined not to let me into the church. I hopped backwards and waited. Sure enough, within a moment, I saw the shadow of the Erl King move behind his eyes.

'Is this the place, Jenny?' he said to me through Cecil's mouth. I nodded.

'I think it's inside. I think I can find it.'

The Erl King nodded with Cecil's head. 'Wait there, I will come now.' His presence faded and Cecil stood there trembling. I stepped back to give him some space.

The Erl King appeared in the distance, hurrying down the road, the parson's black hat pulled down over his face. Cecil went to open the gate into the churchyard. The Erl King swept in without sparing him a look.

'You have remembered?' he said to me, his dark eyes boring into mine.

'Yes, this is the place. I think the entrance is hidden inside, underground.'

'That would be prudent of them. Do you remember where?'

I shrugged. 'I can sniff it out, but we will have to search.'

The Erl King snapped his fingers and Cecil moved to open the church door. I recognised the edge of distress in his face; he really did not want us to enter the church. I wondered if it was the echoes of the magic that had hidden the place, or if he merely objected to such cursed creatures entering onto holy ground.

I followed the Erl King into the church. It was cool and dark after the summer heat, and my eyes took a moment to adjust. I had never stepped inside the church before; it had been built a

few hundred years after the Norman invasion. There was a small
clutch of candles burning on the altar, casting long flickering
shadows on the wall. Faded tapestries showing the stations of the
cross hung on the walls, the woven faces of the saints looking
down at rough-hewn pews. I walked tentatively down the aisle,
my feet quiet on the smooth cold flagstones.

To the side of the main church was a small side chapel, opposite the block that housed the anchorite cells. In the centre was
a large font, carved from blocks of limestone. The Erl King followed me in up to the font, and trailed his fingers through the
holy water. He flicked droplets at me.

'Well, you had better start looking,' he said.

I turned to the walls, trying to sharpen my memories. There
was a faint breeze coming from the main doors but beneath that
was the barest draught, gliding over my feet. It seemed to be
coming from the side chapel.

I crouched down, tracing the edges of the wide flagstones,
worn smooth by the passage of generations of feet. I could feel
the eyes of the Erl King boring into me as I scrabbled around,
trying each stone to see if it was loose. None of them moved
easily, each secure against their neighbours. I contemplated
sending for a tool and trying to lever them up, but it seemed too
forceful. If there was a way in, then it would be subtler.

I continued to squat there, leaning back on my ankles and
chewing thoughtfully on my lip. My eyes flicked to the font.
I looked at it critically then dropped my eyes. Strange, it was
almost difficult to look at it directly. I turned my head to look
again and found my gaze sliding off to the side.

There was definitely something unusual about the font. I kept
my eyes on the floor and reached out with my hands, feeling the
carved limestone pillars that supported the bowl. They were
cold, even in the cool of the church, the stone pulling the heat
from my palms. I remembered something my mother had said
to me once, about limestone being magical. A rock made from
the bones of living creatures, with all the power and energy
trapped inside.

My right hand touched something strange. On the inside of the column, between smooth arches and spirals, there was a small nugget of rock. I ran my fingers over it. The blob was egg-shaped, pointed at one end and with a fine ridge coming from the other that curled back on itself. The pads of my fingers felt tiny semi-circles carved into the top.

I grinned to myself as I realised what it was. A stone fish, tucked into the back of the font. I stroked the back of the fish. As I did so I could feel the rock pulling at me, asking for something, whether magic or a password I didn't know.

I dropped my hand and stood up.

'It's here,' I said, turning to the Erl King. 'Put your hand inside, you can feel the carved fish. That's the key.'

He looked at me lazily. 'Go on then.'

'I don't know how to open it. I think it wants power.'

'Try,' he said silkily. 'This is your place, it shouldn't take too much effort from you.'

I knelt down again and stroked the fish. This time when the pull came I fed it, opening a barrier inside myself and letting the lake flow through me. I felt the fish twitch underneath my fingers then swim forward through the stone. It circled the column, darting through the carved buttresses and spirals. It swam up into the stone bowl, coming up above the water-line and circling around to the rim. The fish circled the rim of the bowl three times, still pulling at the magic of the lake through me.

After the third circle it stopped and sank into the stone. I felt the flow of magic stop and leaned in to try and see what was happening. For a moment everything was silent and then the whole font began to glow. The stone was changing colour, grad-uating from pale gold to purest white. As it changed it began to split apart and grow, unfurling like the petals of a rosebud and then melting into the floor. Where the font had stood was now a wide circle of pale crystal, shooting out veins of calcite into the surrounding flagstones. In the centre was a dark hole, leading down into the earth.

I stepped towards it, already reaching out a hand to lower myself in when I felt a cold grip on my shoulder.

'Wait,' said the Erl King. I hesitated. Letting the Erl King into such an ancient and sacred place felt heretical. But I had done so much already, walked down this path too far to balk at this. I stepped back and let him pass.

He released my shoulder and swept forward. Without turning his head, he crooked a finger at Cecil who grabbed a candlestick from the side of the chapel and hurried forward. The Erl King took the candle and held it out in front of him. He let go and the lighted candle hovered in mid-air. The flame flickered as if in a draught as it began, slowly, to descend into the darkness.

From where I stood I couldn't see much but the Erl King's face twitched with pleasure and he beckoned Cecil closer. He pointed a bony finger into the opening and Cecil sat down and began to lower himself into the gap. For a moment I was concerned that the passage would be too deep for him to reach but then the sound of boots hitting rock emerged and Cecil called up.

'It's not too deep,' he called. 'And there's a passageway, leading south I think.' His head popped back to the surface. 'There are steps carved into the wall, it should be easy enough to get down. Should I keep going?'

The Erl King shook his head. 'Time enough for that. Leave the candle there and come back up. I will summon someone to guard the entrance. Tonight we shall perform the ritual.'

Cecil clambered back out and scuttled back to his post at the wall.

The Erl King turned to me. 'Well done, Jenny. Your task is complete. You may return to the house. When I have come into my power I will fulfil my promise.'

I paused, not wanting to leave him now. 'Is there nothing else I could do? I would rather stay and help if I can.'

He considered, staring at me with narrow, dark eyes. 'Very well. Rest now. I will send for you at the appropriate time.'

*

I watched the night fall on from the roof of one of the cottages. The sweltering sunshine had broken to a damp, grey heat that was even more unbearable. I'd climbed up through the thatch for a last moment of reflection, to try and get the order of things straight in my head.

I kicked my foot at the thatch, releasing a cloud of dust that made me sneeze. I wished more than anything that I could talk to Temperance and Brackus. The last months of travelling had made me dependent on companionship, undoing a thousand years of staunch silence. I rubbed at my nose, wondering for the hundredth time whether Brackus was all right. He was still locked up in the anchorite cells, injured and weak. If I could write, I could have left a note for him. Alas I had never learnt, and didn't dare talk to any of the villagers. I doubted the Erl King was possessing them all at once but it was unlikely my trying to make conversation with them would go unnoticed.

Too late to worry about that now. I picked up a reed and began to clean the grime out from under my nails, wiping the gunk onto the thatch beside me. Satisfied, I filed my thumbnail against a small whetstone I had found downstairs. I honed the talon to a point, tapping the edge against my other hand until it was sharp enough to draw blood. I moved on to my other nails, methodically sharpening and tapping. The task required enough of my concentration that I was able to block out everything else. By the time all ten nails had been filed to dagger-like edges my heart rate had slowed, my racing mind had quietened.

I inspected my hands, flexing each joint and tendon out in front of me in the grey twilight. Time to forget about Temperance, about Brackus, about the world outside Chipping Appleby. Time to remember what I had almost forgotten about myself, since Temperance had fallen into my life.

I wasn't a human, nor a goblin, nor a high fae. I was Jenny Greenteeth, fangs and claws and unholy strength. I was a nightmare, a scary story, the dark shape glimpsed through the weeds.

Below me, the few villagers that had been on the street were beginning to scuttle back inside. Across the way I could see

Cecil coming out of his house, turning to hold the door open. I scrambled to the edge of the roof and climbed down. I padded over to the church and leaned against the wall. A pair of broad-shouldered farmers came around the corner lugging a large wooden chest between them. The closer of the two froze when he saw me, not moving even when his companion knocked the chest into him.

'Allow me,' I said, pushing open the heavy church door to let them past. They looked at each other then back up the road, clearly trying to decide whether it was better to go past me or to risk the Erl King's displeasure. I could see the muscles in their arms twitching at the weight of the chest and eventually they edged past me, eager to put down their burden. I followed them into the church. Since the last time I had been here some-one had come in and lit batches of smooth beeswax candles all along the aisle and behind the altar. The flickering light made the place seem warmer. The farmers turned to the left into the side chapel, where a nervous-looking teenager was shifting from foot to foot. He was trying not to look at the tunnel entrance that yawned beneath him and gave a small yelp as he saw me follow the farmers into the chapel.

The second farmer told him to head home, and he edged past me, vanishing out of the church at astonishing speed. The farmers dropped the chest onto the stone floor with audible relief. They eyed me suspiciously and moved around to keep the comforting bulk of the chest between us. I resisted the urge to roll my eyes at them and turned to peer down into the tunnel. Candles had been placed at the foot of the initial shaft. The candlelight illuminated rough steps carved into the limestone, worn smooth by the touch of numberless hands. The base was five yards or so below the level of the chapel and I could see a tunnel winding away towards the south. I leaned in a little closer, wondering how far it went.

The sound of the church door creaking open split my thoughts and I jumped backwards as the Erl King swept through the nave. Cecil followed close at his heels, a large woollen sack swung over one shoulder. The sack seemed to contain something alive, probably a sheep or goat for the sacrifice.

The bulkier of the two farm lads was sent climbing down the shaft first, with his mate levering the chest after him. There was much muttered cursing as the heavy box scraped against the sides of the tunnel and trapped fingers and thumbs. The Erl King stood watching, impassive. I glanced at him from where I lurked in the shadows. He didn't seem nervous or apprehensive; the same blank expression lingered on his features as always, punctured by occasional flashes of amusement when one of the men yelped in pain.

After several long minutes of struggling to move the chest the second farmer jumped into the tunnel, followed by Cecil, still carrying his sack. The Erl King turned to me, eyes glittering in the candlelight.

'The time has come, Jenny.' He extended a pale hand towards the tunnel.

I nodded, trying to keep my face as impassive as his and moved to pass him. As I bent to swing myself down I felt his cold grip on my shoulder.

'Remember what you are,' the Erl King hissed into my ear. 'Remember what it is you want, what you have already paid for it. Do not falter now.'

I fought to repress the shudder that his proximity triggered in me, managing to nod mutely and drop myself into the tunnel.

The descent was easy enough and I found myself in a low chamber, with the corridor I had seen earlier leading out to the south. The men had huddled along the side wall, waiting for their leader. The Erl King dropped down beside me. He snapped his fingers and we set off down the corridor. The walls were damp, woolly with dark mosses and lichen. The only light was from a burning torch carried by Cecil, lit from a tinderbox, but my night-sight filled in the shadows.

The tunnel had been carved from the rock. Overhead, too dark for human eyes to see, the walls were painted with woad handprints and runes, strange symbols of a lost time. Further up, on the ceiling, ochre stick figures chased boars and deer across the damp rock. I reached up to trace the horns of a giant stag.

'Keep up,' whispered Cecil from where the tunnel turned left. I dropped my hand and hurried after him.

From the bend in the tunnel it took only a moment of walking before we came out into a huge chamber. The rock of the walls was polished to a water-like smoothness, reflecting the candlelight and the image of our group back and forth across the cavern, though other tunnel entrances swallowed up the light, leading into blackness. The ceiling had more of the woad paintings, this time forming a great spiral of stars and leaves, coiling towards a central point – a huge sun coated with gold. The edges of the sunbeams and the spiral's arms seemed to glow in the light of the torches that Cecil's men were placing on the walls.

Below the painted sun was the well of Avalon.

It was surprisingly small, I thought, the housing only three handspans across, and the same length tall. Instead of the rough mud bricks of the village wells, each stone was cut from glassy tourmaline that flashed darkly in the torchlight.

Around the well lay the knights. Each was dressed in full armour; with steel helmets and gleaming breastplates, and each bore a merrily painted shield. Their faces were smooth, untouched by centuries of sleep, though their hair was shot through with silver. Many bore traces of terrible wounds; bloodstained cuffs and rent tunics, but the flesh beneath had long since healed.

We picked our way between them, stepping delicately around scattered swords and arrows.

Against the far wall was a raised plinth. Stone roses twined around its edges, their petals blurred with dust. Arthur slept on. A thin gold band circled his forehead and his hands were clasped together, bright rings on his fingers.

The Erl King leaned over to inspect the sleeping king, checking both sides of the plinth as if looking for something. Satisfied, he straightened and turned back to us.

'Bring the chest over there,' he ordered, pointing towards the well, 'and set it up.'

The farmers obeyed and bent to open the heavy iron clasps. I wondered absently if the Erl King had deliberately avoided touching the metal.

Inside the chest was a long wide stone, buffed into a flat oval shape. The Erl King knelt and lifted it out, holding it in the air while the farmers retrieved a series of pieces of wood and assembled them into a stand, fitting it over the well. The Erl King lowered the stone onto the stand and I understood: it was an altar. I could see reddish stains on the edge of the stone, marks of older blood sacrifices.

I remembered my mother telling me of living offerings, carried out by the druids in the old days, when her mother had been alive. They had made gifts to the fae, to the forests and even to the Jennys of significant rivers and lakes. Those ways had died out before my mother's time, though the memory of those deaths echoed through the lands.

The Erl King batted the farmers aside and retrieved a pair of long knives, one carved from pale bone, the other whittled from black obsidian. Both looked honed to a razor-sharp edge. He laid each one carefully beside the altar then bent to collect more paraphernalia from the chest.

Cecil edged past me. I eyed the spot where he had left the sack and began to edge towards it. Crouching beside it, I pulled it open, then dropped my hand in horror.

Inside, stripped to his breeches and covered in bruises, was Brackus. His hands and feet were bound with iron and a bundle of filthy rags was stuffed into his mouth. His eyes opened and he squinted up, blinded by the sudden light.

Chapter Twenty-Two

My heart skipped a beat and I lurched backwards, dropping the top of the sack back on to Brackus's face. Behind me the Erl King was still supervising the construction of the altar. Brackus wriggled against his ties, managing to flick the rattan cloth off him again. I knelt down, my fingers instinctively beginning to untie the filthy gag that had been stuffed in his mouth.

How could Brackus be the sacrifice? I tried to remember the Erl King's exact words. He'd said Brackus would be kept in the cells till I had completed my tasks. I cursed myself for not securing his safety; I had been so distressed by the order to kill Temperance I had not considered the threat to my other friend.

I got the gag off and he gasped for air, coughing violently. Before he could get his breath back, I heard the grating voice of the Erl King calling to me. I twisted my head around. He was still bent over, melting the bases of the candles and sticking them into place.

'What the hell are you doing here, Jenny?' Brackus hissed at me.

I turned back, 'Brackus, I'm sorry, I—' Before I could say anything more, I heard footsteps behind me. The farmhands were upon us, and, reaching around me, they dragged Brackus out of the sack and to his feet. He looked weak, barely strong enough to hold himself up and the men handled his weight as if it were nothing.

I pulled myself to my feet and hurried after them. I tried to keep my face neutral.

'Jenny,' the Erl King called, 'come over here.'

I scuttled to his side, keeping an eye on the farmhands.

'You still have not learnt to keep your nose to yourself,' he growled at me. 'Still, it is of no matter. I should be thanking you for bringing him to me. Saves me the trouble of luring in another fae. Yes, with the blood of this humble goblin, I will open the well and yoke its power to mine.'

'But he's fae,' I stuttered, trying to form an argument. 'I thought all sacrifices had to be mortal. I thought it would be a boar or a hart of some kind.'

The Erl King eyed me. 'Ordinarily yes, I would have spilt the blood of some lesser offering or perhaps taken a human life. But I mean to bind the well to myself, and therefore must offer blood similar to mine, for at the core of my being I am fae.'

The farmhands had reached the altar now, were beginning to wrench Brackus over it.

'Please,' I gabbled, 'if it has to be a fae then find another.'

'No time for that now.' He brushed me aside, striding towards the altar.

I leapt for the Erl King's arm, but he barely looked at me, flicking out a magical blow that threw me back to the ground. Behind him the farmhands had forced Brackus over the great flat stone, yanking up his chin to expose his throat. I screeched at them, hoping to scare off whatever human part of them was left, but their eyes had gone entirely black and I knew with sickening certainty that the Erl King had possessed them entirely.

'Wait,' I screamed.

I lunged forward but Cecil stepped into my path, his eyes filled with a familiar expression. I dodged to the right, reaching out to slash my nails across his face, the sharpened points raking his flesh. The human part of him winced but he kept coming, wrenching my arm down and pulling me back. I swivelled and aimed a kick at him, planting the blow straight between his legs. He howled and went down.

Brackus was struggling against the grip of his captors, snarling and biting at them. He managed to sink his teeth into one callused hand but its owner didn't release him.

I stumbled forward and crashed into a wall of invisible magic, blocking me from the well. It shocked me and I fell to the ground, sprawling next to the empty chest, smacking my head on the floor.

'Take me instead,' I yelled desperately. 'My blood can be the sacrifice.'

The Erl King paused and looked at me.

'Truly?' he asked, a rare look of surprise crossing his face. 'You would give up your future for this detritus?'

I paused, searching myself, then nodded, 'Yes. Take my blood.'

The Erl King raised his eyebrows, 'It is good to know there are still surprises to be had after eons of existence. No matter, I will not change the order of things now.'

'No!' I hurled myself forward again, rebounding off the magic boundary.

'Hush,' the Erl King snapped at me. 'I will get you another hobgoblin if you are suddenly so fond of them. But we must carry on.' He turned away.

The Erl King picked up the obsidian knife and sliced into the flesh of his left hand. He reached out and scattered the blood over Brackus's chest. The droplets steamed where they hit his skin, and Brackus cried out in pain. The Erl King raised the knife in the air and said something in a language I didn't know. The candlelight illuminated the hard bones of his face, grinning like a skull. Then he brought the knife down with frightening speed.

Brackus screamed. The knife hilt juddered where it had been stabbed into his left shoulder, pinning him to the stone. The Erl King, ignoring the screams, reached for the bone knife and slashed at his other hand. He repeated the incantation and stabbed it through Brackus's right shoulder. The Erl King was chanting aloud now, his voice echoing back from the walls at me. The air shimmered and I sensed that he was baring his soul, ready to spill blood and bind himself to the well.

I tried to get up and slipped, almost falling into the chest. I scrabbled around for purchase inside, and my hand touched something smooth. I blinked at it, realising the object in my hand was the alicorn dagger. This was the moment, the chance I had bought with blood and pain.

I grabbed the knife and hauled myself to my feet. Cecil was still sprawled on the floor, his eyes having returned to their usual blue. The Erl King had his back to me, clearly feeling secure behind his magic wall. I took a deep breath and launched myself forward.

The spiralling point of the alicorn pierced the wall of magic, which shattered like glass. The Erl King began to twist but I had kept moving and the dagger was already stabbing through his back. I felt the blade break through his spine and he crumpled to the side. A thunderclap shook the cavern, and the rock itself seemed to quake. The body of the pastor, now lifeless, was sprawled on the ground.

My momentum carried me forward and I almost fell onto Brackus. The farmhands had tripped backwards, their eyes rolling back into their heads.

'Jenny,' whispered Brackus, his voice cracked and sore.

'It's all right, Brackus,' I said, 'I'm here.'

'Get them out,' he whispered, rolling his eyes towards the knives.

I seized the bone knife; it was icy cold in my grip. 'This is going to hurt.' I yanked with all my strength. For a moment I didn't think it was going to move but then the knife came loose. I reached for the obsidian knife and yelped. It was burning hot, scorching the palm of my hand. I steeled myself and reached for it again, leveraging all of my strength. As it came out I dropped it on the floor with a clatter.

'Thank you, Jenny,' Brackus said, sitting up. The wounds in his shoulders were healing up as I watched. He looked up at me and grinned. There was something about his smile that I didn't like, something behind his eyes.

'Brackus?' I said, haltingly.

'Did you think it would be that easy, Jenny?' His pupils grew until they filled the whole of his eyes. 'Striking down my mortal shell when I have this one to adopt?'

I stepped backwards, looking around desperately for the alicorn knife.

'Don't bother, Jenny. if you smite me again, I shall take your form. You are a fool indeed to try to trick me. There is no knife that can kill me. Alas for you that you have disrupted my sacrifice; I shall have to spill your blood in replacement.'

He beckoned with one hand and I felt my body drag itself towards him. Tears trickled from my eyes as he forced me down onto the altar stone.

'Be grateful, Jenny, that I have this use for you; your suffering otherwise would have been endless.'

I twisted wildly, looking around as he drove the obsidian knife deep into my shoulder, splattering my face with blood. I screamed as a pain I had never felt before ripped through me. It felt like my whole body was aflame, burning and burning. I stopped trying to fight my way free, consumed by the unceasing agony. Only the second pain of the bone knife going into my right shoulder permeated my senses. I lay, pinned, fighting to contain my screams as the face of my oldest friend leered down at me.

'Now to put an end to this,' he said, and picked up the alicorn knife.

A shadow moved in the dark. The Erl-Brackus looked up and I saw surprise flicker across his face.

'You,' he spat, hatred in his voice. 'You should be dead.'

I twisted against my restraints and looked back. Temperance stood at the edge of the cave. Her face was dirty, her clothes ragged and blood-splattered, and her hair hung limp but she was alive. She flashed me a quick smile and my heart sang with joy and relief to see her. I opened my mouth to call out to her but the Erl-Brackus flinched, causing the bone knife in my shoulder to cut even deeper. I yelped and Temperance's eyes narrowed.

'Get away from her,' she spat, raising the old sword in her left hand.

'Drop that silly thing,' the Erl-Brackus said. Temperance lifted the blade higher, the steel glinting in the candlelight.

The Erl-Brackus made a slashing movement with his hand. Temperance flinched but didn't move. He tried again, to no effect.

'I said drop it,' he snapped. 'You must obey me.'

'You should have finished reading the parson's Bible,' she said, raising her right arm. Where the scratched and poisoned hand had been there was only a stump, from where I had swung the sword and cut it off. It was bandaged neatly with scraps of linen.

'If your right hand causes you to sin, cut it off.'

The Erl-Brackus hesitated, doubt crossing his face. His eyes flitted to me and I spat blood from my mouth and smiled at him.

'We put on a good show, didn't we? Did you really think I would kill her? That I could be so easily bought? Or my daughter so easily replaced?' I laughed.

The Erl-Brackus scowled and made towards me, then stopped.

'No matter, I shall deal with you later.' He opened his hand and cast a spell at Temperance, hissing with malevolence.

She twisted the sword and batted the magic away. The Erl-Brackus frowned and tried again. Again, she deflected the attack.

'What is that you have there?' he asked, uncertainty creeping into his voice.

'The sword you should have known was here,' Temperance said. 'The sword that has always been here, entrusted to the lake guardian since before this cavern was built. I didn't realise before I came to this place, and saw Arthur and his knights. But I know now who Jenny is, and I know the name of the sword she bears.'

She stepped forward and thrust it directly into Brackus's chest. 'Excalibur.'

The Erl-Brackus gaped down at his chest then screamed. The blackness in his eyes seemed to burn with dark fire that quickly spread all through his body. He fell to his knees, still scream- ing, writhing in agony. Excalibur shone silver-white through the darkness, burning out the evil. The Erl King gave a final screech and then the cave was lit up with a blinding flash and he was silent.

Brackus toppled backwards, the sword leaving his chest with a wet, sucking sound.

'Jenny.' Temperance rushed to my side, dropping Excalibur. She bent over me and I smiled up at her.

'You're here,' I whispered.

'Of course I'm here,' she said, cupping my face in a bloody hand. Her eyes flitted to the long knives. 'I need to take them out, can you bear it?'

I nodded, keeping my eyes locked on her. She ripped the knives free and hauled me to my feet

'Quickly,' I said, 'Brackus.'

She bit her lip and helped me crouch down next to our friend. His chest was still moving, long rattling breaths that snatched at my heart. Temperance ripped a strip from her skirt and pressed my hands over the wound, trying to staunch the bleeding. His eyes fluttered open, returned to their native blue.

'The Erl King . . .' he whispered.

'He's gone,' Temperance said firmly.

'Thank you,' Brackus said, smiling slightly.

'How did you get here?' I asked her, still dazzled by the flash of the sword.

'When you threw the sword in the lake it was caught in the same currents that dragged me to your cave. I stopped bleed- ing as soon as I grabbed it. That was enough of a clue to make me look at it more closely. There's an old legend that Excalibur prevented the bearer from blood loss. I wasn't sure until I had regained enough strength to heal myself and started to explore the back of your cave. The tunnels lead all the way back here. I felt the magic pulling me; I came through just after you killed the pastor.'

She reached down to place her hand over mine on Brackus's chest wound. She began to mutter, trying to cast a spell of healing but I could tell she was too drained.

'I don't have enough strength,' she said, 'can you share yours?'

I shook my head. 'Not here. I need to get to the lake. Can you carry him?' I looked down at Brackus who was growing paler and colder by the minute. 'He's not going to make it.'

'Can't you call it from here?' Temperance asked, her hands already soaked with blood.

'It's too far.' I gestured at the wounds in my shoulders; it was taking all my strength to stay conscious.

Temperance looked down at Brackus. He was bone-white now, his breath starting to fade. Tears fell from her eyes and landed on his face. The rage I had felt when the Erl King had tried to sacrifice him rushed back into me, the pain of almost losing him; and now, when our enemy was vanquished, I could not save him. The fury at this final indignity choked me, burning the tears that tried to blind my eyes.

'No,' I whispered. 'You're not going. I will not lose you.'

I staggered to my feet. Temperance looked up at me, her eyes blurry with tears.

'Jenny, what are you doing?' she called after me as I crossed the cave. I knelt in front of Excalibur, running a hand over its length. I took a quick breath then grasped it in my hand. I came up on one knee, feeling the power, the strength, the stories of the steel. Then I sank it into the ground.

The blade cleaved the limestone like butter. As I drove it in, I reached out for the lake, for the well, for the water that had made Avalon the heart of Britain.

'Come to me now,' I whispered, 'I am the heir of Avalon, I am the Lady of the Lake. I call your power to mine, not to bind but to borrow.'

Blood from my wounds trickled down the blade and into the

rock. A roaring filled my ears and the world fell away. Water burst from the well, washing away the bloody detritus of the altar. In the south I could feel the lake coming towards me, and a great wave washed through the cavern. Temperance gasped as it washed over her and Brackus, hurrying to conjure quick bubbles of air over their heads.

The water kept coming, from the well, the lake and the river, rising up and filling the cavern. As the sweet, cool water hit me I could feel it healing my wounds. I opened my mouth and breathed it in. The power rushed through me, greater than anything I had felt before. I could feel Temperance and Brackus's heartbeats, and reached out with a tendril of the power to them. Temperance latched onto it and began to channel a healing spell. I felt Brackus's heartbeat strengthen, ringing out clearly now through the water. I wrapped the magic around Temperance's wrist, smoothing away the last of the pain.

The cavern was almost full now, but I couldn't let go of the sword. The power it was feeding me was incredible, and under the water I felt stronger than ever. I saw now that I didn't have to choose between a new world and the old one – that instead, I could forge the world in my own image. The power of the water rushed through me faster and faster. I laughed, bubbles spilling out of my mouth. I turned to wave to Temperance, to share this new gift with her.

She was clinging to Brackus, the both of them buffeted by the raging current that had turned the cavern into a whirlpool. As I watched the air bubbles she had conjured were shrinking, then popped.

In alarm, I reached out towards her, then wrenched Excalibur from the stone.

The water calmed, then began to drain. In a mad tangle of limbs, swords and detritus, the three of us were sucked back through the cavern, down towards the lake. My cave flashed before my eyes, all my trinkets and keepsakes floating around us, before the water crashed down with a huge splash, draining back into the lake.

We sprawled on the cave floor spluttering and coughing amid the chaos. I struggled up, crawling over to Brackus. Temperance and I leaned over, looking down at his face.

For a heart-breaking moment he was still. Then he opened his eyes, looked up at us and winked.

Epilogue

It was an unseasonably hot day in early spring. The frogbit was just starting to regrow, bobbing up and down on the surface of the water, little green buds unfurling into the warm air. I swam through the cool waters of the lake, luxuriating in the feel of it against my limbs. The rays of sunlight filtering through the lily pads flashed on the scales of perch and roach as they grazed contentedly in the shallows.

I heard splashing towards the eastern banks and kicked off towards the sound. As I swam the old pike glided past me, eying me up to see if I had any food. With a twist of his tail he vanished back into the deep.

The splashing was coming from just north of where the Caerlee flowed out of the lake again. I drifted just beneath the surface. A human child, a little girl, was standing in the shallows, her dress hoiked up around her knees. She had dark curly hair and her mother's eyes.

'Jenny, Jenny!' she called.

I sneaked up as close as I dared then burst out of the water. She screamed with delight and clapped her hands.

'Jenny, Jenny, again, again!' she cried, wading over to embrace my legs. She tilted her face up and grinned in that wild unabashed fashion that children do.

'Ursula Crump,' I said, mock-seriously, 'have you run off again? Where is your mother?'

'She's coming down now with the babies.' Ursula said, releasing my legs, her eyes wandering to a patch of newly blooming lilies. 'She said I could run ahead.'

'Did she?' I asked, grabbing Ursula's hand before she ended up out of her depth. She and her brother had only learnt to swim in the warmer days of last autumn, coming down with Temperance to practise their doggy-paddle around the lake.

'Mm-hmm,' murmured Ursula, not meeting my eyes. I sat down, the lake water coming up to my chest, and scooped the child onto my lap.

'Well then, we'll just wait here for her, shall we? Why don't you tell me something you've learnt recently?'

This was a tried-and-true method for distracting Ursula and she immediately launched into a complicated description of some baking she and her mother had been doing. I nodded along as she gesticulated, enjoying the meandering account of flour and butter.

'Ursula!' came a cry from behind us. Ursula twisted guiltily and I picked her up and stood up to wave. Temperance was hurrying down the hill, a baby strapped to her back and a toddler on her right hip. Her right arm held the toddler in place, the silvery scar where her wrist ended gleaming in the sunlight. A picnic basket swung from her left hand.

'It's all right, Temperance, I've got her,' I called. Temperance slowed to a walk and put down the toddler.

'There you go, sweetheart,' she said, then turned back to me. 'Thanks, Jenny, she just took off as soon as I opened the door.'

Temperance reached the edge of the lake and I swung Ursula over towards her and climbed out onto the bank.

'Didn't I tell you not to run off?' she said, retrieving a blanket from a wicker basket and laying it out on the banks.

Josiah the toddler wandered over towards me, his arms stretched up. I bent down and picked him up, swinging him around until he giggled and screamed.

'Here, Jenny.' Temperance unwrapped the baby and held her out. 'Take Val for a moment. I need to catch my breath.'

I put down Josiah and took my goddaughter. Her little face was scrunched up, eyes closed in sleep, one fat hand curled up next to her head. Temperance collapsed on the blanket and began taking her boots off. She dangled her feet over the banks into the lake.

'Ah,' she sighed, 'that feels nice.'

I stretched out beside her, cradling the baby in my arms. Val caught my finger in one of her tiny hands, pressing it to her cheek.

'She's sweeter every time I see her,' I said to Temperance. 'I still can't believe you named her after the dog.'

'I owe my life to that dog,' Temperance reminded me. 'Besides, only you, Benedict and I know her full name is Cavall. The rest of the village think she's called Valerie.'

I started to respond but Ursula and Josiah jumped back into the water and began splashing each other.

'Don't go too far out,' I called, adjusting the currents of the lake to keep them bobbing at the surface. Only more splashing sounds answered. Temperance shook her head.

'I suppose I can't really blame them. It's the first day it's been warm enough to swim since winter.'

'Want to come for a proper dip?' I asked.

'Sure.' Temperance took off her kirtle whilst I unwrapped the baby. She woke up and cooed at me, big hazel eyes and a trace of her father's cleft chin. I stepped back into the water and lowered her in. She kicked her legs and wiggled around happily. When I let her drop below the surface with me she kept her eyes open in the clear water and waved her arms around until I brought her back up.

Temperance waded in and we swam out to the centre of the lake. Josiah and Ursula followed, still splashing each other. I passed Val back to Temperance and took turns throwing the other children out of the water.

When they were tired we all lay back and floated in the water. When the sun was directly overhead Temperance sighed.

'All right you lot, time to get out. We've got lots of work to do back home,' she said.

There was general grumbling and I helped shepherd them all back to the bank and into dry clothes from the basket.

'Thanks, Jenny.' Temperance kissed my cheek. 'Benedict says to tell you he hasn't forgotten about the dredging he promised you, on the south of the lake. Next Sunday he'll come over after church and get it done.'

'You should bring the children, make a day of it,' I said, ruffling Ursula's hair. 'I'll rustle up some fresh trout and we can cook them over a fire. No one from the village will see me from there.'

'Perfect. Send an invitation to Brackus too, if you like. We haven't seen him since before Christmas and I'm sure he's not one to miss a free meal.'

I grumbled at Brackus's name just for tradition's sake and waved as she began to herd her children back up towards the village.

When they faded from view, I grabbed a handful of leaves and whispered a message into them, setting them off down the Caerlee.

I sank back into the water, smiling at the memory of the children's laughter. I swam around, tidying up for a while, then headed back to my cave.

I hauled out into the darkness, the wisplight casting a pale glow over the contents of the cave. I made my way to the back, running a hand over the damp walls.

I picked up a long parcel and began to unwrap the oiled leather. The sword lay before me, still encased in the plain scabbard. I ran a finger over the hilt, marvelling again at the echoes of the power I sensed within it. I grasped the hilt and drew the blade, holding it before me so that the wisplight glinted on the still sharp edges.

I closed my eyes and remembered the faces of the knights sleeping just yards from here. The old man and the king, the Round Table.

'The sword of the once and future king,' I whispered to Excalibur, my breath fogging the blade. 'The candle that keeps the darkness at bay.'

The hilt burned in my hand, but I gripped it tightly.

'I will hold the line,' I said. 'I will not fade. I will keep the faith for Temperance and all her kind. For those who have forgotten the old ways I will remember, and I will defend them.'

The sword cooled and I loosened my hold on it. I replaced it in the sheath and wrapped it back in the leather. Then I stepped back into the water and swam out into the sunlight.

 A note on pronunciation

The Welsh language, whilst beautiful, can be a challenge to an English reader. I have chosen to keep the original spellings where possible rather than anglicise them. Pronunciations vary by tradition but here are the ones I imagined while writing.

Tylwyth Teg – Tul-with Tegg
Gwyn ap Nudd – Gwin ap Neu-th
Creiddylad – Kray-thill-add
Twrch Trwyth – Turk Tru-ith
Penrhyn Ddu – Pen-Rin Thu

Acknowledgements

First thanks must go, as always, to my parents. From teaching me to read to being the first to read this book, you've provided me with unlimited love and support and spell-checking.

Thanks to Ally for all the writing sessions and support, to Annie for first inspiring me to pick up a pen, to Puva for reminding me to celebrate the little wins along the way.

To the Sydney writing group, thank you for your company and encouragement and ice cream sundaes as I finally got this book out of my head and onto the page.

Thank you to my incredible editor Emily Byron for her insightful work on the manuscript – without you this wouldn't be the book it is. Thank you as well to the whole Orbit crew – it's been an honour to work with such a brilliant creative team.

Finally, thank you to my agent Sam Edenborough – I could not have asked for a better representative for Jenny or for me.

extras

orbit-books.co.uk

about the author

Molly O'Neill is a fantasy author and engineering geologist. She was born and raised in the Cotswolds and moved to Australia in 2019. She now lives in Sydney, on the land of the Gadigal People. Molly writes fantasy books inspired by the beautiful landscapes of her two countries, and by the folklore of the British Isles. She particularly loves the darker Arthurian legends and the Welsh myths of the Mabinogion and often uses them as a foundation for her stories. When not furiously scribbling ideas into a notebook Molly can be found looking intensely at rocks, paddling on the Sydney beaches or searching for the perfect taco. *Greenteeth* is her debut novel.

Find out more about Molly O'Neill and other Orbit authors by registering for the free montly newsletter at orbit-books.co.uk.

if you enjoyed
GREENTEETH

look out for

HOW TO LOSE A
GOBLIN IN TEN DAYS

by

Jessie Sylva

*When a halfling, Pansy, and a goblin, Ren, each think
they've inherited the same cottage, they make a bargain:
they'll live in the house together and whoever is driven out
first forfeits their ownership. Amidst forced proximity and
cultural misunderstandings, the two begin to fall in love.*

*But when the cottage — and their communities — are
threatened by a common enemy, the duo must learn
to trust each other, and convince goblins and halflings
to band together to oust the tall intruder.*

CHAPTER ONE

Pansy

The problem with mushrooms, Pansy decided, half-squatting in the damp, forest earth, was that far too many of them looked alike. Take, for example, the crop of orange fungus blanketing one side of the fallen log before her. Was it the delicious, yet exquisitely rare Phoenix Tail mushroom she'd spent most of the morning searching for or, rather, the far more ominously named Bloodletter Shroom? Gods only knew the answer to that one. Because Pansy certainly didn't; not even with a borrowed copy of Fatleaf's Fungal Fancies clutched in one dirt-stained hand.

At this point, the smart thing to do would've been to back away and leave the mushrooms to carry on as they were, undisturbed. But the thought of leaving behind what could very well be the greatest culinary treasure trove this side of Giant's Reach made something inside Pansy shrivel. Not to mention, she'd be coming home empty-handed—on tonight of all nights.

No. Pansy shook her head. She couldn't do that. She wouldn't.

Blowing out a breath, she tucked a stray ringlet of copper-colored hair behind one large, rounded ear and squinted closer at the finger-like frills jutting up from the log's mossy surface. Well, it was certainly orange. But was it the 'burnished orange of a warmth hearth,' as Elwan Fatleaf had put it? Maybe. Though how that differed from the 'dull orange of an overripe pumpkin' Pansy wasn't quite sure.

Perhaps Blossom would know. She was a florist by trade, so mushrooms weren't precisely her area of expertise. But it was her book that Pansy had borrowed. And if Blossom couldn't give her a firm answer—well, Pansy would throw out the mushrooms and come up with something else. Better to be safe than sorry, especially when the alternative meant potentially poisoning your entire family.

"The things I do for a good quiche," she muttered, retrieving a small paring knife from the folds of her apron. There were probably blades better suited for this; foraging knives or some such. But like most halflings, until today, the closest Pansy had gotten to foraging was visiting the local grocer, who, unfortunately, did not deal in anything other than the very ordinary. And Phoenix Tails were anything but.

Still, even with only a paring knife at her disposal, the mushrooms came away without much fuss. Soon, Pansy was rising to her feet, her potentially-poisonous-but-hopefully-not haul tucked safely inside her wicker shopping basket.

As much as she would've liked to keep searching—just in case—the hour was getting late. The sky overhead, glimpsed in narrow snatches through a wild, thick canopy, had already deepened to a soft lilac, edged in equally delicate pinks and golds that continued to thin as daylight waned. Pansy estimated that she had a couple of hours or so before night set in in earnest. Plenty of time to walk the winding trail back to Haverow—if she left now.

Of course, as luck would have it, she managed only a few steps in the direction of home before a new treasure caught her eye: a truffle, white and plump, rising just above the carpet of dead leaves that blanketed the forest floor. Had some animal unearthed it only to abandon their plunder in a moment of panic?

"Huh. Well, you won't find me complaining," Pansy said, hopping off the path once more with aplomb.

It took a little bit of maneuvering on her part, the ground here more gnarled roots than dirt, but soon she reached the shallow divot in the earth the truffle called home. The white bulb was enormous, nearly the size of her fist. With it, she could make enough truffle butter to fuel dozens of recipes, from truffle butter mashed potatoes to this one wonderfully soft white truffle butterbread she'd always wanted to try. None would be as extraordinary as the Phoenix Tail quiche she'd been hoping to prepare, of course, but the truffle butter, at least, she could leave behind. It would be a piece of her heart for her parents to keep close, a reminder that her love for them could never diminish; no matter how much distance might come between them.

Warmth bloomed beneath Pansy's breastbone at the thought. Perhaps, tonight wouldn't be such a disaster, after all—even if the mushrooms in the basket did turn out to be poisonous dopplegangers.

Squatting down anew, Pansy reached for the truffle. However, before her fingers could even so much as graze its pockmarked surface, a pink blur darted out in front of her, and the truffle was gone.

"Thief!" she cried, watching as a conspicuously well-fed—though no less alacritous for it—pig made off with her would-be prize. "Piggy thief! Bring that back!"

Unsurprisingly, her demands fell on deaf ears. But Pansy would not give up so easily.

She surged to her feet, her dress already hiked pre-emptively around her knees. No need to give herself any more things to trip over; the forest already had her more than covered on that front. Still, even with a sea of uneven terrain before her, Pansy managed to keep pace with the pilfering swine. In fact, she was soon gaining on the creature.

"I've got you now!" she shouted, legs pumping harder still.

Pansy's vision had condensed, leaving nothing but the rotund, pink mass ahead of her—plus, the truffle clamps between its jaws. So, when the pig abruptly released the truffle in apparent concession, she gave no thought to what might be around her. She dove.

No sooner had her fingers closed around the squat bulb than another set fingers, longer, greener, and more slender than her own, found hers, pressing nails like flat shards of obsidian into soft, unguarded skin.

For half a breath, hazel eyes met yellow in complete and perfect stillness, where even the world itself seemed to pause on its axis. Then, the moment passed, and both Pansy and her unexpected interloper broke apart, each relinquishing their hold on the truffle in favor of scrambling back several paces (and, in Pansy's case, letting out a less-than-dignified squeak).

A goblin? Here? Pansy hugged her basket close, heart kicking hard against her ribs.

In truth, this shouldn't have been such a shock. Just as the forest bordered Haverow and several other halfling villages on one side, it abutted a vast network of caves on the other, all inhabited—or 'infested,' as the neighboring dwarves might say—by goblins. No doubt, this was one of them, having temporarily abandoned the dank, festering darkness they loved so much to—what? Scavenge? Steal? That's what goblins did, after all. Provided they weren't too busy slaughtering halflings in the name of whatever dark lord or necromancer they'd volunteered to serve.

This goblin, at least, seemed to be unarmed. Granted, the little daggers they sported at the end of each finger could certainly do some damage with the right application; the tiny, pink pinpricks dotting the back of Pansy's hand were proof enough of that. But even those claws seemed to have diminished slightly, as if they'd been retracted. Like a cat's.

Still, it was difficult to know anything for sure. While Pansy had stumbled backwards in a straight line, the goblin had taken a more strategic approach, seeking cover behind the same knot of overgrown roots they'd popped out from. If Pansy squinted, she could just make them out. But in the ever-waning daylight, who knew how long that would last.

In many ways, the goblin looked exactly how Pansy had imagined: green hair; green skin; clothes in varying shades of brown and gray, all held together by scraps of fabric and a prayer. And yet, their features were also softer, rounder, even when doused in the gnarled, twisting shadows of the forest. With full cheeks and a flat, button-like nose, the goblin was almost—dare Pansy say it—cute.

To think, she had an entire bookshelf's worth of Wolf Banefoot books at home, and none of them had prepared her for this. Then, again, she could hardly expect stories about the greatest halfling hero to wax poetic about the very goblins he was fighting.

Speaking of: was this goblin going to fight her?

So far, they had yet to deviate from the strange half-crouch they'd dropped into, their muscles pulled bowstring-taut beneath the gray weight of their cloak. While one hand gripped the curve of one immense tree root, the other extended behind them, palm flat and out. Almost as if they were telling someone to wait.

Pansy sucked in a sharp breath, panic squeezing around her throat like a vice. Her gaze swiveled away from the goblin, searching, instead, beyond. There, she found not another goblin like she'd feared, but a familiar thief, pink and potbellied, standing at the base of another tree, its head cocked slightly to one side. A goblin's accomplice. Of course.

Had the goblin stolen the pig, she wondered, only to nearly scoff at herself for having even deigned to ask such a silly question. They were a goblin. Surely, that was answer enough.

No sooner had Pansy glimpsed the creature than the goblin shoved themselves away from their makeshift shield and back into her line of sight. Don't you dare, blazed the silent accusation, knife-bright behind a tangled veil of moss-green hair. No words had been spoken. Yet Pansy heard then all the same.

"I'm not going to hurt it," she snapped, the hot swell of her own indignation shattering the uneasy silence between them. "I came out here to gather some ingredients. That's all."

A beat. Just long enough for the goblin's ears to unpin from their skull. "I didn't know halflings foraged." Their voice was surprisingly soft—perhaps, even almost pleasantly so—but also oddly devoid of inflection, particularly when compared to the way Pansy's neighbors in Haverow spoke.

"Yes, well. I'm making a quiche," Pansy declared, canting up her chin at a defiant angle; anything to eke out a few extra millimeters against a goblin who thought her so low as to hurt a defenseless pig—thief or no. "A very halfling thing to do, mind you."

The goblin's eyes flicked down to Pansy's basket, still clutched to her chest, the narrow slits of their pupils flaring ever so slightly wider. "You know those are poisonous, right?"

"What?"

"Those mushrooms. You can't eat them. They'll kill you."

Heat flooded Pansy's face, rushing all the way up to the tips of her ears. So, they had been Bloodletter Shrooms, after all. Just her luck. She'd spent the whole day slogging through these woods; all for the privilege of accidentally poisoning her parents with what was supposed to be the greatest meal they'd ever had. And worst of all, a goblin had been the one to tell her just how badly she'd mucked it up.

"I-I knew that!" Pansy stammered. "I wasn't going to eat them."

An awful lie by any measure. The goblin clearly thought so, judging from the way their nose wrinkled. Still, they asked, "What were you going to do with them, then?"

"I—" Pansy floundered, her cheeks burning hotter and hotter with every second wasted scrabbling for some halfway-believable excuse. As if there could ever be one in such a situation! She knew it. The goblin knew it. Perhaps, even the pig knew it! And still the goblin continued to wait for her answer, their expression an inscrutable, unyielding wall.

"Decoration," she forced out at last, miraculously managing to keep a straight face.

"Decoration," the goblin repeated, flatly.

"Yes." Pansy sniffed. "Decoration. Am I not allowed to decorate my home?"

"With mushrooms."

She shrugged. "I like the color orange."

The goblin blinked at her, long and slow, then said, "Take it."

Surprise loosened the knot pulling Pansy's spine taut. "What?"

"The truffle." They gestured towards it, still lying between them. "You clearly need it more than I do."

"What's that supposed to mean?"

The goblin shrugged, their gaze drifting to one side. "I just don't want a bunch of dead halflings on my conscience is all."

Pansy's waning flush roared back with a vengeance; now with a decidedly angry sheen. "I already told you they're not for eating!" Then, just to really drive the point home, she upended her basket, scattering the lingering evidence of her failure across the dirt. "There! Happy? Now you don't have to worry about us stupid little halflings poisoning ourselves with deadly mushrooms!"

For several beats there was nothing beyond the ragged drag of Pansy's breathing, her shoulders heaving as she stood at the center of an orange halo of her own creation. The goblin said nothing, did nothing. And eventually it seemed like it'd stay that way. But then they started towards Pansy, pausing only briefly to retrieve the truffle, which they promptly deposited in her otherwise empty basket, now hanging limply at her side.

"You should go home before it gets dark," they said, now close enough that Pansy could see the smattering of barely-there freckles dusting the bridge of their nose. "The forest is thick and hard to navigate without light, especially for someone like you."

As the goblin stepped away, Pansy considered whether she ought to thank them. Good manners dictated that when someone gave you something you responded with a show of gratitude in turn. But, of course, it wasn't so easy when that someone had been anything but polite themselves. Still, she supposed it was the right thing to do. Take the high road and all.

After steadying herself with an especially deep breath, Pansy opened her mouth to utter two words she'd never expected to say to a goblin. But before she could even so much as form the first syllable, the goblin tapped their cheek and, with a whisper of something like a smirk curling at the corner of their mouth, said, "By the way, you have dirt on your face. A lot of it."

Pansy could've screamed.

Returning to her parents' burrow in Haverow should've been a relief, a much-needed balm to soothe the sting of her earlier encounter with that awful goblin. Surely, there was nothing an hour or two in the kitchen couldn't fix. Unless, of course, someone had beaten her there; someone who, to be clear, was not supposed to be there.

"Mom!" Pansy groaned as she set her basket on the counter, the truffle inside rolling lightly across the bottom. "I told you I was going to cook tonight!"

"Oh, honey, it's fine." Her mother waved her off with one oven-mitt-clad hand as she continued to stir the contents of a heavy, red saucepan with the other. Judging from the state of her hair, which often proved wilder than even Pansy's own curls, she'd just started; the brown ribbon she always used to hold her hair back while she cooked hadn't even begun to slip yet. "You were out all day. You can cook tomorrow instead."

There it was—the very thing Pansy had been afraid of. She swallowed the sigh that welled up in her throat and said, as kindly as she could manage, "Mom, you know I won't be here tomorrow."

Her mother shrugged. "The day after, then."

"Or the day after. I'm moving out. We talked about this."

A beat passed. Her mother said nothing, her gaze fixed ostensibly on the pot in front of her; filling for a pot pie, Pansy guessed, judging from the smell—warm and homey and full of butter. But, of course, her mother's thinking had always been plain to see, etched, this time, in the tightness around her mouth, pulling her lips into a thin, pale line.

Finally, a sigh. "Do you really have to leave?" her mother asked, almost plaintively, hazel eyes a few shades greener than Pansy's own flicking over to meet hers. "You'll be so far away."

"Not that far," Pansy corrected, heading over to the nearby

sink to wash her hands. Just because her mother had already started on dinner didn't mean Pansy couldn't help. "Besides, I already told you I'd come visit. Every ten-day. Like I promised."

Her mother, however, would not be placated so easily. She shook her head, her mouth now screwed into a full-on frown. "It's not right. You should be home. Here. With family. Even your grandmother recognized that in the end when she moved back to Haverow. Granted, it didn't make much of a difference by then, I suppose . . ."

"Mom." Pansy shot her mother a hard look, her hands stilling beneath the stream of cool water from the tap. "I'm moving into grandma's old cottage. Not"—she gestured haphazardly, uncaring of the tiny droplets the movement loosed from her fingertips—"running off to fight in some wizard's war."

Somehow, the notion alone was enough to pull a noise of distress from deep in her mother's throat. It didn't matter that it had been nearly five decades since the last Great War, that the Realm was, arguably, at peace; perhaps, even the most tranquil it had ever been, with the latest in a long line of dark lords sealed away via powerful magic, never to be seen or heard from again, his cruel armies of goblins and orcs equally decimated by the forces of Good. It mattered even less that Pansy had no interest in following in her grandmother's footsteps, whether it meant joining up with some wizard, killing goblins, or saving the world. The fact that she wanted to see more—the slightest, ittiest bit more—of what lay beyond the four corners of this cozy, little hamlet was enough to mark her as a cause for concern in her mother's eyes, an echo of an old wound that had never quite truly healed.

At this point, Pansy's father, who had doubtless been eavesdropping since the start, poked his head through the doorway and said, "Your mother's right, Pans. The forest is no place for a halfling. Not to mention, no one's lived in the old cottage for decades! For all you know, the roof could've been blown clean off by now."

"Then I'll fix it," Pansy declared, shutting off the water with a decisive twist. Her father's favorite nickname for her wasn't going to sway her; not this time. "I know neither of you are happy with my decision, and I'm sorry you feel that way, but my mind's made up."

"But there could be goblins!" her mother all but wailed, her lower lip trembling as a ruddy haze mottled her usual, golden-brown complexion.

Pansy half-wanted to tell her about the goblin she'd encountered earlier, to serve as proof that her mother's concerns were largely overblown. But, frankly, that wasn't what her mother needed right now. Letting out a breath, Pansy quickly wiped her hands off on her apron before pulling her mother into the biggest, tightest hug she could muster.

"It'll be okay, Mom," she said, resting her chin on her mother's shoulder like always. "If anything happens, I'll come right back."

A sniffle. "You promise?"

"I promise."

"Good." Pansy's mother pulled away just enough to lightly dab at her eyes. "I just get so worried, knowing that there'll be goblins living nearby. That cottage is right on the border."

"Hopefully, they'll stay on their side of it."

"But what if they don't? You know, a farmer over in Halfbough found his pasture ransacked just last week. Not a single goat left behind! The work of goblins, no doubt. He swears he heard a whole pack of them cackling outside his bedroom window. But, of course, he was too afraid to go outside and check. Smart man. Who knows what they might've done to him if he had." She shuddered.

Pansy gave her a reassuring pat on the arm. "I already told you, Mom. I'll come home. You're acting like the next time I see you I'm going to be telling you all about my new goblin housemate."

Thankfully, her mother let out a little, hiccupping laugh at that. "You're right," she admitted, now smiling as well.

"I usually am. Now what's for dinner? It smells delicious."

And like it would go well with some truffle. But as to where that truffle had come from—well, Pansy wasn't going to think too hard about that one.

CHAPTER TWO

Ren

There was a halfling outside the cottage.

And not just any halfling, Ren realized with a cold jolt of nascent dread. But the halfling from the forest, the one who would've baked enough Bloodletter Shrooms into a quiche to fell an adult dragon if left to her own devices.

Evidently, she'd taken Ren's warning to heart, despite her less-than-grateful response to it at the time. Given how mule-headed halflings always were, especially about things they knew comparatively little about (because of course that made perfect sense), Ren wouldn't have been surprised if she'd loaded those mushrooms right back into her basket the moment they'd turned their back on her. In some ways, that might've actually been preferable. Ren wasn't particularly enamored with the thought of some halfling tramping around their garden and quickly discovered they were even less enthusiastic about it in practice.

Leave those alone, they thought, eyes narrowing as they watched the halfling prod at the start of their mushroom farm, a number of narrow logs, all stacked in a grid-like formation. Judging from the halfling's expression, she had no idea what she was looking at, rendering her insistence on messing with it all the more infuriating. Exactly. It's not for you.

But, of course, the halfling couldn't hear Ren—what with several paces' worth of garden and a window and, you know,

Ren's skull separating them. So, the inevitable happened: the logs fell over.

"Told you so," they muttered under their breath, sour heat pooling beneath their skin. It had taken them hours to put those logs together, and they didn't relish having to repeat the process once more. But, at least, she hadn't broken anything that couldn't be fixed.

Yet.

Abandoning the mess she'd created, in typical halfling fashion, without even a shred of shame, the halfling clomped over to the other side of the garden, where she promptly vanished from Ren's sight. Smothering a curse between gritted teeth, Ren set down their broom and went to find a new vantage point from inside the cottage. Cleaning up the kitchen would have to be a matter for later. No way they were going to let this halfling roam around unsupervised.

Slinking across the floorboards like a shadow, Ren crept towards the living room window, a half-moon opening along the cottage's front, framed in robin's-egg-blue wood. They carefully nudged aside the thick veins of ivy their family had grown to serve as curtains; enough that only a single, narrow sunbeam spilled across the sparsely furnished space. Just because they'd noticed the halfling didn't mean the halfling needed to notice them. In fact, Ren would greatly prefer it if she didn't. Or, better yet, the halfling could just turn around and leave.

Sadly, things couldn't be so easy.

The halfling, much to Ren's profound chagrin, did not turn around; nor did she leave. Instead, she went right up to the front door and, after a few moments spent digging around in a vast array of bags and satchels that couldn't possibly mean anything good, produced a key.

A key! Not even Ren had a key, and their clan had been taking care of this place for decades!

But the indignation searing the underside of their breastbone would have to wait. The halfling had inserted the key into the lock and, discovering it altogether unnecessary, had settled for simply turning the knob. A low creak then followed, unmistakable in its origin. If Ren was going to have any hope of keeping this halfling out of their house, they were going to have to act now.

"Oh, wow," the halfling said, near breathless with wonder as she stepped into the entry hall, its exposed beam ceilings, each inlaid with loose swirls of living moss, unfurling overhead in a precise geometric pattern. "This place has held up really well. I was expecting some holes in the roof. Maybe some missing floorboards. But this—"

With teeth bared and arms raised, Ren leapt from the shadows and roared. It wasn't the fiercest of sounds—frankly, Ren had heard puppies produce better—but it had the intended effect, nonetheless. The halfling screamed, scrambling backwards without a second thought. Unfortunately, instead of racing out of the cottage like Ren had wanted, she slammed into the wall behind her at full-force, hard enough to send the beams overhead rattling and loose the carefully cultivated moss from their inlays.

Years of work, ruined in an instant.

"Stop! You're destroying it!" Ren shouted, dropping their hands into a far less aggressive gesture. It was one thing for the halfling to break the things they'd made. But the work of Ren's clan—well, that was something else entirely.

The halfling, however, wasn't listening. "Get out of my house!" she cried, kicking at a nearby cluster of moss. Perhaps, she'd meant to launch it at Ren's face, but, as it was, she only managed to send it fluttering weakly into the air.

"Your house?" Ren repeated, incredulous, their ears flattening with displeasure. "No. This is my house."

"Then why do I have a, uh ..." The halfling fumbled for something, temporarily lost in the eye-searingly yellow tangle of her skirts. "A key!" She raised it in a moment of triumph, holding it high for Ren to see.

They scoffed. "Is that supposed to mean something? Move your foot so I can try and salvage what you just broke."

The halfling didn't budge, which was hardly a surprise. She

clearly had no concept of what now lay at her feet, the ruined tatters of moss scattered about her like bits of a desiccated corpse. Ren knelt down anyway, well-aware that doing so pushed them into range of the halfling's kick. But getting a boot to the face seemed a small price to pay if it meant scooping each green tuft into the safety of their palm.

Thankfully, the halfling's curiosity overshadowed her capacity for violence—at least for the moment. "What are you doing?" she asked, as if Ren hadn't already answered her question a second ago. Why couldn't halflings just listen?

They let out a harsh exhale, not even looking up as they continued to pick up bits of moss. "All of this? Came from up there. My clan planted the spores years ago in the grooves lining each of the support beams. That's where they should've stayed, by the way; but apparently destroying my mushroom farm wasn't enough for you."

Confusion streaked across the halfling's brow; and yet, there was something else, too, a glimmer in her eye that Ren might've called interest if they hadn't known better. Because, surely, no halfling would care one whit about goblin agricultural techniques.

Then again, maybe they would. If there was anything else as constant as the halfling penchant for running roughshod over anything and everything, it was their love of food, made manifest in pantries so well-stocked one would've thought these halflings were anticipating a several-centuries-long siege! But, of course, those didn't happen to halflings, 'peaceful,' 'jovial' people that they were.

Obviously, whoever had popularized that particular take hadn't found themselves on the wrong end of a halfling adventurer's sword. But admittedly, neither had Ren, too young to have even constituted a spark in their mother's eye the last time a dark lord had plunged the Realm into chaos. Still, something dark simmered in their belly as they looked upon this particular halfling, her obnoxiously bright clothing as damning as her cluelessness. Ugh. Why couldn't she just leave?

"I'm talking about those logs you knocked over on your way in," Ren explained, even though she didn't deserve it. "But at least that I can fix. This"—they gestured around themself—"maybe not, and definitely not completely. This probably comes as a surprise to you, but cultivating edible moss isn't something you can do on a whim, especially like this."

The halfling's cheeks pinked. "Well, you shouldn't have been doing it here anyway," she declared with a huff, arms crossing over her chest. "This is my grandmother, Angelica Underburrow's, house. A house which she passed down to me, Pansy Underburrow. So, like I said, this is my house." She spoke the last two words emphatically, as if that would somehow make them true.

Ridiculous.

"If this is your grandmother's house, then why hasn't she lived here in over twenty years?" Ren asked, finally straightening back up.

The halfling—Pansy—scowled as she plucked a bit of moss from the front of her sweater. She gave it a quick sniff, then flicked it over to Ren. "Because she was old and needed help. That's why she moved back to town—to Haverow. Now, you have your moss; so, you can go back to—wherever it is you came from."

"I'm not going anywhere," Ren replied, standing as tall as they could manage. Thankfully, this put them at least an inch above Pansy. "Your grandmother left this place to rot. If not for my family, it would be exactly as you said: full of holes and missing pieces. Instead, it's thriving. Look at how much life there is now!"

Bellflower. Creeping thyme. Stonecrop. Selfheal. Impossible to name every plant that coiled along the walls or from in between the floorboards. Then, there were the animals: the fireflies that slept inside paper lanterns repurposed to serve as their nests; the mice with questionable taste that lived in an old, halfling-style armchair far too soft for Ren's liking; and, of course, there was Pig, currently snoring away downstairs, no doubt.

And, somehow, none of this mattered to Pansy.

"This sort of mess belongs outside, you know." She scowled. "Not to mention, no one asked you to do anything in the first place."

Ren stared at her, incredulous. "What does asking have to do with any of it?"

"Oh, right. Yes. Of course. Silly me." Pansy bopped the heel of her palm lightly against her temple. "I'm speaking to a goblin. You lot never ask; you simply take!"

"Better than letting go to waste what others could use!" Ren snapped, teeth flashing as fire roared inside their chest. "My clan needed a place to live. This house was empty. Clearly, no one was using it; so, why shouldn't they?"

"Because. It's. Not. Theirs."

"So, a perfectly good home falls into disrepair such that no one can use it. You honestly think that's better?"

"I—" Pansy snapped her mouth shut, brow furrowing as she considered Ren's words. Whatever heat had ignited between them suddenly cooled, quelled by the need to think rather than simply feel. "Stealing is wrong," she declared at last, albeit without her earlier fervor.

Ren sighed. "Well, at least you had enough sense to actually stop and think about it. Surprising for a halfling. Of course, that doesn't change the fact that you're wrong, which, for the record, is far less of a shock."

Fresh crimson streaked across the bridge of Pansy's nose. "Wrong or not, this is still my house, and I fully intend to live in it." Then, as if to drive her point home, she slipped the vast assortment of bags from her shoulders and allowed them to fall to the floor with a resounding thump.

"What a coincidence," Ren remarked, their tone a touch too biting to be considered droll. "Because I was thinking the exact same thing."

Pansy's eyes bulged. "No! Absolutely not. You need to leave. Go be with your"—she gestured vaguely with one hand—"clan—or however you prefer to call it. I'm certain you'll be far more comfortable there anyway. After all, this is clearly a halfling burrow, not a cave. So, hardly suitable for a goblin like yourself."

Ren's chest constricted at the thought of returning to their clan. If only such a thing were possible. But duty bound them to this cottage, and so here they would stay. How shameful it would be to return now, after only a day, rendering their word barely worth the breath that had fueled it.

Swallowing around the lump that had knotted in their throat, Ren said, "I'm quite comfortable here actually. You'd be surprised how cave-like a so-called 'burrow' can be. But thank you for your concern."

Pansy huffed. "I'm trying to be nice here—"

"Oh, are you?" Ren cocked their head to the side, ears perking up in mock surprise. "I honestly couldn't tell. Because where I come from, we don't call someone who barges in unannounced, breaks things that aren't theirs, and insults others 'nice'; we call them a—"

"Okay! Okay! I get it!" Pansy said, holding up both hands in surrender. "You're right. I haven't been very nice. But, in my defense, I didn't expect to find my grandmother's cottage already—inhabited." She ground out the word with something like a grimace, as if it physically pained her to acknowledge an otherwise readily apparent fact.

"If my presence is such a problem," Ren said, crossing their arms over their chest, "then feel free to go back to your village. That way you'll never have to see me again."

A strange expression took hold of Pansy at that, pinching her features together in a way Ren couldn't quite parse. It wasn't sadness or frustration or anything nearly so simple; but, rather, a current of something old and deep-seated, like an abscess that continued to fester below the surface.

"I can't do that," Pansy said, averting her gaze for the first time. "I need—I need to stay here."

There was a certainty to that statement, a level of conviction that Ren found almost admirable. But there was also desperation, buzzing beneath that hard veneer like a hive of frenzied hornets. Whatever had driven Pansy to this cottage, it would not be so easily dismissed; not even by an unwanted goblin like themself.

It was then that Pansy's expression suddenly brightened, understanding flashing in the brown rings of her irises. "You understand that right? That I need this cottage."

Her stare was back upon Ren; now, with an added layer of expectation that hooked beneath their skin. They eyed her warily, uncertainty itching along their spine. "And? That doesn't change the fact that I need it too." That my clan needs it.

"Okay, but one of us can surely make better use of it than the other, no?"

"Of course," Ren answered quickly, so assured of their own need that they didn't even think to consider where exactly Pansy was going with this. After all, what could possibly trump ensuring their clan survived the coming winter?

"So, that person should get the cottage, then. Easy. Problem solved."

Easy? The gall of this halfling . . . "And how exactly are we going to determine that?" Ren asked, eyebrows arching. "You and I both know that words alone won't suffice here."

Then again, perhaps, they were giving Pansy too much credit. She opened her mouth, then promptly shut it again; whatever she'd meant to say lost beneath the press of her teeth. Ren nearly scoffed. Had Pansy seriously believed that they would simply take her at her word? Relinquish their clan's last and only lifeline because a halfling told them to?

Yes, answered Pansy's expression, the wide-eyed look of panic as her mind scrambled for an alternative way forward. How self-centered she must be to think that her people's distrust of goblins hadn't sown similar seeds among the clans, too used to bearing the weight of their kin's sins that they no longer expected anything else. And yet, at the same time, she'd also displayed a very real capacity for understanding. Instead of digging her heels in and continuing to speak about the cottage in terms Ren neither recognized nor cared for, Pansy had stepped beyond the bounds of her own culture and listened; something the monolithic halfling in Ren's mind would've never done. Maybe, that's why they were still willing to hear her out.

"I've got it!" Pansy exclaimed, her eyes sparking with yet another idea. "For now, we'll both live here. But if either one of us decides to move out, then that person forfeits their right to the cottage. Hard to make use of a home if you don't live in it, right?"

Ren blinked, wondering if they'd simply misheard. "I'm sorry, but did you just say you want to live here—together?"

"Well, it's not exactly my first choice," Pansy said with a shrug that was far too nonchalant in the circumstances. "But, like I said, I really need to live here; so, I'll tolerate it. And just in case you get any bright ideas about forcing me out: no breaking each other's stuff. That's rule number one."

Ah. So, that was the halfling's real plan. She wanted to push Ren out, and judging from the grin on her face, she really thought she could manage it. A laughable thought. It would take more than some unpleasant behavior and halfling decor to convince Ren to turn their back on their clan.

"Fine," Ren agreed, their lips parting around a razor-edged smile; what should've been Pansy's first clue that she'd made a grave miscalculation. "But that rule extends to the cottage itself too. We can only add to what's already there. Unless, of course, something is broken or needs to be repaired. In that case, we both need to decide on a solution together."

"Sounds fair to me!" Pansy chirped, then shoved a familiar hand, soft and sun-kissed, out towards Ren. "So, we have a deal then?"

A strange tremor curled in Ren's stomach as they stared down at the proffered palm. They'd touched it before, of course, the memory of yesterday rising, unbidden, to the forefront of their mind, bringing with it a flash of remembered heat. So, why then, did an entirely similar prospect suddenly root them to the spot?

Probably just unease, they told themself, dismissing the behavior with a silent scoff as they reached out to grip Pansy's hand at last; before their hesitation could turn awkward.

Pansy, meanwhile, gave Ren's hand one quick, business-like pump, then pulled away just as swiftly. Less than a second's worth of contact, and still it lingered, a tingling warmth that buzzed against Ren's skin, ever insistent.

Did Pansy feel it too, they wondered, fingers flexing in a (vain) effort to chase the sensation away. It might've been just their imagination, but Ren swore that Pansy's fingers curled into the folds of her skirts a touch harder than before.

"Great," Pansy said, her voice coming out oddly strangled. "I'm, uh, Pansy, by the way."

"I know. You already told me."

"Oh, right." Red bloomed high on Pansy's cheeks. "I forgot."

"Obviously." A beat. Then, somewhat grudgingly: "My name is Ren."

"Ren," Pansy confirmed with a nod. "I'll remember that. Now, with all that settled, I'm going to go ahead and take a look around. And don't you even think of throwing my stuff out behind my back while I'm gone. That, may I remind you, would be cheating."

"Don't flatter yourself," Ren said with a derisive snort. "As if I'd need to cheat to get you out." Then, with a sharp twist of their heel, they headed for the garden, pointedly leaving Pansy—and her plethora of bags—behind.

CHAPTER THREE

Pansy

Although Pansy had been anything but serious when she'd made that quip about getting a new goblin housemate, it seemed the universe was determined to have the last laugh in the end—even if it came entirely at her expense.

To say that today hadn't gone according to plan would've been a tremendous understatement. Granted, Pansy's 'plan' relied on a rather generous interpretation of the word; its second step, lodged firmly between 'acquire cottage' and 'profit,' little more than a long series of question marks. But even so, finding her grandmother's cottage—her cottage—beset by a longtime squatter didn't seem like the sort of situation any amount of foresight could've solved.

Though, perhaps, said squatter wasn't quite so longtime as they would've liked her to believe. As Pansy wound her way through the cottage's expansive halls, she couldn't help but notice that the vast majority of rooms were pretty much bare. With more plants that furnishings, the cottage seemed more like an overgrown garden than an actual home. And while Pansy could believe that goblins didn't share her own people's propensity for decorating every last shred of available space, surely even they needed more than a tattered, halfling-style armchair and a handful of other equally worn pieces.

So, Ren lied to me. What a surprise. Pansy scowled, more

frustrated with herself than anything else. After all, only a fool would take a goblin's claim at face value, especially when dealing with matters of ownership. But she'd confront Ren about it later. There was still so much to explore.

Because unlike her own parents' burrow in Haverow (and most halfling burrows in general), the cottage wasn't confined to just a single level. Instead, it pushed deep into the earth, leading Pansy lower and lower via a series of wooden steps. There, the polished floorboards of upstairs gave way to rich, black dirt, and the air, once bright and warm, cooled and thickened with moisture. If Pansy hadn't known better, she would've thought she'd just stepped into a cave. But this wasn't a cave; this was a burrow—just one that was a little rougher around the edges than most.

An expansion in progress! Yes, that was definitely it, Pansy concluded with a satisfied nod, smiling at her own good thinking. Clearly, her grandmother—or, perhaps, whoever had owned the cottage before her—had simply not gotten around to putting in proper walls or floors yet. Once those were in place, there would be no question that this was a halfling's burrow. But for now ...

"Well, I suppose a few carpets would go a long way," Pansy mused, surveying the space. "Maybe some nice tapestries too— to cover the moss growing along the walls. And those icky mushrooms too. But then again ..." She tapped a finger against her chin, considering. "They are kind of useful, glowing like that. Who knows how dark it'd be down here otherwise."

Far too dark for any halfling to see; that was for sure. Even now, Pansy struggled to navigate the murky gloom, ever-pulsating with eerie bioluminescence. It was no wonder, then, that she eventually tripped, her foot catching on a bit of raised stonework, jutting just high enough to become a hazard.

She went down hard, landing in a graceless heap. The dirt, at least, was soft where she fell; though Pansy couldn't bring herself to feel grateful for it. The sting of indignity was too great to be soothed by such a small mercy.

Ignoring the slight twinge that had hooked into her ankle—a dull throb that was hardly worth any measure of concern—Pansy staggered to her feet. She dusted herself off as best as she could, grimacing at the dampness that now marred her skirt in twin points by her knees. Hopefully, getting these stains out wouldn't take too much scrubbing . . .

Cursing her own clumsiness, Pansy whirled around in search of her inanimate assailant. Her eyes almost immediately landed on a small, stone circle, jutting out of otherwise unbroken earth; not quite a dais, but too large to be a mere stepping stone. It sat alone, at the space's midpoint, its placement purposeful. But for what, Pansy couldn't say; unless, of course, it was simply there to trip the unaware.

Squatting down, Pansy squinted closer at the flat stonework, her fingertips skimming across its surface. Strange swirls unfurled beneath the pads of her fingers, flowing into one another like the tide. They clung to the stone's edge, creating a circle within a circle. Indecipherable; yet familiar, nonetheless.

"They're runes," she whispered, awe sweeping the breath from her lungs. She'd seen them before, stitched into her grandmother's favorite blanket. Not these same runes, of course—it wouldn't make much sense for a random stone to heat up—but still similar enough that a thread of recollection, nestled somewhere deep in Pansy's brain, pulled taut.

"I wonder what they're for," she murmured, a question her own limited knowledge of magic would struggle to answer. After all, that was the realm of elves and gnomes; not halflings, who generally preferred more tangible things, like crafts and agriculture. But, perhaps, there was a clue in her surroundings . . .

She glanced around, her eyes straining ever harder against the greenish half-light. However, apart from a couple of dusty, old rugs, rolled-up and shoved in a corner, there wasn't much to be found, this part of the cottage equally as empty as the last.

That being said, there was a stone archway embedded into the wall ahead of her, its surface decorated with an intricate pattern of drooping wolfsbane, identical to the plants growing along its base. But it led nowhere, its center revealing nothing but flat, unblemished rock. No seams or anything. So, probably just another unfinished project.

"Add it to the list," Pansy grumbled.

Still, those runes did something. Was it too much to hope that they might help her with her current goblin predicament? Maybe. But that wasn't going to stop Pansy from noting them down on the small notepad she usually kept on hand. Just in case.

Had Ren already come across them, she wondered as she slipped the notepad back into her apron pocket, her shopping list now accompanied by a crude rendition of the runes at her feet. Better not to take any chances, she decided.

Seizing one of the old rugs she'd spotted earlier, Pansy dragged it over to where the stone was. She unfurled it, coughing as the motion loosed what must've been a couple decades' worth of dust, and laid it out over the runes.

"There!" she said, smiling at her handiwork, the slight protrusion that remained easily dismissed as one of many wrinkles. "Totally hidden."

It was then that something solid brushed against her leg, quelling her triumph with a sudden deluge of ice-cold fear. Pansy jumped, letting out a high-pitched squeal of a scream that she hoped wouldn't make its way upstairs. Looking down, she found a familiar pig staring up at her, its head cocked to the side in confusion.

Pansy let out a breath, the tension unspooling from her shoulders. "Oh, it's just you, little thief." Bending down, she gave the creature a light scritch underneath the chin, which it received all too eagerly. "That wasn't a compliment, by the way," she added, when the pig pushed itself more squarely against her palm.

After a few minutes of petting, punctuated by ever-more-pleased-sounding snorts, Pansy finally withdrew her hand, much to the pig's dissatisfaction. When it realized it couldn't persuade Pansy into resuming her ministrations, it snuffled over to the rug and began pawing at it with one cloven hoof.

"No, no, no. Let's not do that," Pansy said, gently nudging the pig away with one hand. "It'll be our little secret, okay?"

Thankfully, the pig's listening skills seemed to have improved since their encounter in the forest. And though it did give her a rather dubious look, as if to say 'you're not fooling anyone,' before trotting off, in this case, Pansy would take whatever she could get.

"Oh, you're back," Ren said as Pansy stepped into the kitchen, a narrow, galley-style room outfitted with dark green cabinetry and whitewashed paneling that had nearly been swallowed whole by the encroaching coil of some variety of plant life. "I thought you might've fallen into a hole or something given that scream of yours."

Pansy flushed. Of course, they'd heard her. Large though the cottage was, it wasn't that large. Honestly, she'd have been better off hoping that Ren might do the polite thing and simply not mention it. At least, that had a chance—a tiny, near infinitesimal chance, but a chance nonetheless—of happening.

"That thieving pig of yours sneaked up on me in the dark," Pansy grumbled, ducking her head to one side in the hope that it would shield the worst of her embarrassment from view.

It didn't. Not really. But, in the end, the effectiveness of her strategy proved largely irrelevant. Ren hadn't spared her more than a passing glance, the kind triggered by reflex rather than genuine interest. Moreover, their attention had long since moved on, shifting, instead, to the reed basket perched on the countertop beside them, its lid rendering its contents a mystery—at least, for now.

Probably more moss, Pansy thought with a slight scowl. As if the cottage isn't already full of it ...

"I don't appreciate you lying to me, by the way," she added, the heat that had once stained her cheeks draining into her voice, where it condensed into a caustic barb.

Ren stilled, their hands clamped on either side of the basket, primed to pull it closer. "And when did I lie to you exactly?" they asked, their gaze swiveling over their shoulder to meet hers.

"When you told me your clan had lived here for years. I looked around, and this cottage is practically empty!"

"Ah. That." A pause, filled with the sounds of restless shuffling, of Ren opening the basket and removing its contents, one-by-one; proof, in Pansy's mind, that she'd caught them red-handed. At last, they said, calm as ever, "I didn't lie to you. My clan has been using this cottage for decades now."

"Then where is all your stuff? And don't tell me that goblins don't use furniture because that's nonsense, and I won't believe it."

Ren let out a harsh breath, their nostrils flaring as they cast a look up at the curved truss overhead—seeking divine guidance or, perhaps, just patience. "Is there any point explaining it to you?" they asked, bitterness oozing from every syllable. "You've clearly already come to the conclusion that I'm a liar, and I'd rather not waste my time beating my head against a rock that refuses to be moved."

Pansy stiffened, not entirely sure whether to take Ren's comment as an insult. It probably was all things considered—even if being called a 'rock' was hardly the worst thing in the world. Still, Pansy wanted answers, not a crash course in goblin put-downs. So, she said, "I'm not so prideful that I can't admit when I'm wrong."

Ren scoffed. "You're a miracle among halflings, then. But—fine. Since you listened to me earlier." They sucked in a deep, steady breath and turned around so they could face her fully, propping their elbows against the stone countertop. "I only became this cottage's Caretaker recently. Yesterday, in fact. This place used to be my aunt's responsibility, but she—she got sick. So, the clan needed someone else to shoulder the burden in her stead."

Seeing the way Ren's throat bobbed, how it snagged on the knot of emotion that had stoppered it, Pansy couldn't help but soften. "I'm sorry," she said, the heat of her earlier annoyance evaporating from her skin as quickly as the early morning dew in summer. "Is it serious?"

"Yes," Ren replied, a hoarse croak that spoke volumes. Far

more than they'd wanted to convey, it seemed, because they immediately rushed to clear their throat. When they continued a moment later, they did so in a far more neutral tone. "As for the furniture, if I'd asked, my aunt would've no doubt left some things behind. But right now, she and the clan can make better use of whatever used to be here. So, I told them I'd be fine with only the necessities."

"And the absolute barest of them at that, given what I've seen ..."

Ren shrugged. "Goblins have all learned to make do with little. I'm no exception."

Pansy paused, thinking. "You called yourself the cottage's 'Caretaker.' That's an interesting choice of words."

"I'm sure you halflings would much rather call me a squatter," Ren snapped, their voice sharpening once again; whetted to a knife's point not out of a desire to hurt others, it seemed, but, rather, protect themself. No doubt, they thought they needed to stave off another attack. And what better way than to lash out first, before the other person even got the chance to strike?

Blood pooled beneath Pansy's skin anew, now with a sick, sour tinge. She had thought of Ren that way—earlier, when she'd been exploring the cottage. But, somehow, listening to them now, the word seemed wrong, ill-fitting; not entirely inaccurate, but—too harsh? Maybe, Pansy was imagining things, but it seemed almost like Ren didn't actually want to be here. They had called it a burden, after all. So, why stay? Unless, of course, they had no other option ...

"That's not what I was implying. I promise," Pansy said, hands held up, palms out, in an attempt to placate. "It's just an awfully weighty word, isn't it? Serious."

"Because it is serious," Ren snarled, not mollified in the least. "I know this will probably be lost on you, but there's a beauty in living with the natural world instead of in spite of it. Do you even know how many trees were felled to build this cottage? How much earth was shifted? How many plants and animals were displaced?"

"I'm guessing a lot, judging from your tone."

"Yes. A lot," Ren said, their voice flattening with contempt. "That's why it's so important to make space for nature, to take only what is necessary and no more. Anyone who refuses to honor this truth is a fool, as blind as the snake that eats its own tail."

Although Pansy was loathe to admit it, there was something oddly captivating about the way Ren spoke. Each world pulsed with an undeniable sort of passion; the kind forged in the very heart of a person's soul. It blazed inside them, as wild and fierce as dragon's breath, until even the green rings of their irises shone like burning halos. The sight shouldn't have been nearly so beautiful; and yet, it was, drawing Pansy in, like a moth to a flame. She wanted to listen to Ren, to hear more.

Except, that wasn't part of the plan, was it? The realization crashed over her like a bucket of ice water, extinguishing what-ever spark Ren's fire had kindled in turn. She couldn't afford to let herself get distracted like this. Her mission was simple: get Ren out. Nothing more. After all, this cottage was hers by right; no matter what Ren or any other goblin thought about it. And Pansy, determined to see her grandmother's final wish—her last gift to her—honored, refused to compromise on this fact.

"Alright," Pansy said, the word scraping across her tongue like an anchor. "But—and forgive me if I'm wrong—you don't seem very, um, happy? To be here, that is. I mean, you called it a 'burden' earlier, so ..."

Ren blinked at her, their ears pricking up in what Pansy fig-ured was an expression of surprise—but only for a beat. Soon, they were drooping once more, falling in time with the heavy sigh that escaped Ren's lips. "What I want doesn't matter."

"Of course, it does!" Pansy protested, the words exploding out of her with more force than she'd intended. But that sort of weary resignation just didn't sit right with her! "What's the point of doing anything if it doesn't make you happy? Honestly, I—" She snapped her mouth shut; words too personal for someone who was still practically a stranger crashing against the backs of her teeth. I would still be back in Haverow if I hadn't put my own happiness first.

"Fine," Ren said with something like a huff. "Then what I want is for you to stop bothering me." And with that, they turned on their heel once more, seemingly convinced that the sight of their back would be enough to deter Pansy from making further conversation.

Unfortunately for Ren, all chances of that happening vanished the moment the rhythmic thunk-thunk of a knife against a cutting board reached Pansy's ears; the pace far slower than what she was used to, but still serviceable.

"Are you cooking?" she asked, her curiosity already propelling her forward as any and all recognition of the concept of personal space was thrown from her mind.

Ren stiffened. The sudden intrusion over their shoulder had not gone unnoticed, and they pointedly leaned away from Pansy, a spark of indignation streaking briefly across their features before a new feeling rose to smother it. Unfortunately, of that, Pansy only got a glimpse. Ren ducked their head away from her, long hair drawing over their face like a veil.

"Obviously," they muttered, an odd tremor hooking into their voice. "Sorry to disappoint, but we goblins don't just scoop our food right out of the dirt and into our mouths."

Pansy jerked back, eyes going wide. "I never said you did!"

"No," Ren admitted after a beat, settling back into the space Pansy had abandoned. "But you were probably thinking it."

"Well, I wasn't." Pansy huffed, arms crossing over her chest. "I just wanted to know what you were making. So, stop putting words into my mouth."

"Fine. But to answer your question, I'm making a warm mushroom salad." They gestured to the mushrooms splayed across their cutting board, tiny white buttons already divested of their stems. None of them, as far as Pansy could tell, had been cut evenly. "And unlike those Bloodletter Shrooms you stuffed into your basket the other day," Ren added, "all of these are edible."

Pansy attempted to mask the fresh rush of scarlet to her face with a scoff. "Edible is hardly the sort of measure you want to use for a dish. As far as bars go, that one is practically on the floor."

Ren scowled, though the downward pull of their mouth was scarcely visible through the thick curtain of their hair. "My cooking is fine. Besides, it's not like I'm making this for you or anything. So, there's no reason for you to have an opinion on the matter."

"Then why do you have enough ingredients for two servings?" Pansy asked, eyebrows arching as she pointed at the cutting board.

"I—I like having leftovers."

Pansy snorted. "That's about as believable as what I said yesterday about using those stupid Bloodletter Shrooms as decoration."

Not bothering to wait for whatever half-baked excuse Ren was going to come up with next, she began rummaging through the kitchen's various cabinets. To her profound dismay, they quickly revealed their contents to be almost as sparse as the rest of the cottage, their shelves devoid of even the most basic of kitchen staples. No olive oil. No vinegar. And certainly, none of the seasonings Pansy had come to rely upon in her own everyday cooking. Instead, she found a small assortment of strange plants, none of which she could identify—maybe not even with a copy of Mister Fatleaf's eponymous guidebook at her disposal.

"Where are all your ingredients?" she asked, unable to mask the shrill note of distress that crept into her voice as she continued tearing open cabinet after cabinet. Because, surely, she'd simply not yet reached the right one.

"What are you talking about?" Ren asked, their brow furrowing. "They're all there—back in that first cabinet you opened. How did you miss it?"

Had she? Pansy returned to the cabinet in question, unable to shake the doubt that had snaked in alongside Ren's words. But when she ripped open the door again, so swiftly it was a wonder the whole thing didn't fly right off the wall, she saw nothing beyond the same odd plants from before.

"There's nothing in here! Just some weird plants. See?" She grabbed a tightly wrapped bundle of reed-like stems from the collection and thrust it out towards Ren. "How am I supposed to make a vinaigrette with a bunch of leaves?"

Ren blinked. "Do you not know what oilflute is?"

"No?"

At this point, Pansy assumed that Ren would offer some kind of explanation. Clearly, she was just as knowledgeable about plants as she was about mushrooms, which was to say not very. However, Ren didn't say a thing. Instead, they laughed.

And this wasn't just a giggle or a small chuckle. No, Ren full-on howled with laughter, to the point where they could no longer stand upright, their body shaking as they doubled over, hands clutching at their stomach.

"Stop laughing!" Pansy protested, heat sparking within her anew. Except, this time it bloomed lower, softer, fluttering against the contours of her ribs. This wasn't the white-hot flash of anger or the sour burn of shame. This was something else; something Pansy struggled to name. After all, it would make sense for her to be annoyed or even embarrassed. Ren was laughing at her! Making fun of her! She should be upset about it. So, why wasn't she?"

Unfortunately, Pansy couldn't even supply a halfway decent hypothesis for that one, much less an answer. Her thoughts had come to an abrupt standstill, unraveled by singular, even less explicable observation. Because, in that moment, all Pansy could thing about was just how nice Ren's laugh sounded. Clear and pure, like the chime of a bell.

Blessed Harvest! What am I even thinking? She shook her head, hoping that this might dislodge whatever strange compulsion had possessed her. A halfling should never have these sorts of thoughts about a goblin; a halfling whose grandmother had spent the better part of her life fighting back whole armies of them even less so.

Thankfully, Ren didn't seem to have noticed Pansy's ongoing internal crisis. They grinned at her, tiny fangs flashing in the last burnished rays of fading daylight that filtered in through a nearby open window. Wiping the last bits of mirth from their eyes, they said, "I knew you halflings were an ignorant bunch, but to think that ignorance even extends to the one thing you can never seem to have enough of. The irony, it's—dare I say it—delicious!"

At last, the heat from before shifted into something Pansy recognized, understood. "Excuse me?" she demanded, an icy jolt now accompanying the fire licking its way up the sides of her face.

Ren's grin, however, only stretched wider. "You know," they said, "we goblins often joke that halflings must've uncovered the secret to time travel magic because you all seem to have more feast days than there are days on the calendar."

"That's not true—"

"Is it?" Ren cocked their head to the side. "Could've fooled me with the state of your pantries, always stuffed to the brim. Though, I suppose yours is rather lacking at the moment. How dreadful it must be to have nothing but 'weird,' 'nasty' goblin ingredients at your disposal. Gosh! What will the neighbors think? Better go back to Haverton, where you can have a 'proper' kitchen with 'proper' ingredients like you so justly deserve."

"First of all, it's Have-row; not Haver-ton. Secondly, never once did I call your ingredients 'weird' or 'nasty' or any variation thereof—nor was I thinking it," Pansy quickly added when she saw Ren predictably open their mouth in protest. "So, stop using your imagination to justify your cruelty towards me. And thirdly, I'm not leaving, so either show me how to use these ingredients properly or get out of the way. You're mangling those poor mushrooms."

If she wasn't so furious, Pansy might've laughed at the wide-eyed look of shock Ren gave her, their lips parting uselessly, like a gasping fish out of water. Had they seriously expected her to turn and run because of a few mean words? Unfortunately for them, her time in Haverow had trained her to weather almost anything, her skin thickened beneath the brunt of a thousand tiny cuts. There, she'd already been 'the other,' the odd halfling girl too adventurous for her own good, and every one of her many facets had, over time, been scrutinized into a flaw.

At least, Ren knew they were being cruel; getting her to leave was the point. But the halflings of Haverow would look upon Pansy's departure with nothing but confusion, wondering what could've possibly pushed her to leave their 'perfect' village behind—as if the decades' worth of unvarnished criticism had been a kindness rather than a constant torment!

"Here," Ren said at last, grabbing a bowl from one of the cabinets and extending it towards her; the closest thing, it seemed, she'd be getting to an apology.

"What am I supposed to do with that?" Pansy asked, confusion knotting deep plough lines across her brow.

"You wanted to make a vinaigrette, right? Squeeze the oilflute in your hand over the bowl."

Her expression turned dubious. "I don't see how a bunch of weeds are going to help with that. But, okay." She did as instructed, eyes widening when a steady trickle of cloudy, milk-white fluid escaped from in between her clenched fingers, pooling in a shallow puddle at the bottom of the bowl.

It wasn't anything like olive oil in appearance, but in terms of consistency, the liquid the oilflute had produced was practically identical. Slick with a definite thickness, though not to the point where Pansy would call it viscous. Her curiosity piqued, she lifted her fingers, now glistening with an oily sheen, to her nose and gave them a sniff. A mild, grassy aroma greeted her; far less pungent than what she'd expected. But what about the taste?

"Oh!" Pansy jerked away, her features fluttering like a pair of shutters, newly cast open. "It tastes almost like olive oil. That's incredible! The flavor's a bit milder, perhaps, but that shouldn't be too much of an issue. What about vinegar? I assume you have something for that too?"

Ren nodded and, after handing off the bowl to Pansy,

retrieved a jug from one of the few cabinets Pansy hadn't searched—mostly because they'd been standing in front of it at the time.

"What's that?" Pansy asked as Ren set the jug down on the counter with a dull thump, enough to send the clear liquid inside sloshing.

"Vinegar," they replied, the corner of their mouth quirking up into a lop-sided smirk that shouldn't have made them look nearly so handsome, especially after the cruelty they'd just lobbed from those same lips. "Made from sugarfern, which, I'm guessing, you've never heard of before either."

"Well, it's a goblin ingredient, right? So, of course, I wouldn't be familiar with it." Pansy shrugged, her attempt at nonchalance thwarted by the visible tightness pulling along her shoulders.

"As you can see," Ren said, with pointed emphasis, "I can manage dinner just fine on my own. Your help is not only entirely unnecessary, but also rather unhelpful."

Maybe, it was. But Pansy was no longer listening. The comfort of the kitchen was a familiar one, and she dove headlong into it, turning her attention to the other ingredients, still stored inside the cabinet. She plucked them out, one by one, arranging them across the countertop, a veritable cornucopia of new culinary treasures just waiting to be beheld.

"What's this one?" she asked, pointing to the first, her mind already spinning with possibilities. "And this one? Can I taste a bit? Ooh. Do you have anything that's citrus-y? And what about your seasonings? You must have some seasonings."

Ren sighed, their shoulders slumping in defeat as they swept the hair back from their face. "You're not going to leave the kitchen, are you?"

"Nope!" Pansy chirped, her lips parting around a too-broad grin that sent Ren's own thinning. "Do you want a hair tie, by the way? I think I have a spare one in my pocket. Easier to cook when you don't have to constantly push your hair out of your face."

"I'm starting to think that I should just cut it," Ren grumbled, but nonetheless accepted the proffered ribbon. With a few deft motions, their hair, which otherwise came down to mid-back, was wound up into a loose bun near the top of their head, leaving only a few lingering strands.

One by one, they explained each of the ingredients, describing not just their flavor profiles, but also how they were normally used. Oilflute. Sugarfern. Beechmoss. Lichenberry. Pansy couldn't believe how many there were. What had once been nothing more than a tangle of strange plants had unfurled into a fresh source of inspiration, seeding beneath her fingertips a desire to cook so great she could barely stand it.

In a way, it was almost ironic. To think that goblin cuisine, something she'd never given much thought until now, would awaken in her that same sense of wonder that had seized her the first time her mother had brought her into the kitchen as a young girl.

"This is going to taste amazing," Pansy said as she poured the mushrooms, now dressed in a mixture of vinegar, oilflute, and lichenberry—the closest thing Ren had to a lemon—into a hot skillet. "Honestly, the smell is already making my mouth water, and the mushrooms haven't even started to brown yet. Have you finished chopping the garlic?"

"Almost," Ren replied, their brow furrowed in deep concentration. Although their knife-work still needed refinement, they'd nonetheless managed to cut each clove into appropriately small pieces. After all, there was nothing worse than biting down onto a massive chunk of garlic mid-meal.

"Okay. When you're done with it, throw it into a bowl with some oilflute, vinegar, and—what was that yellow tomato-like vegetable you showed me again? Ambervine?"

Ren nodded.

"Yeah. Mash that up and then mix it all together. That'll be our dressing."

A beat, punctuated by the sound of a whisk scraping the bottom of a bowl. Then: "This is a lot of ingredients for one meal," Ren mumbled.

"Is it? I think it's a pretty simple recipe, actually," Pansy said with a shrug, now gently stirring the mushrooms while great swells of steam wafted up from the skillet.

Another pause. "I wouldn't have used most of these."

"Then I'm glad I could give you some evidently much-needed instruction." She grinned. "How's the dressing coming?"

"Here," Ren said, passing her the bowl in question, their face an inscrutable mask.

"Thanks," she said and tossed the dressing into the pan; the liquid the mushrooms had released had finally cooked off. A couple more stirs, enough to ensure that everything was properly coated, and Pansy cranked off the heat with a flourish. "Now, to put everything together. You have no idea how excited I am to taste this."

"Me too," Ren admitted after a brief pause, their voice so soft it was nearly drowned out by the sound of Pansy clattering about the kitchen in her haste to assemble the salad in its full glory.

And it was certainly glorious. As the first bite crunched between her teeth, crisp lettuce marrying chewy mushrooms in a salty, sweet ceremony that was both familiar and new in equal parts, Pansy found herself overcome with a sudden unshakable sense of certainty. This was what she'd been searching for.

"It's delicious," she murmured, lips parting around a swell of wonder, bright and airy, like gossamer.

"It is," Ren agreed, perhaps a bit grudgingly, the tip of their fork resting against their lower lip, as if caught between two competing impulses: the first, to keep the flavor, still clinging to the utensil's points, on their tongue; and the second, to prevent a second bite.

All in all, a success, Pansy decided. Hopefully, with plenty more to follow—once she paid the grocer back in Haverow a much-needed visit, of course. But that, along with many others, was a problem for tomorrow.

\#

With her belly now full and the day's exhaustion settling onto her bones like a set of heavy, iron manacles, Pansy decided it was time for bed. The cottage, thankfully, was not without one. It sat at the center of the master bedroom—the only real bedroom, given the cottage's barely-furnished state—an immense, towering structure of cast iron and ornate brass, polished to a near-blinding sheen. Though the craftsmanship was undeniably halfling in origin, with each whorl of brass fashioned into a budding bloom, it, like much of the cottage, had suffered a certain level of—call it encroachment. The four posts that would've once supported a canopy of fabric were, instead, draped in long trails of ivy, and the down mattress that Pansy had been expecting had been replaced by a flat expanse of strange, spongy material.

Pressing a hand against it, Pansy conceded that it was not entirely uncomfortable; though she did wonder whether her form would be forever etched into its surface once she'd laid upon it. An unnecessary concern, it turned out. The material sprang back into place the moment she removed her hand, leaving no evidence that she'd ever touched it.

Either way, this mattress, peculiar though it was, was infinitely preferable to sleeping on the floor, which, admittedly, Pansy had been a touch worried about during her initial tour of the cottage. Truly, she'd never been so glad to see that the 'necessities,' as Ren had put it, included a bed—even if it didn't come with any sheets.

Good thing Pansy had plenty of those. She selected a set in soft, buttery yellow—one of her favorites by far—and spread them across the mattress with practiced ease. A horde of blankets, each woven from nearly a dozen different shades of yarn, soon followed, along with far more pillows than any one person could conceivably use, as demonstrated by the fact that the vast majority of them would've surely migrated to the floor come morning. By the time she was finished, the bed looked almost exactly like the one she'd left behind in her parents' burrow. The ivy, of course, being the one key difference.

Pleased with the fruits of her efforts, Pansy headed into the adjoining bathroom to finish getting ready for bed. She shivered as she crossed the threshold, the terracotta tiles cool against the bare soles of her feet. Perhaps, she should've taken a moment to dig out her slippers, soft, wool-lined things that had warmed her toes through many a winter. But with a small caravan's worth of luggage staring back at her, such a task was easier said than done; the mere thought alone was enough to turn her very bones to lead.

Yet another item for tomorrow, it seemed.

While she waited for the bath, a slate-gray tub crammed beneath the room's sole window, its glass panes lightly frosted for privacy, Pansy organized her sizable collection of toiletries into the shallow cubbies that had been carved into the wall by the sink. After all, this was to be a permanent arrangement; so she might as well get things set up as she liked them. Certainly, before Ren had a chance to take over.

In a way, she found herself in a kind of race. The goal? To infuse as much of herself into this cottage before Ren could do the same for themself. It reminded her of Pioneers of Plainsborough, a game she'd once played as a child, where each player sought to capture the most tiles on the board in a bid to expand their respective 'farms.' Much to her peers' frustration (and her own delight), she'd taken to it like a duck to water, thoroughly sweeping the board every time she played. This situation with the cottage, she resolved, would be no different. After all, she'd already claimed both the master bed and bath for herself. A big win for the Pansy Dominion by anyone's standards.

And yet, somehow, Ren hadn't gotten the memo.

Pansy's eyes bulged as she padded back into the bedroom, the damp ends of her curls frizzing in the lingering steam. Because there was Ren, shoving aside her carefully manicured bedspread in favor of—you guessed it!—more moss.

"What are you doing?" she demanded, rushing over in a flurry of staccato slaps of skin against hardwood. "This is my bed!"

Ren paused just long enough to give her a withering, side-long look, their long, pointed ears flattening against their skull in naked displeasure. "Just because you've thrown your stuff all over it doesn't make it yours." A point they punctuated by tossing one of Pansy's many pillows, a heavily embroidered sham with scalloped edges, at her face.

Pansy caught the pillow easily, setting it back onto the bed with a scowl. "We agreed not to destroy each other's things."

"How am I destroying anything? I'm just making some room."

Room. It was then that Pansy noticed Ren's clothing, a loose beige tunic that came down to their knees; far more like her own pink nightgown than the clothing she'd seen them wearing earlier. Her eyes widened anew, cold shock lancing through her nervous system.

"Oh, no. No, no, no, no, no," she said, shaking her head again and again. "You're not sleeping here."

"Then where am I supposed to sleep exactly?" Ren asked, eyebrows arching. "This is the only bed in the entire house."

"I—" Pansy snapped her mouth shut.

It was the only bed, wasn't it? Of course, she could demand that Ren sleep on the floor; maybe, even on that pad of moss they'd flung over the other half of the bed. But that seemed cruel. Unnecessarily so. Plus, she doubted Ren would even agree to it. They'd already proved themself to be equally as stubborn as her, and Pansy, exhausted as she was from the long trek over, had no desire to get into another pointless argument. Better to just skip ahead to the inevitable end result right off the bat.

"Fine. But you need to stay on your half." Pansy jabbed a finger towards the other side of the bed. "And to make sure that happens ..." She seized an armful of blankets and pillows, now scattered across the floor, and dumped them into the middle of the bed. A bit of maneuvering later, and she'd fashioned them into a makeshift wall; far from impenetrable, of course, but it would have to do.

Ren spared it half a glance before letting out a derisive snort. "The bed's big enough that neither of us will even come close to the other, but—okay. Whatever makes you feel a fraction more secure." They shrugged.

"I'm just trying to ensure a certain degree of fairness," Pansy said with a huff, tossing the last bits of her fallen bedspread onto her side of the bed, which was now as disorderly as a rat's nest.

At least, it's still comfortable, she thought as she burrowed into it. Quickly. Before the strange, fluttery feeling that had bloomed in her belly could root deeper. A beat was all it would take, to charge this moment with something it didn't deserve. For as much as there was an undeniable sort of intimacy inherent in sharing a bed with someone, this instance, Pansy insisted, was different. It didn't count. She wouldn't let it.

Even so, her heart continued to pound as she pulled the blankets up to her chin; so loud it was a wonder Ren didn't hear it, given the way it seemed to echo in Pansy's own ears. Each frenzied thunderclap carried the promise of another, a static-like prickle that whispered across her skin. No amount of deep breathing or calming mantras could assuage it. Every inch of her was alive, buzzing, suffused with an inescapable awareness of her surroundings—right down to the way the mattress dipped slightly beneath Ren's weight.

"Your sleeping arrangements really are . . . excessive," they said, shifting beside her, each movement another jolt. If Pansy hadn't known better, she would've thought their behavior purposeful. A way to aggravate her into abandoning her claim.

"Well, excuse me for preferring to stay warm," Pansy sneered over the tremor that ping-ponged through her chest, jittery and electric. "Now, good night."

And with that, she rolled onto her side, as if turning her back on Ren might put them out of her mind just as swiftly. After all, their sharing a bed was out of necessity. Nothing more. And Pansy would remind herself of this fact as many times as it took; until the words became as second nature as the apathy that should've accompanied them.